PASSIONS UNCHAINED

Their lips met in a slow, arousing kiss. It was rough yet soft, infinitely exciting. A dulcet fire burned through Maggie's body. She wanted him madly.

His lips wandered in a moist trail down her throat as he deftly freed the buttons at the neck of her gown. She couldn't stop him . . . didn't want to. She dug her fingers into his hard shoulders, marveling at the muscles that could so easily crush her.

"Darling," she moaned, writhing as the touch of his hand, his lips, brought unendurable rapture to her body. The sweet torture mounted with every second as wave after wave of exquisite fire scorched through her . . .

WINTER'S FLAME

MARIA GREENE

AVON BOOKS ◆ NEW YORK

WINTER'S FLAME is an original publication of Avon Books. This work has never before appeared in book form. This work is a novel. Any similarity to actual persons or events is purely coincidental.

AVON BOOKS
A division of
The Hearst Corporation
105 Madison Avenue
New York, New York 10016

First Avon Books Printing: June 1990

AVON TRADEMARK REG. U.S. PAT. OFF. AND IN OTHER COUNTRIES, MARCA REGISTRADA, HECHO EN U.S.A.

Printed in the U.S.A.

RA 10 9 8 7 6 5 4 3 2 1

Dedicated to the people at Avon Books,
who brought *Winter's Flame* from manuscript to print.

Special thanks to my editors
Nancy Yost and Ellen Edwards.

Prologue

London, 1895

The envelope with the American stamps was as light as thistledown, and the handwriting had a feminine flair. How strange, Maggie Hartwell thought. As far as she could recall, she didn't know anyone in America—except her mother, if she was still alive, and she had never written before. Maggie slit open the envelope, spread the single sheet on her desk, and looked at the signature: Leonora Winston. The name meant nothing, Maggie reflected, frowning in consternation.

Dear Margaret,

Reading this letter will give you a shock, but I will explain everything. The startling fact is, dear Margaret, we're sisters. As you know, your mother traveled to America where she settled in Claremont, Virginia. She gave birth to me six months after she arrived, and we have lived here ever since. I didn't know the truth until the day Mother died—yes, sad to say, she passed away three months ago. However, I don't believe you will feel much sorrow at her death since no doubt you hardly remember her. While sorting through her things, I found her journal, which she'd kept for years. It seems she

1

and our father had an awful marriage—that's why she left England, although she was expecting me. She often wrote about you, and wondered about your life. She used to call you her "moppet." I know she missed you . . .

Moppet.

Maggie's eyes blurred at the memory of her mother's favorite endearment and of her miserable childhood after her mother left. Father had refused to speak about her mother, had never discussed where she'd gone. But why hadn't Mother ever written, at least to tell her about Leonora?

She had a sister! The thought made her head spin with joy, and she had to brace her fingertips against her temples to steady her thoughts. This must be a dream! But the letter in front of her was solid proof that it wasn't a fantasy.

Maggie continued reading.

Since Mother's demise, I am at a loss as to what to do with my life, but I have decided to visit the country of my ancestors, and to see you in London. If I find employment in England I might be tempted to stay, since you're now my only living relative, and I'd like to know you better. I only wish we had met a long time ago.

There are so many things we need to discuss, but that will have to wait until we meet. I will be arriving by steamer to Liverpool on December 6, and I will be wearing a black toque hat with a tall, purple ostrich feather. I so look forward to giving you a hug when I come to London. May I stay for a few days?

Y'r affectionate sister,
Leonora Winston

P.S. I will bring Mother's journal.

Breathless with wonder, Maggie dragged her hand over her eyes, and read the short letter over and over. Her sister would arrive in *one week*, and there was so much to prepare—not just a room for Leonora, although there were plenty of those at the hotel.

How had Leonora found out her name and whereabouts? She had changed her last name from Merton to Hartwell the day she married Horace Hartwell four years ago. Dear Horace would have been excited, she mused. He'd always been happy for her sake and grateful that she'd agreed to marry him. All he'd ever asked for was companionship during his illness, which she'd been able to offer instead of love. Now she might have the friendship of a sister she'd never known existed. At least Leonora had been spared the ordeal of living with their father. Thank God he was dead, or he would surely have made both their lives miserable.

Maggie drew a trembling breath, remembering her father's heavy hand punishing her for everything and nothing, depending on his mood. Even now, she flinched at the memories of the gloomy rooms at her childhood home, the angry silences, the cowed servants. Maybe her mother hadn't dared to write, fearing her father's retribution if he found the letters. But why had Mother left England without her? Maggie had asked herself that question many times.

Nevertheless, she'd escaped her father's tyranny the day that, at age seventeen, she had left the funereal mansion outside Sheffield and come here to London. From then on she'd been free of him—if not of her distrust of men in general, a wariness that her experience with London gentlemen had done nothing to banish. Horace Hartwell had been a rare and wonderful exception.

Maggie rose and rearranged a red-gold curl that had escaped the tight bun at the nape of her neck and straightened her narrow black skirt. Pushing up her wire-rim spectacles, she caught a fleeting glimpse of herself in the mirror, and noticed the flush on her cheeks and the sparkle of anticipation in her eyes. There was a new spring in her step as she left her office at Hartwell's Hotel. She'd always longed for a real family, and now it seemed her wish would be fulfilled. She would share the wonderful news of Leonora's arrival with her daughter, Victoria, and the staff—they would all help to make Leonora feel welcome—then she would count the days until she could travel to Liverpool to meet her sister.

As she climbed the stairs to her living quarters, she wondered how Victoria would take the news that she had an aunt from America. Her daughter was such an open, trusting girl. She had loved Horace as a father, never knowing that another man had begotten her.

Maggie shuddered at *that* memory. She'd committed such folly, but she had been too young and inexperienced to know better. Victoria's father had been the head groom at the Merton mansion, and his betrayal had forced Maggie to run away to London. Her cheeks burned with shame. Thank God, it was all in the past. She would never be so foolish again, so trusting of a charming man's promises. She had created a new life for herself and Victoria, and she would work hard to maintain her daughter's welfare.

The huge steamer dwarfed the other boats in the Liverpool harbor as it docked at its berth. Dressed in her best fur-trimmed coat and a hat with a spotted veil, Maggie observed the passengers along the upper railing, wondering what her sister looked like. She searched eagerly for the purple ostrich feather. The gangway was secured against the ship before the travelers could begin their descent to terra firma. They milled around Maggie, shouting and waving as they recognized the people they'd come to meet.

Maggie's heartbeat accelerated in anticipation as she made her way to the bottom steps of the gangway. Excitedly, she scanned every face that passed before her and surreptitiously wiped her eyes with a hanky. This reunion had stirred up more emotion than she'd felt in years, it seemed.

Was that a purple feather wagging only a few steps away? She craned her neck, but the plume had disappeared behind a cluster of burly male passengers with top hats. When they had passed Maggie, she found that she'd been mistaken. The woman was wearing a dark blue ostrich feather, and she was at least fifty years old.

The passengers left the pier in a steady stream, exchanging hugs and handshakes. By now most of them had stepped off the boat. Slightly worried, Maggie searched the length of the steamer deck, but she saw no one wearing a hat such as Leonora had described. Had she missed the ship?

An hour later Maggie was standing on tiptoes, truly anxious now that everyone had left the boat, and there was still no sign of a young woman in a black hat with a purple feather. As far as Maggie could tell, all the passengers had departed.

Heavy disappointment settled in Maggie's stomach. She looked anxiously at the few people walking alone on the dock, but they appeared to be employees of the steamship company. She waited for another hour, with no luck. Had she missed Leonora in the throng?

Maggie wished she knew how her sister had planned to go to London. By train? Most likely. She passed through the gates and steered her steps toward the train station with a glimmer of hope that she might find Leonora at the depot. But her spirits plummeted when she still failed to find her there.

Not knowing what to do next, she returned to the

pier. As she approached the gates, she threw a cursory glance toward the cab stand. Something on the ground drew her attention. As she looked closer she saw a mangled purple ostrich plume.

Chapter 1

London, December 8

"My sister is still missing, Constable. I wish to see Sergeant Horridge as soon as may be. He promised to find out what happened to her." Stabbing the floor with the tip of her umbrella and drawing herself up to her full five foot nine inches, Maggie knew she looked intimidating. Her back ramrod-straight, she pinned the blushing young officer with an imperious eye. It was the look she used for the laziest of her maids, and it never failed to get immediate results.

Cringing, the constable twirled one of the brass buttons on his blue uniform.

"He's busy, Mrs. Hartwell, but—"

"Then please tell him I'm here. I have waited an hour already, and I have a business to manage."

"Very well, just a moment." The constable loped down the drab corridor's creaking floorboards. The walls were painted a dingy white, and the gas jets hissed and popped overhead behind frosted glass globes. The yellowish light failed to dispel the gloom of the overcast winter day outside.

Concealing her worry behind a mask of determination, Maggie sat down on the uninviting hard-backed chair and glanced at the watch pinned to her white high-necked blouse. She had dressed with exceptional care in a slim, black serge skirt adorned by silk braiding along the hem and a matching jacket with velvet lapels. Her clothes would remind the sergeant that she was a respectable citizen and not some asylum escapee with a lunatic claim about a sister she'd never known existed. Her toque hat with the spotted veil and a cluster of silk violets was a bit frivolous for the occasion, but lovely hats bolstered her confidence. She glanced at the flat parcel in her hand, the carefully wrapped purple ostrich feather. She knew that Leonora had worn it. There was no proof, of course, but she couldn't dispel the premonition of disaster that had overcome her the moment she saw the plume. Now that she'd learned that she had a sister, she yearned—more than she wanted to admit—to know Leonora. Perhaps her sister would dispel the loneliness she'd felt since Horace's death, and they could form a family. Family spelled security and a feeling of belonging Maggie had so longed for while living in the gloomy Sheffield mansion with her father. Now Victoria would have an aunt, and if Leonora ever married, perhaps cousins.

The constable returned, his lurching gait more pronounced as he hurried toward her. "Sergeant Horridge will see you momentarily," he said.

"Thank you." Maggie stood, straightening her back and breathing deeply to fortify herself—the sergeant might have terrible news about Leonora.

Leaning on her umbrella, she glanced out the window. Rain spattered the back of a dusty horse pulling a hansom cab, and made dark round specks on the cobblestones. She glimpsed one of the soaring red-and-white striped campaniles standing like a sentinel in the corner of the carnelian brick building of the New Scotland Yard. The great turrets, the steep roof with its many dormer windows, and the red-and-white brickwork had initially been erected to hold the new opera house, but when the funds dried up for the project, the Metropolitan Police and the Criminal Investigation Department had moved in.

Maggie drew a quick jagged breath, the oppressive atmosphere making her feel as if her chest was bound by an iron band. Decisive steps echoed along the corridor. She turned from the window and came eye to eye with Sergeant Septimus Horridge.

"Please come with me, Mrs. Hartwell," he said kindly. His round face was framed by bristly mutton-chop whiskers, and his small puffy eyes studied her keenly. He wore a butterfly collar with a Derby tie in a garish shade of red and a black frock coat, shiny with wear.

"Thank you," Maggie said, and hurried after the sergeant, eager to learn what he had discovered.

His office was austere, a potted aspidistra the only adornment among the heavy furniture.

"Have a seat, Mrs. Hartwell." He indicated a worn leather armchair in front of his cluttered desk.

Her previous imperiousness gone, she obeyed, placing her umbrella across her lap. "Do you know what happened to my sister?"

He put his fingertips together in a steeple and pursed his lips, closely observing her face. He cleared his throat noisily. "You say your sister's name is Leonora Winston, of Claremont, in the state of Virginia?"

"Yes."

Silence descended like a dense blanket in the room, and Maggie clasped her hands together. The *tick-tock* of an old clock on the wall reverberated in her head as she waited.

"Well, the American authorities say a woman by that name truly lived at that address. She left Claremont recently."

"You see? She does exist. She must have traveled on the ship." Maggie unwrapped the purple plume and placed it on the desk as a reminder. She had shown him the feather on her previous visit.

He again pursed his lips. "I ordered the passenger list from the steamship company in Liverpool and no passenger by that name traveled on the boat that arrived last week." He glanced up quickly, as if aiming to catch her off guard.

"I don't understand." She took the folded paper from her pocket. "I showed you this letter, so you have seen for yourself that she must have been on the ship." She waved the paper in his face.

He sighed and drummed the desktop with his stubby fingers. "I read it, but it doesn't mean that your sister wrote it. It could be nothing more than a silly prank."

Maggie flinched as if he had slapped her face. "Prank? Why would you think that? You sound very indifferent to my sister's plight, Sergeant. Besides, I don't know anyone in America who could have sent the note." He didn't reply, and she took a deep, steadying breath. "Are you implying that *I* wrote the letter, that I'm taking up your precious time with some kind of cruel charade?" Anger heated her cheeks.

He smiled patiently, as if she were a recalcitrant child. "I'm not accusing you of anything, Mrs. Hartwell, but you must know that these things happen. We get nuisance mail and threats every day. Most likely Miss Winston is still in Virginia. She might even write you again to explain why she wasn't on the steamer. Perhaps she was delayed."

Maggie forced herself to be calm. "I hope you realize I wouldn't waste your time, Sergeant Horridge, let alone my own on a trivial matter. I have far more important things to do. I'm certain Miss Leonora Winston arrived and that something happened to her in Liverpool."

Silence stretched between them in a battle of wills.

Sergeant Horridge sighed and, with a gesture of irritation, shoved some papers across the desk. "See for yourself. There is no Miss Winston on the list."

Filled with foreboding, Maggie scanned the long passenger list, while the sergeant took a cigar from a box on the desk, snipped off the end, and lit it. Maggie's stomach turned at the pungent odor. When she had finished reading she returned the list.

"You're right," she said. "Still, I don't know how to convince you that this matter is of utmost importance."

He puffed on the cigar, and the smoke curled upward in thick, lazy veils. "It's difficult to believe your story, considering the fact that you didn't even know you had a sister until you received that letter."

"I'm sure it wouldn't be the first time someone found a relative they didn't know existed. My mother severed all contact when she left my father."

It was difficult to keep her anger under control. Her calm veneer was slowly cracking. She wanted to cry, but if she displayed weakness in front of this man, he would not listen to her. He was the only one who could help her.

"What else can you do to find out more about Leonora?" she asked, stabbing the point of her umbrella into the floor for emphasis.

He shrugged and surveyed her through the smoky haze. "There's nothing else we can do here, I'm afraid."

"So you're not going to contact the police in Liverpool for further assistance?"

He shrugged, and a note of impatience crept into his voice. "Since there's no evidence that your sister ever set foot in this country, I don't see a reason to waste the time of the Liverpool police." He stubbed the cigar into the ashtray, then rose with an air of finality. "I'm sorry about your plight, but I'm afraid

I cannot help you until we have proof that Miss Winston sailed on the ship."

Maggie pinched her lips together with disappointment. "I suppose I cannot force you to act, but it saddens me that my problem isn't important to you."

He smiled tightly. "I understand your viewpoint, Mrs. Hartwell, but believe me, crime is rampant in London. Missing persons have a tendency to turn up sooner or later."

Maggie rose and pulled on her gloves before retrieving the hat plume. "Well, I thank you for acquiring and reading the passenger list." She wanted to beg him to continue investigating her sister's disappearance, but she knew from his obstinate manner that no argument could change his decision.

"Wait a moment," he said, softening in the face of her distress. He riffled through the middle drawer on his desk and from a welter of strings, paper clips, keys, and smoking implements, extracted a cream-colored card. Dusting it off, he handed it to her.

"This man might be able to help you. But I warn you, his fees are high." He glanced at her immaculate black suit, as if calculating whether or not she could afford to hire assistance.

Recoiling from his scrutiny, she took the card and read: *Mr. Thaddeus Webb, Antique Dealer and Private Detective.* "Detective?" she asked.

"Yes, insurance companies often hire him to recover stolen goods. His father was a chief inspector with us, and his grandfather was a famous Bow Street Runner. Webb worked with me here for five years, but he left two years ago. Detection flows in Webb's blood, I daresay." Sergeant Horridge laughed for the first time. "If anyone can find your sister, he can. He's like a dog worrying a bone once he finds a mystery to solve."

Maggie felt a surge of hope. "Thank you."

"And if you could produce a calotype or a minia-

ture of Miss Winston, I'd like to see it just in case I
come across someone . . ."

Maggie gave him a sharp glance. "You mean if you
come across an unidentified corpse."

He looked uncomfortable and pushed his hand over
his shiny pate. "Well . . . I hope it won't come to
that."

He ushered her into the corridor. "Good luck to
you, and good day." Bowing politely, he closed the
door behind her.

A wave of loneliness and insecurity washed over
her. She had never had to deal with anything re-
motely like this problem before, and it frightened her.
Not one to shirk her duties, she nevertheless wished
she had someone to confide in, someone who could
truly help her.

Stepping onto the Embankment, she waved at a
passing hansom. The rain lashed her, despite her umbrella. The wind was cold and smelled of petrol and
smoke. A motorcar roared by, and Maggie gritted her
teeth against the noise. The hansom did not stop so
she went to find a cab stand on Parliament Street
where wagons, drays, and horse-drawn omnibuses
fought for space with private carriages and pedestrians.

With a sigh of relief, Maggie sank down on the
frayed leather seat of the first available hansom. The
interior smelled of wet horse and damp wool. After
wiping her face with the back of her hand—since she
had no handkerchief—she extracted Mr. Webb's card
from her pocket. It was moist already, the corners
curling.

Antique dealer and detective—an odd combination.
However, the address was stylish Maddox Street, just
south of Hanover Square. Due to the more than nor-
mally congested streets, it took the cabby the better
part of an hour to deliver her at Mr. Webb's door.
She paid him and climbed the two stone steps.

The tall narrow town house had been converted into a shop. The windows at street level were cluttered to the bursting point, and displayed a conglomeration of old furniture, oil landscapes, gilded frames of all sizes, mirrors with mottled glass, a painted wooden statue of a Moor, rolls of fabric, a stack of old moldering books, two ornate bronze candelabras, and, to her surprise, a quite modern bicycle.

Shuddering at the disorganized mess, she faced the dark green door and raised the brass knocker that was polished by much use.

She had to knock twice before steps echoed behind the door. It flew open and she stared at a very tall man with the broadest shoulders she had ever seen. They were covered with a gray tweed sack coat and a striped waistcoat; the muscular neck sported a stiff white collar and a spotted ascot. The gentleman had a dimple in his square clean-shaven chin, and fascinating, lean cheeks that she had a sudden desire to touch. His hair was dark chestnut, straight, thick, and glossy. He had dark eyes of a rich coffee-brown hue, and they seemed to smile at her, jauntily, recklessly, under a set of straight sable brows.

The impact of his gaze made her feel as if he'd actually touched her—not just her hand or fingertips, but—intimately. A sweet yearning that she'd never felt before rushed through her and, for a moment, she lost all coherent thought. He was immensely attractive, and that fact frightened her, made her defensive.

"How can I be of service, madam?" he asked in a deep, pleasant voice that imparted a sense of welcoming warmth. "Are you perhaps in search of a Regency chandelier, a satinwood tea caddy, a knife box with silver mounts, or a plain old girandole mirror?"

She could not help but smile. "No, thank you, you're far off the mark. Mr. Webb, I presume?" She held out her hand for a businesslike clasp, but he took her fingers gallantly and pulled her inside. "At your service, Madam—?"

"Mrs. Margaret Hartwell."

"Mrs. Margaret Hartwell of Margaret Street?"

"No, of Berkley Street—right between Portman and Manchester Squares."

In the process of closing the door, he halted for a second. "Hartwell's Hotel?"

She nodded, pleased that he knew of her establishment. Her gaze traveled around the hallway with its mahogany staircase with turned newel posts. The ceiling was covered with varnished, dark brown lincrusta paper. The walls—or what she could see of them—were papered with a Morris leaf design in gold, greens, and browns. The windows were hung with brown tasseled velvet curtains, and the oak floor had a long wool carpet embroidered in floral patterns. The rest of the spacious hallway was cluttered like the windows, with all manner of furniture and curios. A broken Grecian marble pillar leaned against one wall, next to a rosewood hat and umbrella stand. A dusty potted palm seemed to thrive in the congenial disorder. She didn't know which way to turn.

Thaddeus Webb noticed her confusion. "This is a shop-storage combination, you see. My office is upstairs, as are my living quarters." He motioned toward the stairs, smiling reassuringly as she hesitated. He found this lady with sparkling blue eyes and a proud chin highly intriguing. She was a bit stiff though, as if, at some point in her life, she had erected a thick wall around her. He was curious to discover what had caused her so much disappointment that she needed to adopt such a defensive demeanor. "Shall we step upstairs?"

"Oh." Maggie gave him a suspicious glance.

His eyebrows rose. "You look frightened, Mrs. Hartwell. Rest assured, I'm decorum personified." He waited for her to go first. "I take it you're here on business?"

"Yes, of course." She lifted her skirt and started climbing gingerly.

"Too bad. I had hoped it might be a social call. A lovely lady like you . . ."

Maggie shot Mr. Webb a furtive glance to see if he was joking, but his expression appeared serious—until she met his gaze. Then, an infectious grin spread over his charming, masculine face. His eyes simmered with veiled admiration as he pointed at one of the doors off the landing.

His office boasted the same dark colors as the hallway downstairs, but the predominant tone was green—green woodwork and green carpet. Plants of all sizes and shapes sat on wooden pedestals or hung in woven baskets from brass hooks in the ceiling. His desk was a wild confusion of papers, boxes, and writing implements. Two wooden trays for incoming and outgoing mail were stacked on top of each other.

Mr. Webb lifted a bundle of catalogs from the single chair in front of the desk, and offered her a seat.

"I'm afraid my charwoman is at home with a broken leg." When he saw her doubtful expression, he laughed. "You've seen through my lie! In fact, my charwoman took permanent leave when I brought home the Grecian pillar. She said it was the outside of enough, and stalked off, never to be seen again."

"How do you remember where you put things?"

"Ah! There's order to the disorder, Mrs. Hartwell. I use a system that works perfectly well for me."

As Mr. Webb sat down behind the desk, the spring of his swivel chair creaked alarmingly. The man's sheer size dwarfed his surroundings, but it gave Maggie a feeling of safety.

Relaxing, she leaned her umbrella against the desk. She noticed the sensuous tilt to his lips, which looked as sensitive as his long-fingered hands. This man made her feel not only self-conscious, but exhilarated as well. Her heart pounded harder, responding against her will to his charm. She realized how stiff her back was, and how the steel-reinforced corset chafed the tender skin under her blouse. She felt wrapped up in a cage, and she could barely breathe.

"I take it you have come to order some objects to redecorate your hotel, Mrs. Hartwell. If I don't have what you need, I can find it for you. I have extensive contacts in the city and in the provinces." He smiled apologetically. "I call myself an antique dealer, but I deal in modern bric-a-brac and plants as well."

"I've come to solicit your detective services," she said, her concern about Leonora resurfacing.

Her request evidently surprised him, because he rubbed his chin thoughtfully. "I see. You'd better start from the beginning."

"Sergeant Horridge of Scotland Yard sent me here."

Mr. Webb nodded and leaned back in his chair as if he had all the time in the world. "He's a friend and former associate."

"So he told me. Well, to start from the very beginning, my family is originally from Sheffield. My father was involved in steel manufacturing, as was my grandfather." She paused and looked down at the gloves in her lap. "He was a ruthless captain of industry, but that's neither here nor there." She continued, "My parents never got along. When I was three years old, my mother left Father and me for good, and I neither saw nor heard from her again. Then, out of the blue, I received a letter from a woman in America called Leonora Winston, who claimed to be my sister."

"When was this?" he asked.

"The letter arrived nine days ago." Maggie sighed, still feeling suffocated by her tight corset. His dark eyes were most attractive, distracting her from her train of thought. "Leonora explained that she was born a few months after Mother left for America, and that we're full sisters. Mother never told Leonora about me, but she died three months ago, and Leonora found her journal, where she had written everything about the past. Leonora mentioned that Mother used to call me 'moppet.' " Maggie blushed, embarrassed to reveal such an intimate detail. "That's how I know Leonora is telling the truth. She decided to travel here and visit me—perhaps even live in London."

"She never came, did she?" he asked kindly, combing his fingers through his hair.

"How did you know?" Maggie asked in surprise.

"You wouldn't be here if she had, would you?"

Maggie smiled stiffly. "I suppose you're right."

"Go on."

Maggie told him about Sergeant Horridge's efforts on her behalf. "I looked at the passenger list myself, and Leonora's name wasn't there."

"They wouldn't spend more time on the case and sent you over here," he finished off.

She nodded hopefully, and he smiled. "I'm no magician, alas," he said. "I cannot conjure up your sister."

Maggie placed the broken purple plume on the desk for his perusal, and pulled Leonora's letter from her pocket. "Please read this."

He read aloud the lines that she had underlined: "The startling fact is, dear Margaret, we're sisters . . . moppet . . . I have decided to visit the country of my ancestors . . . purple ostrich feather . . . Y'r affectionate sister, Leonora Winston." Silently, he studied the feather. Compassion softened his features. "It must have been a blow for you to learn that your mother just died."

His words comforted her. "Yes, but I was quite pleased to find out that I have a sister. I have no other close relatives left. Having a family would mean the world to me.'' She gave him a penetrating glance, gauging whether she could trust him with any more confidences. Again he seemed to read her mind.

''You must have resented your mother's desertion.''

Maggie felt a familiar stab of hurt, but she suppressed it immediately. ''Yes, I resented her as I grew up, but I don't remember her much. However, I do know that she must have been desperate to act as she did.'' Maggie clamped her lips shut. She wasn't going to spew out the flood of bitterness against her father that she had carried so long.

She twisted her hands unconsciously. ''I'm telling you this so that you'll understand I'm not making it all up. I know it's a preposterous story, but I'm convinced that I have a younger sister, and that she was on the steamship from New York that docked two days ago in Liverpool.'' She stopped, overcome by uncertainty and fatigue. Telling her story once again, and to a stranger, had drained her. If only she had a brother or a cousin who could help her, instead of this stranger. As a woman operating her own business, she constantly met with resistance and suspicion from men. The fact that she ran a successful hotel made her a dangerous opponent, an intruder in the sphere of male affairs. Therefore, she was doubly cautious when dealing with strangers, especially charming gentlemen like Mr. Webb.

''Leonora is lucky to have you for a sister.''

''Why?'' Maggie asked, slightly flustered.

''You care about her enough to find out what happened to her.'' He rubbed his chin again and stood up.

''You believe my story then?'' Relief made her breathe easier.

''You'd have no reason to come here unless you had a valid story. Besides, the letter seems genuine, and Miss Winston might have worn that plume." He lifted a brass can with a spout and began watering the plants. "The only thing we don't know for sure is if Leonora wrote the letter, or someone else."

"Yes . . . I see your point. Sergeant Horridge said the same thing." Maggie was dismayed. "I don't have any other writing sample to show you." She thought for a moment. "Father never mentioned her. Perhaps he didn't know of her existence."

"It's tragic that you don't have more relatives. I've always been close to my family. Life would be empty without them." He smiled. "Though sometimes a large family is a nuisance."

"Do you think you can find her?" Maggie asked.

His eyebrows pulled together. "I can try. I charge two pounds a day, and this case may take a while."

"*Two pounds!*" Anger swelled in Maggie's chest. "That's pure robbery."

He grinned wickedly. "I'd rather sell you that Grecian pillar for two pounds."

Maggie's imperiousness returned with new force. "Don't change the subject," she demanded, giving him her most daunting stare.

He only chuckled. "The question is, can you afford my fee?"

"Of course!" In her mind she saw her savings, which she had amassed with painstaking care, dwindling at an alarming rate. "There's no question about that. When can you start?"

Chapter 2

*H*e *was starting tomorrow*. Maggie jabbed her wet umbrella into the stand right inside her office door at Hartwell's Hotel. Two pounds a day! What gall. Perhaps she should have tried to find Leonora alone, but she had no idea where to begin.

After taking off her hat and jacket, she flipped through the mail on her desk. Her heart almost stopped as she recognized the handwriting on one envelope and the foreign postmark. Another letter from America. Maggie sank down on her chair, her fingers trembling as she slit open the envelope. In her eagerness, she almost ripped the paper as she pulled it out. She looked at the signature first—Leonora's—then she glanced at the date. Her hope evaporated. It had been written two days after the first letter. She rapidly read the short message:

I thought you might want to know what I look like, so that you'll recognize me when I arrive. I'm eager to meet you, as we've been separated too many years already.

Y'r humble sister,
Leonora

Maggie turned the envelope upside down. A black-and-white calotype fell to the desk. Holding her breath, she studied the sweet face on the picture. It was almost a shock to see a face so like her father's. Despite the lack of color, Maggie could tell that Leonora had his thin, somewhat pale features, his curly blond hair, and his light eyes. There had been an old portrait of her father hanging in the hallway of the Sheffield mansion, a portrait painted for his twenty-first birthday. Leonora could have been his twin sister. There was no doubt now that Leonora had written the previous letter, and that Bulver "Bully" Merton had been her sire.

Her heart hammering uncomfortably, Maggie dropped the picture on the desk. What had happened to her sister? An ominous feeling filled her. Leonora must have been on the steamer, there was no doubt in Maggie's mind about that. But how had Maggie missed her? Was it already too late to find her? The questions were making Maggie's head spin.

Her thoughts brightened as she heard her six-year-old daughter's voice on the stairs leading to the living quarters. "Sweetest Mama, you're back! Miss Lather said I did well at my lessons and that I could come down and greet you."

Maggie held out her arms to Victoria, and the thin girl with wheat-colored braids rushed onto her lap. Maggie smiled, tenderly kissed the downy cheek, and looked into the clear blue eyes. "Mama, Miss Byrne said that a strange man was here asking for you earlier. He looked ever so *foreign*. She said he wore unusual clothes and had such strange eyes."

Maggie hugged her close and rocked her as she had done when Victoria was an infant. "Did you see him?"

Victoria looked at her. "No, Mama."

"You can't tell me more about him, then?" When Victoria shook her head, Maggie said, "I will have to ask Miss Byrne later."

"Mama, why are your spectacles fogged up?"

Thinking that perhaps she and Victoria would never meet Leonora, Maggie blinked away a tear. "Because I'm so happy that I have you, darling."

Thaddeus Webb wore a caped, houndstooth-checked greatcoat, the collar turned up against the drizzle. All afternoon he had been unable to shake the thought of Margaret Hartwell's plight, but more than that, he had been unable to forget *her*.

He chuckled. Prim and proper, like a mannequin in a ladies' fashion journal, she had stood on his front step, her back ramrod-straight, brandishing her umbrella as if it were a deadly weapon.

But she was beautiful.

He loved to watch women. They were the most fascinating creatures alive, and the most mysterious. He guessed that behind Margaret Hartwell's tight chignon, spinsterish clothes, and dainty gold rimmed spectacles lurked a lush beauty—if he hadn't lost his eye for female loveliness completely. He saw hair as the setting of the jewel that was a woman's face, and her hair was a lustrous reddish-blond, a color that could be drab, or wildly exciting, depending on the face set against it.

Mrs. Hartwell had warm gilded skin, a spattering of freckles, and eyes that were disconcertingly blue. Her face was a rare gem, with its delicate straight nose and sweet, vulnerable lips that she desperately tried to hold in a pinched line. In short, her face complemented its red-gold "setting" to perfection.

It was a pity that she strove to conceal every trace of allure. The tightness of her chignon—not to mention her corsets—must be extremely uncomfortable, he thought with a laugh. She was so different from his wife, Rachel, who had died two years ago. Rachel had been utterly soft and feminine, a perfect wife whom any man could wish for, and he had been a lucky fellow to win her love. Since Rachel's death he'd not met any woman who interested him—not like Margaret Hartwell did.

He was pleased to discover that the wounds he'd suffered at Rachel's death had healed at last. He'd stopped blaming himself. His interest in Mrs. Hartwell was invigorating, not disturbing. The hint of vulnerability behind her stiff exterior awakened his protective instincts. She seemed so lonely and desperate.

He decided to eat supper at the hotel. There would be nothing wrong with pursuing something he desired, especially if it was just one more peek at the lovely owner of Hartwell's Hotel. Besides, he might learn something that would aid him in his investigation, and the dining rooms had an excellent reputation. Who would have thought the proprietor was female, and such a lady to boot? Where was Mr. Hartwell?

The rain had almost stopped by the time he crossed Manchester Square, and fog was thickening, obscuring the pavement. Gaslights suspended on wrought iron stands glowed with an eerie yellow light, each globe resembling a pale moon in the mist. The entrance to the hotel was flanked by a cluster of three lights on each side and guarded by a doorman in brass-buttoned green livery. The sign above the door identified Hartwell's Hotel in straight brass letters. No frivolous curlicues there. The double doors were of sturdy oak, and the square Georgian house was whitewashed, though streaky with soot. Moisture gleamed wetly on the facade; the air was raw and cold.

"Evenin'," the doorman greeted him, and tipped his stovepipe hat. He held the door open with a white-gloved hand.

"Evening it is—and a bad one," Thaddeus said, entering. Warmth embraced him, and he nodded to the pretty maid in a black dress and starched white apron who took his dripping coat and bobbed a curtsy. Because the establishment belonged to Margaret Hartwell, he closely examined every detail. The foyer was spotlessly clean, the red carpet swept, the brass rubbed bright, and the dark woodwork polished. A cluster of comfortable armchairs was arranged around tables holding reading material.

A middle-aged woman in a plain black gown stood behind the front desk, speaking on the telephone. So, Mrs. Hartwell didn't hesitate to incorporate into her business the inventions that were appearing almost daily in the lives of Londoners. Was she so daring in other areas of her life?

The hotel was plush and quiet. The dining room consisted of three large rooms connected by wide, arched doorways. The first room, to which a waiter ushered him, was decorated in the style of Robert Adam. It had a ribbed plaster ceiling and plaster frieze, both painted white, moss-green walls and white wainscoting, and a polished oak floor covered with a brown carpet bordered in burgundy. The furniture was stately mahogany, and the linen was crisp and spotless. The effect was pleasing, especially with the added accent of healthy potted palms in the recessed French door that faced a tiny, bricked garden. A fire crackled in the white marble fireplace.

Thaddeus sat down, though he had difficulty pushing his long legs beneath the starched tablecloth. Pretending to study the menu, he glanced surreptitiously at the other guests. Waiters in gray-striped trousers and black tailcoats hurried back and forth, expertly balancing trays on their shoulders. An appetizing smell of roast meat and newly baked bread wafted from the kitchen, situated somewhere behind a green baize swinging door. He ordered a bottle of claret, fish soup and rolls, veal and gravy, potatoes, and peas. Nice solid British fare, which could be topped off with coffee and old cognac in the lounge. His mouth watered.

"Tell me, does Mrs. Hartwell dine with the guests?" he asked the waiter.

"Sometimes," came the noncommittal reply. The waiter uncorked the bottle and poured an infinitesimal amount of claret in Thaddeus's glass. "What's your name?" Thaddeus went on.

The waiter gave him a shrewd glance from under red eyebrows. "Paddy, sir."

"Irish, are you? Well, would you like to earn an extra shilling tonight, old chap?" Thaddeus took a sip of claret, savoring the tartness. "Excellent." He placed a coin on the table. "What do you say, Paddy?"

The waiter poured and slanted a furtive glance at the door. " 'Tall depends, sir. I'm not supposed t' get involved with th' guests outside me duties. No funny business, eh?"

Thaddeus laughed. "No. I'd like you to find a way to bring Mrs. Hartwell here. After that, I'll do the rest."

The waiter pursed his lips, avidly viewing the shilling next to Thaddeus's plate. "If she's in, sir." He made a movement as if to scoop up the coin, but Thaddeus covered it with the palm of his hand.

"Bring her here first," he said. "And, by the way, where's Mr. Hartwell?"

Paddy shrugged. "Dead, sir. Toppled two years ago. Th' marriage to Mrs. Maggie lasted only four years." He eyed the shilling once more and walked away.

The soup was delicious. Thaddeus lingered over the steaming bowl, hoping that Paddy would succeed in luring Mrs. Hartwell to his side. He could, of course, seek her out in the name of business, as he had additional questions about Leonora Winston. But he realized it was plain curiosity about Mrs. Hartwell that drove him. It was clear that her hotel was flourishing, proving she must be an astute businesswoman. He was interested in her past and the strange events that had led to the separation of her parents in Sheffield.

It also intrigued him that she sprang from such a different background than his. He had always lived in the heart of London, and probably always would.

After finishing his soup, he patted his lips with the stiff damask napkin and waited for Paddy to return.

The Irishman winked as he removed the bowl and set the main course in front of Thaddeus. " 'Tis done, sir." He gazed at the shilling covetously.

"What did you tell her?"

Paddy kept his face expressionless. "Told her a gen'leman wanted t' see her in th' dining room, sir."

Thaddeus chuckled. "An ingenuous excuse," he said, and slipped the shilling into Paddy's pocket. "Wasted money."

"Not at all, sir. I'll take me girl t' see th' Magic Lantern. Some bloke's showin' travel memories from Africa. Dry, boring stuff, but me girl likes it."

"Well, make her happy then," Thaddeus said, grinning.

He almost choked on his potato as Margaret Hartwell appeared in the doorway. She looked lovely—if severe—in a brown woolen, high-necked dress adorned with gold braids. The wide, puffy sleeves tightened at the elbows and ended at points on the back of her hands, and her hair was scraped back into a thick bun. He could see, now that her hat had been removed, that tiny curls formed along the hairline on her forehead, no matter how obviously she tried to subdue them.

"Oh, Mr. Webb, I didn't expect you here," she said pleasantly. "Is dinner to your liking?"

He nodded and rose. "Would you care to join me?" he asked.

She hesitated. "Are you here on business?"

He shook his head and smiled. "No, I'm afraid I'm guilty of mere curiosity. A lady owning and operating a hotel is an unusual occurrence, and I wanted to see it for myself."

"You've come to gawk?" she asked frostily.

"No . . . I'm impressed. It takes courage and ingenuity to operate a business of this size." She studied him with those lovely peacock-blue eyes, now narrowed with suspicion. "Please sit down and have a glass of wine with me," he urged. "Or eat dessert."

"Thank you, but I rarely dine with the guests."

"A pity." He hesitated, casting about for something to say that would bridge the gap between them. To his surprise, she helped him.

"However, I have something important to show you. We could meet for coffee in the lounge later."

The disappointment lifted from his heart. "I look forward to it."

She was as good as her word. He had no more sat down in a deep tufted leather sofa in the lounge than she appeared at his side. The golden gaslight softened her pinched features, making her look much less formidable.

He rose and waited until she had settled her rustling skirts. Then he ordered coffee and a glass of sherry for her, while he sipped an excellent cognac. The lounge, located through an arched doorway just off the foyer, had a red, blue, and green plaid carpet and heavy furniture. She looked regal in this setting.

"I have something to show you, another development in the case. This will at least prove that Leonora exists," she explained, and reached into a hidden pocket in the side seam of her skirt. Without another comment, she handed him the calotype, and he raised it toward the light. Leonora's face was sweet, innocent, a pale shadow of her older sister's. There the similarity ended. Leonora possessed none of Mrs. Hartwell's strength.

"When did you receive this?"

"This afternoon. It was mailed only a few days after the last letter, but didn't arrive until today. It was thoughtful of her to send me a picture."

He could hear her sigh, a suppressed, quivering sound as if she didn't dare breathe properly.

"I didn't see anyone like her on the docks in Liverpool, but the harbor was so very crowded. I stayed until everyone had left, but there was no one waiting—"

Her voice faded, and he saw that her hand was trembling as she reached for the sherry glass. The business had obviously shaken her, and he felt a spurt of protectiveness—a sentiment he suspected she would have rebuffed it she had known about it. He vowed to help her find her sister, fast. Her hand looked small but strong and capable as it rested beside the glass. Not knowing what came over him, he placed his own hand over hers.

"Don't worry, I'll start the investigation first thing tomorrow morning, and you'll have Leonora at your side in no time." He wasn't convinced he would succeed that quickly, but he wanted to cheer her up. She seemed so sad.

There was a softening of her lips, but she didn't smile. She pulled her hand away, not angrily but with finality. Her eyes were huge and filled with pain behind the spectacles.

"The past always comes back to haunt you, no matter how hard you try to put it behind you," she said cryptically.

"What do you mean?"

She paused.

"I'm alluding to the hurt that Father inflicted on our family. The fact that he had another child— Leonora—whom he never acknowledged is yet another example of his cruelty. Even though he's dead, his tyranny still rules us. Had I only known that I had a sister, and a mother who loved me, my life might have been very different. I've believed all this time that Mother didn't want me any more than Father did, but according to Leonora, she longed for me as I did for her."

He wanted to hear more about her life, but she fell silent, as if she'd encased her thoughts in a mental corset as rigid as the whalebone one she wore. "I'd better keep the picture of your sister for now," he said, and she nodded. "Tell me Mrs. Hartwell, do you know why your parents separated?"

"No . . . Would it help in the investigation?"

"Perhaps." If she didn't know, she could only speculate on the cause of the rift. He moved to a more neutral subject. "How many rooms do you have here? The dining rooms could easily hold a hundred and fifty guests."

"Merely fifteen rooms and three suites. A few of the rooms are rented by the month. Some of the guests live her permanently, you see. It's not a large hotel, but private and cozy."

He scanned the crowded lounge where cigar smoke curled around the gas fixtures. "You have a flourishing business."

She shrugged. "On and off." She finished her sherry and he was afraid she would leave before he had a chance to know her better.

"Tell me, what are you going to do first?" she asked suddenly, interrupting his thoughts.

"About Miss Winston?" As she nodded, he continued, "I'll speak with Sergeant Horridge, and then I'll start investigating the names on the passenger list. I'm glad we have a calotype to show the other passengers. That'll make it easier for them to identify her."

"But there were *hundreds* of people on that steamer."

"I'll have to discover in what class she traveled. But I'll start by visiting the wealthiest passengers. Perhaps someone can tell me about Miss Winston's circumstances. If she didn't travel first-class, she might have been—er, low in funds at the outset." He

WINTER'S FLAME 31

sighed. "Hopefully I won't have to interview every single person who was on that ship."

She inclined her head. "I understand." Her eyes glittered as if full of unshed tears. He could not be sure in the muted light.

"I'm grateful to you for believing my story," she said with a faint smile, her bottom lip quivering.

Her smile revealed the vulnerable woman behind the rigid barrier of her mind, and it made him draw his breath in sharply. She was lovely! As that wistful smile disappeared, he felt bereft, as if the shutters had once more snapped shut around her, barring him from her.

"I—I might as well confess one more thing," she said. "I've had nightmares that Leonora might have fallen overboard at sea, or that someone . . ."

"Pushed her?" he filled in. It was conceivable, but he wanted to reassure her. "A remote possibility. It's hardly likely Miss Winston made such an enemy aboard the steamer."

"But—" Mrs. Hartwell did not finish the sentence, and he could tell that her imagination was conjuring up all sorts of grim possibilities.

"Please try not to worry. Your sister will turn up safe and sound." He stifled an impulse to start the investigation right away. There was nothing he could do so late in the evening. He finished his cognac, then remembered. "Oh, if you don't mind, I'd like to have Miss Winston's address in Virginia. I have a friend in Richmond who wouldn't hesitate to discover a few facts if I need them."

"Of course." She rose. "Come to my office."

Thaddeus placed some coins on the table and followed her across the foyer. Next to the front desk was a plain door and a plaque with the word OFFICE painted on it. They entered. He had expected the same impersonal elegance as the rest of the hotel and was surprised to find feminine touches, rose damask

curtains with gold tassels, flowery wallpaper, and girandole mirrors. A dimly lit gas chandelier with three
glass domes hung from the ceiling. Where his own
desk was orderly chaos, hers was so clean she could
have used it as a dinner plate.

In a dark corner, close to the bay window, hung a
portrait of a man. He gazed at it furtively, then
crossed the room to study it more closely. "Your father?" he asked her, knowing it couldn't be. This man
was fortyish, handsome.

She gave him a cautious glance. "No, my husband,
Horace. He's no longer alive. He died from a lingering illness."

Thaddeus scrutinized her face, noticing that she
seemed ill at ease talking about him. "Did your father
like Mr. Hartwell?"

"As far as I know, Father never knew about him.
When I . . . left my childhood home to come here,
Father—to put it vulgarly—washed his hands of me."
Maggie blushed, not wanting to divulge the shameful
truth of why she had run away from home. There
was no reason for Mr. Webb to know, was there?

Thaddeus glanced once again at the portrait. "Mr.
Hartwell looks kind."

Maggie smiled, relieved that he hadn't insisted on
hearing the whole truth about her past. "Yes, Mr.
Hartwell was the kindliest man I've ever known. A
slow, debilitating illness made him an invalid, but he
never complained. He lost the function of his legs,
and then his arms, but he was cheerful to the end."
She paused, biting her lip. "We met when he was
looking for a housekeeper, and found friendship. He
talked about this hotel, which he'd inherited from his
father, and I was fascinated. I never dreamt the hotel
business would capture my interest, but it did. Mr.
Hartwell respected me, my suggestions about the hotel establishment. You see, our relationship was

founded on trust, and he knew I wasn't going to abandon the hotel once he was gone."

"I believe trust is the most important part of a marriage," Thaddeus agreed. "But, if you'll pardon my familiarity, you don't seem to trust easily, Mrs. Hartwell."

She lowered her gaze, wishing he couldn't see through her so effortlessly. Those brown eyes of his disturbed her more than she liked. She found him eminently appealing, dangerously so, and she feared she would lose her head, especially if he kept staring at her that way. Every time she looked up, she met that steady, frank gaze. She grew more breathless with every minute as his presence filled her senses, awakening desire in her blood. "No . . . I suppose I don't trust easily, but surely there's no crime in that?"

"No, but I hope you will have confidence in me."

Not responding, she sat ramrod-straight behind her desk and wrote on a piece of paper. "Here is my sister's address." Rising, she handed it to him, effectively silencing his unasked questions.

He glanced at the address. "Claremont?"

"Just west of Williamsburg," she explained. She went to the corner of the room where a world globe sat on a jardiniere. Swiveling it to the mass of land that was the Americas, she traced her finger to the state of Virginia. "There is Williamsburg. Richmond isn't too far to the northwest."

He stood so close he could smell her hair. Its scent was sweet and clean, like a meadow of flowers. He had a sudden desire to span her corseted waist with his hands and drag them upward until they touched . . .

"You said your friend lives in Richmond?" She was looking at him, her eyes suspicious behind the spectacles.

He cleared the haze of desire from his voice before

speaking. "Yes. He'll help us if need be." He returned to the desk, pretending to study the address. Her script was rounded and precise, with an elegant flourish at the end of each word. He pushed the paper into his pocket and looked down. Beside the ornate silver inkwell was a square box made of beautiful, polished rosewood with inlaid decorations of walnut, sycamore, and mother-of-pearl. The surface was so smooth it felt like satin beneath his fingertips. "How exquisite!"

"I suppose," she said glumly. "It's the only thing Father left me in his will."

"It's quite valuable. I'd say it's Louis Quinze. The French had a way with inlays, y'know."

She didn't respond, and he noticed that her lips had taken a decidedly downward tilt. There was something so sad about her, that seemed to go deep, deep into her soul.

"Is it for sale?" he went on.

"Perhaps."

He felt that familiar rush of excitement he always experienced upon discovering an antique treasure. "How much?" he asked intending to haggle her down.

"Your entire fee for finding my sister," she said softly. "However long it takes. It should inspire you not to waste time."

His jaw dropped. She *was* an astute businesswoman, that much was sure. He laughed, delighted with her mettle. "You drive a hard bargain."

"Take it or leave it." She sat down behind her desk and touched a stack of papers, obviously indicating it was time for him to depart.

"I'll leave it for now," he said ruefully, running his hand over the wonderful wood. "But I'll be back with your sister before you can say jackrabbit."

"Before you can say Jack Robinson," she corrected

him with a sudden smile. Her eyes had a decidedly wicked twinkle, he concluded as he gripped her hand in a hard clasp.

"I'll be back."

lively gentlemen who came seeking the hotel proved
a disconcerting sight to Leonora, who was unable, ...
... her discomfort ...

Chapter 3

"*Who* was that elegant gentleman?" Cecily asked, bursting through the office door just after Thaddeus Webb had left. "And so masculine!"

Maggie glanced up from her desk at her housekeeper and assistant, Cecily Byrne. "I've hired him to find Leonora." Cecily was right. Mr. Webb had been quite elegant in a black cutaway tailcoat, gray vest, immaculate butterfly collar, and ascot tied with a flourish. He dressed with great flair, which she wouldn't have expected, given the chaos of his house. She set down her bills and leaned back in her chair with a sigh. "He's such an unusual man." She proceeded to tell Cecily about Webb's antique shop, watching as her assistant's eyes grew wider and wider.

"A Grecian pillar from the Regency period? What nonsense!" Cecily said with a gasp. Then she laughed, threw herself into a chintz-covered wing chair, and clasped a red satin pillow to her flat bosom. "How eccentric of him to operate a shop filled with rubbish. I'm intrigued." Her eyes sparkled. "Why don't you introduce him to me?"

Maggie eyed her friend with amusement. Although Cecily was fifty-two years old, and rather unattractive with her mousy hair and hooked nose, she had infallibly good humor and an overly romantic heart. Every likely gentleman who checked into the hotel received a close scrutiny from Cecily, and when a suitable candidate came alone, she did her utmost to pair him up with Maggie. It was tiresome at times, but Maggie knew Cecily meant well, and she dared not protest, fearing to dampen her friend's good spirits.

"Admit that you liked Mr. Webb. 'Twould be unnatural if you didn't," Cecily insisted.

"Yes, I daresay he's rather attractive, if you like bear-sized gentlemen." She watched as Cecily's eyes grew misty.

"All those *muscles*, and such broad shoulders!" The spinster clapped her hands to her heart and sighed gustily.

Maggie was saved from more romantic ravings as the bell shrilled on the counter outside the office. "Guests," she reminded Cecily. "They grow impatient if they have to wait. By the way, Victoria said a foreign gentleman asked for me earlier."

"He didn't say where he was from, only that he wanted to meet you. I don't recall seeing him before. He said he'll return." Cecily tossed the pillow onto a chair and leaned over the desk. "You listen to me, Maggie. It's unnatural the way you close yourself off from attractive gentlemen. They aren't all like your tyrannical father. Horace Hartwell was kind, after all."

"Go, Cecily. I'll think about your advice—later," Maggie said tiredly. "Now I have to deal with the monthly bills from butchers, greengrocers, fishmongers—they all want their money."

Cecily left the room with her usual noisy aplomb. Maggie shuddered as the door slammed behind her friend. Cecily was a veritable beacon of light, and a very able businesswoman. The guests liked Cecily's unfailing good nature and her eagerness to be of assistance. Maggie didn't know what she would do if

Cecily ever decided to leave her job. Hartwell's Hotel would never again be as cheerful.

Sighing, Maggie leafed through the latest bills and sorted them in stacks. There had been a time when she barely had enough money to eat, let alone pay her bills on time. Those days would never return, she vowed silently, and pushed up the spectacles that had slid down her nose. Horace had been a poor manager, and when she'd inherited the hotel, it had been losing money. She had buried herself in work, forsaking everything else to make the business flourish. And it had, beyond her dreams. It was her pride and her happiness, thanks to her efforts and her loyal staff.

The muted sounds of laughter and clinking glasses from the lounge seeped through the walls. A sudden stab of longing pierced her. What would it be like to belong to a party of friends sitting around a table drinking champagne and talking? She would probably never know, because she had shut herself off from congenial company for work, work, always work. And for Victoria, of course.

A blush flamed on her cheeks as she recalled how she had come to be a mother. At seventeen, Maggie had been a very lonely girl in her father's mansion when the new stable groom had arrived. Blond and broad-shouldered, he'd had a way with women, especially one who had thirsted madly for affection. Their love affair had been short and intense, culminating in despair when Maggie had discovered that she was pregnant. He had refused to take responsibility for the child and had left in the dead of night.

Frantic that her father would beat her to death if he discovered her pregnancy, she'd run away to London. Alone, working odd jobs, she'd managed to take care of herself until she'd met Horace. It had hurt to learn that her father never intended to contact her—as if he hadn't cared the least about her.

Ever since she'd discovered the groom's betrayal, caution had been the principle by which she'd lived. Maggie had sworn never to trust another man. Her one experience had taught her that physical love could be glorious, but that a man's love was fickle at best—and mostly centered on the carnal aspect. Horace had been the exception, but he had been too ill to pleasure her or take pleasure from her in bed.

Maggie strolled across the room and glanced at herself in the girandole mirror. Oblivious to her features, she saw only the pain eating at her from the inside, making her an empty shell. She had locked up her heart so tightly that it was gasping for air and light and love. Even though she enjoyed the world of business, it was empty without the spice of passion. She knew it, but her fear of being hurt was stronger than her heart's feeble pleas for freedom.

Suddenly disgusted with herself, she flung open the door that led up a set of narrow stairs. At the end of those stairs were hers and Victoria's living quarters. When the house had been remodeled to accommodate more hotel rooms, part of the third floor had been partitioned off for her personal use. She had no kitchen, since she ate all her meals downstairs in her private dining room or in the office.

She hurried along the corridor and looked into Victoria's bedroom. Her daughter was asleep, so Maggie went into her own sitting room next door, which was furnished with stately mahogany pieces. Partitioned off on one side was the tiny study with its davenport, and located at the other end of the room was the door leading to her bedchamber. She went inside and glanced through the window which faced the mews at the back. The fog pressed up against the panes like dingy cotton, concealing the world from her view. A spell of breathlessness swept through her, and she began tearing off her clothes, as if to free herself from the stifling boundaries she had imposed on her life.

The skirt and petticoats came off easily enough, but she fumbled with the patent steel hooks of the busk-fronted corset covering her from bust to upper thighs. After it finally lay defeated on the floor, she could breathe more easily. Rubbing her tender skin, she threw herself on the bed clad only in drawers and chemise. Despite her freedom from the confining clothes, she still felt trapped. The fog was ominous, moving outside the window as if seeking entrance to her rooms. Swallowing a sob, she got up and pulled the heavy velvet draperies closed.

Every day, her loneliness seemed to intensify, slowly suffocating her. She had to do something about it. A trip to the Continent might alleviate her problem, but she could not leave as long as Leonora was missing.

Thaddeus Webb tried to intrude into her thoughts, but she firmly refused to think about him. Yet she was powerless against the attraction that needed no encouragement to make itself known. Her body remembered him as if he was actually in the room with her. She panicked at his powerful allure. She recognized in him the kindness that many of her male business acquaintances lacked, and she also sensed that he found her desirable. She wanted to trust him, to enjoy his flirtation, but how could she? He might only hurt her in the end.

Upset, she got up and unpinned her hair. Her scalp ached after the tight restraint of the chignon. She brushed her hair with her fingers, and it fell, rich and unruly, almost to her waist.

Flinging off the rest of her garments, she pulled a flannel nightgown over her head and crept under the puffy eiderdown. She shivered in the chilly air. Pulling the cover up to her chin, she lay staring into the pleated chintz half tester over her head. Would Mr. Webb be able to find Leonora? She fervently hoped so. He seemed a very capable man. She remembered the heat that had spread over her skin when he had looked at her. If she wasn't careful, his presence in her life might become very uncomfortable.

"I hope he finds Leonora tomorrow." She said aloud. "Then he'll be out of my life for good."

The next day at noon, Thaddeus Webb stood at the corner of Parliament and Bridge Streets, wondering whether it was too early to visit Mrs. Charlotte Scott-Aubrey of Upper Belgrave Place. Hers was the first name on the passenger list which Septimus Horridge had given him. Septimus had been in a sour mood this morning, mocking Thaddeus's efforts to help Margaret Hartwell.

"You believe her story?" he had asked, snorting.

Thaddeus had felt an impulse to give his old friend a taste of his fists. But he had let the fit of temper pass. "I don't know why you wouldn't, Septimus. You must be losing your touch," he had rejoined. "Mrs. Hartwell is telling the truth."

Thaddeus chuckled at the memory of Septimus's outraged face. His old friend had always been a curmudgeon, a cynic to his fingertips, and a misogynist. Nevertheless, he was an honest man, and a good policeman.

Tatters of fog still hung in the air, but a bleak sun was trying to penetrate the thinning blanket. The day might become lovely yet. Charlotte Scott-Aubrey, here I come, he thought, and set out on foot, since he always thought better while walking. He would investigate all the passengers who had had staterooms on the steamer. Then, if no clue turned up, he would question the less wealthy passengers.

After walking a little more than a mile and a half, he arrived invigorated at a white town house with wrought-iron balustrades. A maid in a black-and-white uniform opened the door.

"Is Mrs. Scott-Aubrey in?" he asked, handing her one of his cards.

The maid bobbed a curtsy. "Let me see."

Ten minutes later he was kicking his heels in a parlor so cluttered with bric-a-brac that it resembled his own shop. A small, plump, black-clad lady with a bush of white hair partly concealed under a white cap swept into the room.

"Mr. Webb? I don't think I've had the pleasure . . ." She threw a cursory glance at his card. "However, I'm not interested in antiques today."

Thaddeus smiled, cursing himself for using one card for his two businesses. He'd tried to be thrifty, but he'd found out time and again that printing up one set of cards had not been a good idea. "I'm here in the capacity of detective."

Her white eyebrows shot up. "Are you with Scotland Yard?"

She evidently hadn't read his card carefully. "No, I do private investigations. I'm looking for a missing woman."

"Oh? I see. Well, I just returned from a long trip to my brother in New York and have not yet had time to step outside. I have barely seen *anyone* since I returned, so I'm afraid I can't help you."

Thaddeus took out the calotype of Leonora from a protective envelope. "Do you recall seeing this woman on the steamer, Mrs. Scott-Aubrey?" He handed her the picture, closely studying the lady's wrinkled face for signs of recognition.

She pursed her small mouth and lifted a magnifying glass from a workbasket on a chair. Walking to the window where the light was better, she studied the picture for thirty seconds. Her face betrayed nothing.

"I'm afraid I can't help you, young man," she said with a sigh. "There were so many beautiful ladies on board, and they all looked very much the same to me."

Disappointment shot through Thaddeus. What had he expected? It would be too easy if the first person he questioned recognized Miss Leonora. "Are you absolutely certain?"

The lady nodded. "Yes, I never saw her." She returned the picture. "I hope you'll have better luck elsewhere. It would be terrible if something had happened to the young lady."

As Thaddeus prepared to leave, she scooped up a newspaper from a chintz-covered chair. "She couldn't be one of these victims, could she?" Mrs. Scott-Aubrey commented, and handed him the paper. "Such barbarians live among us in London. Have you read about it?"

He scanned the headlines:

ANOTHER BRUTAL MURDER IN THE EAST END

A wealthy young woman—recently married—was found stabbed and burned to death and left on a makeshift altar in an empty building. Is there a connection with the previous "Altar Murder"? Both victims were lovely blondes. Scotland Yard is investigating . . .

He slowly folded the paper. "I don't think Miss Leonora Winston was one of them. It's a remote possibility. Besides, as far as we know, she wasn't married."

"Oh." The old lady came up close and stared at him through the lorgnette suspended on a velvet ribbon around her neck. Her voice lowered to a hoarse whisper. "I sense danger around you, young man. Be careful. Death is close."

The skin prickled on the back of his neck, and a

sudden cold spread through his limbs. He smiled humorlessly. "Are you a soothsayer, perchance?"

She flung out her chubby arms in a disarming gesture. "Oh, no, but I do sense things sometimes."

"I can only hope you are wrong." He bowed. "Thank you for your assistance."

By the time he walked toward Kensington and the second interview, the sun was warming his back. Not only had it dispersed the fog, but it soon dissolved the dark cloud of dread that had enveloped him at Upper Belgrave Square. He shouldn't listen to an old women's talk. It was nothing but pure nonsense.

The next two interviews yielded nothing. At the end of the third, he decided to have tea since it was past five o'clock. He'd better go home and see if his partner, Gavin "Peg" Talbot, had bought anything, or, better yet, sold something—perhaps even the Grecian pillar. He walked from Berkley Square to Maddox Street, which wasn't far. Dusk was swallowing the afternoon as he entered the darkened hallway. Light came from the back parlor, a room which was, as yet, relatively free of clutter. He stepped inside.

He halted on the threshold. Mrs. Hartwell was seated on the edge of an old leather wing chair, and Gavin was serving her tea. Something cringed inside him as Gavin gave Margaret Hartwell one of his smiles, which could charm a ninety-year-old crone into blushing.

Obviously Mrs. Hartwell was no exception. That Gavin had lost one of his arms didn't seem to lessen his appeal to the ladies. He wore his artificial limb with flair, just as he did everything else.

"Thad, old dog, you look like you misplaced your bone," Gavin said. "Tea is steaming hot, just the way you like it. Lemons fresh from Covent Garden. I managed to convince Hetty that we couldn't live another day without her scones so she made us some." He turned to Maggie. "Hetty is our cook."

Thaddeus drew closer, cheered by the heat from the fire and the view of Margaret Hartwell in his favorite chair. "So you've met Mrs. Hartwell, Peg." He winked at her, and she pinched her lips tightly together. "I'm pleased to see you, and grateful to Hetty that we have fresh scones to offer you, Mrs. Hartwell." He felt an urge to touch her, and was surprised by its fierceness.

"I came around to hear if you've found any clues," she explained. "I know I shouldn't pressure you, but I'll go mad waiting at home." She looked embarrassed to be confessing her impatience. What had made her so reserved? he wondered, and sipped his tea. A slice of lemon swam in the red-gold liquid. The tea was almost the color of her hair.

"I'm afraid I found nothing today." He told her about his three visits, omitting Mrs. Scott-Aubrey's strange prediction and the newspaper headlines.

Her cup rattled. "How disappointing! I wish you'd found at least a small clue. This waiting enervates me more than I can say."

He searched for words that would soothe her, but remained silent. Leonora's disappearance was indeed strange—if she had, in fact, reached England—and there was nothing he could say to alter that fact.

Gavin came to his assistance. "You must have faith in Thad, Miss Hartwell. If anyone can find your sister, he can." He offered her a tray of preserves. "These things take time. Thad is very thorough and—"

"And slow, you were going to add, weren't you, Peg?" Thaddeus filled in, schooling his voice to blandness.

Mrs. Hartwell lowered her gaze. "I'm sorry to press you, but you must understand—I can't bear the suspense. Is there some way to speed up the investigation?''

"Don't apologize," Gavin told her, flashing another devilish smile, and Thaddeus wanted to wring his neck. "Perhaps you could help Thaddeus. Four eyes and ears are better than two."

Thaddeus wanted to punch that smiling face now. What wild idea had popped into Gavin's head? What *right* did he have to involve himself? Gavin winked at Thaddeus. Did he fancy himself a matchmaker? Thaddeus groaned silently as he noticed Mrs. Hartwell's face brightening at the suggestion. How could he turn her down politely? He would *not* have his investigation hampered by Margaret Hartwell!

Damn you, Gavin! he swore silently while plastering a polite smile on his face. Gavin was too smooth. Whereas he himself was too large to be nimble, Gavin was all slender grace. Even with a wooden arm, he gesticulated as if he were a dancer. His eyes were expressive, his face lean and elastic. He had a mercurial temper, but compassion as well. Women loved him, and Thaddeus could never keep track of his latest conquests.

Whereas he longed for a permanent relationship, and tried to probe beyond the glittering, heady surfaces of the women he met, Gavin broke hearts with the speed of a summer gale.

Usually Thaddeus was resigned, but this was one instance when he resented Gavin's ready charm. "I'll continue my investigation tomorrow, and with some luck, I should learn something about your sister," he told Mrs. Hartwell, wondering what she looked like without her spectacles "But I warn you, it might take longer than you think."

She nodded. "But there must be a faster way to get results. As Mr. Talbot suggested, I wouldn't mind helping you. You don't know how difficult it is to sit at home or at the office, wondering about your progress. I would truly appreciate it if you let me help."

She sipped her tea, then set down her cup, fixing him with those disconcerting blue eyes that made him feel hot and breathless. "A strange thing has happened."

"What?" he asked, stiffening.

"I'm not sure you noticed, but on my desk, opposite the wooden box that you covet, stood another box, a black japanned box with garish patterns. They were popular a few years back, and I bought one at the market to give to my assistant who'd asked for it, but she had already bought one herself, so mine ended up on my desk, holding paper clips and other odds and ends." She sighed and fingered the cameo at her throat. "The box is gone."

"Gone?"

"As in stolen?" Gavin added.

"I don't know," Maggie said. "I certainly didn't move it, and I trust my staff implicitly." Her voice faded, and there was pallor in her cheeks.

"You . . . think someone entered your office and stole it—today?" Thaddeus leaned closer to her. The same prickly sensation he had felt when Mrs. Scott-Aubrey mentioned the Altar Murders skittered over his skin.

"I've questioned all the servants. They claimed no one was in the office today except Miss Byrne, my assistant, and I believe them. Who would want that box? It's worth next to nothing."

"Who indeed?" Gavin said with a ghoulish smile.

Silence fell as they pondered the question.

"Perhaps I'm overreacting. The box must be somewhere in the hotel." Maggie gazed intently at Thaddeus. "Mr. Webb, please. If you don't mind, I would like to accompany you as you go about your business tomorrow."

He smiled wryly. "I'm afraid that's out of the question. Don't you trust me?"

"It's not that—"

"I'd rather not bring you along. It would hamper my investigation."

Her eyes flashed mutinously. "I wouldn't be in the way." She rose. "I resent your implication—"

"You cannot come. That's final." He stood, too, and when she hurried toward the front door, he was right behind her. She turned to him in the doorway.

"I have the right to accompany you. After all, I'm the one paying your bill. A large one at that."

He spread his hands in apology. "I work alone."

"We'll see about that," she said. "Tomorrow."

Chapter 4

The next day dawned humid and cold. Rising at five, Maggie mulled over the disappearance of the japanned box from her desk. She trusted her employees, but could one of them have been so greedy as to steal a worthless box? All her guests were wealthy and quite distinguished, not liable to stoop to petty theft. Besides, it wasn't the loss of the box that worried her; it was the fact that someone had come, unbidden, into her office.

Maggie sighed as she walked through her rooms clad in a dressing gown of black silk patterned with Oriental birds and flowers. Although she had searched every nook and cranny on the previous evening, she still hoped she would find the box somewhere. But she knew it was gone. It had always stood on her desk, and since it contained only paper clips and other odds and ends, there had never been a reason to bring it with her upstairs.

She knelt in front of her armoire and searched the bottom drawer. Nothing out of order there. *Was* it possible that one of her employees had stolen it? No . . . but the thought made her uneasy.

Straightening from her bent position, she looked through her clothes for a suitable costume to wear while pursuing the investigation with Thaddeus Webb. She *would* go with him, no matter what his

objections. Mr. Talbot's suggestion that she assist Mr.
Webb had relieved her. Mr. Webb must understand
her worry and allow her to participate. She would
much rather be involved than sit at the hotel wondering about Webb's progress. She would stay in the
background, not be in the way.

Taking extra care as she dressed, she thought about
Mr. Webb. He seemed capable, but he also *saw* too
much, sensed too much about her. He also asked too
many questions about her past.

Twitching the black wool of her gored skirt into
place, she swung around in front of the mirror. The
white high-necked blouse with gigot sleeves was immaculate. Every curl of her unruly hair was subdued
and pinned in place. With a last tweak of the spotted
blue silk bow at her collar, she was ready to face
Thaddeus Webb. Carrying her cloak, hat, and umbrella, she stepped downstairs to the private dining
room beyond the kitchen, where she always shared
breakfast with Cecily and Victoria—if her daughter
was awake—before the day began.

"Don't worry, Miss Maggie, I'll take care of everything," Cecily Byrne said over porridge. "Miss Lather
will take Victoria to the zoological gardens today. The
gates aren't open to the public, but Miss Lather evidently knows one of the animal handlers."

"Hmmm . . . Victoria will enjoy that, of course,"
Maggie murmured, her thoughts on other things. "I'll
look in on Victoria before I leave. Don't forget that
the fishmonger will deliver this morning." Maggie
sipped the hot tea and looked at the watch pinned to
her blouse. She would make sure to be at Mr. Webb's
house well before he could possibly begin his investigation for the day. "And tell Gertie to thoroughly
clean Lord and Lady Libcott's suite before they arrive.
You know how particular they are," she added with
a sigh. "And in Lord Libcott's room, place a box of
the obnoxious Havana cigars of which he's so fond."

"You think of everything, Maggie. I pray this business with your sister will be resolved soon. You must be under a terrible strain." Cecily gave her employer a compassionate glance. "You look worn out."

Maggie pictured wrinkles on her pale skin in the unkind morning light. "No matter," she snapped. "I cannot be vain and worry about the effects of stress in these circumstances."

"*I* would like to impress a gentleman like Mr. Webb," Cecily went on, undaunted. "Such a *solid* man, and those brown eyes—"

"That's enough, Cecily!" Maggie rose decisively and carried her cup and saucer to the scullery. She returned, saying, "I have no intention of impressing Mr. Webb one way or the other. My plan is to find Leonora as soon as may be."

She inspected the much-scrubbed plank floor of the kitchen and viewed the larders to see that everything was in order. Satisfied, she hurried up the stairs. Victoria's room was dark, and her daughter slept curled up in a ball under the eiderdown. An old doll was clamped under one arm. Maggie smiled and kissed Victoria's forehead. "Good morning, darling," she whispered, but Victoria did not stir. After placing an orange—Victoria's favorite fruit—on the chair next to the bed, Maggie put on her outer garments and left.

"There's a new bounce in Maggie's footstep," Cecily said to no one in particular as the kitchen maids began assembling to assist the unpredictable French chef, Monsieur André, who often arrived in a foul temper due to a late night of imbibing cognac.

"Bounce?" asked golden-haired Gertie, the youngest of the maids. Only fifteen years old, she acted as both upstairs and kitchen maid since she was eager to learn all angles of managing a household. She aspired to become a housekeeper in the future and, in Cecily's mind, resembled what Maggie would have looked like if she'd ever been as carefree as Gertie.

"Rafferty's already at 'is post by th' front door, Miss Byrne."

"I said *bounce*, not bouncer," Cecily corrected her. "Besides, Rafferty is a doorman, not a bouncer."

With a glint of humor in her eyes, Gertie shrugged her shoulders and watched the other maids bustling about laying out knives of all sizes on a pristine linen towel. "All th' same to me." She rose on tiptoes and peered out the window.

"Gertie, you have chores to do," Cecily reminded her sternly. She opened a cupboard and pulled out a stack of towels.

Gertie sighed. "There goes Mrs. Hartwell now," she said as she continued staring at the street. "I wish I had a hat like 'ers, one with veils and green ostrich feathers." Gertie turned away from the window. "I'd better clean Mrs. Hartwell's flat while she's gone."

Maggie hurried toward the nearest cab stand. Not that she couldn't walk the short distance to Maddox Street, but arriving in a hansom would be more businesslike. She would tell the cabbie to wait to strengthen the effect. She intended to show the stubborn Mr. Webb that she was firm in her decision to join him in his investigation.

Ten minutes later, at six-thirty, she squared her shoulders and stabbed the tip of her umbrella into the pavement as she faced the green lacquered door of Webb's shop. She knew she looked her most formidable, but inside she felt a twinge of insecurity. Webb had a most disturbing influence on her heartbeat, and that was a phenomena she could do nothing to alter.

After several nerve-wracking minutes the door opened and Mr. Webb emerged. His massive shoulders were covered in a caped greatcoat, and his chestnut-brown hair curled endearingly over his collar. He wore an atrociously knitted black scarf that was at least two and a half yards long and wound around his neck twice, its ends hanging down the front. He held a black homburg lightly in one hand as he gesticulated with the other.

"What a surprise," he said sardonically as he closed the door and stepped onto the sidewalk. "I didn't know ladies got up this early in the morning."

Maggie nervously adjusted the spotted veil of her wide-brimmed hat and cleared her throat. "Good morning, Mr. Webb. I've been up since five o'clock." A blush stole into her cheeks as his gaze connected with hers. His brown eyes were direct and compelling, and she smiled with embarrassment.

"Aha! You're one of those tedious people who always gets up at the crack of dawn," he said, his lips widening into a grin. "Mrs. Hartwell, what are you doing here, pray tell? I told you—"

Maggie drew herself up and said in her firmest voice, "You know very well why I'm here. I wanted to intercept you before you left for the day."

He pressed his hat down on his head and swung one of the long ends of the scarf over the shoulder. "I told you last evening—in no uncertain terms—that I work alone. Besides, my investigation might be dangerous, and if not that, you might tire too easily."

"I can take care of myself, and I promise I won't be in the way. It isn't as if we're going mountain-climbing in Tibet or crossing the Sahara desert." She jabbed her umbrella into the stone step. "I have enough stamina to brave a day of investigation in London." She paused. "And you will be there to protect me."

He sighed and studied her stubborn chin remembering how he'd failed to protect his wife Rachel from an early death. Icy dread shot through his veins, but he forced himself to forget the painful memories. He *would* shield Maggie Hartwell from the dangers of London. "I was about to visit a French café in Soho that serves a decent breakfast, but it is a place to which I would never bring a lady."

She tilted up her chin. "I have seen most areas of London, including Soho."

He raised his eyebrows. "You shock me."

His voice flowed over her, thick and seductive, and Maggie felt a weakening in her knees. "So?" she asked coolly.

He threw a quick glance at the gray sky. "Very well. Today you may come. By this evening, you'll be heartily tired of detective work." He grinned at her challengingly.

She gave him her most daunting glare in return. "I asked the cabbie to wait." She stepped inside the hansom and was grateful for the rug Webb spread over her legs before joining her.

"After I've had my breakfast we'll go to Bolton Street. According to the passenger list, a Mrs. Clement of that address traveled on the steamer from New York. The female passengers are the most likely to have spoken with your sister. We'll visit them first, and if their information doesn't lead us to Miss Winston, we'll try the gentlemen." His dark gaze probed her face through the veil. "Are you prepared for this? You may be disappointed if we find no clue."

"This is better than sitting at home waiting," she said breathlessly, deeply aware of his elbow touching hers. He took up most of the cab seat, and his aura of virility and strength was highly disturbing in the close confines. She found that his attractiveness frightened her, broke down her defenses when she most needed their protection. Awkward and shy, she was unable to relax in his presence. The cab traveled down Maddox Street, crossed busy Regent Street, and entered Soho. Great Marlborough Street brought them farther into the heart of Soho, which was noisy and strewn with litter, every lane seedier than the last. Soho was crowded with foreign restaurants, public houses, and gambling salons.

Thinking about her sister, Maggie sighed. How had Leonora passed the night? Was she a prisoner in some ramshackle building in the East End, or . . . ?

"You're worried," he said, more as a statement than in inquiry.

She clenched her gloved hands. "Yes, I am concerned. It's funny that just two weeks ago I didn't know I had a sister."

"Quite a shock, I imagine."

She looked at him from the corner of her eye. "Do you have sisters?"

He chuckled. "Two. Delia, the scholar, who will be married soon, and Amintha, sixteen years old and quite frivolous." He sighed in mock exasperation. "I also have two brothers, Tim and Ben. They're ten-year-old twins and quite a handful—must have shortened my mother's life considerably." He gave her a keen glance. "But you wouldn't know about little brothers."

"That's true," she answered with a smile that transformed her face. "But I have a six-year-old daughter."

His surprise was palpable. "Daughter! You don't look old enough—"

"Oh, stop that," she said lightly. "Victoria was born when I was eighteen."

"Which makes you . . . twenty-four. Hartwell's Hotel has a terribly young proprietor."

"It's rude to mention a lady's age," she admonished.

Snorting, he leaned back against the seat, pressing her further into the corner. "Ridiculous rules! Why should a lady be ashamed of her age?" His eyes were dancing with mischief, and she curled her hand into a fist.

"So you disapprove of common politeness, Mr. Webb?"

His shrug was eloquent. "I'm not ashamed to tell the world that I'm thirty years old. In fact, I'm proud to have survived this long, considering the robberies and assaults in London."

"You sound like Sergeant Horridge, as if you were always keeping an eye on the unsavory characters that make the streets unsafe."

"I am, I am. Like a good citizen, I try to protect innocent victims—women and children, first and foremost—no matter what their age."

She fumed in silence. Every time she said something, he made some infuriating comment.

"But you disapprove of general courtesy?" She pressed her lips together, hoping he wouldn't notice how much he riled her.

"I grant you courtesy is important on occasion, but the fiddle-faddle about age, and which fork to use at a posh dinner, has nothing to do with respecting other human beings."

"I disagree." She squared her shoulders. "I would find it singularly distasteful if a stranger on an omnibus leaned over and asked my age." She stiffened even further as his hand landed on her shoulder.

"Relax, Mrs. Hartwell. This argument will only give you a blazing headache. You're tense as a bowstring." He massaged her shoulder gently.

She tried to squirm away, giving him a glance brimming with reproach. "*What* are you doing, Mr. Webb?"

"It's highly unlikely that some stranger would ask you your age on the bus." He smiled wickedly and removed his hand. "And if he or she did, what would it matter? You could treat the question as a joke and say that you're ninety-two."

"Oh, how can you be so flippant!" She tried to move away from him so violently that her hat slid

askew, the spotted net brushing against her eyelashes. Why couldn't she catch his lighthearted mood
instead of closing up and snapping at him? She just
couldn't trust him . . . not any more than she'd been
able to trust any of the gentlemen she'd ever met.

He gently lifted the offending veil and said softly,
"I told you it was a bad idea to spend the day together." He rapped on the roof, and the hansom
stopped. "Hartwell's Hotel," he ordered through the
window.

"*No!*" Maggie shouted.

They stared at each other. "I promise I won't argue
with you," she added with a sigh.

Thaddeus laughed. "A difficult promise, I take it?"
He spoke to the cabbie. "Very well, François's Café
in Dean Street."

Maggie remained tight-lipped for the remainder of
the trip, regretting her decision to spend the day with
him. The last thing Thaddeus asked before stepping
down outside the café was, "One thing that puzzles
me. If you were married for only four years, how do
you have a daughter who's six?"

Her eyes shot daggers. "*Who* told you that my marriage lasted four years?"

He held out his hand to assist her down. "Silver
can buy almost any information. I use it frequently to
ferret out answers."

She ignored his hand and stepped down. "You
won't tell me who, will you?"

"I'm not a tattler."

Her chin rose a fraction. "I'll find out. It won't be
difficult."

"I admire your determination," he murmured in
her ear, and held the restaurant door open for her.
"But this time you'll bang your head against the
wall."

She shuddered in revulsion as she viewed the
greasy wallpaper and frayed tablecloths of the dining

room. "You come here to eat?" she asked incredulously, and turned beet-red as she recognized what must be a lady of the night openly kissing an inebriated gentleman at one of the tables. They were drinking wine and giggling hysterically. The restaurant was almost full, though it was still early in the morning.

"The food is heavenly. François is the best cook in London."

Her lips quirked. "I'm sure Monsieur André would have a fit of temper if he heard you."

"Your cook, I take it?" He led her to one of the tables and dusted off the chair seat.

"Yes, the most temperamental cook in London." Thaddeus helped Maggie remove her coat, and she sat down and viewed the room surreptitiously. "I'm surprised it's open at this hour."

"François' is open all the time." Thad glanced significantly at the ceiling. "Gambling upstairs, twenty-four hours a day. Illicit, of course." He unwound his hideous scarf and hung it along with their coats on pegs on the wall.

"Gambling?" She gasped and threw a furtive glance out the window.

"The police raid the place frequently." Thad waved at a pale, dark-haired man behind the counter. "François himself," he explained and sat down.

The Frenchman smiled and pointed toward the kitchen. He was as daintily formed as a porcelain figure, and his hair was flat and shiny with macassar oil. He disappeared and returned shortly with two cups and a coffeepot on a tray. Steam curled from the spout. Boiled milk misted in a creamer.

"*Bonjour*, Meester Webb! I will make a lovely omelet *au champignons*," he said, beaming. "No?"

"Sounds delicious, François." Thaddeus eyed Maggie thoughtfully. "And bring a basket of pastries for the lady."

"No, thank you," Maggie said. "I have already

eaten." She indicated the coffee. "I will take a cup, please."

"*Café au lait*," François said. He filled the cups, half hot milk, half coffee, and left.

Maggie sipped, savoring the strong flavor. "Do you come here frequently?" she asked Thaddeus.

"Yes, several times a week. Cooking is a skill I don't possess. As you know from your visit at the shop, Peg—Gavin—and I have a cook. But Hetty usually doesn't arrive until dinnertime. And sometimes she never comes at all."

"You must discipline your servants," Maggie said sternly, peering at him over her spectacles.

He laughed. "Listening to you, I can easily imagine what your father must have been like—a rigid disciplinarian, a martinet."

She bristled, her back ramrod-straight. "Mr. Webb! You must use your deductive powers for the problem at hand, not for prying into my past."

His eyes gleamed. "But I was right, wasn't I?"

Maggie seethed, her lips compressed into a thin line. He wouldn't take his eyes off her, and she cringed with embarrassment. She hated losing control of her feelings, and she wished her heart wouldn't pound quite so hard. "Haven't you learned that it's rude to stare?" she admonished, and tilted up her chin.

He leaned closer, his lips twitching. "Forgive me, but I'm stunned by your beauty," he whispered conspiratorially. "Don't you feel the attraction between us?"

Oh, yes, I do. Maggie blushed to the roots of her hair and refused to look at him. She burned to get up and leave the restaurant, but that would tell him just how much he disturbed her. Finally she had to meet his gaze, and what she read there made her blush deepen. "Shame on you, Mr. Webb!"

To her relief, the omelet arrived and the infuriating

Mr. Webb gave it, and a plate of crusty rolls, his entire attention. She sipped her coffee in silence and watched the gray patch of sky outside the window. The clattering cutlery created a homey atmosphere, and she realized how sweet it would be to share breakfast with a man every morning. Cecily's presence was always comforting, but with a man Maggie would feel . . . intimate. But to share a table with Mr. Webb was an entirely different experience. He was so . . . well, so infuriating. She had never met a man like him before.

She was jerked from her reverie by a shrill whistle coming from outside. The door suddenly crashed open, and a group of men stormed inside.

"Police. Make way!" they shouted, and hurtled up the stairs.

"A raid," Thaddeus said. "We'd better leave or we might end up answering questions all day at the police station—unless I know one of the constables."

But as they rose from the table, reaching for their coats, the panicked diners began to surge toward them, all rushing to squeeze at once through the main door. Maggie's spectacles were suddenly wrenched from her face and she was forced back against the wall, Thaddeus pressed shoulder to thigh against her. She could hardly breathe under the weight of his hard chest. Their eyes met and clashed.

"On second thought, why don't we wait here until the crowd is gone?" he suggested with a grin.

She was deeply aware of his hard, manly form molding to her gentler curves. His eyes were so close to hers, she could see every nuance of his emotions, ranging from annoyance to incredulity and amusement.

"Not a bad place to be crushed, considering . . ." he muttered and shifted his legs so that one pressed between hers, the other on the outside of her right thigh. "Very soft—cushioned where female cushions should be." His eyes were by now glowing with mischief.

"Move back this very instant," Maggie demanded when she could find her voice. Panting with anger, she tried to push him away, but he was as heavy as a sack of cement. His body pinioned her against the wall, and his torso pressed against her chest. Her hat had fallen off, but the veil was still stuck to her face. It tickled her nose unbearably. "Please . . ." Her plea sounded lame. Her eyes widened in shock when at the joining of her thighs she felt the growing, hard proof of his male anatomy.

"By Jove," he growled. "Ma'am, your curves are very provoking to a certain member of my—"

"*Mr. Webb!*" She knotted her fingers into a fist. "I will scream if you don't release me instantly."

He made no move to shift his weight away from her. His darkening gaze drifted lazily to her heaving chest. Maggie knew very well that her tight blouse revealed the contours of her bosom. He rubbed one leg against her and a delicious shiver coursed through her. She lost her breath momentarily as he looked straight into her eyes. He finally seemed to realize that they were now alone in the restaurant, but instead of stepping aside, he lowered his lips toward hers. "So very soft," he muttered.

Footsteps pounded on the upper floor of the building, then rattled down the steps. Curses and shouts rent the air.

Maggie flailed her left arm weakly to draw attention to her predicament, and she soon saw the blue-clad figure of a bobby coming toward them.

"What's amiss here?" the policeman boomed. "Has the lady fainted?"

With that infuriating grin on his lips, Thaddeus Webb slowly released his hold on her. "One more minute and she would have," he drawled, and held out his hand toward her.

She refused his aid. Her hair was coming down around her face, and her black skirt was smudged with dirt. She stumbled away from the wall, grabbed the first napkin she could find, and wiped furiously.

"Aw, miss, you look like you could use a sip o' brandy," the bobby said, and bent to retrieve Maggie's hat. He turned to Thaddeus. "And, Mr. Webb, what are you doin' here? Breakfast as usual?"

"Yes, Jeremy, I hope you won't close down the restaurant."

"We'll see. One of our routine raids. A card-gamblin' party was assembled upstairs. Had been goin' all night, I presume. We'll take 'em down to the station and give François a stiff fine." Jeremy watched Maggie as she struggled to pin up her hair. "I'm sorry about the to-do. See you at the Yard sometime, Mr. Webb."

He left, and Maggie gave Thaddeus a fuming stare. "Of all the gall—"

"Shhh," he whispered. "Don't start. And since my breakfast is ruined, we'd better leave." He bent to pick up her spectacles. Before she put on the hat, he placed the gold rims over the bridge of her nose and pushed the curved wires behind her ears. "There! You look just like before, though I must say I now detect a sparkle in your eyes."

"From anger," she spat, and reached for her coat, pulled it on, and adjusted the veil of her hat over her face. She found her umbrella under a stack of cloaks.

Thaddeus shrugged on his coat and wound the scarf twice around his neck. "I take it you will return home now. This has been a most upsetting morning for you."

She glared at his goading smile, and pounded the tip of her umbrella on the floor. "The day has just begun, and I intend to fulfill what I set out to do. And that's that!"

Chapter 5

Mrs. Clement's home in Bolton Street was a handsome white Georgian town house. Maggie glanced with misgivings at her rumpled skirt and wondered if it was a good idea to enter such an establishment without first making more thorough repairs to her appearance. What would Mrs. Clement think of her?

Thaddeus told the cabbie to wait. He offered his arm to Maggie, but she ignored it with a toss of her head. Smiling ruefully, he let the brass knocker fall twice. Almost immediately, a wizened butler dressed in a black-and-yellow-striped vest and a black frock coat opened the door.

Thaddeus handed him his card. "I would like to see Mrs. Clement," he said.

The servant motioned them to enter. "One moment, please."

Maggie and Thaddeus waited in strained silence. A few minutes later the butler returned.

"This way," he said, and led them into a salon dominated by a huge red carpet, heavy mahogany furniture, and a bird cage containing a plant. "Mrs. Clement will be with you momentarily."

Maggie nodded and moved as far away from Thaddeus as she could. She sat on the edge of an ottoman covered in striped green satin. A dusty potted palm

on a wicker table beside her partly shielded her from
him.

"Are you afraid to be alone in a room with me?"
he chided, sitting down on a spindly-legged chair that
looked as if it might fail to support his considerable
bulk.

"Any sane woman would be petrified after the total
disregard you showed for propriety and . . . *respect* at
the restaurant. Your behavior was reprehensible!"
Maggie fingered the handle of her umbrella, debating
whether to stab him with the steel tip. She was sorely
tempted, but she couldn't reach him from where she
was sitting.

The door opened. "Good morning, Mr. . . .
Webb." A middle-aged woman with a graying top-
knot and pince-nez on her long nose entered. "I don't
believe we've met," she said. She was dressed in
tweeds—jacket, wide ankle-length skirt, and riding
boots. Her back was just as straight as Maggie's. She
gave Thaddeus's ratty-looking scarf a disapproving
glance above the rims of her pince-nez.

Undaunted by her scrutiny, he stood. "Good morning. If you don't mind, Mrs. Clement, I would like to
ask you a few questions about a passenger on the
steamship on which you traveled from New York."
He indicated Maggie. "This is Mrs. Hartwell, and
we're looking for her sister, Leonora Winston, who
journeyed on the steamer." He handed her the picture of Leonora.

Mrs. Clement smiled at Maggie. "Oh, hello. I'm
sorry if I kept you waiting, but I just arrived from a
riding excursion to Richmond Park. So your sister is
missing?" She studied the calotype.

"Yes . . . I'm afraid so," Maggie said. "Did you
happen to meet a woman by the name of Winston on
the ship?"

The other woman shook her head. "No, I can't recall that I did. However, one elderly woman I met in

the lounge told me she had spoken to a young lady who insisted that someone was following her. She was afraid of being pushed overboard some dark night. It was a frightfully gloomy prospect, I thought. Could that young woman have been your sister?"

"How horrible," Maggie said with a shudder. "I do hope it isn't true! The lady you spoke with, do you recall her name?"

"Ghastly crowds on those ships," Mrs. Clement said, pursing her lips. "But wait! I think I might have her card somewhere." She stalked across the floor and rummaged in a desk strewn with papers. While Mrs. Clement flipped through her correspondence, Thaddeus gave Maggie a wink and a smile. She frowned back at him, pinching her lips, and he pretended to look frightened.

"We're grateful for your help," he said to the woman in tweeds, and earned a frosty stare.

Maggie noticed the exchange and smiled gleefully at Thaddeus, whose eyebrows drew together. As his eyes began to smolder, he cleared his throat and twirled his hat between his large hands.

"Ah! Here we are then." Mrs. Clement handed Maggie a cream-colored card which bore the name of Mrs. Hubert Smith-Jones in gold lettering. The address was Park Lane, not too far from Bolton Street.

Maggie slipped the card into her pocket. "Thank you very much." She rose and walked toward the door. Perhaps they could find some definite answers today.

"I hope you find your sister. Surely Mrs. Smith-Jones spoke with Miss Winston. I'm sure you'll find your sister alive and well," Mrs. Clement said before closing the door.

As they entered the hansom, Thaddeus said, "I take it you insist on seeing Mrs. Smith-Jones immediately?"

"Of course! The more we fit into one day, the less I have to pay you."

"I want that inlaid wooden box on your office desk, remember? No matter how long it takes to find Miss Winston."

"Very well, but the sooner this matter is settled, the better," she said. "Let's get on with it."

"Yes, ma'am. Your wish is my command." He chuckled, but there was little warmth in his mirth.

"If you don't watch out, you'll end up like the lady we just met, all starch and no heart."

Maggie drew herself up. "Well! What becomes of me is none of your concern, Mr. Webb."

At Piccadilly, Thaddeus ordered the cabbie to stop. He waved to the paperboy on the street corner and got a copy of the *Times.* Black headlines covered the entire front page: ALTAR MURDERS CONTINUE. IS THE RIPPER STRIKING AGAIN?

Maggie shivered. "They never caught the killer of Whitechapel in eighty-eight. Is it possible he has returned?"

His lips set into a grim line, Thaddeus folded the paper and tucked it under his arm. "Anything is possible, but I think the police will catch the killer this time."

"How many murders have there been?" Maggie asked, thinking about Leonora.

"Three. All young, wealthy women, recently married." Thaddeus shot her a keen glance, sensing the turn of her thoughts. "Don't believe the worst. I'm sure Miss Winston isn't one of them. The women who died were all Londoners."

They drove on in silence, the hansom jostling omnibuses and drays on busy Piccadilly. It started to rain, big drops that made the air miserably cold. "Christmas will soon be upon us," Maggie said to lighten the tension. "How will you celebrate it?"

"With my family at home. We go caroling and drink

hot toddies in the neighboring houses. We know everyone on the street since my parents have never
moved from their flat at Ludgate Hill.'' He paused.
''How about you?''

''I will celebrate with my daughter. We have a
Christmas gathering with all the employees at the hotel on Christmas Eve, then we go to church on Christmas morning.''

Thaddeus smiled. ''I'd like to meet your daughter
someday. And just consider, this year your sister
might join in the festivities.''

''I hope so.'' Maggie viewed the bare branches of
the trees in Hyde Park as the hansom turned onto
Park Lane.

Stately town houses with Corinthian pillars and
clipped evergreen bushes flanking the front steps
lined Park Lane. A row of trees that was the bound-
ary to Hyde Park rose on the opposite side of the
street, their dripping branches swaying in the breeze.

The hansom stopped in front of a house with im-
posing marble steps and an oak door with a polished
brass letter box. ''I hope Mrs. Smith-Jones is at
home,'' Maggie mused aloud.

Thaddeus held out his hand to help her down, and
this time she forgot to ignore him. He squeezed her
fingers reassuringly. ''We can always return if she
isn't.''

She hesitated, then pulled her hand away. His clasp
had felt so comforting. ''Mr. Webb,'' she admonished
lamely, and hurried up the steps before he could dis-
cern her blush.

This door had a bell with a pull on the outside. The
clang reverberated throughout the house. A female
servant wearing a black high-necked gown and a
starched white apron admitted them.

Thaddeus asked for Mrs. Smith-Jones, and they
were shown into a chamber decorated in the Oriental
style with painted folding screens and pictures of

mandarins on the walls. Dragons and exotic flowers adorned the carpet underfoot, and an urn held a cluster of dried pampas grass.

Mrs. Smith-Jones was a wispy, white-haired woman dressed in layers of pastel-colored cashmere shawls and a pink velvet skirt. Leaning on a stick, she moved unsteadily over the carpet, making Maggie fear that the slightest draft would topple her.

"How can I help you?" she asked in a high, thin voice. When she laid eyes on Thaddeus she exclaimed, "Oh, my! Such a large man." She turned toward Maggie. "Large men can be so comforting. Why, my Hubert is a veritable giant, and he makes me feel so *safe.*" She folded herself and all her layers of cashmere onto an ottoman. "Well, sit then, my poor dears. A glass of sherry perhaps?" she asked Maggie.

"It's kind of you to offer, Mrs. Smith-Jones, but we're here to ask you questions about your steamship journey from New York." Sitting on a lacquered black chair, Maggie paused and watched the old woman's eyebrows raise half an inch.

"Steamship?"

"Yes, we just left Mrs. Clement's house in Bolton Street, and she gave us your card. She said she had spoken with you during the trip."

"Ah, yes, of course. Those ship journeys are so tedious, aren't they?" She fluttered her frail hands. "Well, what would you like to know?"

Maggie explained. "Do you recall speaking with a young lady named Leonora Winston?"

Thaddeus handed over the calotype, and the old woman studied it for a long time. "She seems very familiar. However, her name wasn't Leonora Winston." Her voice drifted off as if she was thinking.

Maggie held her breath. "Do you remember her name?"

Mrs. Smith-Jones sighed and closed her eyes. "That

young woman was troubled. I remember clearly, she was frightened of someone.''

''Did you see her speaking with anyone else on the ship?''

''Oh, yes, she spoke with all of the younger set, of course.'' She wrinkled her brow. ''But what was her name? My memory isn't as good as it once was.''

Silence fell as the old woman pondered. Maggie held her breath in suspense.

''Ah! I remember now. Her name was Laura Winter. Miss Winter was from some small town in Virginia. I don't recall the name.''

Maggie stared at Thaddeus, knowing instantly that Leonora Winston and Laura Winter were one and the same. But why would she change her name?

''I wish you would take a small glass of sherry with me,'' Mrs. Smith-Jones said querulously. ''It would be awfully rude of me to send you away without the slightest refreshment, my poor dears.'' She glanced out the window. ''And it's raining in earnest.''

''I would be grateful for the sherry,'' Maggie said before Thaddeus could protest. She suddenly wanted to hear everything the old woman had to tell about Leonora.

''I'm delighted.'' Mrs. Smith-Jones pointed at a decanter and glasses on a silver tray on the opposite side of the room. ''I would be excessively grateful, young man, if you would serve us the sherry.'' She lowered her tone. ''I could ring for my housekeeper, but she puts on such dour airs when I ask her to perform extra duties. You just can't find reliable servants these days.'' She sighed. ''I used to have a butler to serve my guests, but he passed away, the poor dear.''

Thaddeus rose and served them. Maggie noticed how carefully he handled the frail-stemmed glasses. For such a large man, he was certainly adept.

Mrs. Smith-Jones sipped her wine and said, ''Miss Winter was a lively, kindhearted young woman, and very lovely. Just like on the calotype you showed me, she had blonde, curly hair and the widest blue eyes. Her innocence was so endearing, and she was never at a loss for words."

"She didn't explain why she was frightened?"

The old woman shook her head. "No . . . she only mentioned it once. I thought it was strange that she would have enemies. The poor thing, so sweet and innocent. Who would wish her ill?"

"Did she mention her home in Virginia?" Thaddeus prodded. He had set aside his glass without tasting it.

"Oh, yes. Her mother had died recently. Since she was all alone in America, Miss Winter decided to reunite with her family here." She turned to Maggie and smiled, her head tilted to one side. "You know, she told me she didn't know she had sister in London until she read her mother's diary."

Maggie lowered her gaze, embarrassed. "Yes . . . the circumstances are odd, and I won't have a full explanation of my mother's motives until I see Leonora—Laura. Truly, I was pleased to discover that I had a sister, since I always thought I was an only child."

"Oh, you poor dears. All those years wasted!" Mrs. Smith-Jones finished her sherry and eyed the decanter longingly. "I seem to recall that there was a young man who gave Miss Winter more attention then the others. I spoke with him on occasion myself. His name is Anselm Ripley, and he lives somewhere here in London." She made an apologetic gesture. "Not that I know where. A tight-lipped, snobbish sort of fellow, I thought." She snorted. "There are many of his kind nowadays."

Thaddeus was jotting down the name in a notebook he had pulled from his pocket. "Was he traveling alone, or—"

"In company, I would expect. However, I don't

seem to remember seeing him in any group. He was always drifting from one party to the next. If I had a daughter—which I don't—I wouldn't want to see her with one of his kind."

"How often did you see them together?" Thaddeus went on.

"Oh . . . all in all, two or three times. They had dinner together once, and they met in the lounge, I believe."

"You saw nothing, er . . . strange, Mrs. Smith-Jones?" Thaddeus continued.

She fluttered her hands and gave him an affronted glance. "Strange? My dear young man, I usually retire to my bedchamber at nine, so I don't see the late-night goings-on, as you might well understand."

Thaddeus smiled. "Yes, of course. Now, if there are any more details you could recall, we would be grateful."

The old woman pondered at length. "No, nothing out of the ordinary happened. I spoke with Miss Winter on the last evening of the journey, and she expressed only excitement at seeing you," she said to Maggie.

Maggie wanted to hear more, but Thaddeus rose and motioned to her to follow suit. "You have been very helpful," he said. "If we have any more questions about Miss Winter, may we return here?"

The old lady flapped her hands. "Of course! I'm sorry I couldn't be of more help."

"You have been of more help than you know," Thaddeus said, smiling roguishly.

"Naughty young man," she chided, evidently delighted, then addressed Maggie. "If you have engaged Mr. Webb's services, you might regret it when you find your sister, Mrs. Hartwell. She might snatch him from right under your nose."

Maggie's cheeks grew warm. "I have no control over Mr. Webb's actions, and hopefully"—she threw

Thaddeus a veiled glance—"my sister will not be misled by his careless charm."

The old lady rose, chuckling. "They always are, they always are." She led the way to the door. "You have brightened my day considerably. Life is sometimes lonely in this mausoleum."

Maggie had an urge to ask if she could come again, but she compressed her lips. Mrs. Smith-Jones was far above her own station.

"I hope you find your sister," Mrs. Smith-Jones said, and pressed Maggie's hand. "She was such a friendly, talkative person."

Thaddeus and Maggie walked down Park Lane toward the cab stand at the corner of Piccadilly. It was still raining, and Maggie unfurled her umbrella. Thaddeus hastened to take the opportunity to step closer under the pretext of gaining the protection of her umbrella. "I can carry that," he said, and slipped his arm around her waist.

Maggie squirmed aside. "Certainly not!" she said, but reluctantly let him stay under shelter of her umbrella since the rain was falling steadily.

"This morning's investigation was certainly edifying," Thaddeus said, rubbing his chin. "I wonder why your sister decided to travel under an alias."

"What will you do with the information Mrs. Smith-Jones gave you?"

"I'll find Anselm Ripley's address and then visit him." He glanced cautiously as Maggie. "But I think I will proceed to work alone.

Maggie sighed in disappointment. "Why? What have I done to hamper your movements? Because I was present these ladies didn't hesitate to see you."

He smiled. "True, but I don't think I would have had any problem seeing them alone. You know, I did detective work before I met you."

She stiffled an urge to poke him in the ribs with one of the umbrella spokes. "If you hadn't, I would never have hired you, Mr. Webb. Experience is of the essence here," she said haughtily.

"I say!" He sounded exasperated. "What did I do wrong now?" He glowered at her, and she returned his stare measure for measure. The black material of the umbrella shadowed his face, giving it a saturnine cast.

"You, Mr. Webb, are the most aggravating man I have had the misfortune to encounter. You're rude, you stare, you touch me every chance you get, and your smile is . . . well, *naughty*. I find you extremely irksome."

He laughed. "And I find you overbearing, priggish, meddlesome, and bad-tempered, but nevertheless, wholly adorable. I think that under your haughty exterior there lies a warm, loving woman."

"How dare you comment on my character!" Maggie exclaimed, though her heart was thundering in her chest. She momentarily lost her breath at the searing glance that accompanied his veiled suggestion, and she went hot all over. She longed to be free of the corset chafing uncomfortably against her breast. She recalled when his body had pressed against hers at the French restaurant, and grew increasingly flustered. She couldn't help but wonder what it would be like to have his large hands caress her naked skin. Speechless with humiliation at her wanton thoughts, she looked to the ground where water rushed beside the sidewalk.

"I think that under all that starch you're a lonely, love-starved person, Mrs. Hartwell." He took her elbow possessively and steered her across the street to the nearest cab. "Since we haven't finished our argument, I recommend we find a restaurant and conclude it over lunch. That is, unless you want to debate that suggestion first.''

"No, but I want to choose the restaurant," she said regally.

"I expected that," he said with a laugh.

Chapter 6

He listened with half an ear when Maggie ordered the cabbie to drive to Oxford Street, only vaguely aware that she intended to have lunch at one of the fashionable tearooms which had sprung up along the shopping areas of Oxford and Regent Streets to cater mostly to the ladies. Deep in thought, he barely noticed when the hansom halted on the busy street and let them off.

But when Maggie led the way into the tearoom, he protested vehemently. "We cannot eat here!" He gripped her elbow to halt her decisive progress.

"Why not?" She glared at his hand, and he released her. "This is a fine place for a midday meal."

"But only *ladies* eat here! I'll be the laughing-stock—"

"Nonsense. Gentlemen dine here as well—although not very many . . ."

Her eyes began to glitter mischievously behind her spectacles, and Thaddeus drew in his breath. "You're doing this deliberately," he said in a low voice. "That's a dirty trick, Mrs. Hartwell. I didn't expect you to be so underhanded."

With a toss of her head, she took hold of his scarf and pulled him through the vestibule. A rack was filled with coats and hats, and a maid with a starched apron and cap held out her hand expectantly.

A smile curled Maggie's lips. "Divest yourself," she whispered.

"Of all the rotten—" he muttered, but obediently unwound his scarf and unbuttoned his coat, which the maid hung on the rack.

"Since your choice of a restaurant was in singularly bad taste this morning, I thought you would appreciate this establishment. You need to learn where to have a safe meal, Mr. Webb. I assure you that we won't be interrupted by a police raid here." She led the way through the small, round tables whose occupants stared in amazement at Thaddeus through hat veils and pince-nez.

He exchanged a chagrined glance with another man who was squashed into a corner by his much larger mate, a woman wearing a hat that carried a dust mop of ostrich feathers.

"Don't you think—" Thaddeus began lamely.

"Don't argue with me, Mr. Webb. You will be splendidly served here." Maggie turned to a waitress carrying a tray. "Hello, Sara. Please bring us a pot of tea and menus. At once."

Mortified, Thaddeus sat on the spindly wrought-iron chair of a corner table and cursed the day he'd laid eyes on Maggie Hartwell. With difficulty he managed to fold his long legs under the dainty table. Peering at him around a potted palm, a woman at the next table gave him a flirtatious smile over her sable boa, and he cleared his throat in embarrassment. Two elderly ladies eating cream-laden pastries at another table were apparently whispering about him. Thaddeus gave Maggie a murderous glance.

"This was the most devious—"

"You took me to a place that endorses illicit gambling," she reminded him. "In comparison, this tearoom is highly respectable."

"You *coerced* me to accept your meddling in my investigation." His voice rose from an angry whisper

to an offended growl. "By Jove, you informed me that
you had no qualms about visiting Soho restaurants.
In fact, you said you had seen most of London before."

She hesitated. "I have. However, I don't make it a
habit to visit restaurants with dubious reputations."

He glared at her, wanting to grab her and shake
some sense into her. "From now on, you will take no
part in this investigation, Mrs. Hartwell. Your presence saps my energy and, God knows, I need all of
it to solve the mystery of your sister's disappearance."

Maggie's eyes lost their teasing sparkle. "We'll see
about that! Now, let's change the subject. I wonder
who frightened her during the Atlantic crossing.
Could it have been someone she met on the ship, or
someone from her home town?"

"I have no idea. We know very little about her
background. I wish her letter had better described her
plans."

The waitress returned with pots of steaming hot tea
and boiling milk. Thaddeus squeezed lemon into his
cup, and studied the limited menu: all ladies' fare of
boiled eggs, scones, crumpets, Victoria sandwiches,
stewed pears, trifle, and any number of frosted cakes
and jellies. He had envisioned frothing ale with steak-
and-kidney pie in some public house, but now it
looked like he would have to make do with—

"Bring Mr. Webb a plate of cucumber sandwiches,
Sara, and I'd like a plate of warm scones with clotted
cream and raspberry jam."

"Now, wait—" Thaddeus began, but the waitress
had already left with a swish of her taffeta skirts.

"Anything the matter?" Maggie asked innocently.

He gave her a wary glance, knowing she was enjoying herself. She was wearing a suspiciously blank
expression, spreading the damask napkin on her lap.

Narrowing his eyes, he had a sudden urge to strangle her, yet at the same time, he found her daring sweetly intoxicating. "This is torture! Cucumber—"

"Shhh, not so loud. I'm certain you'll find the sandwiches to your complete satisfaction." She smiled. "I promise you won't leave here hungry."

"You devil," he growled. *I'll show you.* A slow grin lit up his features, and he moved his legs under the starched tablecloth until he encountered her foot. His smile widened as he let the toe of his shoe delve under the hem of her gown and upward, until he heard her inhale sharply. Her eyes were magnificent in their glittering fury. He chuckled in delight.

"How dare you!" she whispered, and jerked her foot away. This man was infuriating . . . but she couldn't recall a luncheon she'd enjoyed more—and all because of him.

"Since you're so intent on tormenting me, I have to find ways to defend myself." His foot found hers again, and he hurried to entrap it between both of his own. He slid one foot across her buttoned boot. "Ah . . . such a dainty ankle, and such tiny feet," he said with a wink.

She rose abruptly. The patrons at other tables studied them with avid interest.

"What's wrong? Is this establishment no longer to your liking?" he murmured. "You're making a spectacle of yourself by jumping up as if you'd been stung by a bee."

He had the satisfaction of seeing her blush. Averting her gaze, she sat down, her back poker-straight. He wished he could see her eyes now—they were probably darkened in mortification.

He subtly moved his chair closer to hers. The tablecloth hid the proximity of their legs from curious eyes. She started and her gaze flitted about the room, as if she were a trapped rabbit. As he rubbed his thigh against hers, she made a strangled sound. He chuckled behind his napkin and earned a lethal stare.

He found he liked the shape of her thigh even under all those starched petticoats. She would be an
armful of soft curves, he mused, if she ever took off
the steel-lined corset that cinched her narrow waist.
He would certainly like to find out. He would bet his
last shilling, too, that she wore high-necked flannel
nightgowns to bed, along with an assortment of un-
dergarments whose stiff material the Defense Minis-
try could surely use for their soldiers as effective
guard against stray bullets. Chortling, he pondered
the idea of writing a petition to the Defen—

"What now?" Maggie frowned. "You're laughing
at me, and I resent it," she admonished as she pulled
aside her legs as far as she could without falling off
the chair.

The waitress returned with their repast, and Thaddeus looked askance at the pale, crustless bread triangles and limp cucumber edges. Maggie's hot scones
looked much tastier. He grabbed two of the golden
brown breads before Sara had set down the plate.

Winking at the surprised waitress, he sliced one
scone in two and heaped it with clotted cream, leaving barely enough for Maggie. He could sense her
silent protest—her back was straighter than ever.

"You can have all the raspberry jam," he offered
gallantly, then devoured the scone. As he chewed, he
watched her fume in silence.

"Speechless with anger," he murmured to himself.

"*What* did you say?" she said in a frosty schoolmarm's voice. With deliberately precise movements,
she spread the jam and nibbled daintily.

"Speechless angel," he whispered in her ear. A
wayward curl tickled his chin, and he marveled at the
vibrant, glowing, golden-red color. A sudden desire
to undo the severe bun at her nape came over him,
and he wondered what she would look like with her
hair streaming around her shoulders. He inhaled

sharply at the thought and wondered again why this prim, spinsterlike woman provoked such a fire in his loins. It was inexplicable.

She swallowed the last piece of scone. "You have no right to call me an angel," she said. "And if you don't mind, I would like to continue our investigation when you have finished your meal." She gave the bread and cucumber triangles an expressive glance. "I'm sure the sandwiches are quite delectable."

With a suggestive smile, he held out the plate. "Help yourself."

He laughed at her expression, but she took one. Gingerly. He drank his tea, watching her face as she concentrated on the food. Her eyelashes were gold-tipped and curled at the edges, her nose had a faint sprinkle of freckles, and her cheeks looked peachy-soft, inviting his caress. He wondered if her lips would taste as sweet . . .

"Are you finished?" she asked, her eyes questioning him through the spectacles.

"I could sit here all day," he mused aloud, forgetting for a moment that he was now the only male in a room filled with ladies. The gentleman in the corner had already left.

"Well, I won't pay for your dawdling away an entire afternoon in a teashop," she admonished, rising.

He followed with a sigh of relief, and they stepped onto busy Oxford Street. "I suggest that we part here," he said. "I still have several errands to do, and I'll contact Sergeant Horridge—"

"We have not yet concluded our investigation," she said. "I would dearly like to speak with this person—Anselm Ripley."

"Don't you trust me to ask the right questions?"

"Two minds are always better than one." Without waiting for his answer, she summoned a hansom. "To Scotland Yard first?" she inquired.

Thaddeus heaved an exasperated sigh. It was clear

he would have to use his ultimate weapon—a kiss—
to break her determination. It might shock her amply
enough to put an end to their joint sleuthing.

"Very well," he said to her, but as he climbed onto
the carriage step, he quietly gave the cabbie the hotel
address. Thaddeus hoped he heard the request despite the overpowering din of Oxford Street. He sat
down beside Maggie and gave her a calculating stare.
When he was sure the cabbie had turned north on
Baker Street, he prepared himself to do battle.

"But we were going to Scotland Yard . . ." she began, puzzled.

"Yes, but not this afternoon," he answered.

"Why not?" Her eyes were accusing him, and he
had to laugh.

"Please calm down. I have some pressing business
that can't wait." He almost relented when he saw
worry darken her face, but reminded himself he had
to continue this investigation alone.

"There's no time to lose," she urged, clutching her
umbrella handle. "You must make this case your first
priority."

"I have. Don't concern yourself, Mrs. Hartwell. I
won't neglect my duty."

"If only I could find Mr. Ripley's address . . ." she
thought aloud. Turning to him, she fixed him with a
stern stare. "How do you intend to find him?"

"There are ways," he hedged. If he told her about
the obvious sources of telephone and post office, or
the gentlemen's clubs, and the files at Scotland Yard,
she was likely to rush out and search for Ripley herself. There was the chance that she might think of the
same means on her own, but he hoped he would
reach Ripley's home before she had time to think
about anything.

Silence stretched between them before she said,
"You're only trying to get rid of me, aren't you."

He studied the set line of her mouth. ''But you won't be easily persuaded.''

Just as she was about to answer, he gripped her shoulders and pulled her into his arms. She felt light and insubstantial, despite the contours of her corset. There were too many layers between their living, warm flesh, he thought as he lowered his mouth to hers. When she opened her mouth to protest he silenced her with a searing kiss. At least it was searing for him, because touching those rosy, vulnerable lips sent a shock of wild pleasure through him. Surprised, he concentrated wholly on her alluring softness. Her womanly scent intoxicated him, and after some initial resistance, she melted against him and opened her mouth further. The moist warmth tasted almost unbearably sweet to his senses. He felt as if he could explore her lush secrets forever.

A sharp clout of her umbrella on his head jerked him out of his enchantment.

''Of all the gall! Don't you ever dare to darken my doorstep again, Mr. Webb,'' Maggie said hoarsely as the hamsom stopped and she descended, leaving Thaddeus to continue his journey. Her blue eyes blazed, yet he noted with satisfaction that there was a warm blush in her cheeks and a softness to her lips that hadn't been there a moment before.

Chapter 7

"**M**ama, your face is so red," Victoria shouted as she ran toward Maggie through the hotel foyer, her arms outstretched. "What have you done?"

Maggie blushed even more deeply, her mind still reeling from Thaddeus Webb's intoxicating kiss. She felt curiously weak-kneed and breathless, and shamelessly hungry for more of his kisses. This morning when she'd met him they had been practically strangers, and now—what were they now? *Utter enemies.*

The audacity of that man! Against her will, though, she recalled the many times his body had touched hers: his thigh rubbing against her own, his strong arms holding her tight, and, by far the sweetest, his kiss. So direct, and so forceful . . . so *knowing.* His lips had fitted to hers as if they had been created especially for her.

"Mama, you're not listening. You're daydreaming," Victoria complained.

"Shhh," Maggie said, throwing a furtive glance at the guests in the foyer. Only one man peered over the edge of the newspaper he was reading.

"Mama, will you have tea with me? Please?"

Maggie glanced down at her daughter's upturned face. Her blonde hair had escaped one of the pale blue ribbons, and her pinafore had a streak of paint

83

down the front. How could she say no to the girl whose brilliant blue eyes looked at her with such trust and love? "Of course, darling. We'll have tea in the nursery."

Victoria cradled two dolls, one under each arm. "Then Molly Potter and Zoe Soap can eat with us." Jumping up and down, Victoria held out her dolls for Maggie's inspection. "Look, they're wearing new dresses."

Miss Lather, the governess, entered, her face red as if she had run all the way from the nursery. "*There* you are, Victoria. How many times have I told you—"

"Not to run away," Victoria filled in automatically. "But I saw Mama speaking with a strange gentleman in a hansom—"

"That's quite enough," Maggie interrupted, as more guests became interested in their conversation. "You must always obey Miss Lather."

The governess looked ill at ease and curtsied, the stiff gray taffeta of her gown crackling. "I'm so sorry, ma'am."

"Go on then, and I'll join you shortly in the nursery."

Miss Lather ushered Victoria from the foyer, and Maggie hurried behind the front desk. She lifted the telephone and cranked the handle which would connect her to the United Telephone Company on Coleman Street. She prayed that Mr. Ripley would be on the telephone network, even though the chance was slim since telephones were mostly reserved for businesses. Static crackled on the line, and the voice at the other end sounded metallic.

"Could you connect me to a Mr. Anselm Ripley— possibly living in Mayfair or Belgravia," she said.

"Just a moment." The static returned, and then the telephone rang. Suddenly a male voice came over the wires. "Mayfair four nine six."

Maggie's breath caught in her throat as she wrote down the number. "Mr. Anselm Ripley?"

"Mr. Ripley is not available at the moment. May I take a message?"

Maggie hesitated, then an idea sprang to mind. "I'm calling from Fortnum and Mason's concerning a delivery to Mr. Ripley. Unfortunately, an error pertaining to the address has occurred. Could you—"

"Fourteen, South Audley Street. Use the back entrance," the male voice said, and hung up.

Filled with pride at her cleverness and daring, Maggie smiled as she hurried toward her private apartment. She would show Mr. Webb that she was capable of a bit of sleuthing on her own. So as not to waste any time, she would investigate Mr. Ripley herself. She found that detective work intrigued her. She glanced at her watch, frowning. It would soon be dark, but before going out, she would have tea with Victoria. Her family would always come first. A cursory look at the desk in her office told her that the japanned box was still missing.

In her bedchamber, she took off her hat and placed it in a hatbox. The ostrich feathers looked slightly wilted after the tussle in the French restaurant. She slipped out of her skirt with an angry thought for Mr. Webb. How could one human being be so very arrogant and conceited? Then the memory of his kiss swept away all other recollections, and warmth stole through her. Her breath quivered as she relived every moment in his embrace . . . his strong arms . . . his virile scent. And those lips! Insistent, confident, and warm, oh so . . . warm.

The air felt chilly all of a sudden, as if the house—no, her *life*— was empty without his presence. Shaking off her disturbing thoughts, she put on a clean skirt and shirtwaist, brushed her hair, and rewound it into its customary tight chignon. Her cheeks were still rosy, and there was a sparkle in her eyes. Was that because of him? Her blush deepened.

Maggie walked into the corridor. Victoria's laugh tinkled through the nursery door, and love filled Maggie at the thought of her daughter, the most important person in her life.

She sighed. If gentlemen found her formidable, it was because she kept up her guard, but here in the nursery, she could relax and be just as carefree as she wanted.

The room was made cozy with red-and-white-gingham curtains, colorful cushions on the window seat, and a rocking horse whose mane and paint were almost gone after much use.

"Mama! We'll have currant cake and trifle for tea. My favorites." Victoria's hair was newly braided and she now wore a pristine pinafore.

Maggie laughed and hugged her, then kissed her on the forehead. "What have you been doing today? Did you visit the zoological gardens?" She gave the governess an inquiring glance.

"Yes, Mama, but first I had my painting and reading lessons." She showed Maggie a series of water-colors of bright suns, houses, and birds. "Miss Lather says I read very well."

"Little braggart," Maggie admonished gently, concealing her pride.

"Victoria is right, Mrs. Hartwell. She's rapidly learning her letters." The governess took the tray from Gertie, the young maid, who was smiling widely at Victoria.

Victoria ran across the room and pressed a currant bun into Gertie's hand. A friendship had blossomed between the two girls, and Maggie sometimes found Victoria trailing after the maid as she cleaned.

"Thank you ever so much, Miss Victoria," Gertie said with a wink and left.

"We saw the big elephant, Mama. I wish I could

ride him someday. The children take turns, you know. The elephant wears a saddle with two benches on each side, and the riders sit ever so high up!" Victoria's voice was filled with longing. "When can I ride him?"

Maggie—who was afraid of heights—thought of her daughter atop the huge elephant with a shudder. She would never let her on that beast. What if an accident happened? "Perhaps next summer."

"All the children ride for sixpence."

"It's not that, but the elephant has a terrible temper sometimes. I've heard he's crashed through his guardrails twice."

"That's because he wanted to take a walk on his own," Victoria explained, braiding the yarn hair of one of her dolls. "He got bored in his house."

Miss Lather served tea, and they ate together companionably. Maggie listened with half an ear to Victoria's chatter, which mostly concerned the current health of her dolls. "Miss Lather is making a new nightgown for Zoe Soap," she explained, and the shy governess blushed. Maggie thought how lucky she was to have found such a pleasant woman to care for Victoria. She did much beyond her duties to make sure Victoria was content while Maggie was working.

"I'm certain it will be a masterpiece," Maggie said, and made a mental note to increase the governess's wages.

"Will you read to me later, Mama?"

"When you're tucked into your bed. But first I have an errand to do. I'll be gone approximately an hour." She kissed Victoria's round cheek and rose.

"Where will you go, Mama? To visit the gentleman in the hansom?"

Maggie lowered her gaze. "Of course not! He's only a business acquaintance."

"He was so *big*. I wish he would come with me to the zoological gardens. He would be almost tall

enough to lift me onto the elephant. Could you ask
him to come, Mama?'' Victoria gave her most cajoling
smile, and Maggie had to laugh.

''Mr. Webb will not accompany you to the zoo, but
you and I shall certainly go there together in the summer.''

''Oh, Mama, I wish I could have a . . . a father,
someone like Mr. Webb.''

Maggie blushed. ''I would like to give you a father
someday, but I don't think Mr. Webb is the right
man.''

''But I saw him give you a kind smile, Mama. I
think I want a father like him, who's tall enough to
put me on the elephant.''

Disturbed, Maggie patted her daughter's head. Her
old longing to be part of a close family surged up.
She couldn't blame Victoria for wanting a father, but
how had her daughter already fallen for Thaddeus
Webb's roguish smile? ''We'll see, we'll see.''

Maggie received a hug of gratitude from Victoria,
then returned downstairs. She pulled on a fur-lined
cloak since the afternoon had brought colder weather.
If she wanted to reach Mr. Ripley before dark, she
would have to hurry.

Rafferty, the doorman, hailed a hansom for her and
she set out toward Mayfair, a fifteen-minute drive.
The air was damp and chilly, the rain turning into icy
pellets that made the streets treacherous.

She reached the address on South Audley Street
without mishap, and stepped down. After throwing
a cursory glance at the sky, she frowned, realizing
that the rainy weather made darkness arrive faster.
Shielding her hat from the downpour with her umbrella, she stepped up the stairs of the narrow town
house and rang the doorbell. Mr. Ripley was by no
means lacking in funds if his house was any indication, but it fell far short of the elegance of Mrs. Smith-
Jones's home in Park Lane.

An old man with salt-and-pepper hair and Dun-dreary whiskers opened the door. "Yes?"

Maggie adopted her most formal tone. "Mr. Anselm Ripley?"

"No, Mr. Ripley has traveled out of town. He is expected to return next Saturday. Can I be of assistance?"

"No . . . I only wanted to speak with him. It's urgent." *I have to wait a whole week!* Thinking rapidly, she pulled her card case from her handbag. "It's a business matter, and I would appreciate it if Mr. Ripley could ring me at this number." She handed him a visiting card.

The servant thanked her and said he would deliver the message.

Disappointed, Maggie stepped onto the sidewalk. All her energy seemed to have seeped away. A sharp gust of wind hurled along the street, scattering a few dry leaves. Rain pelted down, and she reopened her umbrella. She looked for a hansom, but the only vehicle coming toward her was occupied. To her surprise, it stopped.

A man alighted, and as he turned his face toward her, she recognized Thaddeus Webb.

"You!" they said simultaneously.

Mr. Webb looked thunderous as he paid the cabbie. "I see you couldn't keep your nose out of my investigation."

She drew herself up, yet still felt tiny beside him. "You appear to think that we have all the time in the world, Mr. Webb. At this very moment my sister might be in a dire predicament, perhaps even dying."

The rain was falling harder, and a murky twilight had descended. She started walking along the street since, in her surprise at seeing Mr. Webb, she had neglected to solicit the jarvey's services. Mr. Webb followed her, his collar turned up against the rain. He was still wearing his disreputable black scarf and his homburg, but he'd changed his coat to a macintosh. Anger emanated from him in great waves.

He gripped her arm, bringing her progress to an abrupt halt. "Let go of me this instant," she demanded, but he was not to be deterred.

"Confounded woman! What did Mr. Ripley say?"

She glowered at him, growing angrier by the second. Water was seeping into her boots from the puddle in which she was standing. In vain, she tried to yank her arm away from him.

"Mr. Ripley is out of town and not expected back until next week."

"Hmmm." He let go of her arm, and she walked away. She had to find a cab stand before her boots were wet through and through.

But Mr. Webb was nothing if not persistent. He followed her, his face dark with annoyance, his eyes glittering dangerously. "Has it never occurred to you that it might be perilous for you to get involved in this investigation? You have no idea what happened between Anselm Ripley and your sister."

She stopped short and turned to him, concerned. "Are you implying that he might have *hurt* Leonora?"

Thaddeus shrugged. "Anything is possible."

Maggie walked on. "I'm sure my visit here didn't do me any harm, especially since Ripley wasn't at home."

"That's not the point. The issue here is your meddling, your stubborn determination to expose yourself to unfamiliar—and perhaps harmful—conditions."

When he had stated earlier that day that he wanted to find Anselm Ripley on his own, she obviously hadn't understood he was only trying to protect her. What if Ripley had lured Miss Winston into his home and then done away with her? It was a farfetched idea, but it wouldn't be the first time a woman had fallen for some glib, handsome man only to find herself either disgraced or dead. Perhaps something had happened to Miss Winston that made her ashamed of showing herself at Maggie's home. The curious circumstances of Miss Winston's disappearance were ominous.

Why had Maggie's sister traveled under an assumed name? Had she been involved in some unsavory business in America? There were so many unanswered questions, and Maggie's interference didn't make his intention to shield her from possible shock, or his work, easier.

"It's not for you to decide what's dangerous to me or not, Mr. Webb."

"Let me remind you, you hired me to investigate your sister's disappearance. But, since you're doing so well on your own, and since you refuse to listen to me, I hereby resign." He lifted his hat. "Good day," he said, then strode down the street.

Aghast, Maggie ran to keep pace with him. "Mr. Webb! You can't just *quit*. What about my sister?"

He gave her a cursory glance. "As I said, you're managing splendidly. I don't know why you engaged my services in the first place."

She was losing her breath, trotting beside him. "I don't know what to do next, but I resent your refusal to let me help."

"I don't insist on running your hotel for you," he retorted.

Sick with fear that she had completely alienated him, she clutched his arm. He stopped, staring at her hand on his sleeve. Rain dripped from the edge of his homburg, making his look almost sinister in his anger.

"How many times do I have to repeat myself?" he asked, gently prying her fingers lose. "I resign."

The wind had intensified, blowing the rain sideways in great sheets. Water was weighing down the hems of Maggie's skirts and cloak. But she didn't care at the moment: she had to convince him she meant no harm. Just as she opened her mouth, a gust of wind turned her umbrella inside out and splashed water over her hat and face.

Sputtering, she fought with the unwieldy apparatus while Mr. Webb looked on, laughing. He crossed his arms over his chest. "Do you want my assistance?"

Her hat blew off and rolled down the street. "Oh, no!" she wailed, and lost her grip on the umbrella. The wind sent it hopping down the road like some grotesque toad.

"There went your last defense," he said with a chuckle. "You'll be better off without it."

Hot tears burned in her eyes. "You could at least have tried to fetch my hat," she admonished, wiping the water from her face. Her hair was drenched, her chignon unraveling.

"Why?" He continued along the street which widened into Grosvenor Square, where a cab stand finally appeared.

She fumed, aching to wallop him. "I keep forgetting that you're no gentleman."

"I sometimes help old ladies across the street. Wouldn't you call that gentlemanly?"

"You probably charge them a shilling for the service." She halted beside one of the cabs, feeling as miserable as the horse, who hung his head in the rain. Taking a deep breath, she launched into a last attempt at persuasion.

"I'm sorry for . . . meddling, but anxiety is my excuse. Under normal circumstances, I wouldn't dream of interfering in your work."

He looked at her for a long moment, noticing the bleakness in her eyes. Every shred of composure was gone, making her look utterly vulnerable. His anger disappeared miraculously. "Apology accepted."

"What now?" she inquired as the wind forced her to take a step back. She stumbled on the curb and tumbled back against one of the hansom's huge wheels. Webb held out his hand, but made no move to pull her back onto the sidewalk, forcing her to place her hand in his.

"First, you need to get dry. I suspect your feet are swimming in your boots."

She wiped her face. Tendrils of hair were plastered to her forehead. "Yes . . ." Embarrassed at her disheveled look, she took a faltering step toward the hansom's entrance, mumbled her address to the jarvey, and climbed in. Turning to say her farewells, she was surprised when Mr. Webb jumped in after her.

"In my most gentlemanly spirit, I will see you safely home," he said, and pressed her into a corner. She was shivering with cold, yet strangely warm inside now that he was close beside her again.

Darkness had fallen completely by the time they reached Berkley Street. The streets were deserted in the rain.

"If this downpour continues, we'll have a pea-soup fog by tomorrow," he mused aloud. "Winter is surely the most miserable time of year, don't you think?"

Her teeth clattering with cold, Maggie could only nod in agreement. A few moments later they arrived at Hartwell's Hotel.

"If you so desire, you can come with me and have a brandy toddy to warm your insides," Maggie said.

Thaddeus's countenance brightened. "Thank you." He paid the jarvey.

Maggie stepped into the foyer, closely followed by her escort. Rafferty was at his post, his brass-buttoned coat spattered with rain.

"A perishin' night, Mrs. Hartwell," he offered in a broad Irish accent and tipped his stovepipe hat. "The lounge is crowded and the dinin' rooms are fillin' up.''

Maggie could hear the sound of many voices and the clinking of cutlery. On impulse, she invited Mr. Webb into her private sitting room.

"We can talk more easily in front of my fire," she offered.

His eyes twinkled as he dashed the water off his homburg. "Really, Mrs. Hartwell. Do you dare to be . . . alone with me?" he murmured in her ear.

"I feel very safe in my own home," she said. "And I hope you will, too."

His appreciative smile warmed her heart and prompted an answering smile.

Rafferty took Thaddeus's outer garments and handed them to the maid in the wardrobe. Maggie led the way through the office, Thaddeus behind her.

"I take it you still haven't found that missing box?" he asked.

"No, I have no idea what happened to it." Maggie stepped up the narrow staircase and entered her sitting room. "Here we are. I see one of my maids has laid a nice coal fire in the grate." She unbuttoned her cloak, and was about to sweep it from her shoulders when she felt his hands at the nape of her neck as he gripped the sodden garment. He shook it out and hung it on a hanger dangling from a rack.

Maggie hastily tidied her wayward hair and secured the curls with pins. Sitting down by the fire, she held her hands toward it. Her teeth slowly stopped chattering.

Thaddeus bent on one knee before her and held out his hands. She stared at him uncomprehendingly.

"Stretch out your feet," he ordered. "I'll help you pull off your boots."

Her lips pinched together as she studied him suspiciously. "I can manage, thank you."

He chuckled. "I'm sure you can, just as you man-

age everything else—including my work." Heedless
of her protest, he lifted the hem of her skirt and pulled
out one boot-clad foot. His glance darted around the
room and came to rest on the coat rack and a basket
behind it that contained shoehorns, shoe brushes, and
other implements. He let go of her to retrieve a but-
tonhook.

She couldn't find a way to refuse him when he once
again lifted her foot onto his knee and applied the
hook to the row of leather-covered buttons. He pulled
off the wet boot and touched her damp stocking. "As
I thought, waterlogged."

He gave her a wicked smile, and Maggie sat bolt
upright when she understood the direction of his
thoughts. "Under no circumstances shall you . . . roll
. . . down my stocking," she said, shocked into
blushing.

"I can hardly pull it down unless I release the gar-
ter." He yanked the toe of her soaked stocking as if
to make his point. The lisle was glued to her skin. His
fingertips traveled up her ankle, and higher . . .
slowly, slowly caressing. A warm, wondrous sensation started in her stomach, spreading through her
until she was nearly breathless. Maggie sat perfectly
still, madly wanting him to go on, yet afraid of what
he would do next.

After a moment's deliberation, his hand halfway up
her calf, he set down her foot and lifted the other to
his knee. His eyes smoldered with suggestion, and
a delicious swooping response shot through her—
longing; wild, exhilarating longing.

"A pity. I would have enjoyed seeing your garters,
ma'am."

She could not help but laugh. "Of all the—"

"But then, I take great pleasure in shocking ladies
like you." He released each boot button with deliberate slowness.

She tried to stand up, but he was holding her foot

too firmly. "Ladies like me? What are you insinuating, Mr. Webb?"

He shrugged and a smile played over his lips. "You know very well what I mean."

He thought she was a . . . priggish prude. The realization hurt so much it brought tears to her eyes. She blinked them away rapidly. "That was unkind of you, Mr. Webb . . . but I agree I must appear unwomanly in your eyes."

He touched her chin. "A bit prickly, yes, but adorable nevertheless. Still, as I said before, I think it would be best if our ways parted. I'm sure you are a fine, capable woman, but I like to work alone." He paused. "I usually do get results."

"You must not stop the investigation," she said, lowering her gaze. She knotted her fingers in her lap, wondering how to convince him. At a loss for words, she stared around the room, her attention landing on the tantalus filled with liquor decanters. She rose. "You shall have the brandy I promised, and we will discuss the matter in a civilized manner." Narrowing her eyes, she studied him. "I'll even go so far as to offer you more money, or another antique if that's what you want. We simply must find my sister."

He took a step closer, almost touching her, and rested his hands on her shoulders. His eyes had darkened. "I don't know if I can trust you, Mrs. Hartwell."

"I assure you, I'm a very trustworthy person," she hurried to reply. Oh, why was she pleading with this infuriating man?

"What I mean is, can I depend on you not to interfere?"

His large hands warmed her through the material of her blouse. She found it difficult to gather her thoughts as she gazed into his eyes. They were magnetic, hypnotizing, and so—warm. She hadn't felt so excited, so intoxicated since she had fallen in love with Victoria's father.

She wasn't about to repeat *that* mistake.

Stepping away, she averted her face. His hands had felt so comforting, his embrace would feel even better. It might be sinful, but God, she longed for a man's touch.

"The brandy," she whispered. "Let me serve you a glass."

As if tipsy, she stumbled against the wing chair in front of the fire on her way to the tantalus. Her hands were shaking as she poured the golden liquid into a snifter. She didn't fill a glass for herself.

She handed him the brandy without looking at him, then sat down before the fire.

"Thank you," he said, and lowered his large frame into an armchair on the opposite side of the hooked, rose-patterned hearth rug. With a hearty sigh, he placed his feet on top of a leather pouf that acted as a footstool.

"You must be cold and wet as well," she suggested, the only thing she could think to say.

"Are you implying I should take my boots off—in a lady's presence?" His voice was gently chiding.

"I wouldn't want you to get pneumonia," she answered with a smile.

He gave a devilish chuckle. "Well, Mrs. Hartwell, since I did the favor of removing your soaked boots, you . . ."

She gasped. "You want me to take them off for you?"

He shrugged. "That was the general idea. But, if you believe yourself above such simple tasks, then they shall remain on."

"By no means." Hot with embarrassment, she fell to her knees and began attacking his boot laces. The boot was of supple black leather and fitted his foot like a glove. She had to reach up his trouser leg to find the knot, and as she flinched at touching warm skin, he laughed aloud.

Sitting back on her haunches, she pushed her fists into her hips. "If you're going to make fun of me, I will stop this instant."

He didn't answer, but his eyes spoke volumes. He prodded her with one toe. "I could get used to this sort of service," he said.

Smiling ruefully and shaking her head, she unlaced one boot and pulled it off. A gaping hole on the toe of his sock stared at her. She touched it. "No one to mend for you?"

"Mother stopped a long time ago, and my sisters—"

"Say no more." She lifted his other foot.

The patter of running feet sounded outside in the corridor, and the door burst open to reveal Victoria dressed in a floor-length flannel nightgown and holding one of her dolls under her arm. "Mama! I wondered if you were still out in the rain," she said. "Oh!" she added as her gaze alighted on Thaddeus. Her eyes widened in curiosity at his foot on Maggie's knee. The girl gave Thaddeus an appraising stare. "You're the man who kissed my mother in the hansom earlier. I saw you from my window. Are you going to marry Mama now?"

Thaddeus laughed. Maggie dropped his foot onto the leather pouf with a thud. "Not at all, darling. Come here. How many times have I told you not to storm into a room without knocking first."

"I'm sorry, Mama."

Maggie pulled her daughter close and stroked the thistledown hair that hung down Victoria's back. "As I told you, Mr. Webb is merely an acquaintance."

Thaddeus's eyes gleamed with humor. He held out a large hand for the girl to shake. "Miss Hartwell, I presume."

"Yes, but my papa is dead." She held out her doll. "This is Zoe Soap. She wants to ride on the elephant at the zoological gardens, but she's too small. She needs someone tall to lift her up."

"But who would hold her so she wouldn't fall off?"

"*I* could. I wouldn't be afraid of the elephant. Would you, Mr. Webb?"

Thaddeus's lips quirked. "No . . . at least, I don't think so."

Victoria smiled. "I *knew* you wouldn't be! You're almost as big as he is."

"Victoria!" Maggie admonished. "You must go back to bed now."

"But you promised to read to me, Mama."

"I will, as soon as Mr. Webb leaves." Biting her lip, she glanced at his boots on the floor. He had made himself comfortable in her chair, drinking brandy. Perhaps he would stay until his boots were dry. She discovered she liked the idea of spending an evening with him before the fire.

"Go and read to her now," he suggested. "I'll find my way out when I've finished the brandy."

"Very well, but feel free to stay as long as you like." As he nodded, she accompanied her daughter to her bedroom.

Thaddeus listened to Victoria's cheerful chatter and Maggie's patient replies as they stepped into the corridor. Something warm curled around his heart, and he had a sudden urge to call them back. He felt a sense of belonging as he watched the crackling fire and listened to the rain outside. It had been years since he'd felt this good. He cared more for Maggie Hartwell than he thought possible after so short a time. Despite her meddling, he truly enjoyed her company. The investigation must go on, if only to erase the anguish in her eyes when she spoke about her sister. He prayed nothing had happened to Miss

Winston. Sighing, he rose. Despite Maggie's invitation, he'd better return home to sort through all the pieces of the puzzle he'd discovered today. Her presence had a tendency to muddle his thoughts.

Twenty minutes later, after reading a story and tucking Victoria in, Maggie returned to her sitting room to find that Mr. Webb was gone. Disappointment washed through her. Under the empty brandy snifter he had placed a note which read: *I will continue the investigation on one condition—that you refrain from interfering. Thank you for the brandy. I thoroughly enjoyed your soft touch on my . . . feet. Yours, Thaddeus Webb.*

She crumpled the paper and threw it on the fire. "Oh, why didn't he stay to talk it over!" Still, she *had* promised to stop disrupting his work, and she would keep that pledge. She would just have to trust him.

All she could think of was his warm smile and the touch of his hands as he caressed her legs. Oh, how gloriously tender his eyes had been . . . She couldn't deny the increasing pleasure she experienced in his presence. He made her feel alive and wholly feminine. She could not ignore the desire that simmered in her blood at the mere thought of him. How long could she go on suppressing that yearning? However successfully she'd buried that side of herself in the past, she was now reminded that she'd hidden from love.

Chapter 8

Three days later, Maggie still hadn't heard from Thaddeus Webb. She burned to know what he was doing to find Leonora, but she refrained from contacting him—to show that she was keeping her side of the bargain. It was, however, a difficult decision. In four days Mr. Ripley would be back in London. Perhaps she could secretly visit South Audley Street then . . .

The next morning, she awakened very early, right before dawn. She wondered what had woken her so suddenly. Sitting in bed, her heart thundering, she listened intently for sounds outside her room. Silence lay heavy in the entire house. Had one of the live-in staff come to visit her? But none of them had stirred yet. Pulling up her covers to her chin, she watched the door until her eyes were dry and aching. She could barely make out the contours of the door frame, but the gleaming brass knob shone like a beacon. A shuffling movement came from her sitting room, and she stiffened in fear. Her whole body seemed to freeze into a block of ice, hampering her movements as she slowly folded back the down cover. Why was she afraid? She had never been frightened in this house before.

The sound returned, and Maggie held her breath. Cold sweat broke out on her palms as she eased from the mattress and took one leaden step toward the door.

Her heartbeat roared in her ears, and a spasm of terror shot through her stomach as a thud came from the other side of the door. With great caution, she crossed the room and, taking a deep breath, touched the cold brass knob. The sitting room was now as silent as a tomb, but she sensed something, someone. Her hand shook as she turned the knob.

She stared into the stygian blackness of the other room.

"Who's there?" she asked, her voice faltering. "I heard you walking around."

She held her breath, but there was no reply. "Answer me!" she demanded more forcefully. She took a tentative step inside the room and gasped as she stumbled over something on the floor.

Fear almost shattered her control, and she had to steady herself against the door frame so as not to fall. Her composure in tatters, she found the box of lucifers on the sideboard, right inside the sitting room door where she always kept them. Fumbling, she managed to extract one and strike it against the side of the box. The flare blinded her momentarily. She stared gritty-eyed into the room, not knowing what to expect.

The chamber was empty. Weak with relief, she lifted the glass dome of an oil lamp on the sideboard and turned up the wick. Igniting it with the match, she replaced the dome. Her hands were shaking uncontrollably.

Her foot once again touched the object close to the threshold. She bent down and found that it was the book she had been reading the previous night. Someone *had* been in her sitting room. The last thing she had done before going to bed was to put the book on the sideboard. It couldn't have fallen so far by itself.

She hurried across the room to the door leading to

the corridor and listened. Nothing. The silence was suffocating.

Trembling, she gripped the base of the oil lamp. With a deep breath, the lamp held high, she opened the door and looked out.

The corridor was empty. Before she could lose her courage, she ran the short distance to Victoria's room. The floor was icy under her bare feet, but she scarcely noticed.

A faint gaslight was always lit in her daughter's room, and Maggie saw instantly that Victoria was sleeping peacefully in her bed. Almost sobbing with relief, she stepped inside and softly closed the door, turning the key in the lock.

"Mama?" Victoria asked sleepily. "Why are you here?"

"I felt lonely without you," Maggie said, her voice cracking. As Victoria moved over to one side of the bed, Maggie slid under the cover. "Shall we pretend you're a baby again? When you were an infant you wanted to sleep in my bed all the time."

"That was only when I was afraid, and I'm not a baby anymore." Victoria rubbed her eyes and yawned widely. "Are you frightened, Mama? Is that why you want to sleep in my bed?"

Maggie pressed her eyes tightly together and breathed deeply. "Not at all, darling. Now go to sleep. Tomorrow we will have cocoa and porridge together for breakfast. Would you like that?"

Victoria burrowed closer, and Maggie cradled her in her arms. "You're the bestest mama in the whole world."

Chapter 9

Later in the day, Maggie looked up from the ledger on the front desk at the hotel as a man sauntered into the foyer. There was something vaguely familiar about his deep-set, slanted dark eyes. His gaunt face was both unusual and riveting, commanding attention; his silver-streaked hair bristled as if with electricity, and his form was tall and narrow. There was a foreign air about him, and Maggie noticed that the guests sitting in the armchairs were also studying him intently.

"Good afternoon," he greeted her pleasantly, and placed his garishly patterned carpetbag on the counter. He held a bowler hat in his hand. He had long, well-shaped fingers, and his left hand was adorned by an intricately carved gold ring with an oddly shaped black stone. Closer scrutiny revealed it was formed like a beetle. His brightly colored, embroidered silk waistcoat looked as if it had been made in the Orient, adding to his exotic appearance.

"Good afternoon," Maggie greeted him, closing the ledger. "Would you like a room?"

His penetrating gaze swept the foyer, and Maggie saw a muscle twitch repeatedly in his jaw, pulling his lips involuntarily to one side. "A suite if you have one." He gave her an endearing smile, and it suddenly struck her why he looked familiar. Her grand-

mother had had the exact same smile, the same
slanted eyes.

"Mrs. Margaret Hartwell, I presume?"

She clutched the edge of the counter. "Yes. Have
we met before?" she asked.

He shook his head. "You probably don't remember. Such a long time has passed." He paused. "I
came two days ago, but you weren't here at the time,
so I stayed elsewhere."

Puzzled, Maggie examined his dark, expensive suit.
He must be at least fifty years old, she thought, but
he looked fit.

Handing her a calling card, he said, "I'm your uncle, Rupert Merton," he said simply, and tilted his
head to one side as he watched her reaction.

Maggie closed her mouth, which had fallen open at
his words, and read the name printed on the card:
Rupert Merton, Fifth Avenue, New York. "Uncle Rupert? But Father said you died at sea years ago. Why
haven't you contacted me before?"

He shrugged. "I should have written, of course,
but your father and I were bitter enemies. I heard
about your mother's flight through Grandmother
Merton, and I'm happy she got away. If she had
stayed, Bully would have killed her sooner or later in
one of his rages." He cocked an eyebrow at Maggie.
"I'm surprised you survived him."

A cold sensation swept through her as she remembered her father's bitter hatred and brutality. "He abhorred women in general." She paused. "I didn't
think I had any living relatives. This is a great surprise." Walking around the counter, she nodded to
Rafferty to take Rupert's carpetbag, but he grabbed it
possessively.

"Sorry, but I have some papers I don't want to let
out of my sight."

"Take care of Mr. Merton's coat, hat, and luggage,
and bring it to suite number two," Maggie ordered

the staring Rafferty. She turned to her uncle. "We have many years to catch up on," she said, coming around the counter and linking her arm through his. "Shall we proceed to the dining room? You must be hungry."

He laughed and accompanied her eagerly, bag in hand. The tic in his jaw intensified. "I fear it will take longer than the span of one dinner to tell you everything, dear Margaret."

"Call me Maggie, everyone does. Where did you come from before you arrived here in London?" she asked, showing him to a corner table.

"The Caribbean." He set down his bag and held out a chair for Maggie. Then he lifted the tails of his coat and sat down on the opposite side. "You own a lovely hotel," he said, glancing around the cozy dining room.

"You know a lot about me. How did you know where to find me?" She handed him a menu.

"The solicitors, m'dear. They're still handling the sale of Bully's broken-down mansion, which they have been unable to get off their hands." He studied the menu with cocked eyebrows. "I'm not surprised—a gloomier house I've yet to see."

"I take it you went back to visit?" Maggie studied her uncle, still dazed from the shock of discovering that she had another living relative besides Leonora.

"Yes . . . the roof is sagging, the chimneys crumbling, and weeds grow so thickly around the walls that you can barely see the building." He shot her a quick glance. "You haven't been there since you left?"

"No, it would bring up too many painful memories." She aligned the crystal vase filled with pink miniature carnations to the exact point where the fold creases on the tablecloth met. "What brings you here to London?"

He sidestepped her question. "How's the pike with anchovy sauce?"

She smiled. "Delicious, of course. I always serve the finest here. Vegetable soup to start with, and the currant pudding would be a perfect finish to the fish entree."

"My mouth is watering already. Shall I have hock to wash it all down?"

Maggie waved at Paddy, the waiter. "Iced hock will be perfect, and brandy with the coffee."

When Paddy came to take the order, Maggie examined her uncle covertly. He possessed an air of power, a certain strange magnetism that she had not noticed in her sour father. But then, Rupert seemed so different from him: confident, worldly, un-British somehow. It must be the time he'd spent abroad that had changed him, she thought. She decided foreign travel had been good to Rupert Merton.

Paddy returned with the hock and poured a glass for Maggie's uncle. "Will you have some, Mrs. Hartwell?" he asked.

"No, but you can bring me a glass of sherry." She turned to her newfound relative. "Now you must tell me everything."

With an enigmatic smile, he smoothed the napkin across his lap. His lips twitched erratically. "Where shall I start?" Then, without waiting for her reply, he continued, "You were about three years old when I left. Do you remember me at all?"

"No, but Grandmother had a daguerreotype of you on her whatnot. I don't know where it disappeared to after she died."

"I've changed a lot since my youth," he said. "You wore looped braids behind your ears and a striped pinafore, and you had the sunniest smile I can remember." He sighed, and swirled the white wine in his glass. "I had a terrible row with Bully, and he told me never to return to Sheffield." Rupert's black eyes suddenly blazed with anger. "He had all the power and money from the steelworks. I had nothing, so I had to take his orders. I didn't visit again until just one week ago. Anyhow, on that day so long ago, I took the first ship to America with some money Mother gave me. As you well know, the ship capsized in a storm, and I was presumed dead." The anger faded from his face. "I was saved by a whaler along the Maine coast and brought ashore."

"What kind of work did you find?" Maggie asked, intrigued.

His eyes glazed momentarily, and the tic slowed. "I worked here and there. Ended up in New York where I got involved in the import business: ivory from Kenya, jade from China, diamonds from South Africa, rum from the Caribbean, and furniture from Europe."

"It sounds as if you carved out a successful life in America," she said.

"I got a percentage at the import company. I worked as a buyer, traveling all over the world. When my employer died, he willed half of the business to me and the other half to his daughter. Her husband bought me out, and here I am."

"You never married?"

"No . . . I would have married the daughter, but she wouldn't have me. Still, it's all for the best. What woman in her right mind would want to settle down with me when I'm never at home?" He stretched his legs under the table. "But my travels are over. London will be my home from now on. I will find a warehouse and set up a business here. Import-export."

The soup arrived, and Rupert gave it an avid glance. "You must tell me about yourself after I've eaten this delicious-smelling dish."

"Yes, there's plenty of time. My life wasn't half as interesting as yours," she said. "I'm glad you decided to stay at my hotel."

He dropped his spoon. "Oh, I almost forgot!" He pulled his bag from under the chair where he'd deposited it earlier. After rummaging for a moment, he straightened and placed a jade figurine on the table. "A small gift for you."

Maggie held it gingerly. It looked like an Oriental deity, with four arms and four legs. A sunburst was carved behind the slim figurine. "Who is this?"

"Shiva, the Hindu god of destruction and reproduction. The many arms are a symbol of the 'dance of life.' Exquisite handiwork, don't you agree?"

Maggie studied the statuette from all angles. "Breathtaking. I've never seen anything like it." She gave him a shrewd glance. "I take it your trunks are filled with outlandish figurines?"

He nodded ruefully. "You're perfectly right. I must confess that I dabble in Oriental religions. There's a wealth of wisdom in the ancient scripts, but I prefer to translate their meaning for myself. All the earth's philosophies converge in the power of the gods. We can't see them, of course, but they are there."

Paddy brought the entrée and took away the empty soup bowl.

Rupert Merton's face had relaxed into a trancelike state. He began eating the fish. "Mysticism's a popular science in our day and age. The British travel farther afield and become influenced by the views of our brethren in the East," he continued. He leaned closer, now very alert. "Do you disapprove?"

She smiled and set the figure on the table. "Oh, no, everyone is entitled to their own beliefs. It's just that the Orient seems so strange, so foreign, compared to what I'm used to here. After all, Paris is the only place I've ever visited besides England."

"Bully wouldn't take you anywhere?"

"No. Father despised me, as he did all women. He turned bitter when Mother left him, and he never shook himself out of it." Maggie hesitated, observing her uncle's face. "Did you ever contact Mother?"

He shook his head. "I had no contact with the family, except sporadic letters from Grandmother Merton, but she didn't know exactly where your mother had settled. And I made her promise not to tell Bully that I was alive. Bully could be awfully vindictive, and he might have found a way to ruin my life, just for the pleasure of it." He threw down his fork and knife. "No one cared where your mother went, did they?"

Maggie lowered her gaze. "I did, but I could not travel to America alone."

"So you came here to escape Bully's tyranny. Well done, Maggie! You had enough gumption to stand up to the old ogre, after all. And you were so young! The solicitors told me everything." He wiped his lips on the napkin. "Bully would have crushed you if you'd stayed at home. You know that, don't you?"

"Yes, Father hated everyone, including himself. The house was like a tomb."

Rupert Merton finished his entrée in silence, and Maggie drained the sherry glass. "You know, it's odd, but an hour ago, I didn't know I had an uncle, and before that, I never dreamed I had a sister."

Interest flared in his eyes. "*Sister?* How intriguing. You must tell me about it."

Just then Victoria bounced into the dining room, interrupting them. "Mama! Mama, I escaped from Miss Lather," she shouted gleefully. Paddy followed, carrying the pudding.

The guest at other tables gave Victoria either fond or annoyed glances, depending on their opinions of proper child-rearing. Maggie scowled. "Shhh," she admonished, and lifted her daughter onto her lap. "How many times have I told you not to interrupt a conversation, let alone run away from Miss Lather. She will be frantic with worry by now."

As if to prove her words, Maggie saw the governess wringing her hands in the doorway, probably thinking that she would lose her position. But Maggie believed in some freedom for children. Why curb their natural ebullience as her father had done to her? All she could remember from her childhood was dark walls and silence, one dreary day following another.

"Victoria, you must greet your uncle, Rupert Merton. He has been traveling all over the world."

Victoria's eyes grew as round as saucers as she viewed the stranger. "Have you seen elephants in the wild?" she asked breathlessly. "In Africa or India, I mean. Miss Lather says that's where they live."

Rupert laughed. "No, I'm afraid I must disappoint you. I only visited the towns, never the wilderness."

Victoria looked disappointed. "I want a pet elephant when I grow up."

"The common belief is that they bring luck." Rupert Merton pulled a small box from his bag. "You're fortunate, young lady. I have something here that will bring you luck when you wear it." He handed over the box, and Victoria opened it reverently. The box contained a small jade elephant on a silver chain. The eyes were beads of black jet, and the tusks were inlaid mother-of-pearl.

"How pretty!" Victoria exclaimed, and demanded that Maggie put it around her neck. Maggie obeyed, and Victoria craned her neck to see the elephant as it rested on her pinafore.

"You must thank Uncle Rupert now."

Victoria slid off Maggie's lap and curtsied. "Thank you," she whispered, touching the jade.

Uncle Rupert smiled and patted Victoria's head.

Maggie watched Victoria leave the room with Miss Lather. She had a good view of the foyer, and her heart skipped a beat as she recognized Thaddeus Webb, who was unwinding his horrid black scarf and hadn't yet seen her. After saying something to the maid in the wardrobe, he aimed his steps toward the dining room.

His face lit up as he spied her, then his gaze alighted on Rupert Merton. Although the smile remained on his face, his eyebrows lifted in surprise.

He bent over Maggie's hand and murmured, "Have you already found a new admirer, Mrs. Hartwell? I'm crushed."

She blushed to the roots of her hair and jerked her fingers away. To hide her embarrassment, she adjusted her spectacles. "Mr. Webb, I'd like you to meet my uncle, Rupert Merton, who just arrived from overseas. Uncle Rupert, this is Mr. Thaddeus Webb, an . . . ah, a business associate."

The two men shook hands and studied each other warily.

"Are you here for supper?" she asked Thaddeus.

"Yes . . . among other things." The glance he gave her was so disconcertingly warm, she had to lower her gaze.

"You are welcome to sit here," Rupert said. "I'm finished, but we don't mind keeping you company, do we, Maggie."

Thaddeus didn't have to be asked twice. "I thought you had no living relatives besides Leonora," he said.

Maggie fidgeted, finding the situation bizarre. What a strange coincidence to discover two close relatives within the short span of a few weeks.

"I didn't know about Uncle Rupert until today." She shared with Thaddeus what her uncle had told her about his life. "Do you have news about Leonora?" she asked.

"Does Mr. Merton know about her?" Thaddeus countered and beckoned to Paddy.

"No, but I was planning to tell him." Maggie turned to her uncle while Thaddeus ordered a bottle of claret and shepherd's pie. She related everything he knew about Leonora. Her uncle whistled under his breath.

"If I had known, I would have tried to find your mother in America," he said. "She must have had a difficult time."

"Leonora said that, because Mother was dead, she wanted to come and live in London," Maggie went on, watching Paddy open the bottle of wine and pour a glass for Thaddeus. She was acutely aware of his long fingers cradling the crystal dome as he sipped. His presence was most distracting. She had difficulty tearing her gaze from his lips as they touched the rim of his glass.

"I wonder if there was something else that tempted Leonora to come to London," Thaddeus said, his gaze warm on her. "An inheritance, perhaps."

"Impossible," Maggie said. "Father sold everything he owned except the old mansion and gambled away all the funds. By the time he died, nothing was left except a decrepit house that falls more and more into disrepair every year. The solicitors confiscated that to cover his debts."

"He didn't leave it to you?" Thaddeus asked in surprise.

"Of course not! He disowned me the moment I left his house." Maggie stared in wonder at Thaddeus, realizing his gentle probing made her spill almost all her secrets. If she wasn't careful, she would tell him everything, and he would know the depth of her shame. He had already figured out that Victoria was born before her marriage to Horace Hartwell.

"That old mansion is nothing but rubble," Rupert said, accepting a glass of claret that Thaddeus offered him.

Paddy returned. An appetizing smell rose from the steaming tray set before Thaddeus.

After placing the sauceboat with extra gravy beside the plate, Paddy left, and the conversation continued.

"So an inheritance would not have been an incen tive," Thaddeus mused, tasting the potato crust tha enfolded the meat.

"No, definitely not. If Father had left anything, I'n sure he wouldn't have willed it to her." She gave hei uncle a long look. "I'm sorry to speak so coldly abou my father, your brother, but—"

"Bully was a cynical old man. He never forgave oi forgot a wrong. He carried the bitterness of a lifetime on his shoulders."

Maggie wondered what her father and Rupert hac fought about, but decided to pry some other time after she'd gotten to know him better. Delight flowec through her as she realized that, though Leonora wa: still missing, she now had family. This Christma: would be a very special one.

Rupert yawned behind his hand. "I must be boring company, but I'm very tired. Do you think my suite is ready to receive me?"

"Yes, of course it is." Maggie began to rise. "I wil show you—"

"No, the doorman or one of the maids can surely show me the way. We shall talk more tomorrow." Bowing to Thaddeus, he left.

"Good night," Maggie called after him. "Please breakfast with me in the morning."

Thaddeus concentrated on his meal, but kept giving Maggie smoldering glances that made her blush to the roots of her hair. She contemplated leaving him to finish his supper alone, then changed her mind as she remembered her night-time visitor.

"I was frightened last night," she told him. "Someone came into my sitting room, then fled when I got up to investigate."

He squeezed her hand in concern. "Someone broke in?"

Maggie furrowed her brow. "I don't think I locked

the door. Perhaps it was one of the servants." She
shrugged. "It might not be important."

Thaddeus brooded for a moment. "From now on
you must lock your door, and Victoria's. Let me know
instantly if something out of the ordinary happens."

She nodded as a frisson of fear shot up her spine.
"I will certainly do that."

"I went to see Sergeant Horridge at the Yard. He
has no more information about Miss Winston. At least
they haven't found a, er—corpse."

"That's slender comfort. Perhaps someone decided
to abduct Leonora, rob her, and abandon her far away
from London. Or what if she was a victim in those
terrible Altar Murders? London is gripped with fear
over who will be the next victim." As her anxiety
returned with renewed force, Maggie moved the
flower vase to another spot on the table.

Thaddeus finished the pie and tossed the napkin
on the table. "None of the victims of the Altar Murders is your sister. Horridge told me their identities."

Maggie glanced at him. "How did you find a way
to worm information out of the sergeant when I was
so unsuccessful?"

Thaddeus's smile was maddening. "I thought no
obstacle was too large for you," he chided gently.

She pinched her lips together. "You're evading my
question."

He sighed and swallowed the rest of his claret.

"Although I no longer work at the Yard, Sergeant
Horridge and I have remained friends. We sometimes
meet at a public house over a pint."

"You've never told me why you left Scotland
Yard," she prodded, wondering if she had the right
to ask.

His mouth lost its teasing smile and his face grew
bleak. "A police officer is supposed to protect the
public." He hesitated. "I couldn't even protect my
own wife."

"Wife?" She paused, hesitant to pry now that he had revealed such a secret. "I didn't know you were married."

"Yes." He studied Maggie intently. "You might as well know the truth. Rachel died two years ago during a robbery. Thieves broke into our house late at night. I awakened and tried to stop them. The blow that was aimed at my head hit Rachel's left temple." His voice grew raspy with sorrow. "She died in my arms. That's when I decided I had chosen the wrong career. I wanted to be a policeman just like my father and grandfather, but I was useless." He sighed heavily. "My grandfather was a famous Bow Street Runner," he added in a lighter tone.

Maggie's heart constricted with sympathy. She longed to hold him close until his sorrow melted away. "Surely it wasn't your fault that the thieves broke in."

"No, but I'll never forgive myself for the loss of Rachel. I will probably never be entirely free of the guilt. She had so many dreams for the future—a large family, her own house."

Maggie didn't know what to say. She shared his sorrow, knowing what it was like to have one's dreams crushed. "The only time I fell in love . . . with Victoria's father . . . I was badly hurt. I decided never to let that happen again. When I met Horace—who became my dear friend—I dedicated myself to the hotel business."

"And became a brisk, decisive businesswoman." He caressed her hand lightly. "I admire your strength and independence."

For a few minutes, they shared a companionable silence. Warmth vibrated between them, a deepening trust.

"Oh, Maggie!" Thaddeus whispered, and set down his glass. His eyes brimmed with feeling, and he clasped her hand convulsively. She squeezed his fingers in return, wanting madly to kiss him. She slowly lowered her gaze in embarrassment at her desire and pulled away her hand. He must have looked straight into her soul, she thought.

As if suddenly aware of other dinner guests, he leaned back and cleared his throat. "To get back to the business at hand, I also spoke with two other passengers, but they didn't remember Miss Winston." He brightened again. "Have I earned my wooden box yet?"

She couldn't help but smile. He kept turning her thoughts topsy-turvy with his mercurial mood changes. "Not quite, but you might admire it tonight, and perhaps touch it once."

He leaned closer to her, so close she could smell the lemony scent of his cologne. "May I touch you as well?"

Maggie rose so abruptly that her chair almost fell over. "There's no need for that, surely." Her own longing frightened her in its intensity.

"But I so enjoyed it," he cajoled, his eyes as soft as brown velvet. "And I think you did, too."

"Mr. Webb," she admonished gently, "You are behaving in a most ungentlemanly manner."

"So you have told me." His eyes caressed her, then he laughed. "My mother would agree with you. She's aghast that I turned out to be so wicked when she's propriety personified."

Maggie looked at him, and realized he was fibbing. "Mr. Webb! You're pulling my leg." Flustered, she looked toward the door, thinking of escape.

He took her hand before she could leave. "Are you going to invite me to your rooms, then?" he murmured. "If I recall, your brandy was excellent."

"Well," she hedged.

"You promised." He rose with alacrity. "I knew you couldn't refuse me. Lead me to the box."

Flushing, she stalked out of the dining room, followed closely by Thaddeus. She couldn't remember when she'd felt more alive. It was as if her blood had turned to champagne, shooting happiness through her.

She entered her office, and Thaddeus closed the door behind them. The gas chandelier shone dimly, and an oil lamp glowed on the desk. The room was peaceful even with the muted sounds of the diners and the guests in the lounge.

Thaddeus crossed immediately to the box and held it reverently. "A master carved this," he said, admiring the inlaid design on the top. Without asking permission, he looked inside, noticing the welter of pencils, erasers, paper clips, and rolls of string. "Sacrilege," he said. With a veiled glance at Maggie, he upended the box on the table, scattering the contents in all directions.

"What are you doing?" she cried, and dived for a pencil rolling off the desk.

"I'd better keep it safe from now on," he said, and tucked the box under his arm. "You're not worthy of such a fine object if you fill it with this junk." He threw a disgusted glance at the debris on the table.

She scrambled to gather the pieces before they could all roll to the floor. "Where shall I store this now?" she demanded, outraged.

He set down the box and began pulling out desk drawers. "Tsk, tsk, there's plenty of room in here. Your desk is so spotless one could easily believe you don't do any work." His gaze danced wickedly. "Let me fill your drawers for you, Mrs. Hartwell. I'm certain I can arrange everything to your satisfaction . . ." He paused to let his words sink in, and Maggie was flabbergasted by the innuendo. *Drawers*, indeed! "What do you think?" he continued.

Maggie burned to slap the grin off his face. "You are the rudest man I have ever met," she said hoarsely. "There's no excuse—"

He gently closed the drawer and sauntered over to where she was standing. Pulling the pencils from her clenched fingers, he placed them on the desk. She shrank away from him, but he only leaned closer and placed his hands on her hips. His touch seemed to burn all the way to her toes, and she gasped, evading his eyes, knowing what she would see there.

"If only you would let down your hair and soften your spine, you would be a wholly delectable woman, Maggie. Now—" His fingers moved upward until his thumbs rested right below her breasts. "Now you're only magnificent. Not bad, considering . . ." He bent his head until his breath warmed her ear. "So very magnificent, a lady in an iron cage." He rotated his thumbs, tickling her through her corset. "What wouldn't I give to free you from that prison," he murmured, his lips brushing her earlobes, "and find silky, warm flesh underneath."

"Mr. Webb!" she forced out between stiff lips. His closeness intoxicated her to a point where all coherent thought was impossible. She pushed feebly against him, but his grip hardened, the palms of his hands now moving up and down her back. The tip of his tongue played on the tender skin just below her ear, shattering her last shred of composure.

Her knees were about to give way, but he held her so tightly that she felt powerless against his formidable strength. "Mr. Webb . . ." she whispered.

One of his hands closed over her breast, and she moaned with untrammeled pleasure. His touch lit fires of need in her blood. His lips moved along her jawline to her chin in a trail of tender kisses. Only an inch separated their mouths, and she was aching for his kiss. Without thinking, she wound her arms around his neck and lifted her face eagerly to his. His mouth covered hers with a force that crumbled any lingering resistance. His tongue caressing the moist insides of her mouth filled her with warmth and longing, breaking down a piece of the wall she had erected around herself. For once she felt completely soft and desirable.

Even as her lips tingled from his kiss, he raised his head a fraction and gazed into her eyes. "Oh, Maggie, you gave yourself willingly. I think I won a great battle tonight," he whispered. "But there are many more to come before you surrender completely." He pulled slowly from her. "And I must step gingerly so as not to startle you into running away like a frightened fawn."

Chapter 10

"Something wonderful must have happened to you," Cecily Byrne said the next morning as she shared breakfast with Maggie. "Your eyes are shining like stars."

"I'm well rested," Maggie said, averting her gaze. She couldn't tell her assistant that Thaddeus Webb's kisses had brought the sparkle to her eyes—to her life. She'd almost been ready to surrender to more intimate caresses, but he was right. The only way to proceed in this relationship was with caution. She wished her mind wasn't poisoned by the doubt stemming from her previous experiences.

Cecily poured steaming fresh coffee. "There's some almond nougat cake left over from last night. Do you want a piece?" she asked, viewing Maggie's buttered toast. "If I didn't stand over you like a mother hen, you'd never eat enough."

Maggie didn't reply. Stirring her coffee absentmindedly, she thought about Thaddeus Webb. Such an attractive man, so warm, yet, so infuriating. He had no manners . . .

"Here it is. And I won't leave the room until you've eaten the whole piece." Cecily placed the wedge of cake beside Maggie's cup, breaking into her employer's reverie.

"I wonder if my uncle is awake yet," Maggie said,

and looked at her assistant who, with an enraptured expression, was eating a plateful of cake. Sweets always made Cecily blissfully happy. "You must meet him today, Cecily. A truly distinguished man." She thought for a moment. "There's something slightly strange about him, but I'm so glad to have found another family member."

"Rafferty said he had, besides regular suits, a huge trunk of outlandish clothes in all patterns and colors."

"He was dressed conservatively enough last night, except for the waistcoat, which was a piece of Oriental art." Maggie laughed. "An interesting person indeed."

"You're gaining more relatives every day," Cecily said between bites.

"Isn't it odd?" Maggie said, tapping her fingers on the table. She drank the rest of her coffee and finished the cake. "I will ask Rafferty to see if Uncle Rupert is awake, and then we ought to start planning for the Christmas season. It's already the fifteenth. We shall have a large tree in the foyer and many special dinners, perhaps a buffet . . ." she mused aloud. "I'll see you in my office in twenty minutes."

Maggie sent Rafferty upstairs to inquire if Rupert Merton desired a breakfast tray. He returned two minutes later.

"He isn't there, Mrs. Hartwell, and he hasn't slept in his bed. I didn't see him leave, but then I don't spend every wakin' minute at the door." Rafferty scratched his head and resumed his post.

"How peculiar." Maggie stared outside, almost expecting her uncle to enter that very minute. "Let me know when he comes in."

A shiver of apprehension filled Maggie as she went into her office. How had her uncle managed to leave without anyone noticing? Ever since the strange intruder who had awakened her two nights ago, she felt insecure in the large building. How many people came and went without Rafferty's knowledge? There were many connecting stairs and two back doors which were kept locked at all times. Victoria now slept in Maggie's bedroom so that Maggie could keep an eye on her. Sighing, she sat at her desk and stared at the debris that Thaddeus Webb had left behind. How like him, she thought with a sudden smile, and arranged the clutter in the drawers of her desk. She had let him take the wooden box with him, although his job wasn't finished. It was her insurance that he wouldn't quit before he'd found Leonora.

Cecily entered, leading Victoria. The child looked sleepy, but she rushed across the room and threw herself into Maggie's arms. "Good morning, Mama."

"What have I said about running heedlessly through the house?" Maggie asked, pressing her face against her daughter's sweet-smelling hair.

"That it's rag-mannered," Victoria said. "I'm sorry, I forgot."

"Miss Lather has a chill and is resting in bed," said Cecily. "Shall I take care of Victoria today?"

Maggie shook her head. "How would you like to go Christmas shopping today?" she asked her daughter. "It's only ten days to Christmas, and the earlier we purchase presents, the less crowded the shops will be."

"Can we travel by horse omnibus?" the child asked, excitedly.

"Yes, I suppose we must." Maggie exchanged amused glances with Cecily. "You may fetch your hat and coat, and don't forget your gloves. It's cold outside."

Giggling, Victoria rushed up the stairs.

"I had many plans today, but I suppose they can wait," Maggie said with a sigh. "We must take inventory of the linen supply, and also make detailed plans for the Christmas festivities."

"If there's a lull during the day, I will personally supervise the linen closet," Cecily said. "You need a break from all the work—and the worry."

Maggie thanked her assistant and promised to bring home a surprise. Fifteen minutes later she was dressed in a tight wool coat edged with fur, carrying an umbrella and a fur muff. After the mishap with her umbrella in the street, she had bought another that was larger and sturdier. On her head she wore a velvet bonnet trimmed with fur and a cluster of velvet violets.

"Mama, you look beautiful," Victoria said, wearing her red wool cloak with matching bonnet. Hand in hand, they walked to Baker Street, where they boarded one of the green-painted buses of the London General Omnibus Company. The driver wore a top hat and a rug over his knees as he wielded the leather reins. A conductor with bushy whiskers lifted Victoria onto the platform, next to the curving metal stairs that led to the open top.

"Can we ride upstairs?" Victoria asked.

"No, it's too cold by far," Maggie protested, and sat on the long wooden bench downstairs. "It also makes me dizzy." She glanced at the sky. "Besides, it might start raining any minute now."

Victoria made a face, but was content to stare out the window as the horse-drawn bus moved along the crowded street. "Look, Mama, that crossing sweeper was almost run over by a cart, and there's a flower girl. Are those real flowers?"

"I don't know, darling."

Victoria commented on a photographer with a tripod, a lame horse, an organ grinder, and a mangy dog before they arrived at Peter Robinson, Ltd., in Oxford Circus, where they would do their shopping.

"May we go to Fortnum and Mason's, Mama? I would like some chocolate."

"I'm sure you would, darling. Perhaps later, but

first we must buy presents for everyone at the hotel. You must help me remember everyone, so that they all receive a gift on Christmas Eve."

"Gertie told me she wants a hair ribbon of real silk." Victoria smiled at the conductor as he lifted her down to the pavement.

Maggie took Victoria's hand in a firm grip and led her through the portals of the store. Right inside the door was a rocking horse decorated with a garland of spruce. Victoria wanted to stop there, but Maggie urged her on. They passed through the department for ladies' ready-made apparel and the department for mourning weeds—for which Robinson's was famous—until they reached the millinery area. A female clerk in a black serge dress stepped forward.

"May I be of assistance?"

Maggie decided to be extra-indulgent of her daughter. She smiled. "Victoria, you may chose ribbons for all the maids—the finest and brightest, mind you. I will look at buttons."

Victoria eagerly followed the clerk to a stack of drawers that contained reels of ribbons, while Maggie watched from nearby. The buttons were attached to the sides of cardboard boxes and sorted by color. She needed ten white ones for a shirtwaist she'd been sewing in the evenings.

She heard the clerk discussing colors with Victoria, who was enjoying herself immensely, if her bright chatter was any indication. Maggie's attention was drawn to a stand of huge hats, laden with silk roses and spotted nets. She especially liked a wide, black straw hat with a pink striped ribbon around the crown and yard-long streamers in the back. Cecily would love that for Christmas, she thought. With a bunch of pink silk rosebuds at the bow, it would be very feminine.

The clerk appeared suddenly at her elbow. "How

many yards of the ribbons do you need, ma'am?" she asked.

"Two yards of each, please," Maggie said. "And I would like this hat sent home in a hatbox. Do you have any rosebuds I could add?" She followed the clerk behind the stand of hats and studied an assortment of artificial flowers under the glass countertop. After much deliberation, she chose one full-blown rose rather than the cluster, which looked overpowering. As she held the rose up to the hat, she called, "Victoria, come look at this. How do you like it?"

There was no reply. Puzzled, Maggie frowned and glanced over her shoulder. Victoria wasn't there.

"Victoria?" she called, louder.

Excusing herself, she went in search of her child. The rooms were L-shaped, and she hoped to find her daughter around the corner, but she saw no one there. Frightened now, she hurried through the various departments toward the main entrance, looking everywhere. Victoria wouldn't have left, she thought. She went to the front door with the aim of asking the doorman if he'd seen Victoria leave, then caught sight of her daughter admiring the rocking horse. Rupert Merton stood beside her.

"Victoria!" Maggie admonished, her heart hammering. "How could you leave without telling me?"

"I saw Uncle Rupert, and we were looking at the rocking horse together. We were coming back to fetch you," Victoria explained, contrite. "Uncle Rupert wanted to surprise you with a box of chocolates, but now you've ruined everything."

Rupert Merton laughed and bowed to Maggie. "I'm sorry to have frightened you, but truly, we were on our way back to get you."

Her legs still trembling with shock, Maggie took Victoria's hand. "How did you find Mr. Merton?"

"I went back to look at the rocking horse."

"How many times have I told you not to leave without telling me?"

Victoria looked mulishly to the floor. "You would have told me to wait for you, Mama."

"And you should have!" Maggie straightened and smiled at her uncle. "I'm sorry, but I was worried."

"I recognized Victoria through the window." Rupert held out a box covered with silver paper. "I bought the chocolate at Fortnum's. Merely a small token of my delight at finding my long-lost relatives here in London."

She thanked him and accepted the box. "I had hoped we could have shared breakfast this morning, but the doorman said you weren't in." She didn't mention that they had looked into his bedroom.

"I left early to take a walk," he explained, the muscle in his jaw twitching. "Didn't sleep well at all."

Maggie gave him a sharp glance. "I hope there was nothing wrong with your rooms?" Was he lying, or had he slept on the sofa in the sitting room of his suite, or, perhaps, made his own bed?

"This climate takes some getting used to," he added. "I'm afraid I have a tendency to turn a bit chesty in cold, humid weather." He patted his torso, which was covered with a cashmere waistcoat and a plaid woolen scarf. He wore a black coat and a stovepipe hat. He didn't seem cold.

"That's unfortunate. Would you have dinner with us tonight in my private dining room, where we can talk without interruptions?"

His eyebrows rose. "Interruptions? Like Mr. Webb, perhaps?"

"Yes . . . I hired him to find my sister, and he's made little progress as yet."

Rupert frowned. "Hired him?"

"Yes, he does detective work on cases that the police won't bother with."

"How interesting. I'm sure he will be successful in his endeavor. He seemed a capable fellow."

Maggie remembered Thaddeus's masterful kiss and blushed. "He's decidedly a forceful personality. He's also an antique dealer, and sells all manner of furniture and ornaments. His partner is an interior decorator."

"Hmmm. I might hire him to decorate my house when I have found one." He took her arm. "Are you ready to leave?"

"No." Maggie glanced at Victoria. "We must finish making our purchases and then find out how much the coveted rocking horse is."

Victoria jumped up and down. "Can we, Mama? Thank you, thank you!" She tugged at Maggie's hand, but Maggie told her to behave. "I didn't say we'd buy it," she added.

"I'll be delighted to have dinner with you two," Uncle Rupert said, and patted Maggie's arm. "But now I must be off to see the solicitors. I'm using the same firm that Bully did."

"We'll see you tonight then," she said, and waved as he left the store. After paying for the ribbons and Cecily's hat, and once again admiring the rocking horse, Maggie allowed Victoria to pull her to a toy shop farther along Oxford Street. The child was enchanted with the dolls with their pale bisque faces and elaborate gowns trimmed in lace.

"Someday Zoe Soap would like to have a sister, one with lovely blonde hair," Victoria mused aloud, and Maggie shivered as she was reminded of Leonora. Would she ever meet her sister, or was it already too late?

Filled with misgivings, she took Victoria's hand and coaxed her from the store. The outing had been ruined by her worry for Leonora.

"Mama, can I have a doll? The one with the blonde hair and pink gown."

"Perhaps later," Maggie said.

Victoria had difficulty keeping up with Maggie's brisk pace. "Where are we going?"

"Home." Maggie glanced at the sky. "It looks like rain any minute. Shall we take a hackney to the hotel?"

"Yes." Victoria scanned the street eagerly. "But there aren't any."

Maggie gripped the small hand harder. "Keep on walking. One will come along soon."

The sky darkened until it seemed like late afternoon. A fine drizzle began to fall. "Mama, we'll get wet."

"I brought my umbrella." Maggie spread it over their heads and hailed an approaching hackney, but, already occupied, it bowled past. They walked without finding an empty cab until they reached Oxford Circus. The streets were more crowded than in the morning, the sidewalks filled with pedestrians. Rain began falling in earnest. Maggie stopped at the street corner and scanned the road for a vehicle, then turned and looked in the opposite direction. To her surprise, a man in a bowler hat and a brown caped coat was staring at her most rudely. He was only a few feet behind her, standing quite still, newspaper clamped under his arm. For some unfathomable reason the man's presence frightened her. There was something about him that said he was walking along solely to stare at her.

"We must find a hansom, or even a horse omnibus," she said, and urged Victoria across the street during a lull in the traffic. The packed buses had been passing at regular intervals without picking up passengers.

Glancing over her shoulder, she saw that the man was still following close behind her. Considering her choices, she remembered that Mr. Webb's shop was only two blocks to the south at Maddox Street. However, the blocks were long, and Victoria could not walk any faster. She was complaining already.

"You don't want to get your feet wet, do you?" Maggie reminded her, slowing down slightly. At the end of the first block, she dropped her muff on purpose and as she bent to retrieve it, she managed to glance behind her. The man was still there, keeping pace with them. He should be walking much faster to get out of the rain, she mused. Why was he following her? She almost turned and confronted him, but lost her nerve at the last minute. What if she was wrong?

Her heartbeat accelerating with fear, she almost ran the last block, Victoria complaining loudly beside her.

"We're going to . . . visit Mr. Webb. He lives right around the . . . corner," Maggie explained. Fear made her short of breath, and she heaved a sigh of relief when they arrived at Thaddeus Webb's green door. As she lifted the knocker, she heard female voices coming from within.

The door was opened almost instantly by an elderly woman with a severe silver-streaked bun at the nape of her neck. She had Thaddeus's kind brown eyes and firm jaw. His mother, no doubt. Maggie momentarily forgot her fear. She liked the woman immediately—especially since the teasing light that always danced in Thaddeus's eyes was absent in his mother's.

"Yes?" the woman inquired.

"I'm here to see Mr. Webb. Is he in?" She gave her name, and the woman called into the parlor. "Thaddeus, Mrs. Hartwell is here to see you."

Maggie's heart hammered so uncomfortably that she thought they must notice her agitation. Once again, all she could think of was the stranger behind her. She peered down the street and saw him at the street corner, staring at her.

Then Thaddeus was there, and when she looked into his eyes, she remembered the passionate kiss they had shared. To her annoyance, she felt a blush staining her cheeks.

She swallowed hard and lowered her eyes. Victoria was regarding her with a child's frank gaze.

"Mrs. Hartwell! What an unexpected and pleasant surprise. Mother, may I present one of my clients, Mrs. Hartwell, the owner of Hartwell's Hotel."

Suppressing a sigh, Maggie smiled politely. Who knew when she would get a chance to tell Thaddeus about the strange man now.

Maggie shook the older woman's outstretched hand, noticing the gnarled fingers and papery-dry skin. Those hands knew hard work. Mrs. Webb was wearing a brown, high-necked gown with fabric-covered buttons, and scuffed black boots. A black fringed woolen scarf hung over her shoulders.

Two young women stood in the hallway. The older had dark brown hair, parted in the middle and curled into ringlets which fell over her slim shoulders. Like her brother, she was tall and had the same velvet brown eyes and firm chin. The younger girl had lighter hair of a warm golden-brown hue, and her face was round and friendly, the teasing light evident in her open stare. All of the Webbs had brown eyes, Maggie noticed.

"These girls are my sisters, Delia and Amintha," Thaddeus said. "Delia is planning her wedding, as I told you before, Mrs. Hartwell." He motioned for her to come in, and lifted Victoria up in the air. "How's the view?" he asked, and she giggled.

"I'm taller than you, Mr. Webb. Almost as tall as the elephant in the zoological gardens."

"That you are, Miss Elephant." He set her down as she squealed in delight.

"Did you hear that, Mama. He called me—"

"We all heard," Maggie said, annoyed by Thaddeus's easy conquest of her daughter. After composing herself, she turned to Delia. "I wish you happiness."

Blushing, Delia smiled warmly. "Thaddeus has mentioned you several times. In fact, he said we should bespeak your dining rooms for the wedding reception since my previous arrangements fell through."

"When is the ceremony?"

"On Christmas Eve. We wanted a festive wedding, and what time of year is more joyous than Christmas?" She turned to her brother. "Why don't you take Mrs. Hartwell's coat and umbrella instead of standing there like a great looby." Delia lowered her voice, but everyone could hear when she added, "You're *staring* at her."

Thaddeus laughed and hastened to close the door and take Maggie's and Victoria's damp outergarments. "If you would care to have a chat with the ladies in the parlor, I will see if Hetty will make us tea and sandwiches." He winked at Maggie and her knees went weak. Her thoughts in chaos, she accompanied the ladies into the cluttered parlor. Victoria was speechless with delight when she found a wagon full of painted wooden soldiers and stuffed rag dolls. Maggie let her go. She'd keep an eye on her.

"Amintha, pull up a chair for Mrs. Hartwell in front of the fire," Delia said.

Mrs. Webb sat down closest to the warm blaze and smiled at Maggie. "I take it Thaddeus is helping you decorate your hotel?"

"No, as a matter of fact, I hired him in the capacity of detective." She told them about Leonora, glad that he hadn't discussed her sister's disappearance, not even with his family.

"That's tragic," Mrs. Webb said, looking worried. "You know, we didn't especially like it when Thaddeus left Scotland Yard."

"He has a successful business here," Maggie defended him.

"Yes . . . of course. Thaddeus was never at a loss for ideas, and he's a hard worker when he sets his mind to something." She smiled reassuringly. "He'll find your sister, if anyone will."

Her confident words relieved the knot of tension that had formed in Maggie's stomach ever since she had seen the man following her in the street. Her unexpected meeting with Thaddeus's family commanded her full attention.

"Can you manage our wedding reception at the hotel then?" Delia asked, bringing them back to the initial subject.

"It's short notice, but I'd be delighted to have you there." Maggie studied Delia's frank face. "It's been a long time since we held a wedding reception at the hotel." Not since my own four years ago, she thought. "What kind of food would you like?"

"We'll make up a list of our preferences, and we can discuss the rest later. Gavin has promised to arrange the decorations, if you don't mind."

Maggie shook her head. "No, that would make it easier for us to get ready on time."

They chatted about the hotel and Christmas shopping. Maggie truly liked the three women. How different her life could have been if she'd had the warmth and companionship of a mother, she thought wistfully, enjoying the closeness between Mrs. Webb and her daughters.

Thaddeus returned, carrying a tray. "Hetty was up in arms again about my many faults. She claims I put a dirty saucer in the cupboard and a clean one in the sink."

"I don't blame her for complaining," Mrs. Webb muttered tartly, glancing pointedly around the messy room.

The tea was strong and the sandwiches delicious.

Victoria was offered tea at an antique child's table and chair that Thaddeus had on display in the room. She chattered away, delighted at the attention paid to her comfort, and discussed the toys with him at some length. Maggie suddenly realized how hungry she was after shopping. She hoped Cecily wouldn't worry about her if the parcels arrived at the hotel before they did.

The apprehension she'd felt in the street had slowly seeped away in the fire's warmth and the company of the Webb family. It was obvious the sisters adored their elder brother, and everyone clearly loved Mrs. Webb, who exuded quiet dignity and pride. As Maggie observed Thaddeus's mother, a lump formed in her throat, and some emotion battled to come out. She took a deep draught of tea to dispel the unfamiliar sensation.

Victoria finished her tea, slid into a corner of Maggie's chair, and tucked her hand into her mother's. It was as if she sensed her mother's emotional struggle.

"Who's sewing the wedding gown?" Maggie asked Delia.

"Mother is." Delia smiled. "You can come and visit us at our home in Ludgate Hill if you're interested in seeing it."

"I wish my mother would get married so that I could have a papa," Victoria said.

Maggie wished the floor would open under her. "You once had one," she murmured, hoping the child would leave the subject. "Go back and play with the toys."

"I take it you're a widow," Mrs. Webb said, compassion in her eyes.

Maggie nodded. "Yes. My husband, Horace, died two years ago from a wasting disease."

"How tragic," Delia said. "I don't know where you find the strength to carry on his business."

"It's not difficult to run a hotel once you know how.

Horace was a kind and patient man. He taught me everything."

They all nodded sympathetically, and once again she had the sensation of being drawn into the warm security of the family. Finally Mrs. Webb rose. "We must take our leave now. But we'll meet again soon." She turned to Thaddeus. "If you're ever in the vicinity of the bakery shop at Covent Garden, Thaddeus, bring Mrs. Hartwell along. I'm sure your father would like to meet her." She smiled and held out her hand to Maggie. "You must have a hard life, raising your daughter alone and managing a hotel. I will include you in my prayers."

The lump was back in Maggie's throat, and she could not respond. Her lips trembled, but with great effort she forced a grateful smile.

When the Webbs had left, Maggie glanced at Thaddeus. A new kind of tension had sprung up now that they were alone, except for Victoria. "I'm sorry if I interrupted a family gathering, but—"

Sobs clogged her throat, and she tried her best to suppress the misery that had lodged in her chest. It stemmed from the worry about Leonora that had built for days, but also from seeing such a loving family. The Webb ladies had proved to be the undoing of her usually rigid emotional control.

Walking across the room, she pretended to stare at a dusty Stubbs painting of a man in a pink hunting jacket on a horse, but tears blurred her eyes. Her shoulders slumped. Vaguely, she heard Thaddeus move toward her. The touch of his hands on her upper arms unraveled her last shred of composure, and she began to cry in earnest. He turned her slowly so that she was facing him, pulled a folded handkerchief from his pocket, and dabbed at the tears cursing down her cheeks.

"There, there," he soothed. "What's wrong?"

"Mama, why are you crying?" Victoria asked,

clinging to Maggie's skirts. "Have I been a bad girl today?"

Maggie glanced down at the child's concerned face and could not help but smile through her tears. She caressed Victoria's soft hair. "No," she said, "you've been a good girl all day." She blew her nose on Thaddeus's handkerchief. "Now go and play while I speak with Mr. Webb. We'll go home in a minute."

"I wish you would stay for dinner," Thaddeus murmured, and Maggie had to look into his eyes. They were soft with tenderness, taking her breath away.

"Are you crying, too, Mr. Webb?" Victoria asked, and pulled his trouser leg.

Thaddeus chuckled. "No, but I will be soon if your mother doesn't stop."

Victoria tugged at Maggie's skirt. "He says you must stop crying, Mama."

"Yes . . . I will." Maggie shooed her daughter toward the toys in the wagon.

"May I hold you?" Thaddeus whispered.

"No . . . please don't," she said. "It might instigate another flood."

Nevertheless, he rubbed his palms against her thin white batiste sleeves, and goose bumps of pleasure formed on Maggie's skin. Whatever emotion the Webb ladies' kindness had stirred up, Maggie had found her composure at last. But Thaddeus Webb was doing his best to inspire quite another sensation—desire. It moved swiftly through her, and she longed to be crushed against his masterful chest and taste his mouth again.

To break the seething tension, she told him about the man who had been following them since they'd left Robinson's. "I have never seen him before, but I'm sure he was keeping pace with Victoria and me. It was frightening, and when we couldn't find a hansom, I decided to come here."

Thaddeus nodded. "That was good judgment on your part, Mrs. Hartwell." He walked to the window and moved the lace curtain aside to stare from one end of the street to the other. "There's no one loitering outside right now. However, I will escort you home to be on the safe side." With a suggestive glance, he added, "Nevertheless, I wish you would stay for supper, and perhaps—"

"Out of the question, Mr. Webb," Maggie whispered in shock. Her body, however, reveled in his suggestion.

"I feel I know you quite well, Mrs. Hartwell. In fact, I wish we could dispose of these unwieldy last names."

Maggie drew herself up. "Very well, you may call me Maggie . . . Thaddeus."

He chuckled and pinched her chin as he passed her on his way to the hallway. "Maggie," he whispered. She lowered her gaze. No matter what she did or said, he always managed to turn everything topsy-turvy.

After calling Victoria, she followed him to the foyer. She wished he hadn't seen her tears. Now he would tease her forever.

But she was wrong. He only mentioned it once, in a whisper. "I'm glad you can cry, Maggie. I worried that you were too iron-clad to reveal any emotion." His breath tickled her ear as he helped her on with her coat. "And I hope it wasn't the last time. Softness suits you immensely, Maggie—darling."

She whirled on him, but he was only laughing and pulling on a cloak. Blushing, she helped Victoria with her red coat.

"You have too many things here, Mr. Webb," Victoria commented as she viewed the welter of artifacts filling every space in the hallway. "You need a large toy chest to keep them in."

Thaddeus laughed. "But then I wouldn't be able to admire them as I go by," he said.

"Don't you *stumble* over anything? I always fall over my toys, and then Mama makes me put them in my chest."

Thaddeus winked. "Your mother is very wise. However, as you can see, there's a clear path to the door." He held out his hand to her. "May I escort you, Mademoiselle Victoria?" he asked with an exaggerated bow.

Victoria giggled. "Yes, sir, if you promise to let me ride at the top of the horse omnibus."

Thaddeus quirked an eyebrow at Maggie, and she nodded with a wry smile. Where had Victoria learned to be so coy? Yet the thought of her daughter and the protective Mr. Webb—Thaddeus—being friends warmed her heart.

Chapter 11

Two days later, Thaddeus arrived at Hartwell's Hotel carrying a bunch of mistletoe tied with a red satin bow. He stepped into Maggie's office and held it over the door. She stood at her desk thinking that her knees had turned to water at the exact moment he smiled at her.

"Come here, Maggie, and help me attach this. Bring a chair."

"But it isn't Christmas yet."

"The flower girl on the street corner seems to think it is. She had a whole basket of mistletoe and holly. Bring a chair and a thumbtack."

Maggie obeyed, knowing that he had mischief in mind. "I'm sure you didn't come here just to decorate the hotel," she said suspiciously.

He balanced on the chair and fastened the red ribbon to the molding of the door frame. Then he stepped down and, rubbing his hands, he lifted the chair aside and dragged Maggie into his arms. "The first kiss of the Christmas season. May it last forever." He pulled her unyielding arms around his neck. Then he traced the outline of her face and gently pulled off her spectacles. Folding the wire frames, he dropped them into his pocket.

Maggie's eyesight was blurred, but she was well aware of the smile on his face and the mouth that came closer with every breath. A moan started deep in her throat as the tip of his tongue teased the outline of her lips. The velvet touch stirred a frenzy of longing within her, and she had to cling to him so as not to fall. His mouth was hard and demanding, yet curiously tender and kind. She melted inside as she eagerly accepted his wonderful gift. Life and love pumped through her, growing stronger the more his mouth cajoled and entranced her, breaking down more of the iron barrier inside her.

She gasped in disappointment when he raised his head. "I didn't think you'd mind a Christmas kiss," he said hoarsely. With his fingertips he traced her hairline and tickled her earlobes until she squirmed away, embarrassed at her reaction to his caresses.

"Giving up so soon?" he chided.

"I have other things to do, what with the Christmas season soon upon us." Wishing she had dared to suggest more intimate caresses, she sat down behind her desk. To her chagrin, she realized that her spectacles were still in his pocket. Holding out her hand, she demanded them back.

"Perhaps, but you look rather vulnerable without them, so I might refuse your request for a few minutes, just to admire your lovely face. Your eyes aren't shooting daggers at me for once."

She sighed. "You're the only person I know who can mix insult with compliment."

He chuckled and she could see that he had sat down in the wing chair on the other side of the desk. "I came here for two reasons—in addition to kissing you. Mother and the girls wonder if it's convenient for you to meet with them here on Monday next."

"Yes, I've already alerted the staff to the fact that we have a wedding reception to prepare. I will personally show your family around. Is the groom coming?"

"I don't know." He paused. "I wish I had some more news about your sister, but I don't at the moment. But, in a spirit of goodwill, I wondered if you'd care to accompany me to South Audley Street this afternoon. Mr. Ripley has finally returned. I rang him this morning, and he's willing to see us."

Maggie's heart took a double leap. "Do you think—"

"It's too early to speculate. We'll know more once we've seen him." He rose abruptly and handed back her wire rims. "Could you be ready in five minutes?"

"Of course." She put on her spectacles and ran up the steps to her rooms. After making sure her chignon was tightly wound and her starched blouse immaculate, she flung a cloak over her shoulders and put a plain bonnet on her head. Her hands would be warm in the fur muff.

The day had been cold and windy, with a pale sun brightening the horizon of jagged rooftops. Snow clouds loomed on the horizon.

"Four minutes and thirty seconds," Thaddeus said as she returned downstairs. He was holding his pocket watch in his hand, and a mischievous light gleamed in his eyes. Maggie had brought her umbrella, and, with a rueful smile, Thaddeus offered to carry it. "It might come in handy."

"You never stop teasing, do you?" she asked with a glare.

"Where you're concerned, it would be a mistake. I'll break down your resistance and make a woman out of you yet." He held the door for her.

"As outrageous as ever, I see," she said, wanting to kick his shin.

Thaddeus wore his houndstooth-patterned greatcoat and a soft-brimmed fedora. The long black scarf was in place, as usual.

When they were safely ensconced in a hansom, Maggie asked, "Why do you always wear *that*?" She flicked the scarf.

"It was the last thing my grandmother made for

me before she died." He caressed it tenderly. "I know it's ugly, but it's full of love, and it warms my neck."

Maggie marveled at this man who seemed to have such a large capacity for love and compassion. He was dangerous; she might fall deeply in love with him. There was no use denying that possibility. If she kept seeing him, she was doomed, wasn't she? A twinge of unease coursed through her because he so easily stirred her emotions. He had such power over her . . .

"I wish you could have met my grandmother. She was truly grand."

"Don't forget your mother, who's also a wonderful lady."

"I'll take you to visit her bake shop. She works there from four in the morning until late at night. When Father became an invalid, she supported the whole family until I started working at the Yard."

Silence fell between them, and Maggie suspected his thoughts had turned to his dead wife, Rachel. Had she been a real woman in Thaddeus's eyes?

"How do you define a *woman*, Thaddeus?" she asked recklessly.

He shot her a quick glance and chuckled. "Brooding, are you?"

She didn't answer, only gave him a challenging stare.

He leaned back, pressing her farther into the corner. "A real woman is a vessel of love and softness, of kindness and patience."

"Sounds more like the description of a saint," Maggie scoffed. "No woman is that perfect."

"For hours at a time, perhaps. Sometimes they can be womanly for days, for months, for a lifetime, like my grandmother."

Maggie wouldn't support his theory. "You're idolizing her. What about you wife?"

He paused. "She could be as stubborn as a mule, but, yes, she was loving and warm most of the time."

"You're romanticizing your memories of her." Was that jealous voice really hers? she wondered.

His eyes met hers, making her heart race. "It all depends on how the woman is treated." She sensed a promise behind his words, a promise that he would show her how. Her breath quivered in her chest, and her heart ached with longing. She wanted desperately to experience what he was talking about.

"A woman should be cherished and loved," he continued.

His simple statement touched her deeply, leaving her speechless.

The hansom stopped and Thaddeus became businesslike. "Ah! Here we are."

The manservant who had opened the door on Maggie's previous visit led them through a gloomy hallway whose walls were covered with dusty old paintings.

The salon to which they were shown had a bow window with wicker seats upholstered in golden velvet. The heavy drapes matched the fabric, and the carpet was dusty and threadbare. In the corner was a whatnot filled with strange objects, and the paintings depicted unusual Oriental charts. Where had she seen them before?

"Have I had the pleasure?" came a voice from the door. The high-pitched tone suited perfectly the tall willowy man with wispy blond curls. He had an arresting face with a square jaw and a sharp nose. His gray eyes were keen, and slightly cruel, Maggie thought. Ripley was dressed in a sack coat, a brocaded waistcoat of dull red velvet, and black trousers. The clothes looked elegant, yet oddly feminine.

"No, we haven't met, but we're here to inquire about a certain Miss Winston," Thaddeus said. "She traveled across the Atlantic on the same steamer as you, Mr. Ripley. Does her name sound familiar?''

Maggie wondered why he hadn't used Leonora's alias.

"Miss Winston?" Mr. Ripley pulled a cigar from a humidor on the wicker table and lit it. Puffing thoughtfully, he studied Maggie. Why was he taking such a long time to answer? she wondered uneasily.

"Miss Winston," he repeated. "I don't recall such a name."

Thaddeus took out the calotype of Leonora from an envelope he carried in his hand. "How about Miss Winter?"

"Ah! That name I do recognize," Mr. Ripley said. He looked at the calotype, and nodded. "That's Laura Winter. She was traveling alone all the way from Virginia to see her sister in London." He smiled at Maggie. "Are you the sister?"

"Yes, I am. When did you last see Leon—Laura?"

"I bought her a glass of wine in the lounge. Actually, we were assigned to the same table in the dining room." He sighed and puffed on his cigar. "A charming young woman."

"Did you see her leave the ship?" Thaddeus asked, his eyes narrowed suspiciously.

Mr. Ripley pondered the question as he crossed the room and glanced out the window. "We said goodbye on the morning of our arrival at Liverpool. After breakfast she went back to her cabin, and I to mine." He shot Maggie a veiled glance. "I believe that was the last time I saw her. Relatives met me in the harbor, and I left with them."

Disappointment filled Maggie. She glanced at Thaddeus and saw that he was studying Mr. Ripley closely. "Did Miss Winter tell you how she planned to travel to London? Had anyone offered to help her?"

Mr. Ripley laughed mirthlessly. "Are you implying that I shirked my duty as a gentleman?"

Thaddeus wasn't smiling. "No, but I'm certain you inquired about Miss Winter's situation."

Anger flared in Ripley's eyes. "Naturally. If you must know, Miss Winter thought her sister"—he glanced at Maggie—"might meet her."

"I did, but she wasn't there." Maggie shifted the muff from one hand to the other. "What happened to her? She must have arrived, since you saw her at breakfast that morning."

Silence fell, and Maggie once again sensed an odd uneasiness.

"I'm sorry I can't help you further," Ripley said, his eyes blank. "Perhaps she accepted an invitation to visit someone else for a few days or weeks."

"That's illogical," Maggie said. "She knew I would be expecting her."

Thaddeus moved toward the door. "Come, Maggie. Thank you for your time, Mr. Ripley. If you remember some other important detail, please contact me." He handed the man his card.

Ripley bowed and escorted them to the door. "It's certainly a mystery. Do the police suspect—?"

"They will after I have a talk with them," Thaddeus said grimly.

Thaddeus held Maggie's arm as they walked in silence toward the cab stand on the corner. What could have happened to her sister? Maggie wondered. She'd been missing for almost two weeks now.

"What next?" she asked.

Thaddeus sighed heavily. "I'll find out if anyone left the ship on a stretcher. Perhaps Miss Winston was abducted by someone." He paused. "This is most puzzling. At least we know that she was alive on the day of arrival."

"If Mr. Ripley was telling the truth," Maggie responded. "I didn't like him."

"One of the moneyed young set; spoiled, bored, and arrogant. I've met his type before." Thaddeus shot Maggie a sideways glance. "He wouldn't be above using your sister and then . . . leaving her."

"Those were my exact thoughts," Maggie said bleakly. "I have a feeling something terrible happened to Leonora, or she would have arrived in London days ago."

"Don't think in those terms. We'll find her."

They stopped at the cab stand, and Thaddeus studied Maggie's face for a long time. "I won't rest until I've removed that anguish from your eyes," he said. "Now, go home. I will continue on my own. In fact, I have a meeting with Sergeant Horridge, and I'll relate to him what has happened. He might want to start an investigation now that we have two people who met Leonora and know that she called herself Laura Winter."

"How can I stay at home waiting—"

"Do it!" He helped her into her hansom and closed the door behind her before she could protest, and somehow her anger and fight went away. She trusted Thaddeus. If anyone could help her, he would. On impulse, she leaned forward and kissed his cheek.

"Thank you." She blushed. "Do you want to come for dinner tonight?"

A slow, lazy smile lit his face. "Can't wait to hear what Sergeant Horridge has to say, can you?"

"It's more than that . . . I enjoy your company."

He placed his hand over his heart. "You're reducing me to a blithering fool."

She smiled and leaned back against the seat. "You already *are* one," she said sweetly, delighted to get him back for all the times he'd teased her.

" 'Til tonight then." Smiling, he gave the address to the driver and watched her leave. He felt as if a piece of him left with her, and a wave of such tenderness overcame him that he felt dizzy. He shook his head and started walking. He'd never discover what had happened to Leonora Winston if he had a befuddled head. His lips thinned into a grim line. He feared that Miss Winston was in great danger, if not already dead.

He crossed Regent Street and sought one of the noisy public houses on a side street in Soho. Although the building was grimy with soot and the woodwork filled with dry rot, the atmosphere inside was warm and friendly. The tables had frayed yellow tablecloths, but the brass rail around the bar gleamed, and the green shades on the oil lamps were clean and sparkling. A piano tinkled in the background, and the smell of meat pies wafted through the air.

"One of the usual, Roger," he said to the publican behind the counter, and looked around the room, which was half full. "Have you seen Sergeant Horridge today?"

"Meetin' 'im 'ere then?" Roger asked, and placed a pint of lager in front of Thaddeus. "Ye look right solemn today, Mr. Webb," he added, staring owlishly at Thaddeus through a pair of thick spectacles.

"I have problems to solve, and no solution in sight." Thaddeus tasted the frothing lager and, over the rim of the glass, saw the sergeant enter.

"I'm taking a table. Bring over a pint of the same and two meat pies with mashed potatoes for Sergeant Horridge."

"Th' sergeant'll appreciate that. 'E likes 'is food, 'e does," Roger muttered, and disappeared through a swinging door.

Thaddeus shook hands with his old friend. Septimus Horridge looked with pleasure at the pint that Thaddeus placed before him as he sat down. "Just what I was thinking of as I came through the door." He took a deep swallow. "Ah! There's nothing like a glass of cold beer to slake one's thirst." He gave Thaddeus a probing glance. "I take it you haven't invited me here to ply me with beer."

"I want to talk about Leonora Winston."

The sergeant unbuttoned the heavy gray coat he was wearing. Pulling out his cigar case, he shot a glance at Thaddeus. "No leads, eh?"

"She called herself Laura Winter on the ship, and we've talked to several people who saw her and spoke with her. According to one passenger, Mr. Anselm Ripley, she was alive and on board the steamer on the day it docked at Liverpool." He paused and drank some of his beer. "I would appreciate it if you could find out if the Yard has any records on Mr. Ripley. I don't like the fellow by half. While you're at it, could you check any records of a Rupert Merton of Sheffield?"

Roger returned with a tray. He placed the meat pies and a bowl of steaming mashed potatoes in front of the sergeant. "Are ye havin' a pie as well?" he asked Thaddeus, who eyed the food with interest.

"Can't. I was invited to dinner tonight."

The sergeant filled the plate that the publican had placed before him. "To your parents'? Mrs. Webb is a first-rate cook," Horridge said.

"No. As a matter of fact, Mrs. Hartwell issued the invitation. I'm quite taken with her, and I'd say she's taken with me."

"That poker-backed schoolmarm," Horridge scoffed. "You can do much better than that, Thad."

"I might just be the man to remove the 'poker', and some other steel barriers as well." He chuckled as he thought about Maggie's stiff corset.

"You were always one to accept a challenge." The sergeant supped with great appetite and washed down the food with more ale. "Ripley?" he repeated.

"South Audley Street. Lots of money there, or he had some at one time. He has a nice house, and arrogance to match."

"Don't recall anyone by that name, but I'll take a look through our files. He could be connected to someone else."

"There was something strange about him, though I can't explain it exactly." Thaddeus leaned his chin in his palm and looked at his friend. "Since we have now proved that Miss Winston traveled on the steamer, you could launch an official investigation."

The sergeant creased his brow. "I suppose so, but I think you might get results faster. We have too many cases at the moment. Everything except the Altar Murders ends up at the bottom of the files. Seems we're dealing with another Ripper, perhaps even the same man."

"Too farfetched."

"I wish you were back at the Yard, Thad. Then we might find the murderer." Horridge cleared his plate meticulously with the knife.

"Thanks for the compliment, but I'm happier now. The antiques business offers a great deal of excitement."

"Still thinking of Rachel, aren't you, Thad?"

"Sometimes. She would be hard to replace as a wife." Thaddeus thought about Maggie, missing her already.

"Are you considering marriage, my friend? Will I be invited on the great day?" the sergeant teased, lighting up a cigar.

"Marriage is a serious step, don't you think? That's why you've stayed a bachelor all these years."

"I like my freedom, but you—you would make a good father, Thad. You need someone to take over your business one day."

"You're looking too far ahead, old friend. I think I enjoy my freedom just as much as you do."

Horridge puffed thoughtfully on the cigar and studied Thaddeus with a humorous glint in his eye. "So you want us at the Yard to find this Leonora Winston to impress her sister." He patted Thaddeus's shoulder. "We will, we will, unless you find her first." He rose. "I wish you luck with Mrs. Hartwell. She seems a formidable woman. It will take a man like you to tame her."

Thaddeus snorted. "You should be careful what you say, Septimus. If you weren't such an old friend—"

"Touched a raw spot, did I?" Horridge laughed and shrugged on his coat. He waved at the door. "See you here next week, same time. I'll stand for beer and dinner."

"You'd better find some answers," Thaddeus muttered to himself.

After paying the bill, he left. It was barely teatime, yet dusk already filled the city. Rain mixed with snow had begun falling, and he pulled up his collar. Septimus was right—Maggie had become more important to him than he'd ever dreamed possible. Her vulnerability behind that formidable exterior provoked a longing within him to take care of her. Only after meeting her had he realized how empty his life had become since he'd lost Rachel. After the initial grief and self-recrimination, the wounds had slowly healed, and he'd thought he'd never need another woman in his life. But now he'd found he couldn't live on memories alone. Not until Maggie had wandered into his life did he understand that she was the one he had been waiting for, ever since his wife's death.

He crossed Regent Street and turned onto Maddox. There were lights in the shop windows. Gavin must be home.

To his surprise, the front door was open a crack. A moan sounded from within. Flinging open the door, Thaddeus rushed inside to see Gavin lying on the floor in the parlor, clutching his head. Blood was caked at the hairline above his ear, and his face was as pale as linen. "Damn . . . damn," he swore, and staggered to his feet.

"What happened?" Thaddeus demanded as he assisted his friend to the nearest chair. He pried Gavin's fingers from the wound and studied the ugly lump. A portion of skin had been broken, causing the now matted bloodstain in his hair.

"Two . . . blokes came in here a while ago carrying truncheons. One asked: 'Mr. Webb?' Before I could . . . answer, they had . . . overpowered me and hit me in the head. I fainted, and only just came . . . to." He swore again and raised his head. "But I'll live."

Thaddeus fetched a glass of brandy and a towel, which he'd dipped in cold water in the kitchen. He pressed it gently against the lump, and gave his partner the brandy glass. "I'm sorry this happened to you."

Gavin shot him an irate glance. "Evidently they thought I was you." He gulped the brandy. "Someone doesn't like your work. Have you sold any fake antiques lately?"

Thaddeus shook his head. "Not to my knowledge. But as you know, I'm not exactly a full-fledged expert in the business. Not yet anyway."

"Then it must be the deuced detective business. Someone considers you an enemy." Gavin glared at him. "I might regard you as one myself if this ever occurs again."

"I have a suspicion that someone doesn't want me to continue my investigation into Miss Winston's disappearance."

Gavin grimaced and removed the towel. "Perhaps you should heed the warning."

"Come on, old fellow. I'll take you home, unless you'd rather stay here."

Gavin's eyes were grim. "In your bed perchance, and face another attempt on my person? No, thank you. I value my life too much." He finished the last of the brandy and rose. "You shouldn't stay here if you value yours, Thad."

Thaddeus rubbed his chin thoughtfully. "Perhaps you're right. I think I'll move into a hotel after I've settled you at home. Just let me pack a few things." He bounded up the stairs.

"I have a good idea just which hotel he'll pick," Gavin said gloomily to the empty room. "Thaddeus never lets an opportunity slip through his fingers," he added, and viewed his forehead in a mottled girandole mirror.

Chapter 12

Rupert Merton hailed a hansom and gave the jarvey an address in Golden Square, Soho. The house was grimy and run-down, but its marble steps and pillars proclaimed its former elegance. He knocked once, then, as the door was opened by a young man, slipped inside the hallway.

"You followed her like I asked you, Theo?" he asked the man.

"Yes," Theodore Fowler-Foss answered. "She noticed me, however. Surveillance never was my forte. Evidently, she knows someone on Maddox Street and went into a shop there."

"Webb, of course," Rupert muttered.

Theodore led him along the narrow corridor toward the back of the house. A room which might once have been a luxurious library spread out before them. It was sparsely decorated, but the trappings of the sacred ceremonies were still there: the altar, the candles, the incense. They would be moved to Richmond soon enough, Rupert thought with immense pleasure. The Twilight Brotherhood would make their headquarters in a lovely old house that had once belonged to the family of one of the members. They would no longer have to move from house to house, like thieves, to hold their ceremonies.

The walls were hung with scarlet cloth, as was the

sacrificial altar. Incense sticks in holders emitted a sweet odor that made the Voices that were now part of his mind, his every waking thought, stronger. The Voices were there even now, filling his head with their chatter. He welcomed them like old friends. He'd planned the success of the Twilight Brotherhood for a long time in America. Since he began visiting the group of acolytes in London he'd known the young men were perfect for his purpose of spreading the Brotherhood across the world. The weddings and body sacrifices had already started. Money was pouring in, and the Voices were growing louder and more insistent. Soon they would take over.

"Ripley is bringing an adept who wants entry into the Brotherhood." Theodore snorted and crossed his arms. "He thinks he has the power of a magi and wants to attain the seventh circle."

Rupert was only listening with half an ear. The Voices were speaking to him, chattering so intensely that he had to clutch his head with his hands. They demanded more every day. It was both ecstatic and painful. He knew that soon he would disappear, dissolve, become the highest, a Voice himself. He would be the greatest of them all. He would rule.

"As long as he's a young, *handsome* man. They must all marry wealth, so that we can get the means to spread the Brotherhood. Then the whole world will listen . . ." Rupert slowly dragged on his crimson robe, leaving the hood hanging down his back. He crossed the room to a trunk that leaned against one wall and raised the domed lid. From among the welter of books and charts he pulled out a hookah with two thin rubber hoses.

"I will concentrate before the others arrive. Will you join me?" he asked, and set the pipe on the table. The smoke calmed him, and it made it easier to differentiate the Voices from each other.

They sat opposite each other on the floor in front

of the altar. The patterned red carpet beneath them depicted seven circles, and they placed the pipe in the middle of the smallest circle. Rupert filled the bowl with a ball of sticky opium and lit it, inhaling in small puffs. He reached for Theodore's hands as water bubbled in the container attached to the pipe. After exhaling, his body slumped forward until his forehead almost touched the floor. The Voices crowded in, babbling frantically, louder than ever. Rupert could barely stand it. He went rigid with muscle spasms, his eyes rolling, his jaw clenching. Then the Voices receded, leaving a clear, golden, empty field where he could see beyond everything. He was master. He perceived all. Throwing his head back, he laughed in exultation. The Voices would bow to him. The whole world would one day bow.

"They are here now," Theodore said from far away. For a moment his voice reminded Rupert of his hated father, and he had a powerful urge to squeeze Theodore's throat until the sound stopped. Father had been the one to stand between him and the Voices, but Father's whip and his harsh words would no longer suppress his inner friends, Rupert thought. Father had dissolved into the black void where he could do no more harm. Bully had joined him there. Rupert laughed. He'd been stronger than them in the end, no matter how they had taunted and beaten him. Bully had called him a pale, cowardly bookworm, a dreamer. But Bully hadn't known about the powers.

Feeling strong, invincible, yet at the same time ethereally light, Rupert rose and pulled his hood forward. He was the Reformer—he would change the world.

Soon, the adepts of the Brotherhood glided inside, all silent and solemn. The room flickered with a red light. Was there a fire? Dazed, his head suddenly splitting with pain, Rupert looked around. There was no fire, but the air seemed to vibrate with flames.

Gasping, he cried out, "Behold the power of the Voices!"

He pointed at the man whom Anselm Ripley had brought into the room. The young man looked frightened but also curious. The members of the Brotherhood swayed around him, babbling in trancelike ecstasy.

"You want to join the Twilight Brotherhood, the vehicle of the Voices?"

The young man nodded, wringing his hands.

"Are you prepared to offer everything?" Rupert thought he was flying through the room, hovering near the ceiling momentarily, then landing in front of the bemused man. The red light intensified. A buzzing sound tormented his brain.

"You will die and pass into your new spirit," he said to the young man. "Are you prepared to die?"

The man swallowed, sweat dripping from his forehead. "Must I leave this existence?"

"Your body will be a vessel for the Voices, for the powers of the seven circles, but first your Self will be purified. You must pass through every circle before you will attain a state of emptiness where the Voices will take over." Rupert shook his arms in the air, his breath hissing between his teeth. His eyes were burning and every breath was painful. "Are you prepared to lose yourself?"

The man nodded and shifted his weight to his other foot.

"Your name shall be Shadow until you have obeyed the laws and become accepted by the Voices. Your first test is to marry. The female sacrifice must be wealthy, and you must bring her wealth to the Voices, for the good of their work." Rupert's voice was changing, growing thin. A leaden fatigue spread through him and he lowered himself before the altar, kneeling, as he used to kneel against a chair as Father whipped his bottom. But this time he was the one in

power, and no one was ever going to take it away
from him. Yet the Voices beat him, beat him, never
stopping . . .

Thaddeus entered Hartwell's Hotel carrying two
carpetbags. Maggie, who was standing behind the
counter, stared in amazement.

"What—?"

"Do you have a room?" he asked, and set down
the bags. As he told her what had happened to Gavin,
she paled. "A break-in most likely. Gavin surprised
the burglars," he lied to protect her. It had just occurred to him that *she* might be in danger as well.

"I don't know . . ." she said hesitantly. It would
certainly complicate matters to have Thaddeus staying under her roof. She turned to Cecily, who had
just finished a telephone conversation.

Cecily had overheard Thaddeus's request. "Of
course we have a room for you, Mr. Webb," she said.
"Number three is available, and there is one closer to
your flat, Maggie, number seven."

"Number three will probably suit Mr. Webb better," Maggie said hastily. She waited until Cecily had
gone to ask Rafferty to take up Thaddeus's luggage,
then said, "If it was only a break-in, why are you
moving in here?"

He glanced guiltily to the floor. "Ah! Well . . ."

"You're afraid that some mischance might befall
me, aren't you?"

He took both her hands and regarded her steadily.
"Yes, perhaps. Gavin seems to think that the attack
was meant for me, because of my current detective
work."

Maggie inhaled sharply. "There *is* something
strange going on that might involve Leonora. I
thought I was imagining things—like my night visitor, and that man who followed us from Robinson's.

But now there's been the attack on your friend Mr. Talbot.''

He nodded, clearly worried. "I doubt it involves Miss Winston. Nevertheless, I don't want anything to happen to you. You mean too much to me, Maggie.'' He squeezed her hands and smiled reassuringly. ''For whatever it's worth, I'm here to protect you.''

She felt uneasy, as if a nebulous thereat was hovering over their heads, ready to enfold them, but she tried to smile. ''At least you won't be late for dinner tonight. I'll send Paddy for you when it's all organized.'' She paused, blushing. ''The meal will be served in my rooms, and Victoria will join us for the meal, if you don't mind.''

''Not at all. As a matter of fact''—he patted his coat pocket,—''I have something for her.''

''A bribe?'' Maggie regretted her words when his smile faded. ''I'm sorry,'' she added, ''it's just that—''

''—you always think the worst of me,'' he filled in. He moved toward the stairs. ''But by thinking the worst, you protect yourself against our love. It's true, isn't it?''

Maggie wanted to shout *No!* but she only nodded. ''Ever since I was a child I've eyed gentlemen with suspicion. It takes time to let go of old habits.'' Her lips quivered as she added, ''I'm sorry. It isn't your fault.'' To save herself from more embarrassment, she walked quickly into her office. She didn't know how to explain it to him, but she cared for him more than he knew.

The hours before supper dragged on endlessly. Maggie searched her wardrobe for a suitable dress to wear. She tried on and discarded half a dozen before settling on a dark green silk gown with a high neck, gigot sleeves, and an inset of lace from the collar to the swell of her breasts. The cuffs were long and narrow, and fastened with a long row of buttons, as did the back of the bodice. The skirt was gathered closely at the waist, then flared over starched petticoats. In her tight chignon, she wore a rhinestone comb to which was attached an ostrich feather dyed in the same color as the gown.

"Mama, you look lovely," Victoria said as she entered a while later. She wore a white cotton dress with frills around the yoke and collar. Black ribbed stockings and patent leather boots covered her legs, and Miss Lather had brushed her fine blonde hair and tied it back with a blue satin bow.

"You're very pretty yourself," Maggie said, and gave her daughter a hug. "You must behave with Mr. Webb, and not chatter through the meal."

"Children should be seen and not heard," Victoria intoned, and Maggie laughed. "Miss Lather says that every day."

"She's right, you know." Maggie patted the unruly red-gold curls along her hairline.

"But it's so *boring* and *unfair*. I don't like to sit and stare while everyone else talks."

"Once you grow up, you may speak as much as you want. In the meantime you must listen and learn to converse properly."

"Mr. Webb teases you, Mama. Is that good conversation?"

Maggie blushed. Her daughter saw too much. "As long as he doesn't use abusive and foul words, I suppose it's acceptable."

Gertie put the finishing touches to the dinner table in the sitting room, and Maggie praised her.

"I want it to be special-like," Gertie said with a small curtsy. "Mr. Webb is ever so 'andsome and kind." She winked at Maggie, who smiled grimly.

"You are a cheeky one, Gertie."

"But I always speak the truth, Mrs. Hartwell."

Blushing, Gertie hurried to the door. "I'm ever so sorry if I offended you."

Maggie shook her head ruefully as she listened to the giggles coming from the passage as Gertie closed the door. That maid was a minx. Still, her cheerfulness was infectious.

As a centerpiece for the table, Maggie had earlier filled a crystal epergne with sprigs of holly. The glasses and silver sparkled, and the damask tablecloth with its matching napkins was faultless. As soon as Thaddeus arrived, she would pull the bell chord and Paddy would bring up trays of food.

She was as nervous as a schoolgirl as she waited for the clock to strike seven. He would soon be here . . . How would she dare look at him when she knew she carried her heart in her eyes?

She almost jumped with fright at the knock on the door. "Come in," she called and glanced at the clock. Five minutes early.

Thaddeus entered with a smile, seeming to fill the room with his presence. He was immaculately dressed in a black suit, pearl-gray waistcoat, and a white shirt with a high starched collar. His hair was brushed carefully to lie flat, though it tended to fall forward and curl at the ends. He looked endearing, Maggie thought, and stifled a sudden yearning to trace his features with her fingertips.

"Mr. Webb!" Victoria cried, and ran to take his hand. She curtsied as she'd been taught and stared at the parcel in his hand. "Is that for me?"

He laughed and shook his head. "It's for your mother, but I have something for you, too."

His gaze wandered tenderly over Maggie as he handed her the parcel. When she unwrapped the red paper, she discovered a box of fine chocolates. "Sweets for a sweet lady," he said gallantly, and then pulled out a package that was protruding from his pocket.

Victoria squealed when she'd torn off the paper. "A set of painted wooden animals! Mr. Webb, I saw them in your shop and wished they were mine." Impulsively, she threw her arms around his legs and squeezed hard. "Thank you!"

"Victoria," Maggie admonished. "You're forgetting your manners."

Victoria thanked him properly. Then the animals absorbed her attention as she formed them into groups beside her plate on the dining table. Maggie would usually have objected to that activity, but tonight she only had eyes for Thaddeus.

"You didn't have to bring anything," she said, and with a smile offered him the bonbons. He took one, but instead of eating it, he held it against her lips until she opened her mouth. A shiver of delight coursed through her as his fingertip caressed the soft cushion of her bottom lip. Blushing, she took the chocolate into her mouth.

"This should be dessert, not an aperitif."

"We don't have to keep such strict rules." He went to the tantalus where she kept the liquor. "What will you drink?" he asked as if he owned the house.

"Sherry, please."

He studied the bottles and grunted. "How can you drink that sweet-acid wine?"

"How can you drink Scottish whiskey?" she asked in return as he pulled out a brown, square bottle.

He chuckled and poured himself a good measure. "The same way you drink sherry, through the mouth."

"Oh, you! I warn you, don't get started."

His expression softened. "I can think of other wonderful things one is apt to do with a mouth," he whispered as he handed her the sherry.

"Shh," she warned. She glanced at Victoria, who was happily playing with her new toys. "How do you like your room?" she asked in a louder voice.

"Ah! Fit for a king. I even have a private bathroom, and the brass is polished so bright that it's likely to blind me. And what service! A pretty little maid called Gertie brought me a stack of warm towels."

"You're exaggerating about the comforts," Maggie said dryly. "However, I do take pride in my hotel and like to keep it spotlessly clean."

He sighed. "If I had only one member of your cleaning staff, I'd be living in paradise over at Maddox Street. Do you think you could spare—?"

"I wouldn't wish that cleaning job on my worst enemy."

He laughed, his eyes glittering with challenge. Another knock sounded.

"Did you invite someone else?" he asked.

"No. It must be Paddy with the food. But I didn't ring—" She opened the door to see her uncle Rupert.

He glanced at Thaddeus and the table. "Oh, I didn't know you had company." He turned as if to leave. "Shall I come at another time?"

Disappointed to have her evening with Thaddeus interrupted, Maggie politely motioned him inside.

"A glass of whiskey?" Thaddeus called out. "Maggie stocks only the best brand."

Rupert smiled and accepted. "How could I say no? But I'll stay for only a moment." He sat down on the striped ottoman and accepted the glass from Thaddeus.

"I say! That's an unusual ring," Thaddeus commented, staring at Rupert's left hand. "Where did you find such an article?"

"In Egypt, as a matter of fact." Rupert held his fingers toward the light. "The onyx is carved as a scarab. In ancient Egypt it was the symbol of resurrection."

"I seem to recall that the ancient Egyptians believed that death is a long journey."

"Something like that. I believe in the resurrection

of the body, don't you?'' Rupert's dark eyes bored
first into Thaddeus, then into Maggie. "I believe your
old, limited Self dies, and then you return, reborn in
the same body."

Thaddeus swirled the whiskey in his glass. "Well,
I truly don't know. There's an upsurge in mystical
and religious movements; but I'm not familiar with
the particulars of each philosophy." He glanced at
Maggie. "What's your opinion?"

"Like you, I have no knowledge of resurrection,"
she said, sending an uneasy glance at Victoria. "Perhaps we should discuss this matter at another time."

"Of course. There are many interesting theories in
modern religion." Rupert lowered his voice. "Death
can sometimes be a blessing, I believe—if the person
in question lived a fruitless and wasted life." He
drank the rest of his whiskey.

"Did you have something else to discuss with me?"
Maggie asked crisply. "I take it you've been ex-
tremely busy with your new business venture here in
London?"

"Yes. I found a warehouse for my imported goods,
and now I'm looking for offices and a showroom. I
have also found a business partner, and a town house
in Cavendish Square. Workmen are repairing it before I move in." He held out his glass as Thaddeus
offered him more whiskey. "I came to tell you that
I'll be gone from London for a few days, if you care to
rent out my rooms during that time."

"Oh. Thank you for telling me." Maggie wanted
to ask him where he was going, but she didn't want
to pry since she barely knew her newfound relative.

"Today is Saturday. I'll return next Sunday night."

"I'll have Rafferty pack and store your things while
you're gone."

Rupert rose. "That would be a burden off my
shoulders." He upended the glass and set it down on
the table with a bang. "Excellent whiskey, m'dear.

Goodnight, Victoria," he called to the little girl, who
waved.

As Rupert left, Paddy entered with the food tray.
"You didn't ring, ma'am," he complained. "Food's
gettin' cold."

"We must eat then," Maggie said, grateful for the
interruption. Rupert had somehow cast a pall on the
evening, yet she was still thrilled at having an uncle
who would visit her from time to time. They would
be neighbors when he moved to Cavendish Square.
She looked forward to getting to know him better;
perhaps then he wouldn't seem so eccentric.

She supervised as Paddy placed the dishes with
their silver domes on the sideboard. "That will be all
for tonight, Paddy. Thank you."

"I'm hungry, Mama," Victoria said, yawning.

"And sleepy, too," Maggie added. "Perhaps I
should call one of the maids to serve at the table. I
gave most of them the evening off."

Thaddeus strolled over and held out a chair for
Maggie. "Allow me to serve the meal," he said. "An
intimate dinner for just us—three is more relaxed."

Maggie knew he'd been on the verge of saying a
dinner for *two*, and she was grateful that he'd in-
cluded Victoria.

"Where shall I start? The soup?" He lifted the lid
of a tureen and inhaled the fragrant scent.

"Fish and vegetable soup," Maggie commented.

"What's for dessert?" Victoria asked.

"Shhh, you must wait and see," her mother said.

Thaddeus served the bowls of soup and passed
around a basket of warm crusty rolls. The butter pat-
ties were imprinted with a leaf pattern and arranged
in perfect symmetry on a plate. Victoria voiced her
opinion that it was a pity to ruin the pretty display.

"But if we don't eat we'll go to bed hungry." Thaddeus said, and buttered her roll.

"You're not going to bed here, are you, Mr. Webb? Your room is at the other end of the house."

Maggie blushed, knowing that Thaddeus was looking at her, but she refused to meet his glance.

"If you don't eat your supper, I must send you to bed promptly, Victoria."

"But, Mama—"

"Just obey." Maggie patted her lips with her napkin, barely able to swallow any of the soup, however delicious. All the time, Thaddeus's amused gaze was burning into her, and she wished the floor beneath her would open up. They finished the soup in silence, then partook of a dish of fried filet of haddock with sprigs of dill, a wedge of lemon, sauce, and small white potatoes.

The main entree consisted of lamb cutlets and steamed vegetables. Victoria complained that she couldn't finish her meal if she wanted to save room for dessert.

"Well, I suppose you must taste the trifle that the cook made especially for us," Maggie said with a smile as Victoria forgot her manners and started to jump up and down.

"Trifle is my *favorite*," she told Thaddeus, returning to her seat.

"Mine, too."

Victoria looked at him in awe. "I *like* you, Mr. Webb."

"Your liking probably stems from the fact that I brought you a present and that I enjoy eating trifle."

Victoria giggled and squirmed on her chair. "You're naughty, Mr. Webb. But Mama likes you even better than I do," she concluded, and gave Maggie a frank stare.

"And I like your mother better than trifle."

Victoria whooped with glee. "But you cannot *eat* her."

"Perhaps, perhaps not," he said enigmatically.

After they had finished the delicious trifle, Maggie said, "I will call for Miss Lather to take you to bed, Victoria. You should have been asleep an hour ago, but since we have a guest, I let you stay up late."

Victoria yawned and patted the wooden animals on the table. "It was the best dinner ever since Papa died," she said.

Maggie flinched and sent Thaddeus a furtive glance. He was leaning back in his chair, puffing on a cigarillo, and sipping from a tumbler of cognac. His eyes were unreadable, but she knew he was aware of her every feeling, as he always was.

"Can we go to the zoological gardens tomorrow, Mama?"

"You have tickets? They are usually restricted," Thaddeus said.

Maggie nodded. "We belong to the Zoological Society," she explained. She turned to Victoria. "But we don't visit the zoo in the winter. Perhaps we can skate on the Serpentine if it's cold enough. Mr. Webb might like to join us."

A smile played on Thaddeus's lips. "Only if I can skate, too."

"Oh, yes." Victoria squealed. "Can I ride at the top of the horse omnibus to the park, Mama?"

Maggie threw Thaddeus an exasperated glance. "We shall see. I wish you weren't so stubborn, Victoria."

"I shall be very good," the little girl promised. "If you call for Miss Lather, I will go to my room without whining," she added.

Thaddeus laughed. "You're a rare little minx, aren't you, Victoria?"

"What's a minx?"

"A person like you."

Victoria giggled and gave Thaddeus a playful shove.

Miss Lather arrived a few minutes later, and Maggie gave strict orders that the governess sleep in Victoria's room. She hadn't forgotten the fright she had received at the stranger's intrusion into her rooms.

"Is Victoria frightened of the dark?" Thaddeus asked, having overheard the conversation.

"No, but I fear that someone might . . . hurt her after that night-time visitor I had."

"Who are you afraid of, the staff?" he asked, his eyes narrowed in calculation.

"No . . . that's the strange thing. I trust all of them, and the guests don't come up here. Rarely, anyway."

"Why didn't you tell me how frightened you are?"

"I saw no reason to," Maggie said, and shivered as if a cold draft had crossed the room. She sat down at the table and stared at Thaddeus. He puffed on his cigarillo and studied her.

"Someone is watching you, m'dear. But who? And why?" he said in a low voice.

Maggie's breath caught, and she sent a furtive glance to the dim corners of the room.

Thaddeus took her hand and caressed it, then rubbed it to bring the warmth back to her skin. "You're as tense as a bowstring." He rose and went to stand behind her. "Now relax. You have nothing to fear here." He laid his hands on her shoulders and began a rhythmical massage of her knotted muscles.

She wanted to protest, but found that his touch was too soothing, too welcome, to resist. As tension slowly drained from her body, warmth seeped in. She was intensely aware of his strong yet tender hands, and of his closeness. A whiff of his lemony cologne wafted past her nose, and it stirred a delicious sensation in her stomach.

An intense longing for more caresses flooded her. It was as if her skin was on fire, her perception of his every movement heightened.

"You're so confident in everything you do," she said, closing her eyes. She absorbed his nearness like a starving person would devour food.

"You haven't told me much about yourself, Maggie. All I know is that you're a shrewd and capable woman who, when her mind is set, cannot be moved." He paused, rubbing her shoulder blades with slow, circular movements. "You're a lovely, desirable woman and I wonder why you haven't married again. But it must have been difficult to be twice widowed."

Maggie hesitated to bare her secrets to him, but she knew she had to trust him if they were to build upon their relationship. "You might have heard that I was twice widowed, but that's a lie I keep up for the staff." She bit her bottom lip and concentrated on his magic touch so that she wouldn't panic when she told him the truth. "Victoria was born six years ago here in London. However she wasn't conceived here, but in Sheffield, at my father's mansion." Her voice trembled, but she forced herself to go on.

"I knew Horace Hartwell wasn't Victoria's father," Thaddeus said gently.

"When I was seventeen, I fell head over heels in love with the new head groom of our stables. He was handsome, blond and muscular, arrogant—the type of young man who would turn innocent maidens' heads." She took a deep breath. "You must know that I was very lonely after Mother left. I grew up in the company of governesses, and I didn't see Father except at the evening meals, or when he punished me for childish pranks. I was literally kept a prisoner. Perhaps Father was afraid that I would leave like my mother did."

"You must have been a lonely and unhappy child."

"I was, but I was also headstrong and full of dreams that I vowed to fulfill someday. To start, I was going to have a large, happy family." She clasped her hands in her lap. "The groom talked with me and rode with me." She sighed. "I was so . . . so foolish. He flirted with me, and I fell in love. He was a knight who had come to take me away from Father's tyranny." Her voice faltered, but she forced herself to go on. "Within a month, I had become his lover. We concealed our love from everyone, meeting in meadows, in caves, in the forest. I thought he would love me forever and ever, and I him." She sighed heavily. "Such delusions! I finally got in the family way."

"That must have been frightening."

"Yes . . . When I confronted the groom with the news, he disappeared that same night and was never seen again. I thought of killing myself. I knew I couldn't tell Father—he would certainly have beaten me to death. He would have seen only the disgrace, the sullying of the Merton name."

She clasped her hands tightly, her entire body tensing, remembering old abuse. Thaddeus caressed her shoulders once more, then gently unbuttoned the topmost buttons of her bodice to rub along her spine. His fingers insinuated themselves under the frill at the top of her corset, and her breathing grew labored.

"I felt such shame—I still do. I decided to escape," she continued. "It was the only way. I took the train to London, planning to go into domestic service, save as much money as I could, then have my baby where no one would recognize me.

"Yes, I was very naive to think that I could find work instantly without references. Things weren't easy in London. They never are, are they?" She didn't wait for his reply, but went on. Telling him about her past seemed to lift a burden which she had carried for so long that it had become a habit. All at once, she felt years younger.

"I was constantly propositioned in the streets. The slums were appalling, but I could afford only the cheapest lodgings while I sought employment."

"You had no relative who could help you?" He slowly undid the rest of the buttons at the back of her gown.

"No . . . Well, two distant cousins, but they would have informed Father right away. I was too frightened to face his wrath."

"He never found you here in London?"

"No, he probably thought I was just like my mother, and never bothered to look for me. The solicitors contacted me when he died two years later, by then a poor and miserable man." She paused as he pulled the silk from her shoulders, baring her lace-trimmed chemise straps. She almost protested, but his hands were warm and comforting on her skin.

"I went to several employment agencies where at last I met a man who was looking for a housekeeper. That was Horace Hartwell. He was kind—he complimented me on my hair."

"It is very lovely," Thaddeus whispered, and unpinned the tight chignon. It fell in a thick, lustrous mantle of reddish-gold down her back, and he wanted to bury his face in it, inhale her heady fragrance.

"So I was fortunate. He not only hired me, but helped me with my work, taught me everything about the hotel business. When my belly began to show, he offered me marriage, his name for my child—no questions asked."

"A man of honor," Thaddeus said. He wound his hands in her hair, aching with the need to crush her to him and kiss away the pain of her memories.

She blushed and lowered her head. "I didn't love him, though."

"But he couldn't help loving you." Thaddeus chuckled. "I'm not surprised. You're lovely and desirable." He inserted a finger under her corset and tried to pry it gently loose. Embarrassed, she squirmed away.

"My responsibilities grew at the hotel, since Horace's health was unpredictable. I found that I enjoyed the work immensely." She paused, then added dreamily, "The bustle of guests, people from foreign lands, fine cuisine . . . I've never tired of it. There are much larger hotels—the Victoria, the Savoy, and the Grand, for instance—but I give my customers the very best of everything. That's why I keep the hotel small and cozy. Most of my guests already know each other. We're like a big family, and that's what I want.''

She rose and turned to Thaddeus, her eyes huge and luminous. He gripped her arm and slowly pulled her toward him.

''I hope you don't think less of me for taking what Horace offered,'' she whispered.

''No . . . we all have to survive.'' He pulled his hands through her silky hair. ''To do that, you married Horace Hartwell.''

''Yes . . . he was such a thoughtful man. I did love him in a way—like a good friend. Of course, the staff knew he couldn't be Victoria's father since she arrived only two months after the wedding.'' She studied Thaddeus's face, wondering if he would be repulsed by the knowledge that she'd borne an illegitimate child. Shame burned through her, but his face showed nothing but concern. She thought about Horace, who'd saved her from destitution. ''Besides the disease that deteriorated Horace's bones, he had a bad chest and had to rest constantly.'' Tears gathered in her eyes. ''He loved Victoria from the start and treated her as if she were his own daughter. I think we eased his loneliness.'' She dabbed at her eyes. ''He left me the hotel in his will.''

Thaddeus caressed her cheeks with his thumbs. ''Since his death, you've changed this hotel and made it truly prosperous. Horace Hartwell would have been proud of you.'' Without another word, Thaddeus pulled her to him and lowered his mouth to hers. She tasted so sweet, so warm, that his head reeled. She was everything he'd longed for since Rachel had been torn from him.

''Oh, Maggie, darling . . .'' he murmured against

her throat. She trembled in his arms like a frightened fawn, but he knew she would soon relax once she realized how much he cared for her.

"No man has touched me intimately since the groom at my father's estate," she murmured, stiff with apprehension. "I don't dare to . . ." She wanted to let go of her inhibitions, to allow him to lead her down the path of physical loving, but the fears that had held her back from any romantic involvement were still strong.

She sank down on her chair at the dinner table, not daring to look at him. He remained standing behind her, and since the bodice had fallen from her shoulders, he slid his hands from her neck down over her chest. With fingers that were as gentle as the touch of a butterfly wing, he unsnapped the hooks of the hard busk at the front of her corset. Closing her eyes, she breathed in deeply. A current of cool air touched her skin as he parted the corset at the top and took her breasts into his hands.

Her heart hammered, and her breathing again grew labored. A sweet ache swelled within her as he took one of her nipples between his thumb and forefinger and massaged it gently until it hardened. Her thoughts whirled as his tender homage sent waves of uncontrollable excitement to every part of her being, reminding her of the heady passion she was capable of feeling. His touch became almost unbearably sweet, making her yearn to tear off her clothes so that nothing stood between them.

He bent over her shoulder and kissed her throat and collarbone, then traveled further down, until he reached the gentle swell of her breasts. He looked at the turgid pink nipples and a wave of such raw desire engulfed him that he thought he would lose his balance.

"Come, dearest," he coaxed, reluctantly pulling his hands from the warm, inviting mounds. God, he wanted her so badly he could barely breathe. Her scent, her satiny skin, the tilt of her chin beckoned him, intoxicated him with need. She had let him come this far . . . There was not much left of her iron control, and he believed she would be the softest, the most abandoned siren he had ever held in his arms.

She half-rose from the chair, instinctively wanting to follow him, to invite him into her bed, but a nagging doubt held her back. Once in her life, she had followed her emotions blindly, and the result had been Victoria; her seemingly insurmountable problem had found a blessed solution. This time, however, she would not give herself without at least a promise that he wanted more than just her body.

"Come," he urged again, his voice husky, his eyes veiled with smoldering desire.

She fought a silent battle within herself, but reason won in the end. Clutching the edges of her corset together, she shied away from him. "I won't let this happen," she whispered. "The dinner invitation didn't include a dessert of this kind. I'm not ready for it."

He clasped her face between his large hands. "You're a lovely, desirable woman, Maggie, and I believe you need to be loved. I need you."

"Every human being needs love," she said, and pulled up her bodice. "But I cannot let my emotions rule me."

He struggled for a moment, hoping to gain a measure of control over his desire before he tried to speak again. "I didn't come here to take advantage of you, Maggie. I came because I enjoy your company immensely, and, if you must know, you entrance me. You're magnificent, vibrant. In you I see an energy that you've kept tightly bottled up behind that prim exterior." He traced her jawline with his fingertip. "I wish you would dare to live fully, to believe that life isn't all an evil conspiracy."

How could she ask him about commitment? It was he who should offer her the shelter of his name before he asked her to give her body. Yet the yearning of her body was almost unbearable. Saying no to him was the most difficult thing she'd ever done.

He smiled guiltily. "I suppose it was ungentlemanly to give in to my feelings and suggest a night of loving. Don't look so frightened, Maggie. Rest assured, I have no intention of ravishing you—although the temptation is destroying me."

He righted his ascot, and walked toward the door. Longing wrenched Maggie's heart as he bowed. "The dinner was excellent, and the . . . dessert more delicious than a man could ever describe."

Just before he closed the door, he whispered, "Good night, sweet Maggie. I know I will dream about you tonight."

Still clutching her bodice with stiff fingers, Maggie nodded and said good night. *Maggie, you are a coward!* she berated herself. Why are you such a prude? You bared your shameful secret to him, so what difference would it make if you gave away the gift of your body? There are ways of protection . . . She blushed at her thoughts. Her body was almost *demanding* her to give up every ounce of self-preservation she still possessed. "Oh, no," she moaned, her determination faltering. Her hands were trembling and her blood pounding with longing as she undressed and crept into bed. Frustration and loneliness would be her companions tonight.

Chapter 13

❦

A strange noise outside her bedchamber awakened Maggie from an uneasy sleep in the middle of the night. Clutching the covers, she wondered fearfully if she'd forgotten to lock her door when Thaddeus left. For once, she hadn't worried about the unspoken threat she felt every night when she went to bed. Victoria was safe with Miss Lather, and the governess had promised to lock her door.

The sound came again, like cloth rubbing against the panels of her door. She wanted to call out, but kept silent. If she waited, she might find out who was in her sitting room.

Cold with fear, she pushed aside her eiderdown and slid from the bed. Her long flannel nightgown hampered her movements as she crept toward the door. The only light in the room was the red glow from the coal fire in the hearth. There it was again, a dragging sound against her door. Collecting her scattered thoughts, she remembered that the sideboard was right outside, and that the food was still there. Perhaps one of the maids had sneaked in to carry out all the dishes before Maggie rose in the morning. No, why would anyone be working in the middle of the night? She started as the clock on the mantelpiece chimed twice.

Who would be in her room at this ungodly hour?

175

And why hadn't he or she knocked on her door? Her heart hammering, she pressed her ear to the oak panel. She heard the sound of someone pulling out a drawer. This might be the person who had stolen her japanned box in her office! Even though terror held her in its numbing grip, she had to discover who it was.

She kept her sewing implements in a basket on the small table beside the door. As silently as she could, she pulled out her scissors and clutched them tightly—they would serve as her protection. She didn't dare contemplate the fact that she was vulnerable, a woman alone. Holding her breath, she turned the key in the lock slowly. It made a slight scraping noise, and she waited until she heard yet another movement outside, the sound of the door of the sideboard opening.

Her hands clammy and her legs weak from fear, she peered through the crack in the door. In the weak moonlight streaming through the windows, she could make out the dark shape of a man. The wide shoulders and the height were impossible in a woman.

"What do you want?" she asked, when she found her voice.

The shape whirled and faced her momentarily. She saw a pale face, limp hair hanging down on both sides. The man fled headlong to the door leading to the corridor. Maggie ran after him, her scissors held high. "Who are you?" she called hoarsely.

Without responding, he sprinted across the threshold and slammed the door behind him. By the time Maggie had found the courage to open it and face whoever was waiting outside, she was trembling so much she could barely remain upright. The corridor was bathed in eerie white moonlight, and the shadows of the few pieces of furniture lining the walls were huge.

The doors to the nursery and Victoria's room were

closed, as was the one at the end of the passage, leading to the guest rooms at the front of the house. Maggie hurried after the man. Had he been one of the guests? She gingerly opened the door and looked into the dim hall beyond. Gas lamps on the dull red walls were turned low, casting shadows on the floor. The passage was empty, and not a sound came from the stairs. Was he even now waiting for her in some dark corner?

Viewing the closed doors of the guest rooms, she hesitated before venturing further. Thaddeus's room was at the other end, and she thought that if she could travel that far, she would alert him.

Her throat dry with fear, she advanced. It seemed that the very walls were breathing, watching her. She jumped as a sound came from one of the rooms, but after one petrifying moment, recognized it as a snore. Clenching her teeth in determination, she continued, aware of the silent threat with every breath.

She could have cried with relief as she reached Thaddeus's room. She knocked without hesitation, praying that he wasn't a heavy sleeper. After the second try, the door opened and she could have kissed his dear face topped with sleep-tousled hair.

"It's me, Maggie. May I come in?" Was that ragged voice really hers?

He flashed a wide, wicked smile, and opened wide the door. "What a pleasant surprise."

Without another word she stepped inside. "I had a visitor again tonight. I confronted him, but he fled before I could find out who he was." At the end of her tether, she would have collapsed if he hadn't steadied her. He led her to a chair and eased her down, then pried the scissors from her stiff fingers.

"I'm glad you came here. I'll go and investigate. For your protection, I want you to lock the door from the inside while I'm gone."

"It's no use, Thaddeus. The man has vanished."
She drooped against a stuffed chair.

He pulled up a footstool and placed her feet on it.
After spreading a blanket over her, he fetched a tum-
bler of brandy and pressed it to her lips. "Drink this.
You'll soon feel better."

She obeyed, still so tense with terror that she could
barely open her lips. The brandy burned down her
throat and warmed her stomach. Her breathing grew
steadier, and her muscles gradually relaxed.

Thaddeus massaged her shoulders as he'd done
earlier in the evening. He didn't speak, but his presence was immensely comforting. She downed the rest
of the brandy to dissolve the memory of what had
happened in her room.

"If only I knew what he was looking for," she said.
"I have nothing of much value in my rooms, only
some silver cutlery and a few semiprecious stones."

"If we knew, we could apprehend the villain,"
Thaddeus said. "I must go and take a look at your
rooms. Don't be afraid. I won't be a minute."

He left, and she locked the door behind him. Maggie poured herself another glass of brandy, and this
time the liquor filled her entire body with a comfortable glow.

Leaning back her head, she sighed deeply. Her
limbs felt strangely weak.

Thaddeus returned in a few minutes. Only then did
she notice his dress. He wore a wildly patterned, blue
and green silk dressing gown over—nothing! His bare
legs showed under the hem, as did the dark mat of
hair on his chest. Maggie fought a longing to touch
him.

"No one was there, as you said. I locked your
door." Thaddeus handed her the key and she put it
on the table.

"I don't want to go back there alone," she said.

"You can stay here." He paused. "In fact, I don't

want you to sleep in your room tonight. The intruder might come back." He stretched out on his bed. "Come here," he said softly. "I will hold you until you go to sleep." He patted the mattress beside him and held up the cover. "Don't be afraid. I won't take advantage of you."

She was too tempted to resist his offer. Nothing could make her return to her bedchamber again until morning. For just this one night she wouldn't be alone and miserable, worrying about the identity of her sinister caller.

Her legs unsteady, she stepped to the bed and sat down on the edge of the mattress. Drawn to his warmth, his reassuring smile, she lay down, stiffly at first, but when he tucked the cover around her and pulled her resolutely into his arms, she yielded. He was so close she could feel the heat of his skin through her nightgown and smell the aroma that was his alone, a heady, virile fragrance that made her head spin more than the brandy had done.

Intoxication. With a sigh, she burrowed her face against the strong column of his throat.

"Sleep now, Maggie, you're safe. Don't worry, no one is going to hurt you here," he crooned softly, stroking her hair. He nuzzled her cheek. "You smell so good, like fresh linen that has dried in the sunshine."

She chuckled. "It's my nightgown."

"No . . ." he protested. "It's your skin." He continued caressing her hair, and she gradually drifted into exhausted sleep. She didn't hear what else he said, but the sound of his voice soothed her.

She awakened some time later. The room was dark except for moonlight trickling through a crack in the draperies. Thaddeus's scent enveloped her, and as he moved, throwing a leg over hers, she discovered that he was awake. He moved so that she was completely locked in his embrace. His arms were strong around her, and his warmth enfolded her. She turned her head toward him, showing that she was awake.

He touched her face, his fingertips tracing the outline of her chin. With a groan he buried his hands in her hair, and an immediate response flared in her. She could not deny herself the love of this man. For much too long she'd been starved for a man's care and companionship. Shutting her mind to the doubts that threatened to destroy the moment, she wrapped her arms around him, drawing him even closer. Surely he would not abandon her tomorrow? She ought not be afraid. He was an honorable man.

"Oh, my darling," he muttered as she responded to his ardor. "I love you so much, Maggie." Their lips met in a slow, excruciatingly arousing kiss. His tongue invaded her mouth as if ravenous for all the sweetness she could offer. It was rough yet soft, infinitely exciting. A dulcet fire swooped through her body.

His lips wandered in a moist trail down her throat, and he deftly unfastened the buttons at the neck of her nightgown. She couldn't stop him . . . didn't want to. She dug her fingers into his hard shoulders, feeling the silk of his dressing gown slipping beneath her touch. The belt had loosened and the material fell away from him. Eagerly exploring the springy hair on his chest, she marveled at its breadth, the muscles that could easily crush her if he weren't so immeasurably tender. Yet the banked-up urgency she sensed in him had a potent, provocative effect on her. She could barely breathe as he parted her bodice and explored her breasts.

"Soft as velvet," he whispered, massaging her nipples.

Her breath changing to shallow gasps of pleasure, she caressed his hard hipbone, sliding her hands over the silk of the dressing gown. The hot proof of his excitement was pressing against her thigh, but she could not yet touch him intimately. *She wanted him madly.*

He laved her nipples with his tongue until they were taut with almost unspeakable pleasure. Wave after wave of exquisite fire scorched through her. He moaned as she raised her hips instinctively, rubbing unwittingly against the throbbing center of his desire.

She didn't seem to realize what her wholly feminine, vulnerable body was doing to him. He could barely contain himself when she began rubbing her leg up and down his, massaging him, her every move making contact with his member. The covers had fallen to the floor and he could see her pale thighs as her nightgown slid up. He was acutely aware of her hand wandering over his belly, making the fiery tightness in his loins more unbearable every second. In an innocent, yet painfully arousing movement, she raised her hips to his, over and over, as if in an attempt to appease her mounting desire.

He inhaled raggedly and let his hand ride on the sweet mound between her legs. Holding his breath, he inserted one finger into her secret haven and discovered the moist, velvet warmth he knew he would find. His pounding heart made it difficult to breathe. He massaged her hidden treasure gently, then more urgently as he could no longer restrain his ardor.

"Darling," she moaned, writhing as the touch of his hand brought unendurable rapture to her body. The sweet torture mounted with every second, and she held her breath lest it disappear. It was as if something inside her was pounding, pushing to come out, to break loose from the restriction of her body. The thought of touching him, encircling the smooth, hard shaft that taunted her, made her even more excited.

"I can't bear it . . ." she whispered, holding his buttocks and pressing herself against him. She parted her legs, and his fingers slid into her effortlessly. Cry-

ing out in sweet agony, she undulated her hips to get
more of him. His breaths were coming in gasps
against her neck, and she longed for the moment
when he would take her, make her his. But he waited.
He pulled the nightgown over her head and flung it
aside.

He kissed the inside of her thigh, the tender skin
that was the forecourt to her secret eden. She gasped
when he took her into his mouth, teasing her with
his tongue, branding her with an ecstacy more tantalizing than she had ever dreamed. Something burst
within her and she hovered on the precipice of rapturous liberation. Then he rolled over her and between her legs. As she lifted her hips to meet his
thrust, she was panting, every fiber quivering with
yearning.

He was big and hot, so fulfilling she had to cry out
as the first wave of release rocked her. He moved hard
and swift within her, not tiring until she clung limply
to him after another sweet wave of delight overcame
her. A hoarse moan rose from his throat as he pushed
into her with savage force, then quivered in her arms,
and collapsed against her.

He caught his breath, laughing in delight, kissing
her over and over. "Oh, how I've longed for this
night," he said. "I knew that dreams of you would
haunt me from the first moment I saw you."

"I, too, fought the attraction," she whispered, "but
it didn't take you long to destroy my defenses."

"That's because I was the right man to do it. I knew
that your prim and daunting demeanor hid a vulnerable heart." He took her mouth in a fiery yet tender
kiss. "I can't get enough of you," he said as he raised
his face from hers. "You intoxicate me beyond reason." He slid his hands along her body. "You're
beautiful and warm, your body a masterpiece."

She snuggled closer to him, reveling in every inch
of the muscular frame that touched her. Wanting to

tell him how much he'd pleased her, she sought for the right words, but ended by saying nothing. This was too rich, too new, too fragile to put into words. In his presence she was always aware of everything about him, his smile, his form, his movements—yes, even his thoughts.

"How wonderful," he murmured, and his arms tightened. "Let's make love all night. Let's cross the sea of rapture to its peaceful shore again and again, so that we won't forget it in the merciless morning light."

Maggie closed her mind against her doubts. Tomorrow she would worry about the future, but tonight she was a princess in an enchanted land where the prince of her dreams was determined to give her all the pleasure he could conjure. She intended to enjoy it fully.

Chapter 14

When Maggie awakened the next morning in Thaddeus's bed, he was gone. She glanced at the clock on the nightstand. Eight o'clock! She couldn't remember the last morning she'd slept so late. Stretching catlike on the mattress, she inhaled his scent, which lingered in the bedclothes. In the warm cocoon of memories and a comfortable down cover, she luxuriated in the satisfaction he'd given her. She felt as if he'd caressed every inch of her, inside and out, leaving her relaxed and rejuvenated.

Where was he? Twenty minutes later, she slid out of bed and pulled the nightgown over her head. She could not find a note on any of the tables. Viewing the room, which was decorated with a green Morris wallpaper, she caressed the four-poster bed with burgundy velvet hangings where she'd known such rapture. She touched one of his coats, draped over the back of a chair. It, too, smelled of him, and a rivulet of excitement shot up her backbone.

She wanted to wake up beside him every morning, but for that to happen, they would have to follow the conventions. Marriage.

Uneasy now, in the sharp light of morning, she wondered what he meant to do. She didn't need a man to provide food and shelter for her. Thank God she was financially independent, but how she would

adore to have him by her side, every morning and
every night. But did he want her as mistress or wife?
Her rigid upbringing and her own experiences had
taught her that love outside marriage was disastrous.
Probably Thaddeus had no idea how difficult it was
for a woman in her situation. She would have to go
more slowly and not allow her desires to overrule her
reason until she knew where they were headed.

Sighing, she glanced again at the clock. It was Sunday, and she would have to hurry to get ready for
church. The thought of running through the corridor
dressed in only her nightgown gave her a moment of
unease, but taking a deep breath, she opened the door
and plunged ahead. Luck was with her; she reached
her room unseen. But where had Thaddeus gone?

Thaddeus walked through his house at Maddox
Street. He had awakened in the morning to make love
to Maggie again, but she had been sleeping so sweetly
that he hadn't had the heart to awaken her. Seeing
her there, her hair spread around her like a red-gold
halo, he had been breathless with awe and love. He
was going to make this woman his wife if it was the
last thing he did!

He scratched his head and studied the contents of
a box in one of the storage rooms at the back of his
house. "Where did I put that blasted ring?" he said,
and dug through the box once more.

The items in the box had belonged to his grandmother, and the heavy gold ring with a square-cut
ruby that had been her engagement ring should have
been there. He wanted to give it to Maggie when he
proposed. Where was it?

As he stepped upstairs to his office, his gaze fell on
the exquisite inlaid box that Maggie had given him. It
reminded him that he had to find Leonora Winston
without delay. He watered his wilting plants and
flipped through the mail. Gavin had been working in

the shop and had evidently sold some of the furniture downstairs.

Thaddeus rubbed his hands together in delight. Although it didn't exactly make him wealthy, the antiques business brought in a steady income.

He looked in the middle drawer of his desk and came across a dusty velvet-covered box. Inside was his grandmother's ring. The ruby was covered with grime and the gold looked dull.

"With a polishing you'll be as good as new," he said, and pocketed the ring. Frowning, he realized he would have to postpone his marriage proposal until the jeweler had cleaned the ring. He shrugged. That gave him time to make the event the most romantic experience of Maggie's life, creating a memory to cherish for the rest of their days. He wanted to give Maggie the very best because she was the very best woman a man could marry.

Patting the pocket where he'd put the ring, he went back downstairs. Gavin was in the parlor studying three rugs of different patterns and colors.

"I'm overworked. You haven't been much help here lately," he grumbled, and shot Thaddeus a shrewd glance. "That Hartwell case is taking up too much of your time."

"It's a complicated case," Thaddeus said, thinking of Maggie in his bed last night.

"I believe you're focusing on the wrong *angle* of the mystery. You were to investigate Miss Winston, not Mrs. Hartwell."

Thaddeus laughed. "Peg, you're too sharp by far." He pointed at a red rug with a border of green leaves and huge yellow flowers at the corners. "That one."

Gavin gaped. "You don't even know what I'm working on," he said. "You've spent so much time away from here, it seems that I run the business alone."

"Red goes with everything today. Can't go wrong with that carpet. However, the green—"

"I'm creating a Grecian seaside effect, with wall frescoes, a ceiling full of clouds, Ionic pillars—"

"Pillars! Did you sell the one we have? I know where we can find more of the same."

"Of course I sold it. Lady Belkinsop was ecstatic. But a red carpet?"

"I see your point. The green would be better." Thaddeus wound his black scarf around his neck, shoved a fedora on his head and a coat over his shoulders. "Business is calling."

Gavin shouted after him, but Thaddeus made his escape. Forgetting it was Sunday and that the shops would be closed, he headed toward the jeweler's shop around the corner.

After dressing her hair in a less severe chignon with soft loose curls at the temples, Maggie went to church with Victoria and Miss Lather. She had barely slept a wink, and she was still feeling the afterglow of lovemaking.

"Mama, you're so sleepy this morning," Victoria commented as Maggie failed to answer some of her daughter's questions on the way home from church. "Miss Lather said she'll build a barn for the wooden animals that Mr. Webb gave me," the child said.

"I'm only using a discarded box," Miss Lather said in her timid way. She sometimes reminded Maggie of a fearful rabbit, her ringlets hanging like floppy ears on either side of her face.

"And we'll paint it with my watercolors," Victoria added.

"It sounds most entertaining. I must see it when it's ready. I might even lend you my assistance—if you want it," she added with a smile.

They entered the hotel, and found Thaddeus there, reading a newspaper in one of the chairs in the foyer.

He rose, smiled at them as they entered, and gave Maggie a long, searching glance. Again, that pounding longing surged through her, and she grew breathless. Did their secret show? She blushed and lowered her gaze guiltily. Part of her wanted to throw herself into his arms; another part was aghast at her wantonness.

"Shall we go skating this afternoon as planned?" he asked.

"Yes!" Victoria exclaimed. "Mama, you promised."

Maggie nodded. "Let's meet here at three o'clock." She paused. "Or are you having Sunday dinner here with us, Thaddeus?"

He looked at her speculatively. "No . . . I'd better dine with my family as usual. And remember, Mother will bring Delia to discuss the wedding reception tomorrow."

Maggie blushed, remembering her own thoughts of marriage. "I haven't forgotten." She relinquished Victoria's hand to Miss Lather. "You must refresh yourself before dinner, Victoria, and so shall I." With a shy look at Thaddeus, she walked toward the office door. She'd seen such longing in his eyes, but also a teasing light.

" 'Til later," he called after her, and only she heard the underlying suggestion in his tone. "I look forward to sharing the excitement of skating with you," he added with a wicked smile.

She didn't see him again until it was almost time to leave for their outing. He entered the hotel foyer as she was speaking to Rafferty at the door. "Did you pack and remove Mr. Rupert Merton's belongings?" she asked the doorman.

Rafferty scratched his head. "Yes, I put them in the attic, but there wasn't much to pack. He left carrying one carpetbag."

"Thank you," Maggie said. "Please ask Gertie and

another maid to clean the rooms so that we can put some other guest in there."

Maggie turned her attention to Thaddeus. Her knees went weak as he gave her the widest of smiles. "I hope you're in the mood for a cold afternoon outdoors. I, however, can think of another pastime that would be more rewarding," he growled in her ear.

"Your mother should have washed your mouth out with soap, Thaddeus." But Maggie couldn't help responding with a warm smile. "You're the most unmanageable man I've ever met."

"The one who lit your fires, Maggie," he whispered, "and hopefully the only one who can quench them."

She blushed to the roots of her hair. "I expect you to behave in my daughter's company. One word like that, and we'll leave you to fend for yourself."

"Will you let Victoria ride on top of the bus if I accompany her?" he asked as the little girl entered with Miss Lather.

"Perhaps . . . as long as you keep silent. Victoria is at a very impressionable age, and I wouldn't want her to hear any of your sly remarks."

He shrugged, a smile tugging at his lips. "Your wish is my command, ma'am." As they went to meet Victoria, he took her arm. "By the way, I want to let you know that I'm meeting Sergeant Horridge tomorrow morning. He might have some new information about your sister."

"I would search day and night if only I knew where to look," Maggie said.

His eyebrows rose. "Are you complaining about my methods?"

She shook her head. "No, I'm just worried and impatient." Impulsively, she gripped his hand. "If Leonora was alive and well, she would have come here. Don't you agree? Something must have happened to her."

He sighed. "I'm afraid you're right. The more time that passes, the more I fear that she met with an . . . accident of some sort."

"I must know. I imagine all sorts of terrible things." Misery welled up in her at the thought of her sister.

He squeezed her fingers. "I know."

"Mama, are you ready to go?" Victoria was beaming at the prospect of visiting the park. "I'm wearing a new bonnet, Mr. Webb."

Thaddeus chuckled and viewed the hat, which had a large black bow at the front of the crown. "Very lovely, Victoria. What if one of the cab horses thinks it's a patch of hay and snatches it off your head?"

Victoria looked horrified, and Thaddeus laughed. "It was only a joke. He wouldn't like the taste of the velvet bow anyhow."

Victoria wagged her stubby finger at him, although a smile lit her face. "You're pulling my leg, Mr. Webb," she scolded.

Thaddeus hoisted the bag with the skates in one hand and took her hand in the other, leading her out of the hotel. "Perhaps I am, perhaps not." Laughing, he walked down the street with the girl, Maggie following.

Her heart constricted with tenderness as she viewed them together. A bond had sprung up between man and child, and she wished she could give Victoria the father she so longed for. Yet . . . what sort of plans for the future were going through Thaddeus's head? He adjusted the straps of the skate bag, and Maggie remembered his large hand on her naked breasts. The memory made her weak-kneed. If he touched her like that again, she would melt without the least constraint; she would be even more enmeshed in his web of passion.

He turned slightly and caught her glance. Desire simmered palpably between them, forcing a blush to Maggie's cheeks. His eyes had a smoldering predatory quality, stalking her, reading her every thought. She had to force herself to look away, and was relieved when they arrived at the bus stop.

The day was windy, but not especially cold. Maggie held onto her black wide-brimmed hat adorned by a cluster of red silk poppies and a spotted veil which she had pulled down over her face. "Do you think there's ice on the pond?" she wondered aloud.

"I don't know." Thaddeus assisted Victoria upstairs and settled her on the bench, then came back down to help Maggie inside. Victoria squealed in excitement at finally riding at the top of the bus, and the other passengers laughed. Maggie stepped inside the bus, grateful that she didn't have to join them so high off the ground. She exchanged a glance with Thaddeus before he stepped back up the narrow iron ladder onto the roof. The electricity crackling between them as their eyes met made the air in the carriage seem hot, but Maggie knew the heat was inside her.

The park was filled with families. Children in sailor hats and fur-trimmed coats darted here and there among the more staid adults. Although the nights had been cold for a week, the Serpentine was not frozen, and Victoria almost cried with disappointment. "What shall we do now?"

"We can stroll in the park, then drink hot cocoa at a teashop," Thaddeus suggested.

At a coffee stall, they watched sparrows hopping along the sandy lanes looking for crumbs. A vendor of roasted chestnuts called to the passing strollers, and Thaddeus bought a paper cone filled with the hot, salty nuts.

The three of them sat on a park bench and munched on the chestnuts. The wind wreaked havoc with headgear and newspapers, and Victoria screamed as her hat flew off and rolled along the lane. After she had caught it, she came running back.

"Mr. Webb! Can I travel on top of the bus on the way home as well?"

"You'd better ask your mother." He added to Maggie in an undertone, "She wants to ride it."

"She may—if you go with her."

Thaddeus laughed and patted her hand. "You're a remarkable woman, don't you know?"

"No, I don't," she said. "I certainly won't ride, but now that you're here . . ."

They drank hot cocoa and had their picture taken by a photographer who had set up his tripod under an old oak. Time disappeared at lightning speed in Thaddeus's company, and Maggie wished the day would never end.

Evidently, Victoria enjoyed his company almost as much as she did. "Can we travel from Hyde Park Corner to Piccadilly Circus, and then up Regent Street?" Victoria asked beseechingly. "Or else the trip home will be over much too soon."

"What do you say, Maggie? An extra-long ride on the horse bus?"

"I can think of better ways to travel," she grumbled. "I don't know where Victoria got this passion for horse buses."

"Now, don't be a spoilsport." The bus arrived, and the conductor jumped down to collect the fare. Before Maggie could protest, Thaddeus had carried her up the rickety ladder and deposited her on the hard seat at the edge of the roof. She clutched the armrest in panic, her stomach lurching as she looked down.

"No!"

"Victoria's next," he said to suppress her protest. He lifted the giggling child up next to Maggie.

"Mama, you'll be frightened, won't you?"

Maggie could not find her voice as the bus moved under her. Thaddeus jumped up on the seat beside them, laughing. Maggie gasped as the carriage seemed to sway to one side. She was among the tree-tops, and the ground looked dizzyingly far away.

"How could you," she whispered faintly into Thaddeus's ear as the horse ambled down Piccadilly. The benches wobbled, and Maggie became slightly queasy.

"It's almost like being on a ship on a stormy sea," he said with a teasing smile. "Ouch, your eyes are scorching me."

She would gladly have strangled him if they hadn't been on top of the decrepit horse omnibus. Closing her eyes, she prayed the ordeal would soon be over.

"Mama doesn't like heights," Victoria said after giving Maggie a searching glance. "She says they make her sick."

"I didn't know that," Thaddeus said guiltily. "Why didn't you tell me?"

"Because I never dreamed you would take matters into your own hands and cart me around like a piece of baggage," Maggie said angrily.

He looked sheepish. "I'm sorry."

Maggie moaned, and Victoria shook her sleeve. "He said he was sorry, Mama."

The two horses turned frisky as they passed another carriage and the benches seemed to tilt over the very edge. Maggie paled and held her breath. Nausea swept through her. She wished she could go downstairs but the ladder was on the outside of the carriage.

"It'll soon be over," Thaddeus said.

"Look, Mama, the crossing sweeper looks like a midget," Victoria cried, and everyone except Maggie laughed.

When the ride was over at Oxford Circus, Victoria had stars in her eyes. She hugged Thaddeus's legs impulsively. "Thank you, Mr. Webb. You're the best-est man in the whole world," she said.

Thaddeus's eyes were infinitely tender as he lifted

Maggie down. Her legs were stiff and her head still reeled. He carried her to a bench and set her down. "Wait here with your mother, Victoria. I'll fetch a glass of water."

Cursing himself for his stupidity, he walked to a coffee stall on the curb and ordered coffee and a glass of water. While downing the lukewarm coffee, he looked at the other customers. Two men were chatting under the awning, their backs turned to him. His gaze fastened on a familiar face.

One of the men was Anselm Ripley. The young man was dressed in a dark overcoat and a black beaver top hat. He was laughing as he raised his cup, and Thaddeus's gaze was caught by Ripley's left hand. He wore an intricately carved golden ring inset with a black stone. Wondering where he'd seen such a ring before, Thaddeus recalled the evening several nights ago, when he'd met Maggie's uncle. Merton had been wearing an exact replica of the ring.

Was it a new fashion, or could the ring hold a certain meaning? Was there a connection between Rupert Merton and Anselm Ripley? He had to find out, Thaddeus thought as he set down his cup and wiped his mouth. But not from Ripley, not directly anyway. To learn Ripley's secrets he would have to use stealth, since the young man had not volunteered any information at their first meeting—nor had he worn the ring . . .

Chapter 15

The outing ended on a strained note, Maggie still angry with Thaddeus for forcing her to ride on top of the horse bus. Claiming he had business to discuss, he left them at the hotel only half an hour after he'd seen Anselm Ripley. With a quick smile of farewell, he hastened off to the waiting hansom that had brought them from Oxford Circus.

Maggie told Victoria to go inside and ran after Thaddeus, who had just stepped into the carriage. "Does this business involve my sister?" she asked.

He hesitated. "It's possible."

"I'm coming with you," she said. "Wait until I have settled Victoria with Miss Lather."

"No! You will not accompany me this time." He gave the cabbie the address. Maggie recognized Ripley's street number instantly. Fuming, she crossed her arms over her chest. "You're keeping information from me," she accused him.

"No." Before he could explain, the hansom had moved forward. Steaming, Maggie listened to the *clippety-clop* of the hooves as she made her plans to follow him.

After ascertaining that Victoria was in good hands, she put on a pair of heavy boots, remembering her previous visit to Anselm Ripley's house and her walk in the rain later. Thaddeus Webb wasn't getting rid of her that easily. She had a few choice words to say to him once she caught up with him! Bringing her umbrella, she hurried outside.

When she climbed into a hackney which had just set down two guests at the hotel, Thaddeus was already at his post, in a dark portal leading to a courtyard on the opposite side of Ripley's house. Maggie would have liked this adventure better than the horse bus, he mused, and she would have kept him company. But how could he have told her about his suspicions that Rupert Merton and Ripley were somehow connected? Not that it might mean they had been involved in a joint *crime*. Yet . . . instinct told him otherwise. But Maggie wouldn't believe his hunch that Merton wasn't quite what he appeared to be; she seemed pathetically pleased to be reunited with her uncle. This time, Thaddeus sensed he was on the right track. Would it lead to Miss Winston? If he was lucky, Ripley might point him to her.

Darkness was falling rapidly, and the wind had increased in strength. Thaddeus grew bored and contemplated lighting a cigarillo, but realized that the glow of the burning tobacco—not to mention the smoke—might give him away, if Ripley happened to walk by.

A hackney stopped at Ripley's door, and a woman alighted. As she paid the jarvey, Thaddeus recognized Maggie. Outraged, he darted across the street and yanked her back with him to the portal.

"What do you think you're doing?" he demanded. "You could have ruined everything."

"What are *you* doing skulking out here in the dark?" she retorted, pulling away.

"Watching Ripley's house, you fool." He made himself breathe deeply to cool his ire. "You're the most inquisitive, most exasperating female I've had the misfortune to encounter," he growled.

"And you're the most intolerable, high-handed—"

"Shhh," he whispered, and pointed at the street. "He's coming home."

Maggie watched the tall slender figure of Anselm Ripley. He was whistling and swinging his umbrella. Without so much as a glance in their direction, he entered his house and slammed the door.

"What now? Do we have to wait here for long?" she asked, already feeling the icy fingers of a winter draft worming their way under her skirts.

"We'll stay here until he leaves. I'm sure he'll go out later." Thaddeus eyed her sardonically. "If you don't like waiting, you can always return home."

Maggie tossed her head, ignoring the cold. "I want to discover what you're so eager to learn about Mr. Ripley."

Watching the house carefully, they stood in silence for about twenty minutes, before Thaddeus spoke.

"How much do you know about your uncle, besides his involvement in the import-export business?" He could barely make out her shape in the darkness, but he sensed that she was thinking.

"Like everyone else in the family, he had a quarrel with Father before leaving on a ship bound for America twenty years ago. He was saved miraculously from shipwreck."

"He had no contact with your sister?"

"No. I asked him. He didn't even know of her existence until I told him." She turned her head toward Thaddeus, but it was too dark to see his features. "Why?"

He shrugged. "I find it strange that he would turn up on your doorstep so suddenly, and right after you expected your sister to arrive."

"He said he'd come from the Caribbean, not America," she explained.

"What else do you know about him?"

"He told me stories about his travels, and he has many curious souvenirs to show. He learned many foreign customs on his trips.'' She paused, thinking. ''He's a bit odd—has those penetrating eyes, you know, and says many peculiar things, about religion especially. Nevertheless, he's always courteous, he's kind to Victoria, and he's paid his hotel bill.''

''Have you seen evidence of his so-called business?''

Maggie shook her head. ''No, but he has promised to take me on a tour once everything is settled. And, if you recall, he's found a town house in Cavendish Square.''

''A moneyed fellow by all accounts.'' Thaddeus rubbed his chin. ''Tell me, did he leave the hotel at any specific times, like every day at two or seven o'clock for instance?''

''No . . . not that I remember. Why?''

''He might have some rituals or habits that he's brought with him from the Orient.''

''He hasn't told me anything like that. But the first night he didn't sleep in his bed, and later he explained that he'd taken a walk.''

''Unusual. Perhaps he's an insomniac.'' They stood in silence for another twenty minutes. Maggie was starting to shiver. She sighed with relief when Anselm Ripley came out, pressing a top hat onto his head. He was dressed in dark evening clothes and a heavy overcoat. Swinging a walking stick, he sauntered down the street. Maggie wanted to follow him instantly, but Thaddeus held her back until Ripley had reached the street corner. They kept to the shadows, which wasn't difficult since darkness had fallen. The gas lamps cast only a dim yellow light on the cobblestones.

Ripley hailed a passing hansom, and, keeping his head down, Thaddeus moved close enough to catch the address. When Ripley had left, Thaddeus flagged down another carriage, and helped Maggie inside. ''Ripley's going to a music hall in Whitechapel. I hope it won't embarrass you too greatly to visit such a common place," he teased.

"No more than it will embarrass you," she said with a toss of her head.

He chuckled and pulled her close. She stiffened as he pressed his lips to hers. Tension escalated between them, a sweet agony that strove to be quenched. "God, woman! You have bewitched me," he said, his breath hot on her face. His mouth swooped down on hers, silencing any protest that might have surged to her lips. His touch sent her blood pounding recklessly. She opened to him, her whole being crying out to him.

"So help me, I could take you right here on this dingy seat, woman," he growled, his voice evoking a hot prickly sensation in her.

She wanted him to take her, wherever, whenever, every day . . . but she fought to remember her earlier resolve.

"Why are you struggling? Are you already tired of my touch, Maggie?" He let her go, and she righted her hat and straightened the lace at her throat.

"No . . ." she whispered. "But not *here*, surely?"

He laughed, and, smiling wryly, she pondered the possibility of banging his head with her umbrella.

The hansom took them through Soho and the City. They passed Holy Trinity Church into Whitechapel, the beginning of the meaner areas of London.

"Ripley certainly likes bawdy entertainment," Thaddeus commented grimly as he viewed the painted women in garish clothes on the streets. Loud singing and laughter came from the pubs and the houses of assignation.

The hansom stopped before a building that had only two torches burning on either side of the door. There was no name on the wall, and the windows had been barred with shutters.

Thaddeus paid the cabbie. "I wish you had gone

home,'' he said to Maggie as he helped her down.
"This is no place for a lady."

She gave him a mocking smile. "With you here to
protect me, what could happen?"

She gasped, however, as they entered the dingy
foyer. Before them spread a large room filled with tiers
of seats. People of all classes and ages sat in the rows,
singing with the bandmaster who was swinging his
baton extravagantly.

The stench of old sweat and vomit fouled the air,
making her hold her breath. The floor was unspeak-
ably filthy, and the draperies in the door opening
were a tattered velvet of indeterminate color.

"I can tell the entertainment is not to your liking,"
Thaddeus said close to her ear. "A glass of wine will
quite restore you, and I always down a pint in the
evening."

His eyes teased her. "Wait until you see the female
dancers. All legs, and they are not too shy to show
them."

"I take it you revel in this kind of entertainment?"
she said scathingly, but entered bravely on his arm
after he'd purchased tickets.

"Sometimes, but I like a leg I can touch—not only
watch," he murmured, and caressed her thigh as they
sat down in the back rows, so they could unobtru-
sively keep an eye on Anselm Ripley, who was seated
by the side exit of the theater, near the front.

She pulled away as if stung by a bee, and color
surged into her cheeks. Her retort was drowned by
the shouts that rang out as a row of women dressed
in short satin skirts and barely anything else entered
the stage.

Maggie stared in outrage while the orchestra, which
was partly hidden in a pit below the stage, struck up
a bawdy cancan.

Arm in arm, the girls formed a row. They wore
scandalous black net stockings, and their lips were

painted bright red. They began flinging first one leg, then the other into air. Maggie's eyes widened in shock. They were wearing some kind of minuscule drawers, and they were *black*. It was the most indecent thing Maggie had ever seen.

"This is wicked," she hissed to Thaddeus.

"I find it most fascinating," he parried, the devil back in his eyes. He leaned closer. "But none of these girls have as lovely legs as you do, Maggie." To stress his point, he reached between their seats and slid his hand slowly from her knee to the top of her thigh.

She almost jumped up, but the gesture was curiously exciting. This man to whom she'd given her body in wanton surrender last night, was a man of great . . . appetites. And he kindled hers.

"You have no shame, Mr. Webb," she scolded, but her voice had lost its edge.

"Mr. Webb? I thought we had come much further than that, Maggie."

"The progress can always go backwards if you're not careful." Maggie averted her eyes as the line of girls danced across the stage. She threw a glance at Anselm Ripley. "It's hard to believe that Mr. Ripley has a longing for such *cheap* entertainment," she added.

Thaddeus laughed, his voice startlingly close to her ear. If she didn't discourage him, he would end up in her lap.

"Many society bucks like this kind of tawdry amusement. I could point out quite a few who are here tonight."

Maggie shook her head. "I'd rather not know." The girls were leaving the stage, and Maggie glanced at Ripley, noticing that he was clapping heartily and smiling.

A male singer in a black tailcoat and white shirt entered and began singing patriotic songs. The audience joined in the refrains and, after linking arms with their neighbors, swayed from one side to the other in their seats. Maggie found her arm clasped by a portly, older man in a Norfolk jacket and knickerbockers, who urged her to sing. The songs turned to lewd ditties and, judging by the enthusiastic response, the audience was very familiar with the lyrics.

She closed her mouth tightly as Thaddeus joined in the chorus. He winked, and she lowered her gaze in shame. How could he be so *vulgar?* He was only doing it to tease her, but she would find a way to repay him, she vowed.

Acrobats followed the singer, and then a ventriloquist entertained with a wooden doll wearing an exact replica of his scarlet cloak and top hat. The show ended with the reappearance of the cancan girls. Maggie almost left before the spectacle was over, but she remembered their true reason for coming here, and contained her urge.

Ripley rose as soon as the curtain had fallen.

"He's leaving," Thaddeus said. "We must follow him." He stood so rapidly that Maggie barely had the time to collect herself. As she stepped out in the aisle, her black gored silk skirt snagged on a seat. She bent to pull it free, and when she glanced up, Thaddeus had disappeared in the crowd. His head was bobbing above the others some way ahead. He turned and waved at her frantically to follow. Evidently, he was about to lose his prey.

Maggie was jostled back and forth by the crowd and when she arrived in the lobby, there was no sign of either Thaddeus or Mr. Ripley. Uncertain, she stood right by the door, staring from one end of the dingy room to the other. Men of all ages and walks of life passed her, many offering their company for the rest of the evening. Maggie was mortified. Where was Thaddeus?

Sighing in fear and exasperation, she stepped outside. The street was lit only by the torches beside the door, and there was no sign of Thaddeus. Had he taken a cab to follow Ripley? Dejected, she waited another ten minutes before hailing a passing hansom. This was not an area in which to remain alone, she thought grimly, viewing a drunk reeling toward her. She tightened her grip on her umbrella, but the man didn't accost her. Whatever had become of Thaddeus? Just as she was about to step into the cab, her toes kicked something on the ground. She looked closer and recognized the knitted black fabric. A shiver of fear coursed through her as she lifted Thaddeus's scarf from the muddy cobblestones. It was sticky and as she held it closer to the cab lamp beside the door, she found a smear of blood. A sob caught in her throat. Had someone overpowered him? She glanced along the street where two drunkards lurched from side to side. The music hall crowd dispersed, leaving an ominous silence behind. There was no sign of Thaddeus, and she had no idea in what direction he'd gone—or been taken. The fog curled in the air, and she knew there was nothing she could do but go home and wait.

The hansom drove through the dark streets. A cold draft seeping along the floor made Maggie shiver. Apprehension filled her more with every mile that passed, and tears gathered in her eyes. Something terrible might have happened to Thaddeus.

She arrived at the dark hotel. Only a gas lamp glowed above the front desk. The night porter, Rafferty's nephew, was nodding in a chair by the door, and Maggie nudged him awake.

"Mrs. Hartwell!" he exclaimed, and jumped to his feet and righted his livery. "I didn't know—"

"You should not sleep on your post, Monty." She could barely suppress the tremble in her voice. "The moment Mr. Webb arrives, let me know. I'll be in my office."

"Yes, ma'am" he said.

Maggie walked into her dark office and turned on the gaslight. With a sigh, she took off her coat and hat. She could not sleep until she found out what had happened to Thaddeus. Her hands trembled as she poured herself a glass of sherry. She sipped it and discovered that she could barely swallow due to the fear constricting her throat. Sitting behind her desk, she stared at the bloody scarf in her lap, unable to concentrate on anything but the question of Thaddeus's disappearance.

Thaddeus's head felt as if it would explode if he so much as opened his eyes. He was lying on a lumpy soft surface, and the air was filled with a strange odor that reminded him of exotic flowers. A smoky haze swirled lazily in the room. He lifted himself up on one elbow and tried to recognize his surroundings. His wrists were tied to a bedpost, but with a mighty heave, he managed to dislodge the turned wooden spindle and free himself. With his teeth, he undid the knot of the rough cord.

The room was furnished in different shades of red, and the walls were black. Huge pillows of Oriental patterns were spread on the floor, and chimes tinkled in the draft from the partly open door leading to a hallway. Groaning, he heaved himself to his feet. Jagged flashes of pain cut through his skull. He lurched against a bookcase, overturning a potted plant next to it. After shaking his head to clear away the grogginess, he tottered toward the door. All he could recall was that he'd followed Ripley out of the music hall. He'd lost Maggie in the crowd, but he'd planned to wait for her outside after discovering where Ripley was headed. The young man had taken him by surprise in the shadows outside, delivering a hard blow to his head, then attempting to strangle him with his scarf. Thaddeus had managed to fight him off, then ran after Ripley, who had hurried south on Bishops-

gate. Thaddeus had followed some distance to see
that Ripley wouldn't disappear down a side street.

But he had. Thaddeus had had the choice of pursuing Ripley—as had been his goal from the start—or
waiting for Maggie. He'd calculated that ten minutes
alone in the foyer wouldn't harm her. But as he
turned the corner of Union Street, three men had
suddenly overpowered him, beaten him, and dragged
him into an alley. That was all he remembered until
this moment.

Pausing at the door, he pulled the watch from his
pocket. It was already past midnight, two hours since
he'd left Maggie. Swearing under his breath, he
slipped out of the room with its cloying scent. In the
hallway, the odor was even more pronounced. His
head ached like the devil, and the smoke didn't im-
prove it. He touched the side of his head, finding his
hair matted with dried blood. He had to find a way
out of the house. Had it been a mistake to follow Ripley? But Ripley might present a significant lead to Miss
Winston. Was this it?

Thaddeus stared down the passage lit by gas lamps
that popped and hissed. At the other end were two
doors, one half open, the other closed. Surely one of
them must be the exit. The layout of the house confused him, and he didn't know if he was in the attic
or on the ground floor. Taking deep breaths to fight
the weakness weighing down his limbs, he walked
slowly toward the open door. He could hear the mur-
mur of male voices as he moved closer. After a quick
look through the door, he saw stairs leading down.
The sounds were coming from what seemed to be the
basement. He tried the other door and found a room
filled with clothes and discarded furniture. No way
out there. Where was the front door?

Swearing silently, he tried the stairs. They groaned
under his weight. He waited for the inevitable attack,
but the voices continued, rising and dipping in a

strange cadence. His grogginess returned, and Thaddeus blamed the thick flowery fog wafting around him. He realized where he'd smelled it before—it was like the incense used in churches. Frowning in consternation, he leaned against the wall to gather his strength. The strange intonations drew him downward, toward the sound. An eerie red light glowed brighter with every step he took.

He got downstairs without too much noise, and hid in the shadow of a large armoire. What he saw through the door opening made his stomach lurch. Men in black robes and hoods were swaying around an altar in time with the incantations. Whirling incense and undulating candle flames added to the eerie scene. The red light came from the candles, which were cupped by crimson glass globes on the altar. Thaddeus could not see the faces under the hoods. The men wore masks depicting the faces of animals, the grotesquely contorted faces of jackals, wolves, and bears. Thaddeus counted seven men, and his eyes widened as he discerned another form on the altar, a female shape wrapped in a shimmering red cloth. The body lay perfectly still, and Thaddeus's mouth went dry with fear. The *Altar* Murders . . . He remembered the headlines in the newspapers. Cold sweat ran down his spine, and he swallowed repeatedly, clutching the edge of the armoire to remain upright.

The dance halted abruptly, and Thaddeus watched as the tallest man, who wore a scarlet hood instead of a black one, raised a glittering dagger above the shape on the table. He mumbled some high-pitched harangue, but Thaddeus could only make out a few words—*behemoths of voices . . . king of the seventh circle . . . eternal servants . . .*

Thaddeus recoiled from the ghastly scene and lumbered toward the stairs. If he hadn't felt so weak and disoriented, he might have tried to stop the ceremony, but he knew it would be futile. He had to escape to report his findings immediately. Unwittingly, he'd happened upon a gruesome secret, and it was his duty—

"Shadow, bring down the man," a harsh voice called out. "The Voices demand the sacrifice of his blood."

Thaddeus didn't wait to meet his captors. He stumbled up the stairs, cursing because his head was still foggy. There had to be a way out. Steps pounded behind him as he ran into the room where he'd awakened. He looked out the window, but it was pitch-black outside. Then he saw a door at the other end of the room and hurried toward it.

Just as he fled to another set of stairs beyond the chamber, three hooded men entered, their robes swirling around them. "Shadow, stop him!" one called out and hurtled after him. Thaddeus had just climbed the steps and seen the front entrance—his way to freedom—when one of the men threw himself over him. Thaddeus wrestled with the attacker, and the jackal mask came off in the fight. He stared into Ripley's glazed eyes. There was no recognition, only a fanatic light. Thaddeus braced himself against the blow directed at his head.

Maggie stared unblinkingly at the glow from the gas jets in the ceiling until her eyes ached. Her thoughts were sluggish due to her lack of sleep, and her muscles ached with tension. All she could think of was Thaddeus's strange disappearance. What had become of him? She wanted to cry with the agony of uncertainty, but no tears came to her eyes. Mesmerized by the flickering light, she could only stare and stare.

The clock chimed four in the morning. She'd been sitting at the same spot behind her desk ever since midnight and all she could do was pray, pouring all the agony of her heart into her prayers. Nothing happened. There was no relief, no appeasement of her anguish. Her thoughts reached out across the vast silent night toward Thaddeus, asking him where he was, but her mind remained empty, waiting.

If he didn't come back soon, she would splinter into tiny pieces.

The only sound in the room was the ticking of the clock. Soon the streets would fill with morning noises, but this was the dead of night, when evil thoughts prowled and nightmares abounded. *Tick-tock, tick-tock.* Another fifteen minutes passing, the half hour striking, and still she couldn't move.

Thaddeus managed to deflect the fist aimed at his head, then he delivered a shattering blow to Ripley's jaw, and the younger man rolled aside, unconscious. With great difficulty Thaddeus rose to his feet to meet the other attackers. His knuckles pounded with pain, but he clenched his fists to deliver another blow if necessary, and another . . .

The two robed men moved stealthily toward him. The gleam of a blade shone amid the black folds, and Thaddeus knew he had to overpower that man first or his heart would be pierced by steel. No one spoke. There was only the sound of labored breathing behind the bizarre masks.

Thaddeus's head ached and his eyesight blurred, but he recognized that he was much larger than the other men. Surely he could overpower one! Ripley stirred on the floor, moaning in pain. Thaddeus realized he had to act, or become a prisoner anew—a corpse.

With a shout of fury, he threw himself through the air and landed on the first man, bringing him down to the floor. The blade flew in a glittering arc to land on the other side of the shadowy hallway. In a fit of rage, Thaddeus pounded the man's head twice against the floor until he went limp. Just as Thaddeus turned to face his other attacker, the man jumped onto his back and got a stranglehold on his neck with some sort of soft, twined cord. Staggering to his feet, Thaddeus struggled to free himself from the murderer clinging to his back. His head seemed to swell from the blockage of the blood, and wind seemed to rush in his ears. His lungs aching with the strain, Thaddeus closed his hands around the cord and pulled with all his might. Just as he thought he would faint, the rope loosened. Gulping for air, he doubled over so that his tormentor rolled off his back. Gripping the man's neck, he lifted him clean off his feet and hurled him against Ripley, who was advancing unsteadily. Both men fell down and Thaddeus made his escape through the front door.

The night air was cold, and he shivered as he sought concealment in the shelter of a hedge growing in front of the house. It was so dark he couldn't find the road. As he studied the facade, or what little he could see of it, he heard the irate voices of the men who now pursued him. They would probably follow the direction of the drive, and if he listened to their steps, he would know where to go. Crouching on the cold soil under the hedge, he waited and listened. Although he wanted to run, he knew it would be safer to wait here in silence.

The men returned a few minutes later, their footsteps very close by. Then he heard one of them pause almost right next to him and call out, "I've found him. He's hiding in the hedge."

Maggie shifted her burning eyes toward the clock. Five already. The staff would stir any minute to check on the coal fires in every room. A dry sob wracked her throat, and she forced herself to stand. Staggering to the window, she looked between the tasseled velvet drapes. All she could see was the minuscule tiled garden at the back and the high stone wall. The sum-

mer-blooming plants now stretched their bare spindly
arms toward the gray dawn. They looked as desolate
as she felt. She sensed that something awful had happened to Thaddeus, and sorrow sat like a leaden
weight in her chest. A sigh escaped her throat as she
dropped the drapes back in place. She had an awful
premonition that he wasn't coming back to her. Her
steps heavy, she climbed up the stairs to her living
quarters above.

Thaddeus stiffened in his crouched position, dig-
ging his fingers into the frozen earth. The man who
claimed that he'd found him moved toward the other
end of the house.

"Well, where is he?" another voice asked.

"I mistook a stack of wood for a sitting man. But
he must be here somewhere. He couldn't have disappeared into thin air."

When the men moved further into the garden sur-
rounding the house, Thaddeus decided it was time to
leave. He moved from the shadow of one bush to
another, in the direction of the drive. When gravel
crunched under his boots, he knew he was on the
right track. Unable even to see his hand before him,
he moved away from the house. He would have to
take stock of his environment to be able to retrace his
steps later, but when he heard the voices returning,
louder this time, he decided it was more important to
flee while he still could.

Pain pounded through him as he staggered forward. In his mind, he saw the human shape on the
altar again, and he had an urge to retch. He'd never
seen anything so revolting, so wholly *evil*.

He followed a winding road, stumbling into the
ditches three times, for about fifteen minutes, when
dawn's first light finally brightened the horizon. He
discovered that he was outside London. Hedges bordered the lane, and beyond them, huge roofs told

him that he was in an expensive suburban neighbor-
hood, but he had no idea where. Not until he recognized the gilded entrance gates to a park did he realize
he was in Richmond. The Thames flowed lazily
through the village, and Thaddeus's steps were more
energetic as he entered the local constabulary's headquarters. He was shivering in the cold morning air,
since his overcoat and hat were missing—and his
scarf.

The constable stared at him bleary-eyed, as if the
slamming of the door had awakened him. "What—?"

"Good morning, Sergeant. I'd like to report that I
was incapacitated and abducted last night." Thaddeus bent over the desk to show the lump on his
head.

"Tell me everything from the beginning," the policeman said, pulling a notepad toward him and licking on the nub of a pencil.

Thaddeus reached across the desk, and grabbed the
officer on the front of his uniform. "We don't have
time for that. Bring some of your men and I'll show
you where the Altar Murders have been taking
place."

"The Altar M—murders? Here in Richmond?"

"Right in your idyllic haven. Come along."

An hour later, when the constable had arranged for
a police team, Thaddeus was leading the five bobbies
back along the road he'd just walked. He'd carefully
measured the time he'd spent on the lane, but no
matter how close to the mansion they came, he
couldn't find it. He studied every house, every drive,
and growing angrier and angrier as he realized he
was unable to recognize his prison.

"So where are the murderers?" the sergeant asked,
crossing his arms over his ample chest. He was sweaty
with the unexpected exertion, and now glared accus-
ingly at Thaddeus.

"I'll find the house in a minute."

An elderly gentleman walking a poodle stared a the blue-uniformed group that had gathered so earl in the morning. He touched his hat and mumbled "Good day."

"It's further down—somewhere," Thaddeus sai firmly, although he had begun to doubt his judg ment. The hedges bordering the lane were all th same, the gardens almost identical.

Twenty minutes later he still had not located th right house, and realized he had to give up. The con stables were fuming, thinking they were the target o a tasteless practical joke.

"You'll be arrested for this," the sergeant grum bled. Thaddeus wondered how the hell he'd get ou of this predicament.

Chapter 16

Maggie splashed cold water on her face, knowing that, despite Thaddeus's disappearance, her life must go on as usual. Her limbs leaden with fatigue, she tightened the sash of her dressing gown and sorted through the gowns in her wardrobe. She chose a dark brown dress with no lace or ribbon accents. Sighing, she spread the dress on the bed and searched for a fresh shift, petticoats, and stockings.

A knock sounded on her sitting-room door, and Maggie's heartbeat accelerated. Running through her rooms, she threw a glance at the mantelpiece, seeing it was seven o'clock. She flung open the door.

There he was, hatless, coatless, but nevertheless, intact. "Thaddeus!" She threw her arms around his neck. He lifted her off her feet and swung her in a circle, laughing wildly.

"If only you knew—" she began, tears surging, at last, to her eyes. Her heart soared with the relief of finding him safe and sound. "I found your scarf—it was all bloody!"

"I'm glad you missed me." He set her down. "Come inside and I'll tell you what happened." After closing the door behind them, he led her to the ottoman and made her sit down. "I was attacked by Ripley and his cohorts in an alley off Union Street." Then he told her everything he knew, except his suspicions about her uncle's possible involvement with Ripley's gang. "The men in robes were the most frightening sight I've ever seen." To protect her, he also withheld his knowledge of the human offering on the altar, knowing that Maggie would not sleep if she heard that Ripley was one of the altar murderers. After all, Leonora Winston had spoken to him on the Atlantic steamer.

"Unfortunately, I could not recognize the house in daylight. The constabulary at Richmond almost arrested me then and there, believing the whole thing was a prank." He laughed. "It took me the better part of an hour to make the sergeant ring Horridge at Scotland Yard so that he could vouch for my identity and sanity."

"Which I take it he did," Maggie said wryly, as she stroked his hair and examined the wound that was now covered with a white sticking plaster.

"The sergeant in Richmond patched me up," he explained. "Nothing to worry about. The lump is almost gone."

"I can't tell you how happy I am that you're safe." She could not sit close enough. Leaning her head against his shoulder, she sniffed his sleeve. "You smell strange."

"Incense. They were using it in their ritual."

"I've heard there are many strange spiritual societies in London, but I've never known anyone actually involved. Supposedly, they seek enlightenment."

Thaddeus remembered his ordeal earlier. "This group was worshipers of the darkness."

Maggie shivered as if a cold wind had blown through the room. She hugged his arm closer, and Thaddeus turned to her and hauled her into his embrace.

"I worried about you," he said, "but I had to leave you alone in order to follow Ripley."

"Yes, I understand. Besides, I'm used to fending

for myself. I won't venture outside again without my trusty weapon—my umbrella.''

He kissed her hair. ''My brave Maggie.'' Tenderness shone in his eyes and she swallowed convulsively. Her heart was so full she thought she would burst.

''My lovely Maggie.'' He undid the pins holding her hair up and the rich, shining mantle fell over her shoulders. Then he gently lifted the spectacles from her nose and placed them on the table. ''You look like you didn't sleep any more than I did,'' he whispered. He caressed her face. ''Pale and wan. Your eyes have dark circles.''

''It was the longest night of my life. I was certain something terrible had befallen you.''

Thaddeus thought how near he'd been to ending up as an altar offering in Richmond. He drew a sigh of deep relief, grateful that he was here to feast his eyes on the woman he loved.

She rose, color glowing in her cheeks. Holding out her hand, she said, ''Come, I want you to hold me, to love me,'' she said. ''When you didn't return last night, I realized that life is too short to waste on fears and doubts.''

He stood, strangely abashed yet intoxicated. Beside her slender beauty he felt like a big, bumbling bear. He let her lead him into her bedchamber, and he gazed around the room in wonder, admiring the feminine touches everywhere. She had created a calm haven of soft colors, where he knew he could forget the harsh world outside. He touched the potted plants by the window, sensing in her a kindred soul.

''Come.'' She led him to the bed and pushed him down. She pulled off his sack coat and wool vest. He blushed as she ran her fingertips along the opening of his shirt after unbuttoning it. She pulled it out of his breeches, and he sucked in his breath as she eased open the top button of his waistband. Her dressing gown parted slightly, and he could see the swell of her breasts, her pale, creamy skin. Losing his shyness, he crushed her to him. "My lovely flower, you're naked underneath," he whispered against her breasts, and slid his hand the length of her back to cup one firm buttock through the silk.

Maggie nodded. "Yes, I just undressed." She scooped up her dress and underwear from the bed and placed them over the back of a chair. Without hesitation she folded back the covers and the crisp sheet and lay down on the mattress. With a smile, she untied her sash, ravenous now for his lovemaking. She had been close to losing him, and now that he was back, she wanted him completely.

She spread the robe wide, revealing her naked body to his simmering brown gaze. It darkened with desire, and he tightened his lips as if the view was too much for him. With a groan, he crawled into her bed after discarding his boots, socks, and trousers. His shirt was still hanging loosely from his shoulders, and she wound her arms around his waist inside it.

"Kiss me," she demanded, and he complied with a moan deep in his throat.

She slung one leg over his hips and rubbed her thigh along his muscular side. Her toes teased his thigh, and he moved against her, pushing the rigid proof of his arousal against her abdomen.

"I can't wait," he complained between gasps of pleasure as she kneaded his buttocks. Her skin was like the finest mother-of-pearl, her turgid nipples sweet berries that he couldn't suckle enough. Only to think of the treasures that hideous corset had hidden made him shudder. He dragged his hand the length of her body, along the dip at the waist, the flare of her rounded hip. He knew he would worship this woman for the rest of his life, if she would let him. These eyes, that could sparkle with delight as well as anger, were the only true sapphires in the world, he

mused, as he gazed deeply into them. They had softened with the smoky haze of desire. He knew he
could never describe the depth of emotion that overcame him every time he met that blue steady gaze.
He was a drowning man, drowning in his love for
her, and he hoped that no one would ever save him.

She pulled his hand down to the throbbing center
of her desire, and let him caress her until pleasure
spread molten through her blood. Her breaths grew
shallow, and she was aware only of his masterly
touch, his scent, the rough texture of his day-old
beard. She guided into herself that hard part of him
that searched for solace. Groaning, he sagged against
her as her softness enfolded him warmly, his breath
fanning her left nipple until it tingled. As the fires
built within her, she wrapped his buttocks with her
legs so that she could feel him more deeply.

He held her tightly in his arms, and she entwined
her arms around his massive shoulders. He began a
slow, excruciatingly sweet massage, not only within
her, but of her entire being—or so it felt. His love
washed over her and inside her, releasing her from
all restraint. She sensed that he was struggling to
contain his own stormy desire, but he waited, he held
back, until her mounting hunger could be assuaged.
His sweet, deliberate torment stirred up a tempest
within her until everything was centered on him inside her, attuned to his song of utter rapture.

Simultaneously, they reached that point where all
sensation became a crescendo of enchantment, a
shuddering release until only stillness remained,
peace and happiness. Cradled together, heads close
on Maggie's lace-trimmed pillow, they slept.

A frantic knock on the door awakened them two
hours later. ''Maggie, are you ill?'' cried Cecily Byrne.
''Please open up. Did you forget you had an appoint-

ment with Mrs. Webb and her daughter? They're downstairs now.''

Maggie gasped and sat up in bed, pulling the sheet to her chin. "I slept late," she called back. "Tell them I'll join them in ten minutes."

"Very well."

Maggie glanced at Thaddeus, who had his arm slung over her lap so that she couldn't move. She softened inside as he smiled sleepily at her, but duty tugged at her conscience. "I must get up. What if your mother happened to find out that you spent the night here?" Blushing, she slid toward the edge of the bed, but he tightened his hold over her thighs so that she couldn't move.

"I live here temporarily. No one except you knows in which bed I slept." His brown eyes gleamed wickedly. "I'm glad it wasn't in mine." He burrowed closer to her naked body. "Yours is so much *softer*."

Maggie blushed as his gaze roamed over her body, stopping most indecently at her breasts. "I must go down. It's rude to keep your mother waiting, especially since we had an appointment."

He muttered something unintelligible and stroked her thigh. Her skin tingled and her breath caught in her throat, but she fought the impulse to surrender to his caresses. However, as she struggled to get out of bed, he slid his hand over her hip, upward past her waist, until he cupped one full breast.

"My God," he groaned. "Stop fighting . . . who knows when we'll have another chance." He played with her nipple until it grew hard, but she resisted the delicious sensation.

"Thaddeus! Don't you have the slightest feeling of shame?" She managed to get one leg over the side of the mattress.

"Why should I?" He dragged her back, but she got a good grip around the tester post and dragged herself away from him, laughing as he tickled her mercilessly behind her knee.

"Thaddeus Webb! Of all the incorrigible men, you take the cake." She stood naked on the floor, valiantly meeting his lascivious stare. His eyes simmered with desire, but she refused to be drawn in. At last she found the wits to scramble into some clothes, a simple shirtwaist and gored woolen skirt. After brushing her hair and pinning it into its usual chignon, she put a pair of pearl drops on her earlobes.

"There! I don't think I've ever dressed this fast." Looking at herself in the mirror, she noticed that her eyes sparkled and her cheeks glowed from hours of lovemaking. Observing him in the reflection, she stepped into a pair of soft leather pumps.

He was leaning on his elbow, watching her, that infuriating grin still on his face.

"I would appreciate it if you left my room before the maids arrive to tidy up."

"I know it would embarrass you to have them find me here." He slid out of bed and sauntered over to her. "Don't worry." With a twist of his fingers, he pulled the pins from her bun, and her hair cascaded down her back.

Shying away, she glared. "What are you doing now?"

"This is so much better," he said, pulling his hands through her hair.

"But highly inappropriate for a hotel owner."

He shrugged. "Very well. Let me at least help you. You don't have to look like a schoolmarm, you know." He turned her around, then dragged the silver-backed hairbrush through her tresses until they crackled. He deftly twisted her hair into one thick braid, looped it up, and fastened it with a tortoiseshell comb at the back. He fluffed the curls at her temples.

"There. Now you look like a lovely young woman who has just arisen from a night with her lover."

Maggie snorted, but she was secretly pleased with the change. Her whole body felt different with the rearrangement of her coiffure.

She was about to leave when he caught her a last time by the door. He pressed her to his naked chest and rubbed himself against her. "Now you can go," he said, chuckling at her outrage.

She righted her glasses and stalked through the sitting room. "You made me *only* one hour late instead of twenty minutes late, you scoundrel."

"Mother is a patient woman."

"Oh . . . *you!*" She slammed the door. Miss Lather came out of the nursery as Maggie hurried along the corridor.

"Mrs. Hartwell, I want to ask a favor of you," she said breathlessly, and fell into step with Maggie. "I meant to visit my mother in Margate, and would so much like to bring Victoria. Would that be possible? We could spend a few days by the sea, and Victoria would be away during the hectic Christmas preparations."

They had arrived at the top of the stairs leading to Maggie's office. "Hmmm, it might be a good idea. I will think about it, and tell you later today. Tell Victoria that I'm sorry for not waking her this morning. I will share tea with her instead."

Maggie didn't wait for the governess's reply as she ran downstairs. The Webb ladies were sitting in her office, and Maggie blushed with guilt, remembering that she'd just left Mrs. Webb's son in her bedroom. Her lover.

"I'm so sorry that I'm late—"

"Don't apologize," said Mrs. Webb with a kind smile. "Your assistant told us that you are extremely busy at this time of the year."

Maggie's cheeks grew hot. "Yes . . . busy indeed."

She studied Mrs. Webb, who sat straight and still in
the wing chair by the desk. Wearing a dark gray fitted
coat, fur muff, and a black hat adorned with one os-
prey feather, she looked proper and solid. Delia reminded Maggie of a delicate spring flower in pale blue
coat and matching hat on her brown hair. "Where's
Amintha?" she asked as she pulled out a stack of papers with ideas for the reception.

"She's much too excitable for this kind of outing,"
Mrs. Webb said with a smile. "She talks too much,
and always asks awkward questions." Mrs. Webb
paused. "Tell me, is my son . . . er, living at the hotel
now? Gavin Talbot told me Thaddeus had moved in
here."

Maggie swallowed hard as she met the searching
brown gaze. "Yes, but strictly as a guest, of course.
I'm afraid it's my fault—it concerns the investigation
I hired him to do." Hating to lie, she walked toward
the door. "Shall I show you around? We ought to
choose one of the dining rooms for the reception."

"I want the very best for my daughter's wedding,"
Mrs. Webb said, pulling Delia with her to the foyer.
The bride-to-be blushed, and excitement shone in her
eyes. Seeing Delia's happiness, Maggie felt a sudden
longing for a wedding of her own. Thaddeus surely
felt the same way after their wonderful night together.

She led the ladies from one dining room to the next,
and they decided that the middle one, with its tiny,
tiled outside garden, would be perfect.

"My regular customers will be dining at the hotel
as usual, but another door leads to the larger dining
room, so this can easily be blocked off."

"Gavin will see to the delivery of hothouse flowers—pink roses and carnations," Mrs. Webb explained. "Now, what about the menu? Can the food
be prepared here?"

Maggie suggested canapés and champagne since it

would be an evening wedding, and she suspected that the Webbs couldn't afford a full-course meal. "How many guests?" Maggie asked, her pencil poised.

"It will be just a small assembly, about twenty-five invited. Mostly relatives and friends." The older woman hesitated, then turned her clear gaze toward Maggie. "You might wonder why I want to have the reception here, and not somewhere closer to home." She paused. "You see, I wanted to create a cherished memory, uncluttered by the commonplace reminders of everyday life."

Delia blushed. "Oh, Mother!"

"I'm flattered that you considered my hotel for such a special event." Maggie felt tears gathering in her eyes. This tightly knit family touched her in a way that broke through her defenses. The Webbs were proof that happy families existed.

"I've written down all the spreads to put on the canapés: salmon mousse, lobster . . ." She riffled through the papers, but could not find the menu. "Excuse me a moment." She hurried to her office just in time to see Thaddeus descending the stairs in the lobby. He looked magnificent in a dark brown suit, a blindingly white shirtfront with high collar, and a red-striped ascot tied jauntily under his clean-shaven chin. He looked so handsome that Maggie's heart ached. As she stepped into her office, he winked, making her hot all over.

It took her the better part of ten minutes to find the menu suggestions. She came out of her office just in time to see Thaddeus press a fedora on his head and leave. His black scarf, which she had sponged clean at dawn, whirled around him in the brisk breeze. Where was he going? she wondered.

Maggie entered the dining room to hear the last words of a discussion.

"—Thaddeus will never marry again, you mark my

words," Mrs. Webb said. "He couldn't find another
woman like Rachel, and he won't settle for less."

"But, Mother, Mrs. Hartwell would be perfect for
him."

"I agree, but I'm not sure Thaddeus does. He
hasn't made it clear that he has any serious intentions
toward her. They only have a business agreement as
far as I know."

They noticed Maggie coming toward them and
stopped abruptly. Their words had made her uneasy.
Did Thaddeus think she wasn't good enough to be
his wife, or could *any* woman compare with Rachel?

"You look so pale, Mrs. Hartwell. What's wrong?"
Delia asked shyly, and caught the papers as they
began to slide from Maggie's hands.

"I . . . I'm not feeling very well," she said truth-
fully. "I'm afraid it might be the influenza that is rampant in London." She handed the young woman the
sheet with the menus. "Please read these, and if you
have any other suggestions, let me know. We can accommodate almost any kind of request." Her voice
faltering, she led the way to the foyer. She forced a
smile to her lips, ignoring her pounding heart. "I
hope you'll make the wedding cake yourself, Mrs.
Webb. Your son has told me how wonderful your
pastry is."

Mrs. Webb laughed. "Thaddeus is too biased to
judge my cooking," she said. "But I will naturally be
pleased to make whatever Delia wants at her reception."

"I hope you'll feel better tomorrow," Delia said
kindly. "I will send some of Mother's special broth
when we return home. It cures everything." Impulsively, she laid her hand on Maggie's arm. "I hope
we may become friends."

Maggie wanted to cry at Delia's thoughtfulness.
"We already are."

After they left she ran to her office where she indulged in a hearty bout of tears. She couldn't remember the last time she had cried—except for that time in Thaddeus's shop. *Idiot!* she chided herself, wiping her nose.

She sat down behind the desk, and thought about what the Webbs had said concerning Thaddeus's marital plans—or lack of them. She'd been so eager to see in Thaddeus what she wanted to see that she'd given herself without any commitment from him. But she had wanted to, and she didn't regret it. She'd never considered that her past made her unworthy, but would Thaddeus think of marrying a woman who had borne an illegitimate child? She didn't know any man who would. She pushed away the grim thought.

She dried her eyes and settled down with the accounts, a boring chore she hoped might bring back her composure. But even as she worked, the ache in her heart reminded her of her foolish dreams of marriage.

Thaddeus met Sergeant Horridge at the public house in Soho. "This time the meal's on me," the sergeant offered.

"Do you have anything on Ripley or Rupert Merton?" Thaddeus asked as he took a bite of his steak.

"Nothing in the files." The sergeant studied Thaddeus's face. "Did you expect that they would be wanted by the police?"

"No . . . not exactly, but Merton might have left England because of some crime."

"What exactly happened in Richmond?" Horridge asked. "I was surprised to get a telephone call from an irate police sergeant, claiming you were ready for Bedlam."

Thaddeus chuckled, then grew serious. "I was taken to a den of devil's worship in Richmond last night, but I couldn't find the exact place again when I returned with the law. Anselm Ripley was one of the participants. He wore a ring exactly like one I saw on Rupert Merton's hand. I suspect that all the men in that group wear identical rings. In fact, I shall prove it.''

Horridge rubbed his chin in thought. ''Hmmm. Odd indeed. But why would they want to hurt you?''

''Because I'm trying to find Miss Winston.'' He sighed. ''I'm convinced that she's somehow involved with Ripley—and the mysterious cult.'' Thaddeus remembered the human shape on the altar and the glittering dagger in the hooded man's hand. ''I also fear she might be dead.''

''A hideous thought, but likely. She's been missing for a long time.'' Horridge swallowed some ale and studied his friend. ''You're eager to solve this puzzle, aren't you?''

Thaddeus scrutinized Horridge's face, gauging how Septimus would take his next words. ''I might have stumbled onto the men who perpetrated the Altar Murders.'' He told Horridge about the enshrouded body on the altar and the knife.

The sergeant rubbed his chin. ''Are you sure? It sounds farfetched. You were probably befuddled after that blow to your head. It could have been anything. These cult rituals are usually harmless. Besides, they're rampant in London. I've witnessed a few myself.''

So Horridge wasn't ready to believe him. ''Very well, I'll find proof.''

''If you need more information, I'm at your beck and call. I understand that you want this case behind you as soon as possible.''

''Yes, I would like to take the burden from Mrs. Hartwell's shoulders.''

''So you take it on your own?'' Horridge smiled. ''I'd say you get too involved in your work, Thad.''

Thaddeus tossed his napkin on the table. ''I'll send

you an invitation to the wedding, but first I have to ask Mrs. Hartwell to be the bride."

Horridge's face brightened even more. "I say!" He rose and slapped his friend's back. "You certainly don't let grass grow under your feet. This calls for a celebration."

Thaddeus placed a detaining hand on his arm. "The bride has to accept my offer first." He furrowed his brow. "I'll be forever grateful if you can discover anything more about Ripley's background."

"We'll investigate his friends and business associates. But remember, if nothing untoward happens during our inquiry, I cannot afford to waste a constable on another wild goose chase, especially since you don't recall the address in Richmond. We can't search every house for an altar and a body."

"Of course. But I assure you, something is about to happen."

Thaddeus returned to Hartwell's Hotel, possessed by an urgency to solve the mystery of Maggie's missing sister. He knew he would have to travel to Liverpool to discover if anyone saw what had happened to Leonora after she disembarked. Perhaps Ripley had been the last person to have contact with Leonora Winston.

It was raining, and Thaddeus raised his collar. The air was cold, and a fog was gathering over the city. He longed to sit with Maggie before a cozy fire, but it would have to wait. The only reason he was returning to the hotel was to alert Maggie that he would be working without a break until he had some definite news about Leonora—good or bad.

His tenderness for Maggie sat warmly in his chest, and he marveled at the strength of his feelings. The prim and proper Mrs. Hartwell had turned his entire life upside down the moment she stepped across his threshold in Maddox Street.

Should he propose to her now, or wait until this

usiness with Miss Winston was over? The ruby ring
/as still at the jeweler's, but all he had to do was to
·ick it up this evening. However, he wanted to make
the most romantic moment of their association, and
ecause of this puzzling case, he couldn't plan the
·erfect moment to go down on his knee.

He decided to wait. Maggie needed time to get used
o him, and she must know by now that his inten-
ions were honorable. Women usually sensed these
hings, and he was sure she would be happy to as-
ume the conventional bonds of marriage. He found
hat he was looking forward to it as well. Coming
ome to Maggie after a hard day's work would be as
lose to paradise on earth as any man could imagine.
he was magnificent.

His coat was damp and his feet were wet by the
ime he reached the hotel. Where would he find Mag-
ie on this dreary day? Working, most likely.

Rafferty touched the brim of his stovepipe hat as
'haddeus stepped through the door and shook the
aindrops from his fedora.

"Mrs. Hartwell is in her office," the doorman said.
'She works too hard if I may say so," he added.

"Did Mrs. Webb and my sister leave?" Thaddeus
nwound his black scarf and gave both it, and his
odden coat, to a maid.

"Yes, over an hour ago."

Thaddeus smoothed down his hair and righted his
scot. Clearing his throat, he knocked on the office
loor. His heart thudded in anticipation, as he hoped
t always would when he saw her. He never wanted
o see their sparkling love fade.

"Come in," she called, and he stepped inside, feel-
ng suddenly shy. What did she see in a great bum-
·ling bear like himself?

Maggie raised her gaze to her lover's face, and was
ereft of her breath. She loved this man so much it
/as almost unbearable. With his hair wet and curling

over his collar, he looked adorable yet reckless. It wa
no wonder she'd foolishly let him take her body, he
heart—yes, even her soul. Her whole being reache
out to him, and she wanted to cry for the pain an
the beauty of her love.

"I missed you," he said, and she tingled all ove
But she had to be strong and withstand that charmin
smile and those large tender hands that were abou
to pull her from her chair and drag her into his arm:

"No! Don't touch me." He studied her closely an
she averted her eyes. The warmth in his grin wa
replaced by bewilderment.

"What? Why?" He loomed over her where she sa
at her desk. "Look at me, Maggie. What change
since this morning, when we were so close? Di
Mother say something to hurt you?"

"Of course not!" Yet it was true that Mrs. Webb'
doubt that Thaddeus would ever marry again ha
hurt her. Why would he want to marry a woman wh
had a sordid past? Would he want to be the father o
a child who'd been conceived out of wedlock? Sham
burned in Maggie's cheeks. If he discovered that sh
desired the respectability of marriage, he might reco
with outrage, and if he took her in his arms, she kne
she'd blurt out everything she was feeling and think
ing.

"Do you regret our—intimacy?" he asked.

She whipped her head around. "No . . . I have n
regrets." And she meant it.

"Something has evidently upset you," he insiste
and placed his hands over her shoulders. "I wish yo
would confide in me."

"It's only the work," she lied. "It's been hecti
lately, and with Leonora's disappearance . . ."

"Yes, I know. The reason I came here to see yo
was to tell you that I'll be extremely busy for the ne
few days. I will not rest until I find Leonora, an
that's a promise."

She looked at him with tears in her eyes. "That's very kind of you. Do you have any new leads?"

"Not at the moment, but I have some ideas to pursue." His eyebrows quirked. "You're not insisting on accompanying me any longer, Maggie? Had enough of the music hall, I take it?" The old teasing note was back in his voice, but Maggie could not relax.

"No, I've learned to trust your judgment implicitly. I have my own work to think of."

"How cold and distant we sound," he chided, crossing his arms over his chest.

Maggie glared through her spectacles and shuffled some papers on the desk. "If you're angling for adoration, you must go elsewhere. I have many problems to deal with before the day is over."

"Tsk, tsk, I see the schoolmarm is back." He paused and studied her face closely. "If you're overworked, you should take a few days' holiday. Your assistant is capable—"

She stalked across the room and pulled out a drawer full of files. "I didn't ask for your advice, and I'd appreciate it if you didn't give it out so—so smugly."

"Smugly?" He crossed the floor to tower over her. "That was uncalled for."

She dared to face him, noticing that his chin had grown decidedly pugnacious and his eyes smoldered—with anger, no doubt. "I asked you calmly and succinctly not to tell me how to live my life," she continued.

He gripped her upper arms and stared at her. "That was rude, Maggie. You know I care about your welfare. I like to know about your problems here, and your personal problems, if there are any."

She pulled away from him. "You know too much already. Soon you'll start playing the master, ordering everyone around." Anger and misery boiled

within her. Her words were ruining everything now
but she couldn't stop them. "I won't have it."

His face hardened, and she flinched. She wante
to take back everything, but it was too late now
"Why shouldn't you consult with me about your life
Maggie? A relationship is give-and-take. I wouldn
hesitate to listen to your advice." The sweep of hi
arm encompassed the room. "In fact, I'm sure yo
know more about business than I do, and I wouldn
hesitate to listen to your opinion in matters that con
cern my antiques."

"This discussion will not lead anywhere," she said
"Our businesses are in no way connected." He
hands trembled as she laid the files on her desk. Al
this fuss because she didn't dare to confront him
about their future together? "I think you'd bette
leave. I have better things to do than quarrel wit
you."

He strode to the door. "I find it highly aggravatin
that you won't share your everyday life with me. No
only did you tell me how to investigate Miss Win
ston's disappearance, but you actually *hounded* me ev
erywhere. And I let you."

Maggie cringed at his anger. She wanted to run
across the room and throw herself into his arms, bu
pride held her back. "Please go," she said quietly
"We should think about our . . . future and our per
sonal needs before we meet again. I hope that th
next time I see you, you'll have something to tell m
about Leonora."

He tore open the door so violently that Maggie
feared he would pull it off its hinges. "Maggie, I wish
you wouldn't shut me out." He stalked out and
slammed the door.

"No!" she called after him, but it was too late
Don't go.

Chapter 17

The next day, after asking Cecily to take charge of the hotel for a day or two, Maggie took the north-bound train at King's Cross station. It would stop at Sheffield, and from there, she could hire a hackney to take her to her old home. She hadn't been there for almost seven years, and it was on the spur of the moment that she had decided to visit the mansion. After Thaddeus had left, a thought had come to her that Leonora might have traveled up to the Midlands for some reason.

Maggie knew she would have time to ponder her future during the trip. She wished she had parted with Thaddeus on a friendly note, but the damage was done, and only time would reveal the strength of their relationship. As she settled herself in a private compartment of the yellow first-class Pullman car, she thought about him, missing him.

She watched the scenery change from gray roofs and tall rusty chimney pots to meadows and woods. After much deliberation, she had let Victoria go with Miss Lather to Margate. It was better for her daughter to be out of the way while the investigation into Leonora's disappearance continued. Thaddeus's life had been threatened, and Maggie was unsure whether her mysterious nighttime prowler had anything to do with her sister.

As she thought about Thaddeus, and what their next meeting might bring, she drifted off to sleep to the rocking of the train, her head propped against the cushion fastened to the wall. She didn't awaken until the train stopped at Nottingham, where she bought some sweetmeats and nuts from a hawker with a tray outside the station house. The day was sunny and unusually warm. It was hard to believe that Christmas was just six days away.

The landscape grew hillier as the train crossed into the Peak District, and Maggie felt a twinge of nostalgia. These had been the vistas of her childhood. She wished her father hadn't been such a cruel and implacable man, so that she could have returned earlier, visited him while he was still alive. But her wishes were useless now, and she knew he would never have changed.

She arrived at Sheffield, a rapidly expanding industrial town, a center for steel manufacturing. Huge, ugly warehouses and factories marred the landscape. All the colors were gloomy brown, beige, and drab gray. It struck her that London, even with its teeming life and ramshackle buildings, was ten times lovelier than this cheerless pit of misery.

Carrying her carpetbag herself, she walked to the railway hotel, which was right next door. It was clean inside, if slightly musty due to the cool, humid air. At the desk, she pulled out the calotype of Leonora which Thaddeus had returned to her after their visit to Anselm Ripley, and showed it to the clerk.

"Have you seen this woman—staying at the hotel lately, or perhaps dining here?"

The thin, bald man with pince-nez perched on his nose stared at the picture. "No, never."

Dejected, Maggie signed the ledger for a room and the doorman carried her carpetbag upstairs.

The coal fire in her room was pitifully small. Maggie longed to go back to her own comfortable abode.

As soon as she had rested, she would have dinner, and then, perhaps, travel to her childhood home. It was located only five miles outside of the town.

However, as soon as she stepped into the dining room, the first person she saw was her uncle. Her eyes widened in surprise. "Uncle Rupert! What are you doing here?"

He frowned in consternation and his napkin dropped to the floor as he stood. "Margaret? This is truly unexpected, but a pleasure all the same." He indicated the table. "Will you please join me?"

"Yes, of course." She sat down as he pulled out a chair for her. Fixing him with a curious stare, she added, "Why didn't you tell me you planned to come up here? We could have traveled together. And why didn't you take any of your luggage from Hartwell's?"

"It happened on the spur of the moment. I was investigating the remote possibility of restoring the old mansion, but it looks like a futile mission." He shrugged and poured a glass of wine for her. "I'm getting sentimental in my old age." Heaving a deep sigh, he emptied his glass. "I was thinking in terms of a summer residence, y'see. Bully left the mansion to his solicitors in lieu of his debts, and they're frantically trying to get rid of the heap."

"My, you've been busy establishing yourself and your business, and now this," she said, sipping her wine. She ordered soup, whitefish, mutton, and a rhubarb tart from a waiter in a dark coat with a towel hanging over his forearm. She was famished.

"Yes, but it looks like I'm just about finished with my endeavors. The workmen will have completed the restoration of my town house in Cavendish Square when I return to London, and I can settle down for good. I've moved most of my luggage there, and when I go back, I'll fetch the rest at your hotel." He patted her hand. "You must, of course, come to dinner one night at my new home."

"I look forward to it." Maggie studied the strange scarab ring on his hand and wondered if a world traveler like her uncle would be satisfied settling down.

"What are you doing here, Margaret?" he asked, his eyes narrowed in speculation. The muscle twitched in his jaw.

"I wanted to get away from London for a day, and thought there might be a slim chance that Leonora traveled here."

"Well . . . ? Is there any indication that she did?"

Maggie shook her head. "No, I asked at the desk here and at the train depot, and no one recalled seeing her. But there are many train travelers, so her presence could have been overlooked." She paused. "But don't you think that a foreign lady like Leonora would stand out from the other passengers?"

Rupert Merton toyed with the stem of his glass. "Yes, it's highly likely."

"I'll ask at all the hotels in town, just to make sure she didn't stay here in Sheffield." She sighed. "I'm still worried about her."

"It's understandable, but at least you found one lost relative." He pointed to his chest. "Me."

She laughed. "Yes, a nice twist of fate." She had a sudden urge to know him better, and since he was family he might not be averse to explaining some things that had preyed on her mind. "Rupert . . ." She hesitated. "Would you please tell me why you left England those many years ago?"

His knife clattered on the plate as he laid it down. "An abrupt question, m'dear."

"No one has ever disclosed what happened between you and Father."

"We never got along very well, but the straw that broke the camel's back was his accusation that I . . . er, had a liaison with your mother."

Maggie gasped.

He nodded. "I assure you, it wasn't true. Bully had

a fertile imagination. He guarded your mother's every step. When he found us wandering together in the garden one day, he assumed that we were involved." He stared at Maggie. "Your mother was a lovely woman, and you look like her—the same hair color, the eyes. But again, I was not enamored of your mother. She was too high-strung, too bitter."

The very air seemed to grow still as he paused. Maggie had a sudden sensation of doom, raising goosebumps along her arms. She watched his face intently as he continued. "Bully beat your mother constantly; she told me so herself. I wasn't surprised when she left, never to return." He sighed, his eyes glittering strangely. "You know, I believe that Bully thought I had fathered your sister, but I swear," he laid his hand on his heart, "that it isn't true."

Maggie shivered as if touched by a cold draft. "You told me you didn't even know of Leonora's existence."

He poured more wine. "That's right . . . I had no idea. Your mother might have led a difficult life in Virginia—fending for herself and a small daughter, but at least she wasn't abused. She must have changed her name to Winston to forget the Mertons, and I don't blame her."

The waiter returned with a soup tureen. Maggie automatically took a swallow, but was so intent on her uncle's words that she didn't even taste the soup.

"Had I known about your mother's plight, I might have tried to reason with Bully."

"But what about me? Why did she leave me behind?"

Uncle Rupert's smile seemed fixed on his face, like a painful mask. "I suspect Bully threatened to kill her if she took you—his only true offspring—away. Bully was a strange man, Maggie."

"He treated me horribly all those years, ignored me, belittled me. He could not have loved me."

"I think he did, in his own warped way. Perhaps,

deep down, he worried that someone else had fathered you. He had grown into a bitter man, you must remember that.''

After chewing a piece of meat, Merton continued thoughtfully, ''It took great courage to strike out on your own, Maggie.''

''I . . . I was mortally afraid of Father.'' She couldn't tell him the true reason for her flight from Sheffield, not until she felt more comfortable in his presence. There was an odd stillness in the room, as if someone was listening to their conversation. Maggie looked at the other diners, counting five couples and one lone gentleman at a table in the corner behind a large aspidistra in a wicker planter. They couldn't hear a word across the room, which hummed with conversation.

''You seem distressed, m'dear. Are the memories bothering you?''

Maggie glanced into his eyes, struck by the certainty that the strangeness came from him. Something drove her to say, ''Tell me, Uncle, are your religious beliefs . . . er, Christian?''

His fork stilled and he stared at her in with a peculiar expression. ''What an extraordinary question, Maggie. What in the world—?''

''I didn't mean to insult you in any way,'' she added, embarrassed. ''It's only that you've been away for so long, and you've a certain *air* that appears so, well, exotic.''

He relaxed visibly, as if all the starch had gone from his body. The tic on his face slowed. ''If you must know, I have studied various religions extensively.'' He leaned closer to her, and murmured, ''Truly, I find them all sadly lacking in many respects. Their rituals are not what I call *worship.*''

''Worship? Well, then pray tell me, what is worship?'' Maggie was uncomfortable under his strange, magnetic stare.

"It's sacrifice, m'dear." His voice turned conspiratorial again.

"Sacrifice?" she echoed. "What do you mean?"

"To give up something in deference to a greater cause. Simply to sacrifice your own needs and desires to follow a greater plan."

Maggie could not take her eyes off his face. "It sounds difficult. Give up one's own *self*?"

"Tell me, what sacrifices do regular churchgoers have to make?" He grew peevish. "There's no longer any true test, no show of courage, no pitting of strength against evil." He flung down is napkin. "In ancient days, a knight had to earn his honor through valor, through combat and challenge, or lose his life."

"But who is to decide what sacrifice is proper to gain that honor?"

"Someone who understands the greater scheme of things."

Silence hovered between them until Maggie broke it. She didn't like the smile lurking on his lips.

"Are you implying *you* know that plan?"

He shrugged. "One must find out for oneself. Even a woman who cannot gain honor through combat can make a sacrifice."

Maggie laid her napkin on the table. "I find this discussion highly upsetting, Uncle Rupert. You're glorifying savagery and violence, and I cannot agree with such disturbing views."

"A human can only gauge his true strength when he is tested. Death—"

Maggie shivered. "I have no idea what you're talking about, but I suppose you're entitled to your beliefs."

"I can explain it to you if you're interested, Maggie."

"It sounds intriguing, but the hotel business takes up all my time. However, you could lend me some books to study."

He smiled enigmatically. "I would be delighted." He drank the last of his wine.

She paused, watching him. "I would like to understand you better."

He patted her hand soothingly. "We have years ahead of us yet, I hope. I certainly look forward to knowing you."

They finished their meal in silence. "It has been a long day. I'm tired," Maggie said, and rose.

He stood, his face shadowy with regret. "I was just beginning to enjoy our conversation." He led her to the door of the dining room. "I hope my convictions won't ruin our newfound friendship."

"Of course not. You have the right to your opinions." Maggie slanted a glance at him. "When are you leaving?"

"In two or three days, but I will endeavor to share another meal with you before you go. I'm glad that we met here."

Maggie said good night, crossed the foyer, and ascended the curving mahogany staircase. The wavering gaslights' reflection against the dark green wallpaper made the corridor eerie, and she hurried inside her room and locked the door. Filled with uneasiness, she sat down on the only stuffed chair in the room. She didn't know what to make of her uncle, but she thought him more eccentric every time they met.

She glanced out the window. The day was passing into late afternoon and it would get dark around four o'clock. The visit home would have to wait until tomorrow.

Filled with nervous energy, she paced the room. She had no desire to discuss religion with her uncle again, so she decided she would have to stay in her room all evening. Thank goodness she had brought a book to read. Stretching out on the bed, she turned up the gaslight and started on the first chapter. Before long she drifted off to sleep.

She woke around eight, and ordered a late supper to be served in her room. As she sat alone in front of the fire, she realized how much she missed Thaddeus. How had she lived without him before? It had been half a life, a monotonous life.

Whatever difficulties they might have to resolve in their relationship, she wanted to make the effort. With that thought, she went to bed and fell into an exhausted sleep.

The next morning brought snow flurries and a cold breeze. She hired a gig to take her out to her childhood home. Outside town, the rocky hills loomed as far as the eye could see. Patches of snow covered the higher parts, and the wind howled over the ground. The gray ceiling of the sky seemed to sag all the way to the earth, and a few storm-whipped trees added to the vista of desolation.

The gig stopped in front of the crumbling gates of the mansion, which rested on the crest of a rolling hill. Maggie remembered the spectacular view with nostalgia. The tumbledown wall around the overgrown park was covered with scraggly vines, and the gravel drive was pitted. Tufts of dead grass stuck out of every crevice, even out of the stone foundation of the house that her grandfather had built with such pride. The granite he'd used for the walls was intact, but the Gothic window frames had rotted, and broken glass was everywhere. The slates on the roof were either dangling from the steep, rotting eaves, or covered with green moss and lichen. The devastation brought sadness to Maggie's heart. Such neglect!

It has been her father's wish to let it go to ruin. If only he'd given her the house, she would have kept it in good repair, but he'd wanted everything to die with him, the last Merton—or so he'd thought, not knowing that Rupert had survived the sea disaster. Maggie told the cabbie to wait for her.

"Father, how could you be so cruel to everyone?" she whispered as she pushed open the front door. It was hanging from one hinge, and there were bird droppings everywhere inside. Wildlife and vagrants had taken over the property. Before long, grass would grow where there once had been a gleaming parquet floor.

She heard a crash from the upper floor and started in fear. "Who's there?" she called out as she heard footsteps above. No answer. Swallowing hard, she walked halfway up the creaking stairs. Her palms grew clammy and she wiped them on her skirt. "Is anyone up there?" she called louder. She picked up a brick before going inside.

The house had ten bedrooms on the second floor. Perhaps some derelicts were even now living there. What was there to be afraid of? she chided herself. Pinching her lips in determination, she walked up the rest of the steps before she could lose her courage. The twisted tree limbs blocked the windows outside and the hallway lay in shadows.

She heard another sound as if someone was sliding a heavy object. She walked stealthily toward the noise, to the room that had formerly been her father's bedchamber.

Fearing what she would find, she peered around the door frame, and instantly saw her uncle on his knees as he searched the lower part of a cupboard. She dropped the brick and crossed her arms over her chest.

He jerked around, his dark hair covered with dust. "Margaret! You almost frightened me into an apoplexy." He rose and dusted off his knees.

"What are you looking for?" she asked, and stepped inside.

"I thought I'd make sure that none of the family

heirlooms had been left behind,'' he said with a fleeting smile. His face was red with exertion, and his clothes were rumpled and gray with dust. He appeared to have spent all morning going through the rooms.

"I'm certain the tramps would have taken anything of value.'' She looked at the debris on the floor, old magazines and newspapers, pieces of wallpaper, cracked china.

"There isn't as much as a stick of furniture here, not even in the attic. I walked through it this morning.''

"You have been busy then.'' Maggie had a nagging suspicion that he was keeping something from her. "Why won't you tell me what you're really searching for?'' she said, fixing him with a penetrating stare.

He wiped his hands, the color receding from his face. A shutter seemed to have fallen over his eyes, and Maggie was surer than ever that he was hiding something.

"We all have secrets, don't we?'' she prodded. "But if yours concerns the family, then I have a right to know.''

He shrugged, and walked back to the cupboard whose contents he'd dragged out on the floor. "If you must know, I had hoped to find letters, or a diary of some sort that would have explained why Bully was so bitter and let everything go to rack and ruin.''

"I don't think you'll find anything,'' she said, poking a toe at a newspaper clipping. "Father was not one to express himself, so I doubt that he kept written records of anything.'' She read the yellowed paper. STEAMER SUNK AT SEA, NO SURVIVORS. "Look, this is about the accident in which you were involved.''

"Yes, I saw that,'' he said. "Bully kept *some* things.'' He snorted. "He probably kept that out of glee, knowing he would never have to see me again.''

Maggie picked through the rest of the newspapers, but there was nothing else of interest.

"A desolate place, don't you think?" he said, and righted his ascot which was askew. "It gives me the willies." His gaze darted to the somber corners of the room.

"Yes," she admitted, slanting a glance at him. "It was strange to see you on your knees peering into cobwebby cupboards."

He laughed. "You know how it is when you begin going through old things. One find leads to another, and you won't stop until you've sorted through the entire pile." He took her arm and led her out on the landing. "You look so suspicious—as if I was committing a crime."

"No . . . it was unexpected, that's all." Somehow she still doubted that he'd told her the entire truth.

They stepped outside and the wind grabbed their coats with ferocious playfulness.

"The carriage is waiting for me," Maggie said. "How did you get here?"

"I walked across the hills. Highly invigorating, but I wouldn't mind sharing the cab back to town. If you don't mind?"

"Of course not. It's too cold to be outside on a day like this." She glanced at the sullen sky. "It looks like more snow is heading this way."

In silence, they rode along the rutted road which was bordered by stone walls. When the first chimneys of Sheffield appeared, Rupert Merton said suddenly, "Your father had a great deal of power. He commanded the lives of all the workers in his steel mill."

"Yes, but he wasn't a good employer. The workers suffered terribly, toiling at least twelve hours a day, and you remember how hot it was inside with the furnaces blazing. I hear the new owner of the mill is a kinder man."

"Bah! What does it matter? The mill put food on
the table for the workers. They lived in decent cot-
ages that your father saw fit to erect."

"They were jerry-built; they lasted only five years
before falling apart."

"Nevertheless, the workers listened to Bully. He
would stand on a chair at one end of the factory and
shout his message, and the people looked up at him
as if he were God."

"They probably hated him for his cruelty, but dared
not protest for fear of losing their employment."

Rupert struck his thigh for emphasis. "Yet he held
their lives in his hand to do with as he saw fit."

Maggie gave her uncle a searching glance. "Not an
enviable position, surely. At the hotel, I always have
to make sure I'm fair to everyone employed, and I
find I must constantly juggle the priorities from day
to day."

Her uncle pinned her with a strange stare. "You
perhaps lack the vision for greatness."

Silence hovered between them, and Maggie wondered what was going through his mind. "You compare power to greatness?"

"They walk hand in hand." He drew himself up,
and inhaled until his chest expanded visibly. "One
day I will combine the two."

Maggie wasn't sure if he was serious. "A dictator
might voice such a statement. Are you planning to
have a factory where you can play God with the
workers, perchance?"

His smile was enigmatic, but Maggie sensed the
hectic energy behind his smooth facade. "I might, but
my plans are on a much . . . larger scale."

Maggie pinched her lips together. The conversation
was getting ridiculous, just like their talk last night at
the dining table.

"What exactly are your plans?" She searched his

face for clues, but all she could see was his obvious delight at his own thoughts.

"If my calculations are correct, my ideas will be widespread, across this country, yes, perhaps even throughout the world."

Maggie's jaw dropped. "You're anything but provincial, Uncle Rupert. I suppose it's due to your traveling. Are you going to set up offices in every capital?" She waited for his reply, wondering what it would be.

He chuckled. "Hardly offices, m'dear, but it's still too early to discuss. First I have to become established in England."

The carriage pulled up in front of the hotel. "I never realized you had such vast ambitions, Uncle Rupert," Maggie said, and, before he could assist her, she had stepped down. She spoke before going into the lobby. "Your plans seem to require a great deal of money."

He nodded and paid the cabbie. "Yes . . . that's a problem, of course, but I adore a challenge."

He led her inside and bowed gallantly over her hand. "Your company is as delightful as ever," he said.

She replied, "We must part here. I'm traveling back to London tonight after inquiring at the rest of the hotels for my sister."

"Do you need assistance?"

"No, I can manage on my own, and I don't want to ruin your time here."

"I will return to London shortly." He smiled and bowed once again. "Until then."

After a light luncheon, Maggie went outside, her sister's likeness at the ready. She visited the rest of the hotels in town, but knew, even before she started, that it was futile. Leonora had never come here.

She boarded the evening train for London, more confused than ever. But one thing was clear in her mind—she never wanted to be separated from Thaddeus again—no matter what his intentions for her were, honorable or dishonorable . . . Their love was the most important thing in her life.

Chapter 18

It was snowing heavily as the train pulled out of Sheffield. The wind whipped the flakes around in a mad dance outside the window. Maggie wondered if London was covered in white as well.

The compartment was cozy, and she was so tired. The day had brought too many memories from the past, and her encounter with Uncle Rupert had been odd, to say the least. What had he been looking for so purposefully in the cupboards of the ramshackle mansion?

She drifted off to sleep as the train swayed from side to side. An hour later she awakened to the screech of the brakes as they reached Nottingham. Maggie looked outside and saw a hawker selling hot tea from a kettle on a spirit lamp. Beside it, was a covered tray with buns, and she realized how good one would taste. In fact, the vendor was beckoning to her as she opened the door. Gripping her handbag in one hand, she struggled against the wind that tunneled along the ground.

"Perishin' day, ain't it?" the hawker said, and poured tea into a cracked cup.

"Yes, terrible." She paid him and took a bun from the tray. It was still warm in the middle and its filling of raspberry preserve tasted heavenly.

"Me old lady made 'em," he boasted when she made a sound of delight.

Other travelers joined them on the platform, and Maggie moved aside. After a few minutes she had finished her pastry and tea, but as she was about to return to the Pullman car, two men stepped off the train and halted her progress.

"Mrs. Hartwell?" one of them asked. He was old, with hunched, rheumatic shoulders, and his clothes were ragged. She gasped as she recognized the other, younger man. It was he who had followed her and Victoria that afternoon in London. Fear crawled over her. She retreated a step and looked toward the other passengers, but only two remained, and they weren't watching.

"What do you want?"

"There's something we want to show you," the young man said, rubbing his mittened hands. His gaze darted along the platform.

"What—?" How had they found her? No one except the staff at the hotel and her uncle knew her whereabouts. "Please step aside," she demanded, trying to pass them, but they grabbed her arms and hauled her around the corner of the station house. Before she could emit a scream one of the men placed his hand over her mouth. She was powerless against their strength as they led her toward a waiting carriage.

"The coach is there, just like he promised," the younger man said. As they rounded the next corner that faced the open yard in front of the station house, the ferocious wind leapt at them, driving snow into Maggie's eyes. Pressing her head down, she struggled to stay upright. They pushed her relentlessly forward. The carriage was covered with a layer of snow—even the horse had a thin, white mantle.

"What do you want?" she shouted as the man took his hand from her mouth. She was shoved up against the door opening of the coach and lifted inside. Before she had a chance to struggle, the young man gripped her and held her down against the seat. Crying out in pain, she fought against his superior strength. "What are you doing—?"

He covered her mouth with a scarf and the older man bound it hard at the back of her neck. She struggled to scream as the carriage moved forward with a jerk, but no sound escaped the scarf. Craning her neck as she partly reclined on the seat, she tried to see where they were heading. One of the men leaned over her and tied her hands together. She knew it was futile to fight them, and she sagged against the squabs. Tears gathered in her eyes, and she could barely breathe for the scarf pressed so tightly over her nose and mouth.

She trembled uncontrollably, knowing that someone was out to hurt her, but who? It had all started with the disappearance of her sister, then the silent visitor in the night, and now this. What did she have that they wanted? Her body? Would they mutilate her like the Whitechapel killer's victims in '88? Her head swam, and she was afraid she would faint from fright. The tears trickling down her cheeks cooled in the icy air, chilling her face. Her limbs grew cold and numb.

They traveled for what seemed an eternity. Then the carriage turned off the main road and stopped in a drive. She could barely make out the shape of a thatched cottage roof and a tall tree in the yard.

The men jumped down without speaking, and dragged her outside. She stood on shaky legs that threatened to give out at any second. One man on each side, they gripped her arms and led her past the low door. The room was warm, and a fire glowed in a hearth, but there was no sign of occupants. The cottage had an unused look except for the blaze in the grate.

They set her down on a sofa, her hands still bound

together. One of them tossed her handbag on the table beside her. Without as much as a glance, they turned and left, locking the door behind them.

Maggie shook so much she could not move for many minutes. But she drew a ragged breath of relief when the carriage pulled out of the drive. It looked like she would have a chance to escape if they didn't return soon. She wished they had removed the scarf.

When she'd collected her scattered wits, she walked around the tiny room. There was a dining table and a set of hard chairs, an overstuffed sofa, and gingham curtains at the windows. As far as she could see, the room held no personal belongings of any kind. Perhaps someone had rented the cottage to hold her prisoner.

All she had to do was to find a sharp edge to cut the rope around her wrists, and then climb out of a window. She walked to the one by the door and glanced outside, noticing to her dismay that it was barred. She glanced at the side of the cottage to see if there were any neighbors to alert, but the house was surrounded by a tall hedge.

Her legs still trembling, but her mind planning ways of escape, she searched the room for anything sharp enough to cut the ropes. A door at the back led to the kitchen.

There must be a knife somewhere, she thought, shivering. It was so dark she couldn't see anything except the dark shapes of the cupboards. Were the men who had brought her here going to leave her without food? And for how long?

She fumbled along the lead sink and pulled out several drawers, but they were empty. After a while she gave up, knowing she wouldn't find what she sought in the darkness. To preserve the warmth of the other room, she closed the door behind her. When the fire went out—she refused to carry that thought to its conclusion.

There was another door that led to a lean-to shed
attached to the house. Hope flared in her heart, and
she tried the door leading to the garden, but it was
barred with a piece of lumber, she noticed through
the cracks. She could see nothing in the shed since
there were no windows to let in light. If there were
any tools, she wouldn't be able to find them until
dawn.

Dispirited, she returned to sit by the fire on a chair.
A narrow, spiral staircase led to the loft above, but
she knew it would be pitch-black up there. Short of
gnawing off the ropes with her teeth, it was impossible to free herself. To escape, she would need both
her hands.

Her mind swirled, struggling to understand the
reason for her imprisonment. Could her uncle be behind this? There was no reason for him to incarcerate
her, and just because he was odd, it didn't make him
responsible for her abduction. Did one of her staff
want to extort money? With the hotel making a good
profit, she was a rather wealthy woman. But there
were so many others, more prosperous than she. Still,
she lived alone with her young daughter, and was
thus more vulnerable. Thank God Victoria was in
Miss Lather's good care!

The night wore on, and Maggie's head slumped
against the back of the chair. A sound outside roused
her temporarily, but it subsided. Fear was her con-
stant companion, tightening her muscles until her entire body ached. Finally, she slept heavily for an hour
or two, and when she awoke, the first dawn light
filtered through the windows. The fire had gone out,
and she was shivering with cold.

Would her abductors return today? she wondered
as she stretched her stiff limbs. She wouldn't rest until she found a way to freedom. Her stomach growled
with hunger, but she gave it only a fleeting thought.

She climbed the spiral staircase and found two

empty bedrooms. Not a stick of furniture, and the windows were bare, no iron bars here. Elated with that discovery, she looked outside, noticing that the drop to the ground from the dormer windows was high. She would have to slide along the steep thatch roof and fall as she may.

Not wanting to lose more time, she made her way back down. There had to be something that could cut the rope. Her hands were stiff and bluish due to the lack of circulation. She could barely open the door to the lean-to shed.

I will find a tool out here, she thought. I will not give in to this predicament.

Almost immediately she saw the handle of an ax leaning against a chopping block, partly hidden by a stack of wood. There was the answer to her prayers.

The shed was freezing cold, and she shivered uncontrollably, although she was still wearing her coat. She sank to the ground and fumbled with the ax until it lay flat on the ground. Then she clamped the long wooden handle between her knees, and stood the blade sharp end up. Leaning over it, she began to saw the rope back and forth over the edge.

She worked until her quickening circulation brought some warmth to her limbs.

"There! I did it!" The rope had snapped in two and she'd pulled off the scarf. Her captors had been careless to leave the ax or perhaps they hadn't noticed it. Bending her fingers and rotating her wrists, she felt the flexibility return to her hands. Then she went back inside and closed the door. The only thought in her head now was escape.

She rushed up the staircase and chose the window which would give the best chance for a soft landing, but discovered that all but one was painted shut. It took all her strength to pry that one open. She leaned out and tried to see what the ground looked like below, but the jutting thatch eaves obscured her view.

Just as she'd decided to step over the sill, the carriage returned. The drive was at the other side of the building, and Maggie crossed the room. She saw the younger man alight. Sucking in her breath, she tiptoed across the floor. There was no time to lose her courage. Gathering her skirts, she lifted her legs over the sill and stepped onto the roof. Her feet slid from beneath her instantly, and she got a frantic hold on the window frame. Lying flat on the thatch, she knew she would glide down without anything to halt the speed of her fall. Her heart thudded with fear, and cold sweat broke out on her forehead. If she started thinking, she would never dare to let go. The crashing of the doors inside helped her make up her mind.

Help! she screamed silently as she squeezed her eyes shut and loosened her grip. The thatch was smooth and soft as she sailed downward, then over the edge. Gasping, she soared through air, and landed on the ground with a thud which knocked the breath from her body. She lay perfectly still for a moment. Had they heard her, or seen her?

Her backside ached terribly, but other than that, she was unhurt. As she fought for air, her head seemed filled with helium. Dizzy, she closed her eyes and tried to relax. Within seconds she had regained her equilibrium, and she forced herself into a sitting position. Victoria would never believe her if she related this adventure—not that she would tell her anything. It would only frighten her.

Standing on shaky legs, she steadied herself against the wall, listening intently for sounds inside the cottage. She brushed the mud off as well as she could and steered her steps toward the hedge, skirting the occasional snow patches. Thank God most of the snow had melted in the rising temperature. Then she remembered that she'd forgotten her handbag on the table inside.

"How will I get back to London?" she mused aloud

as she hid in the shelter of the hedge. The door slammed shut on the other side, and the young man stalked around the garden. She threw herself flat into the ditch on the other side of the hedge, grateful that the water was frozen solid under her. Praying fervently he wouldn't find her, she lay perfectly still. He circled the yard twice, then stepped into the carriage once more. When it pulled away, she darted back behind the hedge lest they see her in the ditch. They passed her and she drew a deep sigh of relief. But would they come back when they didn't find her along the road? She had to get away before they did.

To her delight, she found the key still in the lock. Her abductors hadn't expected she would escape, and now that she was gone, they hadn't bothered to remove the key.

She unlocked the door and retrieved her bag, then headed in the direction from which the carriage had turned into the drive on the previous evening. The road was lined with cottages and spruce hedges. She knew she must be some distance away from Nottingham, and she had to return to the train station at any cost. All she could think of was to get back safely to London and Thaddeus. Walking along, she prayed she wouldn't meet her attackers on the road. They would recognize her instantly. She had no idea who the men were, but the young man had been welldressed; she'd noticed that.

The snow had almost melted during the morning hours, but it was beginning to flurry again, and the wind had grown colder. The snow was adhering to the wet tree branches. If she hadn't been so upset, she would have admired the lacy loveliness of the white-powdered twigs.

She must have walked for two miles before she saw the first smokestacks on the horizon. Carts and carriages were traveling along the road, and she kept her eye on every passing vehicle. The lane made a bend around a tall stone wall, and she found herself alone yet again. Suddenly she heard a clatter of hooves behind her, and she whipped her head around, instantly recognizing her abductors' coach. It had been standing behind the wall—lying in wait for her perhaps. Her heart in her throat, she sped along the road, praying that she would meet someone who would help her. The carriage rattled behind her, coming inexorably closer. She pulled up her skirts and started running faster. The new snow on the ground made the surface slippery, and she stumbled several times. She rushed onto a field that looked smooth. The road made a huge bend coming up on the other side of the meadow, and it would take the coach a long time to circle it. She would run through the dead grass and gain a greater lead. To her relief, no one followed her across the field: perhaps the men were afraid of drawing attention to themselves. She scrambled up on the other bank, onto the road. Another bend in the lane took her past a hedge, and there before her was a wagon filled with potato sacks.

Shouting and waving, she caught the attention of the young couple in the wagon, and the man halted the horse.

"Are you going into Nottingham?" Maggie asked between gasps.

"Aye, that we are. Want a lift, missy?"

"Yes, please." Maggie scrambled onto the wagon and sank down among the sacks. "There are some men in a carriage following me," she explained, looking anxiously behind her. She felt she had to explain her mad rush. "I was visiting an old friend when I decided to take a walk and was pursued."

"Some young bloods out for mischief," the farmer's wife said knowingly. She stared at Maggie. "Don't ye worry none, we won't let them harass ye."

"Bad day to take a walk," the man said to Maggie as he spread a blanket over her knees.

"Yes . . . I deeply regret this little outing," she said, mostly to herself. "When's the next train to London?"

"This morning sometime. We'll drop ye off at the station," the woman said with a kind smile. "Hope yer friend won't worry 'bout ye."

"I'll send her a note." Maggie's lips trembled. "One would think the countryside would be a safe place to visit."

"Aye—it's them young gentlemen from town. A mischievous lot," the man said.

The carriage came into view, and Maggie's heartbeat escalated. Would they stop the wagon and demand that the farmers release her? Maggie closed her eyes in prayer, feeling totally exposed and helpless.

She stared at the menace behind her, but it kept its distance. The farmers let Maggie off at the train station, and Maggie hoped the men wouldn't dare attack her in a throng. She bought a ticket to London and sat in the most crowded part of the waiting room. The two men who had abducted her appeared once, but she pretended not to see them. Yet she felt their stares. When they left, she knew she was safe.

The train departed an hour later, and Maggie was grateful to be on it. In two hours, she would be back in London, and she would buy herself a hearty breakfast at the first available tea shop.

The train journey was uneventful, and it was midday when Maggie arrived at King's Cross. Snow flurries danced thickly in the air. London would have a white Christmas after all.

Maggie ate ravenously, then hurried back to the hotel, worrying for some strange reason that everything would be gone, building and all. But no, it was still there, Rafferty at the door, brass-buttoned coat and hat in place.

"Good day, ma'am," he greeted her with a wide smile. "We're delighted t' have you back."

"Has anything happened while I was gone?" She unbuttoned her coat, and glanced around the quiet foyer.

"Aye, the yule tree has arrived. A tall thing it is, and terribly prickly." He pointed to one corner of the lobby. And he was right. The spruce reached all the way to the ceiling, and the bottom branches were wide and sweeping.

"It smells fresh, like the forest," Maggie said. "You must help me decorate it later."

"A pleasure, ma'am," he said, beaming.

Maggie spotted Cecily behind the counter and hurried up to her. "Have you heard anything from Victoria?" she asked instantly, forgetting to greet her assistant.

"My, you are in a dither!" Cecily said, and shuffled the mail. "Here, a card came with the afternoon post."

"Anything else of importance?" Maggie asked as she scanned the governess's neat hand. Her daughter was evidently happy and unhurt at the seaside.

"Is something wrong? You seem awfully tense," Cecily said, studying Maggie's face closely. "And tired."

Maggie decided to tell her friend about her ordeal. "Come with me upstairs for a glass of sherry." As they climbed the steps in the office, Maggie asked, "Any news from Mr. Webb?"

"He came in late yesterday and said he was going to Liverpool. He didn't say why, but he told me he'd probably be back late tonight."

"Will he .. ahem, be staying here, or has he moved back home?" Maggie unlocked her door, finding the movement of the key difficult, as if the lock was jammed.

"He didn't say," Cecily answered, and gasped as Maggie turned up the gaslight. "*Whatever* happened here?"

Maggie's jaw fell as she surveyed the mess in the room. Everything except the furniture had been turned upside down and strewn over the floor.

"What in the world—"

"I will ring the police," Cecily said. "There must have been a break-in here."

Maggie stood as if rooted to the floor. "Wait!" she said. "I need to think."

Cecily stared at her uncomprehendingly. "Think? I'm sure the police must be notified."

Maggie gestured to Cecily to sit down while she viewed the havoc carefully. She went to the tantalus that held her liquor bottles and poured a large measure of sherry for them both.

"Here, drink up. It will calm our nerves."

Cecily was pale as she stared at the mess. "Who would do such a thing?"

"I want you to assemble the staff downstairs in the office. I will speak to them in half an hour, and then we'll notify the police."

"Why?"

"Someone might have seen something unusual, and I want to ask them myself. They'll be too frightened to tell anything to the police." She picked up a chintz-covered letter box from the floor and began stuffing the letters back into it. "I wish Mr. Webb were here."

"What do you think the thief was looking for? Money? Valuables?"

"I don't know." Maggie grimaced as she retrieved another box, this one of leather which had been cut to shreds. "It looks to me like someone has been searching for something in particular." She poked her toe at the cutlery heaped on the hearth rug. "They didn't steal the silver." She walked swiftly into her bedroom and found her jewelry case opened, but none of the pieces were gone.

Cecily stood in the doorway. "It's almost as bad in

here. It's strange, nothing but the boxes you own have been torn apart.''

"I noticed that, too." She sighed. "It all started with the japanned box that disappeared from my office desk." She glanced at her assistant. "Please assemble the employees. They're all still here, aren't they?"

Cecily looked at her watch. "Yes, most of them will be here 'til five." She shook her head in puzzlement as she left.

"I'll be down in half an hour." Maggie was so tired she could hardly imagine she'd stay awake that long. Still, she knew she would be unable to sleep until this mystery was solved.

After washing, she donned a fresh gown of blue wool with a touch of lace at the collar. She recalled the way Thaddeus had fashioned her hair once before and copied the loose arrangement, which felt better than the tight chignon she usually wore. Her longing for Thaddeus sat like a pain in her chest.

Appalled by the chaos in her rooms, she tried not to look at it as she went downstairs.

The servants were lined up in a long row, Cecily at the head with Rafferty, and the rest according to rank. Gertie, the little kitchen maid, stood closest to the door.

Maggie studied the group. Tension hung in the air, and they all stared at her with wide, frightened eyes. They were a hardworking, cheerful lot, and Maggie prayed that none of them had stooped to thievery.

"I called you in here because someone has broken into my rooms." Scrutinizing each face, she marched down the row like a general surveying her soldiers. "The thought that one of you—loyal employees whom I've trusted for years—could have done this to me, makes my heart ache. But, if you confess now, I will let the matter rest without notifying the police. The

ulprit will lose his or her employment, but I promise
will stop at that." She sighed defeatedly.

Silence lay heavy in the room, and they all stared
t her, dumbstruck.

She walked down the row once more, then up. No
ne spoke as she sat down behind her desk, her lips
et in a tight line. "Well? If I report you to the police,
nd you're found guilty, you might hang."

A collective sigh of terror swept through the crowd.
"Ma'am, I didn't do it," Gertie piped up, and started
rying. "Cross my heart."

The others shuffled their feet uneasily, and looked
t each other.

"I believe you." Maggie wanted to cry herself. "It
ll started when the japanned box disappeared. Please
ell me what you know, even if you weren't involved
n the theft of that box."

Paddy, the waiter, stepped forward. "Begorra," he
nuttered softly. "I don't think any of us is guilty,
Mrs. Hartwell. If ye take a look at the key board by
he larder, ye'll find one o' them missin'. The extra
key t' the back door, ma'am."

Maggie gasped and stared at Cecily, "Is this true?"

"I hadn't noticed," the older woman said, wring-
ng her hands.

Maggie's eyes bored into Paddy. "And you didn't
ell me or Miss Byrne?"

Sheepishly he shook his head. "If I did, I would be
suspected of stealin' it since I noticed it."

"I wouldn't have blamed you, Paddy."

The others murmured, everyone now claiming their
nnocence. "I believe you," Maggie said, "I've never
nad any reason not to trust you. But perhaps one of
you saw something unusual, or some strangers hovering?"

The servants shook their heads, and Maggie's hope
was dashed. She wished they could have told her
nore, but at least she'd learned about the key. "Go

back to your chores. But keep your eyes and ears ope
for unfamiliar details—and, Rafferty, keep a clo
watch on strangers entering the hotel lobby.'' Sh
paused. ''Notify me instantly if you find anything
or anyone—where they shouldn't be.''

Relief filled the air as the staff hurried out of th
office. ''You're too soft by far, Maggie,'' said Ceci
with a sad droop in her shoulders. ''I don't kno
how that key could be missing.''

Together they investigated the board which hel
the keys to the wine cellar, larder, and linen close
There were extras for all the doors.

''What shall you do now?'' Cecily went on.

''I shall ring Sergeant Horridge at the Yard.''

Chapter 19

A fter returning from Liverpool, Thaddeus went home to Maddox Street to change clothes. In the parlor, Gavin and a customer were discussing a carved dining room set. "You must see that this would suit your needs perfectly," Thaddeus heard him say.

Thaddeus laughed as he leaped up the stairs two at a time. No one could resist buying when Peg was the seller, he thought. Especially if the customer was female.

Thaddeus tore off his clothes and opened the faucets of his bathtub. He couldn't wait to see Maggie again. It seemed an eternity since he'd last held her in his arms. The spat they'd had was ridiculous, and he would make her see that. They needed each other. He soaked in the bath, enjoying the warmth and relaxation it brought to his limbs.

Half an hour later he'd dried himself and was buttoning his shirt when Gavin knocked on the door and stepped inside.

"Any luck with your investigation?"

"Yes . . . as a matter of fact—"

Gavin interrupted him, "Oh, before I forget, a gentleman was here to see you yesterday. I took an instant dislike to him when he looked down his nose at me and demanded to know your whereabouts."

Gavin snorted and sank down in a leather wing chair. "I told him I didn't know."

Thaddeus frowned. "What did he look like?"

"Tall, frail, blond, with the coldest gray eyes I've ever seen. He was poking his nose into the corner cupboard in the parlor when I happened upon him. I had been talking with Hetty in the kitchen, and didn't hear his knock on the door."

Thaddeus wondered if the visitor could have been Anselm Ripley. Before leaving for Liverpool, he'd made sure Horridge had arranged to have Ripley's house watched.

"Did he wear any striking jewelry?" Thaddeus asked.

Gavin was silent for a long moment. "Now that you mention it, he wore a massive gold ring on his left hand. The stone appeared to be onyx, if I'm not mistaken."

"It must be Ripley," Thaddeus said with a grim smile. "He's after me because I'm investigating Leonora Winston's disappearance."

Gavin pushed back his hair. "How do you know?"

"I can't tell you exactly, but for some reason he doesn't want me to find her." Thaddeus tied his striped ascot and tucked it under the front of his waistcoat. He combed his hair and tested his newly shaven chin. It was soft—for Maggie's lips, he thought with a sudden smile.

"How are you, old friend? Still having a headache after the blow?" he asked Gavin as he shrugged on his tweed jacket.

"No, but there's something strange going on. I feel like this house is being watched." Gavin cursed under his breath. "I don't like it one bit, especially since I seem to have been the recipient of blows meant for you." He rubbed his head. "I prefer my brains intact if you don't mind."

Thaddeus went to the window, pushed aside the

elvet drapes, and stared down at the street. He could ee nothing untoward, and no one was lurking in the ortal across the street. "No one there now."

Gavin went to the door. "If you need help with this ase, let me know. The sooner it's solved the better. Besides, your regular customers at the shop miss your xpert advice." He reached into his pocket. "Here, a messenger brought this from Scotland Yard."

Thaddeus took the envelope and placed his arm round the slighter man's shoulders. "I couldn't have a better friend than you."

Gavin punched him lightly. "Ever since you got involved with Mrs. Hartwell, you haven't been yourself. She's really turned your head."

Thaddeus nodded, his heartbeat quickening. "She has." He patted his coat pocket where he'd slipped he box with his grandmother's ruby engagement ing. "If Maggie will have me, I intend to marry her."

Gavin grinned. "You sly dog! Have you told your amily?"

Thaddeus wound his long black scarf around his neck twice. "Not yet. Can't say anything until Maggie says the word, y'know."

"Are you going to ask her tonight?"

Thaddeus lowered his eyes with sudden shyness. 'Perhaps. But, Gavin, do you think she'll accept a bloke like me? I don't have much to offer except a moderate bank account and odd pieces of antiques."

Gavin laughed. "Probably not, but you won't know until you ask. Go and ask her now, you silly fool." He left the room and closed the door. Thaddeus pulled out the letter. It was from Septimus Horridge.

Thad, old chap,
    I have discovered that Ripley is a close friend of a certain Theodore Fowler-Foss. We've been trying to locate his whereabouts without success, but his last address, a town house at Golden Square, was

deserted, and no one has lived there for years, a
cording to the neighbors. As for the cult rituals y
saw in Richmond, the chance is very slim that th
would be connected to the Altar Murders. We ha
found absolutely nothing to implicate Rupert Merto
His business is legitimate, his connections in Ne
York prestigious. I'd say he dabbles in black magic
like so many others in this day and age. Are you su
you saw a human form on the altar? I'm sorry, bu
have no more time to waste on this case. You mu
work on your own until there's solid evidence. W
have twenty other leads to investigate concerning th
Altar Murders. Your claim is only one of many, so
cannot give you more support.

With a curse, Thaddeus flung the letter onto h
dresser. He hadn't been mistaken. There had been
body ready for sacrifice. He sighed in exasperatio
He'd find proof that Merton and Ripley truly we
involved in the Altar Murders.

His face grim with determination, Thaddeus aime
his steps toward Hartwell's Hotel. Just as soon as he'
seen Maggie, he would continue his work. The cas
was more complicated than he had ever anticipated

He fingered the velvet box in his pocket. Would h
dare to propose after the argument they'd had at the
last meeting? He wanted the event to be extra-specia
Visions of a room full of roses, soft violin music, an
a delicious meal flitted through his mind. How woul
he find a way to set that up without her knowin
about it?

Thaddeus sighed with pleasure. Maggie was
woman in a thousand. She was lovely and warm, in
telligent and kind. Every sterling attribute he admire
belonged to Maggie. Thaddeus, you besotted fool, h
told himself.

It was snowing heavily by now, and the win

whipped around the street corners. He clutched the
box with the ring, and then the idea came to him. He
would hire a room at the Savoy and set up the proposal celebration there. The staff would arrange everything, and the only thing he would have to do
was to ask Maggie out to dinner. But what if she said
no . . . ? He would have to take that risk. She was an
independent woman, and he'd goaded her beyond
endurance.

When he arrived at the hotel, he was surprised to
find a blue-uniformed bobby standing beside Rafferty
at the door.

"Good evening, Larry," Thaddeus greeted the
policeman. "What are you doing here?"

The bobby lifted two fingers to the rim of his hel-
met. "Evening, Mr. Webb. A matter of business. Sergeant Horridge is inside with Mrs. Hartwell."

Thaddeus didn't wait to ask more questions but ran
inside, through the foyer, and up the stairs to Maggie's private rooms. The doors stood wide open, and
Horridge, along with another bobby, was on his knees
in the middle of an incredible mess. White-faced, her
lips pinched together, Maggie was standing by the
bedroom door. He hadn't expected such a frightful
turn of events.

She lifted her gaze to his, then flew across the room.
"Oh, Thaddeus!" she cried, throwing herself into his
arms.

Warmed by her welcome, he hugged her tightly.
"I've missed you sorely, darling." He looked at her
pale face, but she held her eyes clamped shut as if in
pain.

"What happened here?" he asked, inhaling the familiar, sweet fragrance of her hair.

"Someone broke in." She pulled him inside, and
he stepped gingerly among the rubble of Maggie's
belongings.

Sergeant Horridge looked up from his task of sort-

ing through the debris. "Hello, Thad. It looks like
regular break-in, but Mrs. Hartwell insists that noth
ing was stolen."

"Except the back door key, but I don't know whe
it was taken," Maggie said. "I realize you have to as
my staff some questions, but they swore no one ha
taken the key—or perpetrated the break-in." He
voice trembled. "And I trust them. Nothing like thi
has ever happened before."

"Could one of the guests have taken the key?"

"Well . . . it's possible, but they usually don't g
into the kitchen area where the keys are hanging."

Thaddeus lifted the tattered chintz-covered box. "I
seems this person is especially interested in boxes."

"That's what I noticed," Maggie said. "It all starte
with the japanned box I told you about when we firs
met."

Thaddeus thought about boxes and Anselm Ripley
Was there a connection?

"Let's go into your bedroom," Thaddeus said t
Maggie. "I need to speak with you."

They went inside and closed the door. Sitting or
the bed, Thaddeus pulled Maggie down beside him
and held her hand. "I'm sorry for the argument w
had last time," he said.

Her lips quivered. "*I'm* the one who should apol
ogize," she said. "I was too hard on you."

"Anyway, I have some good news. Since w
parted, I went to Liverpool to discover if someon
actually saw your sister disembark, and I spoke witl
a porter who carried her bags to a waiting cab." He
paused. "The reason that Horridge could find no trac
of your sister was because this porter was ill at the
time of the inquiry, and he's the only person at the
steamship dock who remembers her."

Maggie leaned against him and slid her arm
around his waist. "But where is she now?"

"The porter said there were three men in the hack

ney waiting for her. They were talking with her, arguing, but the porter couldn't hear the words."

Maggie drew in her breath sharply. "It's strange. I went up to Sheffield to discover if Leonora traveled there instead of London. While the train stopped at Nottingham, I was abducted by two men, one of them the man who followed me from Robinson's the day I ended up at Maddox Street." She told Thaddeus about the rest of her trip and her meeting with her uncle.

"I managed to escape from the cottage." She thought for a while, furrowing her brow. "I have no idea how long they planned to keep me. No one was there to guard me. There was no food, no extra firewood, and they returned the next morning—perhaps to collect me. They were not out to rob me since they left my handbag with me, and I carried quite a large sum of money for the trip."

"What was your uncle doing in Sheffield?"

Maggie sighed. "Who knows? The man has revolutionary ideas—plans—which he insists will eventually change the world. But whatever wild ideas he has, he's still rather a quaint man, always polite." She smiled. "I rather fancy an eccentric in the family."

The memory of the robed men at Richmond flashed through Thaddeus's mind, but he didn't want to voice his suspicion that Rupert Merton was involved. She seemed to have a real soft spot for the man—understandable, given her strong family feelings—and he oughtn't say anything until he had proof. Besides, Merton had had plenty of opportunities to harm Maggie if he'd wanted to, so she was probably safe from him. The problem was, what was the connection between Merton and Ripley and Leonora Winston? Why had Miss Winston disappeared and Maggie been abducted? Did the two sisters have something that Merton and Ripley wanted?

"I don't like this one bit," Thaddeus said grimly. "I'd like to take you away from here until this is solved."

"Unthinkable!" Maggie said. "I have to arrange your sister's wedding reception on Christmas Eve, and the usual Christmas dinners. Besides, we have to decorate the hotel."

"Can't the staff take care of that?"

"They will, but I have to make sure it gets done. Anyway, I like to decorate the yule tree with Victoria."

"Victoria should not be here now."

"I know. I just sent Miss Lather a telegram and asked her to stay a bit longer and return on Christmas Eve. That gives us three more days."

"Good." He tilted her chin and studied her vulnerable mouth, now relaxed. A wild urge to kiss her came over him, making him think about the ring in his pocket, but a knock interrupted their moment of intimacy.

Maggie opened the door for Sergeant Horridge. "I can't find any more clues here," he said. "Are you sure nothing is missing, Mrs. Hartwell?"

Maggie gestured toward her open jewel case. "Not a thing. I don't have very valuable jewelry, but I daresay a thief could have pawned it and gotten a few pounds if he was desperate."

The sergeant shook his head. "It's most puzzling. It doesn't look like the work of a regular thief to me. No, more like someone tore your things apart in a fit of rage."

Maggie paled even more, and clutched the door frame. Thaddeus hurried across the room to steady her. "That's enough, Septimus. You're frightening Mrs. Hartwell." He told Horridge about Maggie's ordeal in Nottingham and the sergeant whistled through his teeth.

"Do you think there's a connection?" Thaddeus continued.

Horridge rubbed his chin in thought. "Possibly. Someone might have wanted Mrs. Hartwell away from the hotel while he, or she, searched through her things."

"But why?" Maggie whispered. "I have no enemies."

"There might be someone from your past," the sergeant said. "Think about it. In the meanwhile, I will continue the investigation into your sister's disappearance. If she didn't return to America on another steamer, she must be somewhere on this island.

"I will see myself out." He put his bowler hat on his head and ambled out the door.

"I'll help you clean this mess up," Thaddeus offered as Maggie's shoulders slumped. He gathered all the scattered papers and letters and put them in neat bundles on the table for Maggie to sort through. She discarded the broken items and fetched a large empty cardboard box from the storage room, in which she stacked the rest.

"What's going to happen now?" she asked.

"I'll keep Ripley under close watch. He'll eventually lead us to the center of this problem, and there, I think, we'll find your sister."

Maggie's hands were still. "Dead or alive, I wonder?"

Thaddeus didn't dare voice his fear that Leonora Winston had been the human form on the altar at Richmond.

It was late evening before they had finished the cleanup. "I'm glad I decided to spend the night at the hotel," he said. "Is my room still available?" He was hesitant to ask to share her bed when she was so upset.

"Yes . . . yes, of course. I believe some of your clothes are still here." She blushed, then dropped her gaze. He seemed to sense her thoughts of their shared nights.

"Maggie, I'd like to take you out to dinner tomorrow night," he said, not wanting to delay his proposal any longer. He couldn't very well keep crawling into her bed without offering her his name. "At the Savoy."

She gasped. "The Savoy?"

"Yes, I thought we deserved some time away from all the horrifying events. I want the evening to be very special for us."

She raised her gaze to his, and he could read the question, the shyness there. As he enfolded her in his arms, he hoped she understood what surprise was on his mind.

Chapter 20

Maggie spent the next day decorating the hotel with the rest of the staff. She had to do something to keep her mind off her sister's fate and the other mystifying occurrences. As time moved on leaden feet, she wound garlands of spruce around the mantelpieces and the doors in the dining rooms, and placed armfuls of holly in shiny copper urns. But she didn't have the Christmas spirit, especially with Victoria gone. Her daughter loved to help place the flags and the paper angels in the yule tree. Maggie glanced at the bare tree in the corner, and decided she would save it for last. She placed a basket of Christmas crackers on the counter. The crackers opened with a bang. Each contained a sweet and a motto. They were the children's favorite treat.

Cecily was polishing a silver candelabra that would hold four red wax candles and sit on the front desk on a red embroidered tablecloth. When the telephone rang, Cecily answered it, then called out to Maggie, "It's for you. Your uncle."

Maggie held the earpiece to her ear. "Uncle Rupert?"

"Margaret, I'm so glad I got hold of you."

There was such terrible static on the line that Maggie could barely hear him. "Is something wrong? You sound ill."

"I caught a horrid cold in Sheffield. My business partner, who lives in Richmond, insisted that I stay with him. I wonder if you could pack some of my things and bring them out here. Besides, my partner would like you to stay for dinner."

"Today? But I have other plans . . ."

"Is it possible?" His voice turned pleading. "I'm in bed, and the doctor advised me to stay prostrate for three days, or until the fever goes down." He coughed, and Maggie felt a twinge of compassion.

"You'd better heed the doctor. This cold, wet weather might give you pneumonia." Maggie sighed and looked at her watch. It was getting dark outside, but she could easily catch the Underground line to Richmond at Victoria station. "I'll be glad to come. Do you want anything special packed?"

"My books, and two changes of clothes."

Maggie hung up, and went to the attic. Her uncle's trunk, along with an empty carpetbag, were stacked in one corner. She found some shirts neatly folded and, on the bottom of the first box, two books. She noticed that they were about Oriental religion, and one had some charts she didn't understand. Placing everything into the carpetbag, she returned to her office.

She glanced at her watch again, planning to go out to Richmond right after tea. After ordering a tray in her rooms, she climbed the stairs. The maids had cleaned and polished everything so that no trace was left after the break-in. The rooms looked almost impersonal in their neatness.

A knock sounded, and Thaddeus stuck his head inside. "May I enter?"

"Thaddeus! I'm so glad to see you," Maggie said, smiling. His cheerful presence was exactly what she'd been missing all day. The surroundings that, before, had seemed colorless and bleak took on a rosy hue.

He caught her in his arms. "Remember that dinner I promised you at the Savoy?"

She nodded and clasped his waist tightly, never wanting to let him go.

"Well, they don't have any private dining rooms except for tonight. They'll be fully booked until after Christmas, and I wouldn't want to wait that long for an evening alone with you," he murmured. As she stiffened in his arms, he added, "I know it's short notice, but you didn't have any other plans, I hope."

"It won't work," she said. "Uncle Rupert called. He's ill, staying at his business partner's house. I promised to deliver some things to him, and his partner wants me to stay for dinner."

Thaddeus groaned, thinking of the ring burning a hole in his pocket. "No . . . can't it wait? Merton isn't dying, is he?"

"No, but I promised, and, though he wouldn't say it, I think he needs my support."

"Please . . ." Thaddeus begged, kissing her hair. He couldn't bear the thought of having to wait to propose until after Christmas.

Glaring, Maggie pulled away. "Don't pressure me! I won't break my promise to a sick uncle."

Thaddeus crossed his arms over his chest. "So he's more important than I am, is that it?" How could he tell her he abhorred the idea of her spending time with her shady uncle, who could very well be involved in Miss Winston's disappearance, not to mention the Altar Murders?

"That was childish," she said, drawing herself up. Her magnificent eyes sparkled with anger, and Thaddeus's heartbeat quickened. God, she was lovely . . .

"Can I accompany you then? Perhaps we could have a late supper together later."

"No, you weren't invited. Besides, I don't know how long it will take. Our tête-à-tête must be postponed, Thaddeus." She opened her wardrobe and flipped through the dresses on the hangers. "What would be appropriate to wear to a dinner?'' she murmured.

She chose a green velvet dress with short puff sleeves, a tight bodice with a wide lace collar, and a flaring gored skirt. A velvet sash of contrasting green accompanied the outfit, along with long green gloves.

Thaddeus thought of ways to detain her. He couldn't just ignore his suspicions. What if something happened to Maggie while she visited her uncle, and he wasn't there to protect her? He couldn't stop the stupid words before they slipped from his lips. ''You cannot go, Maggie. I forbid it. I can't prove anything just yet, but I believe your uncle might be involved in your sister's disappearance.'' He couldn't mention the Altar Murders. Not only would she think the idea preposterous, but Merton was her uncle, the lost family she'd never had. ''Your life might be in danger, not just your possessions.''

There was a flicker of fear in her eyes, but he instantly noticed the mulish set of her chin. She pushed past him when he blocked the path to her dressing table.

''What makes you believe my uncle—? Why should he—'' She refused to look him in the eyes as dismay filled her. She'd been so pleased to have found Uncle Rupert, and now, Thaddeus had poisoned her happiness.

He sank down on the bed. ''Number one, he came to the hotel at exactly the same time Leonora was expected. Mere coincidence? It's difficult to believe.'' He gave her a beseeching glance. ''Number two, he and Anselm Ripley wear the exact same type of ring, the scarab, if you recall. Another coincidence?''

''It's possible,'' she countered. After brushing out her hair, she put the hairbrush on top of her dressing table.

He nodded. ''Yes, but such coincidences are seldom innocent. I don't know his reasons, but he might have abducted Leonora—then you, because he's looking for something, perhaps something of value that is connected to his past and yours."

"It's only conjecture," she said defensively.

He sighed. How could he mention his conviction that Merton was involved in the Altar Murders without completely alienating her? To prevent her from going he was hard pressed to tell her. If only he had proof. "It might be supposition on my part, but you should heed my warning. I fear Anselm Ripley might be involved in the . . . the Altar Murders." He held his breath as he walked toward her, and placed his hands on her shoulders. "What if I'm right?"

"Altar Murders? No, no! My uncle and Ripley?" She refused to believe such awful things about her uncle. "They started happening before Uncle Rupert arrived in England."

"He might have been here much longer than you know."

Maggie averted her face. "I pray you won't criticize my uncle any more. I'm prepared to overlook a few odd quirks in his character, and I cannot believe he arrived here to put my life in danger." She snorted. "That's absurd,, Thaddeus! He has always been friendly and treated me with utmost politeness. He's the only family besides Victoria that I have, and I mean to be loyal—like you would be loyal to your family—unless you can prove that I'm wrong." Her voice faltered. "I hope to God that you can't."

Without another word, he gripped her arms and hauled her to him. He crushed her against his chest and caught her lips with his, overwhelming her with his kiss until she went limp in his arms. Then he eased the pressure and reveled in the softness of her mouth and the moist sweetness of her tongue. The same weakness he always felt when holding her in his arms came over him.

"Oh . . . Maggie . . ." he whispered against her ear as he managed to tear himself free from the intoxicating kiss. She was so soft and yielding, and he squeezed her closer. Her heartbeat was as rapid as his. She struggled feebly to get away, but soon gave up.

"Darling," he continued, tasting the soft flesh at the base of her throat. "Arguing about your uncle is madness." Her scent made his head spin and his loins tighten in anticipation. He held one rounded breast in his hand, and cursed the stiff corset that prevented him from exploring her better.

"No . . ." she moaned. "I don't have time for this." She wriggled out of his grip, and he felt shockingly bereft. Crestfallen, he watched her cross the room and pull her gown from the hanger.

He felt the velvet box containing the ruby ring in his pocket. An urgency filled him, fear that he would lose her if he didn't propose now. He couldn't let this moment slip by.

"Maggie, come here," he said urgently, holding out his hand toward her. "This is important."

She gave him a penetrating glance, then crossed to him. He couldn't remember a time he'd felt shyer as he led her toward the ottoman in the corner. Bewilderment evident in her eyes, she sat down, and he slid down onto one knee. Dragging his hands over her thighs and hips, he circled her waist and looked deeply into her eyes.

"Maggie, dearest, will you be my wife?" His breath rasping in his throat, he lifted the box toward her and flipped open the lid. The ruby gleamed richly against the black velvet.

Her eyes widened, and her cheeks paled. Maggie thought her heart would stop at the exquisite thrill that shot through her. She couldn't keep her lips from trembling, nor could she halt the gathering of tears in her eyes. They ran in two rivulets down her cheeks, and he gently lifted her glasses and held his handkerchief against the flow.

"I love you more than I can say," he said, his voice hoarse with emotion.

She nodded and her voice was thick with tears as she said, "Yes, I accept. Gladly."

Hands fumbling, he pulled out the ring from its velvet bed and tried it on her ring finger. It fitted perfectly, the ruby glowing against her pale skin.

"It's as if it was made for you," he said, smiling. "It belonged to my grandmother—the one who knitted my black scarf."

"It's lovely," she said, admiring it.

"I wanted it to be a perfect moment at the Savoy, after a delicious meal."

She caressed his hair. "Nothing could be more perfect than the actual moment of you asking me, wherever or whenever."

He held her waist and pulled her close, burying his face between her breasts. "I never thought it possible to feel this strongly about any woman," he murmured. "It's all-consuming—"

"Bell-ringing," she said wryly, and looked down into his eyes. "Angel chorus."

With a low growl he rose and pulled her up to him, then held her face between both his hands. "I was afraid you wouldn't accept."

"And I feared you would never ask." As if in a trance, she lifted her lips to his. Her love soared through her, in a dizzying, delicious swoop of rapture. He pulled his hands through her hair and kissed her tenderly.

She felt vulnerable with her hair down, and even more disarmed when he undid the cloth-covered buttons of her blouse and spread it open.

His eyes dark wells of desire, he pushed the blouse from her shoulders, and she shivered delicately, her stomach tightening with yearning.

"Maggie, look at me," he asked as he unfastened the steel clasps of her corset, and closed his hands around her breasts which were now covered only by the thin silk shift. "I want to see the desire in your eyes."

Shyly, she lifted her gaze to his, and gasped at the tenderness tempered with raw longing she saw in his brown eyes.

He caressed her breasts. "Peaches," he whispered, and bent his head to take one turgid nipple into his mouth through the shift. "Ripe, rosy peaches." He suckled her, and she could barely stand as a hot wave of craving crashed through her. She fumbled with the buttons of his waistcoat and shirt, tossing aside the ascot.

Greedily, she dug her fingertips into the thick mat of hair on his chest, and breathed in his warm, masculine odor. His lemony cologne enticed her senses.

"You smell like a summer meadow, but your skin is like something forbidden, dangerous, wholly intoxicating," he said. "And your form . . . there are no words fine enough to describe its perfection."

"Are you trying to turn my head, Mr. Webb?"

"Well, fair is fair, because you've already turned mine." He kissed her shoulders and undid the hooks of her waistband. Her skirt puddled around her ankles and he lifted her petticoats over her head. The last one, lace-edged silk, got tangled in her hair, and she laughed.

Groaning with desire as her curves were revealed through the whisper-thin shift, he lifted her up, her head still swathed in white silk. She sighed in pleasure as he laid her down on the bed and ran his hands over her enchanting body. Her shift slid erotically up until a tuft of red-gold hair was visible at the joining of her thighs. He nipped her there and slid his tongue rapidly between the folds before she could protest. Instead, her thighs widened in welcome. Such a shaft of desire drove through him when he viewed her most secret place that he could barely stop himself from invading her tempting wetness right then and there.

He closed his eyes momentarily, and gritted his teeth in self-control before kissing her inner lips again.

She emerged from the hampering petticoat and flung it aside. His tongue's movements created the most exquisite torture within her. She arched against him again and again, seeking release from the sweet, ever-mounting wave building between her legs and radiating to every corner of her being. His muscles tensed as he hugged her thighs, and he was taut as a bowstring when he slid up the length of her body. His weight crushed her against the mattress, but she embraced his body and tantalized him by rotating her hips until the tip of his hard shaft was at the opening from where her dulcet ache stemmed.

She cried out in pleasure as he entered. He pushed himself into her with tantalizing slowness until she was squirming urgently beneath him. His face set, his eyes burning with desire, he began to move inside her, bringing her to the edge of ecstatic insanity.

"Damn," he swore hoarsely and arched against her, biting down on his bottom lip. "I can't hold back."

She bucked, wiggling from under him and pushing him over on his back. Straddling him, she rode him as he kneaded her breasts, until she crested into a shuddering cry of ecstasy. He gripped her hips and pounded into her, calling out her name as a rapturous release swept through him.

Satiated, she lay down on his stomach, still cradling him inside her. He bunched up her hair which shielded him from the world like a heavy curtain.

"I want it again," he said, kissing her slender neck, "And again . . . and again . . ."

She straightened her legs and lay completely on top of him. He bent his head forward and kissed her love-ruised lips.

Her eyes were slumberous after their lovemaking. "What's stopping you?"

"Siren," he replied fondly, wondering if a man could die from too much love.

Chapter 21

Maggie thought she was gliding on clouds as she grasped her uncle's carpetbag and waited in the lobby while Rafferty hailed a hansom cab for her. Thaddeus was still asleep upstairs, and she had washed and dressed without him noticing that she was gone. Better to do this than have some heated argument about her decision to go out. He had a tendency to be autocratic, and she had no desire to bend to his every whim. Before he'd come into her life, she had been perfectly capable of taking care of herself. And yet . . . his concern warmed her heart, and, as he had said, there was something sinister afoot. But how could he suspect Uncle Rupert of perpetrating the most hideous killings in London?

The snowfall had stopped, and the ground was soggy with slush. No picture-book Christmas in London this season. The wind had grown bitter cold, and Maggie shivered, although she was wearing her heaviest coat with fur lining and a hood. Her boots were warm, and on her hands were knitted mittens that Miss Lather had given her for Christmas last year.

"There's one now," Rafferty said, waving at the cabby whose eyes were barely discernible above his muffler. The hansom stopped on the opposite side of the street, and Maggie climbed inside. "Victoria station, and hurry," she ordered through the window.

What was the address Uncle Rupert had given her? She took off one mitten and searched her handbag, although the intermittent light from the gas lamps was hardly strong enough to read anything. Frowning, she pulled out everything, purse, comb, handkerchief, keys, hairpins, and a pencil. No address. She clearly remembered writing it down on the pad beside the telephone, but she had most likely forgotten to tuck the paper into her handbag. Thinking hard, she remembered the street, Sparrow Lane. But was the number 544 or 542?

"You idiot!" she chided herself. Should she return and risk an argument with Thaddeus? No, better not. She might see something that would show her to the right house in Richmond, and if she happened to knock on the wrong door, she could always apologize. Filled with a sense of well-being, she thought of Thaddeus and twirled the ring on her finger. Mrs. Margaret Webb, she mused, or Mrs. Thaddeus Webb. Both sounded fine, and she already missed his smile and his embrace.

Thaddeus had awakened the moment Maggie closed the door to the bedroom. "Damn!" he swore and swept aside the bed covers. Viewing his naked ness, he realized he couldn't very well rush out afte her. Why did she have to run off to her uncle? She was too trusting, that was why.

He dragged on his clothes in a frenzy and tied hi ascot willy-nilly. After a cursory pull of Maggie's brush through his hair, he flung on his overcoat and ran dow the stairs, just in time to see the hansom leave.

"Was that Mrs. Hartwell?" he asked Rafferty "Where was she going?"

"No idea, sir. Said she would visit her uncle. Live in Cavendish Square now, doesn't he?"

Thaddeus nodded and hurried outside. He woul have to catch up with her. As she had done when h started the investigation, he would force himself on her, demanding to accompany her.

Panting, he ran along the street to keep up with the hansom. Since the traffic was scarce at this time of night, the carriage moved at a good clip. Thaddeus clenched his teeth, refusing to let the cab out of his sight. When another hansom came along, he waved forcefully until it stopped.

"Wot's yer 'urry?" the jarvey asked with a cackle. "Got fire in yer be'ind?"

"Don't let that hansom out of your sight," Thaddeus ordered, and jumped inside. "It will be a few bob extra for you if you don't lose it."

The jarvey began whistling a shrill tune, and Thaddeus realized the wizened man had warmed himself excessively with some brandy bottle hidden somewhere in his voluminous clothing.

Rubbing his chin in consternation, Thaddeus noticed that Maggie's carriage didn't make the turn to Cavendish Square. She wasn't going to Rupert Merton's house after all.

But where was she headed? To his surprise, the hansom turned down Regent Street, and drove in the gathering fog to Piccadilly, and then west to Hyde Park corner. Thoroughly puzzled, he watched as it traveled the length of Grosvenor Place to Victoria railway station. Where was she going?

"Stop some distance behind the other hansom," he ordered the jarvey who was now singing enthusiastically to himself, and stepped down. He paid the fare, adding a generous tip.

Gaslight streamed through the portals of the station, and Thaddeus stepped inside the huge echoing waiting hall. There was no sign of Maggie. He scanned the area rapidly. He had recognized the ostrich feather of her black hat as she had stepped down from her cab, but it was nowhere to be seen at the moment. He pushed through the thinning crowd, his gaze darting from one woman to the next.

A train whistle blared and, too late, he realized that she might have jumped onto a train that was part of the Underground line. Its end station was Richmond. He must have just missed her in the throng, since she wasn't to be found on the platforms. How had that happened? Had she seen him and stayed hidden? He watched as the train left the depot, then stalked up to the only open ticket window.

"Did you see a young woman with red-blonde hair, spectacles, and a black hat with a plume?"

The hunch-shouldered old man nodded. "Aye, she was just here. Bought a ticket to Richmond, round-trip."

"Give me the same," Thaddeus said grimly. "When's the next train?"

"In an hour."

Thaddeus paid and wandered amidst the crowd, clutching the ticket. *Richmond?* Why was she going there? A sensation of doom swept through him. If Rupert Merton was involved in the altar slayings, there was no guarantee that Maggie wouldn't be the next victim. Would she be the person to lead him back to the house where he was attacked? He had an overpowering urge to protect her, but if she found out that he'd followed her, she would be furious.

Cold sweat trickled along his spine at the thought of Maggie walking into danger. While he waited, he decided to send Septimus Horridge a message. He wondered what to write as he hauled out a lead pencil and an old envelope from his pocket.

The station house was emptying. Gentlemen in bowler hats were reading the papers, and some country females from the vegetable market were carrying baskets of rutabagas and parsnips. They were red-faced from being out in the cold all day, and neither mittens nor threadbare coats could conceal their discomfort. Two urchins darted past Thaddeus where he was sitting on a bench beside the tracks, and he decided to trust one of them with a shilling and the message. There simply was no time to hire another messenger.

He scribbled a note for the sergeant to meet him at the Richmond station as soon as possible. Another train entered the depot, letting off a cloud of steam and a hiss.

Thaddeus grabbed one of the urchins rushing by, and stared down at the pale, gaunt face and stringy hair. "Want to earn a shilling?" he asked.

"A whole bob?" the urchin asked, round-eyed.

"Yes . . . but you must promise to deliver this message to Sergeant Horridge at the Yard."

"I ain't goin' there," the urchin said, his chin jutting.

"For a bob you will. If the sergeant isn't there, give this to one of the constables and tell him it's from Mr. Webb. Most urgent."

The urchin eyed the shiny coin in Thaddeus's hand and pulled his grimy cap down low over his eyes. He licked his lips in anticipation of the food the money would buy.

"Arright, then." He grabbed the message and the coin, and was out of the building so fast that Thaddeus blinked in surprise.

"Septimus might never see that," Thaddeus mused to himself, "but at least the lad gets a good meal tonight."

He was startled out of his reverie as the engine hissed again. He glanced at his watch; forty minutes before the train would leave. Hopefully, he would catch up with Maggie in Richmond, but he doubted it. After buying a newspaper, he jumped into the first railroad car to wait for its departure. He spread open the paper, but he couldn't concentrate on the news. Tapping his fingers on the windowsill, he waited, glancing every five minutes at his watch. Just before the train was about to leave, Sergeant Horridge flung open the door and jumped inside. "What's going on?"

"I believe Maggie Hartwell will lead us to the altar murderers," Thaddeus said grimly. He drew a sigh of relief as the train finally jerked forward with a piercing whistle. He hoped he wouldn't be too late.

Richmond, a sleepy, ancient town on the outskirts of London, was pitch-black as the train stopped. Only a few gaslights dotted the lanes and Maggie saw that it had started to snow again.

She got off, holding her head down against the blast of icy wind welcoming her. Three other passengers got off, and struggled beside her toward the station building.

"Excuse me," she said, "but can you advise me as to the location of Sparrow Lane?"

The lady, who was holding the hand of a young boy, smiled. "Yes, 'tis right around the corner from here. Go the length of this road, past the gardens and the park, and counting five gas lamps, turn left, and then another right—Sparrow Lane. Won't take you but ten minutes to walk there."

Maggie was relieved to hear that, since there were no hansoms waiting outside the station. She would have to trudge through the snow that was gathering rapidly into banks against the hedges. The fog which had hung over London was not yet covering Richmond. She walked from one light to the next viewing the tall brick mansions behind their hedges. Richmond was the wealthy merchants' and doctors' paradise. They built their dignified homes outsid London, where they stashed their wives and children, while spending more time at their town club than at home.

Maggie found Sparrow Lane without difficulty. The street had even fewer lights than the others, but she could make out five houses along it. She read the numbers on the wrought-iron gates; 544, and beside it, 542.

Peering through the bars, she tried to figure out which was the right house. Both of them looked dark, but the lights might be burning on the opposite side of the house. Straightening her back, she stepped up the paved path leading to the door of the first residence. In the gloom, she found the knocker. After the hollow bangs had died down, the stillness around her was eerie. She wished she had listened to Thaddeus's advice and accepted his company.

There was no sound of footsteps so she lifted the knocker again. It thudded dully, the sound reverberating inside. No one was at home. She glanced at the dark facade, wondering if the other house was the one she sought. Through the hedge, she could see a flickering light in the basement area. Someone was at home there.

Shivering, she walked back out to the street, and up the gravel path to the next house. It was set farther back, the approach lined with evergreen bushes and trees. There was no light at the front. One would think that someone expecting guests would leave the light on outside, she thought.

"Please be the right address," she whispered, unenhusiastic about investigating every house on the street.

It had a knocker just like the house next door. She let it fall hard three times, vowing she wouldn't leave until someone opened the door. As she stood there staring at the wood, she realized that a weak light was coming through a crack. The door was ajar. Perhaps her uncle was too ill to let her in. But where was his friend? Worried, she nudged the door open.

A strange, sweet odor reached her nostrils, an aroma that was curiously familiar. Where had she smelled it before? The house was hot inside, and light came from below the stairs curving past an open door at the end of the hallway. She stepped into the foyer, uncertain what to do. Waiting, she hoped someone had heard her knock.

"Anyone at home?" she called out, but the house was shrouded in silence. A room was to her left, a parlor of some sort. All she could see was the shapes of heavy furniture and drapes. In the feeble light she noted that the predominant color was red, even the walls in the hallway. There was nothing unusual in that, but it gave the house an oppressive atmosphere.

As far as she could tell, this wasn't a place where Rupert's partner would have his dinner party, or was it? Strange. There were no smells of dinner cooking, nor the chatter of guests. She turned as if to leave, when she heard a noise.

It sounded like a high moan, voiced by an animal in pain. Frozen to the spot, Maggie listened for more sounds, but there were none. Something propelled her toward the light, an urge to relieve that pain. Was there a sick dog in an otherwise empty house? She couldn't stand to see animals suffer if she could help it.

Another groan made her hair stand on end, and she clutched the door frame which separated the hall-way from a set of stairs. To her surprise, she noticed that the light came from a smoking flambeau in a holder on the wall. How barbaric, and how hazard-ous. The wall of the basement was made of stone, but nevertheless there were flammable materials close by. The torch filled the passage below with smoke, and it stung Maggie's eyes.

Another moan came, weaker now. Then there was a sudden babble of voices, and Maggie grew icy with fear. She knew if she had any sense, she should turn around right now, but something held her back, a nagging suspicion at the back of her mind, a thought which had to be taken through to its end. She had overlooked something all this time since Leonora's disappearance, and she suspected that she now had reached the heart of the matter.

Her legs trembling, she took a step downward, then another. The sweet, sickly odor grew stronger with every move, and she blinked against the irritating smoke. As she neared the bottom, the air was hotter and filled with strange sibilant sounds, a thousand whispers. The light changed as she drew closer to the end of the passage. Now it flickered red, a bright crimson that reminded her of blood.

Pressing herself close to the wall, she breathed deeply to control her terror. What was she afraid of? She had entered a house belonging to strangers, and they would throw her out when they discovered her presence. What in the world had induced her to step inside?

The voices rose and fell as if chanting a rhyme. What were they saying? She advanced three steps, then another two, until she could touch the door frame if she stretched out her hand. The pungent odor of incense hung more heavily in the air, and the torches popped and flickered in their brackets.

She couldn't understand the words, with the voices rising into a wild babble. Afraid, yet unable to leave, she stepped forward until she could peer around the corner. Her eyes widened in shock as she eyed the strange scene before her. Hooded figures swayed back and forth to the sound. They wore robes of different colors, silver and gold and black. In the middle was an altar, and the tallest form behind it was robed in scarlet velvet with an odd sign embroidered in gold thread on his chest. Due to the tallness of the swaying forms, Maggie surmised they were men. This must have been the ritual Thaddeus had seen. An opium hookah stood among a scattering of cushions on the floor. She had seen pictures of such things before.

The man in red lifted both his arms, the voluminous sleeves sliding back, exposing his pale, sinewy forearms. He held something in his hand, and as the hand shifted, a steel blade was revealed by the reflection of the many red candles burning in branched candlesticks at the four corners of the altar.

Maggie almost screamed when she saw the still shape on the altar. A woman with long, blonde hair was lying almost naked on the red cloth of the shrine, her arms folded over her chest, her hands clasped as if in prayer. She was wearing only a thigh-length shift and a pair of lace-up boots. Her face was deathly white, and Maggie saw that her eyes were open, staring in mindless terror at the blade that glittered above her head. Clearly she was too frightened to even try to escape.

Maggie knew that the robed man was going to plunge the dagger into the woman's heart. A strange, unbearable tension mounted as the babbling voices increased in volume. Maggie glanced around frantically for some weapon. She couldn't bear to watch the woman die without at least trying to help her.

At the opposite end of the passage, she noticed some three-gallon glass bottles with cork stoppers on a shelf. Focused only on aiding the victim, she partly forgot her fear, although her limbs seemed increasingly sluggish as she ran along the corridor. Her hands trembling, she pulled the cork out of the first bottle, and sniffed, instantly recognizing the heavy odor of lamp oil. The other bottles also contained oil, and she hoisted two of them, one under each arm. Panting under the load, she prayed she would be in time.

Without hesitating, she set down one bottle and gripped the other with both hands and stepped across the threshold just as the voices were rising to a crescendo.

"Stop!" she shouted as loudly as she could.

The chanting came to an abrupt halt, and the robed

men turned their faces toward her. All she could see
of their features were the eyes that glittered fanati-
cally from the slits in their hoods. Something golden
glimmered on the hand that held the dagger, and
Maggie recognized that ring in a flash; it was the onyx
scarab that her uncle wore. "Maggie," he hissed.

Thaddeus had been right about her uncle . . . "Let her
go!" Maggie demanded hoarsely, almost dropping
the bottle from sheer fright. Instead, she heaved it
over her head and across the room. It landed against
the altar and shattered. Oil splattered over everything, and glass shards rained to the floor. The
woman on the altar screamed in terror, and Maggie
snatched up the other bottle and hurled it after the
first. The floor gleamed wetly with the oil that now
soaked into the hems of the robes and the carpet in
front of the altar.

The men began to advance slowly toward her, and
the woman on the altar was struggling against the
red-robed man's grip on her arm.

Maggie thought she was lost, but she grabbed the
nearest torch, which sat right next to the door, and
held it inside the room.

"If you don't let her go I will throw this torch, and
you'll all go up in flames. You won't be able to save
your robes from igniting instantly."

Was that high-pitched, trembling voice really hers?
She breathed shallowly, believing she would crumple
any second. Every fiber of her being seemed to be
unraveling slowly, and she braced herself against the
door frame as the men stared at her, unmoving. They
could reach her within seconds, but she could throw
the torch faster. She sensed they feared a fire that,
even if they escaped, would surely burn down the
house.

Maggie stared unblinkingly as the woman slowly
rose from the altar. Her hair was streaming around
her, the candlelight flickering over her deathly-white

skin. She stumbled as she slid once on the oil, but steadily gained control over her legs. Her face glistened with tears, and her eyes were dilated with shock. There was something familiar about her, the blonde hair . . . the chin . . .

Maggie waved the torch over her head to remind the men of her threat. The woman reached the door, her chest heaving in dry sobs. She seemed lost to the world.

"Run outside!" Maggie ordered fiercely. "Now!"

The woman scrambled up the stairs, her sobs increasing now that she was so close to freedom.

Maggie could not tear her eyes from the scene in front of her. It was straight out of a nightmare. How would she get away? As soon as she turned around, they would pounce. Her only hope was to run faster.

She took one step back, then another, and the men advanced an equal distance. Her gaze flickered to the door, and with a desperate last action, she whirled and slammed the door in the faces of the men. Bracing herself against it, she dropped the torch on the floor. Relief darted through her when she saw the key was in the door. She turned it, and the lock clicked into place at the exact moment the men launched themselves against the barrier.

The torch forgotten on the floor, Maggie ran up the stairs and out of the house. Without a glance behind her, she sprinted to the lane. She heard the crash of the door breaking as she reached the gate. The blonde woman stood huddled in the shadow of the hedge, waiting.

"Don't just stand there! Run!" Maggie shouted, noticing that the lady had wrapped something around herself. Thank God for that, because the cold was fierce penetrating even Maggie's thick coat. Yet she was sweating with fear, and her breath came in tortured gasps as she rounded the corner of the next street. The woman was right behind her, still sobbing uncontrollably.

They heard shouts behind them, and Maggie urged the woman, "Run faster! If they catch us, we'll die!"

Chapter 22

The sound of stomping boots behind them drew steadily closer, and the men were shouting to each other. Maggie realized that she would lose her breath any second, unused to running as she was. They would just have to outwit their pursuers.

They passed a street lamp, and Maggie thought they'd better stay out of the light. She pulled the woman with her into the shelter of a hedge.

The woman stumbled in the snow and fell to her knees, her hair straggling around her face, but Maggie urged her to her feet. "Hurry, they're almost here," she whispered.

Without a word, the woman followed as silently as she could. They crossed a garden, weaving around thorny bushes, trees, and a fountain with a stone ledge. The men were even closer now—Maggie could see their dark shapes on the lane.

Maggie halted her companion behind a concealing tree trunk. Their breaths rasping, they listened tensely for sounds that the men had seen them, but the pounding steps receded down the lane. The men had run past.

"We must walk from one garden to the next until we're sure the men have stopped searching for us," Maggie said quietly. "If we reach the station house, we'll be free. They won't dare attack us there."

Taking the woman's trembling hand, Maggie dragged her through the hedge to the next garden and made her run again. At the station house they would somehow summon the police. The stationmaster must have a telephone.

Maggie didn't even dare to consider her uncle's involvement, but the awful truth left her weak with horror. Thaddeus had been right, after all. Rupert was part of the Altar Murders. Her uncle . . . She burned with shame, but also bitter disappointment. She had been so happy to finally be part of a family.

"What's your name?" she asked the woman as the welcoming light of the depot appeared in the distance. "How did you get here?"

"They kept me locked up for weeks," the woman said between sobs.

Maggie stared at her in curiosity, noting the foreign twang of her voice. "Leonora . . ." she whispered between lips that were stiff with cold.

"Yes. I'm Leonora Winston. I traveled to England to meet my sister in London."

At last they reached the station. Leonora's face looked blue with cold, and she was shivering uncontrollably.

"I'm Margaret Hartwell," Maggie said, choking. Inside the waiting room, she pulled her sister into her arms and held her tightly. Tears gathered in her eyes as she loosed her grip and looked into her sister's pale, dazed face. "Leonora, you're my sister. If only you knew how I have worried about you. I feared you would be—dead. I can't tell you how relieved I am that you're safe."

"Margaret?" Leonora whispered, and gently touched Maggie's cheek. Her hands were icy. "I would have been dead if you hadn't arrived. They were waiting for the perfect moment to execute me. They said they wanted me to ponder my sins before

I died." Her voice trailed off, and her shoulders slumped.

"We have so much to talk about," Maggie said, wishing she could wipe away the terror lingering in Leonora's eyes. She embraced her once more and rubbed Leonora's stiff back. "If only you knew how much I longed all these years to have a sister, a family."

"I, too," Leonora whispered. She returned Maggie's warm hug, and Maggie uttered a silent prayer of gratitude that her sister was unharmed. "You saved my life, and I will always be beholden to you. Thank you." She gave Maggie a watery smile, and Maggie knew that their friendship had been sealed at that moment. Looking into Leonora's eyes, she felt as if she had a distant connection with her mother, with a part of the past that had not been fouled by her father's tyranny.

The train from London puffed into the station, braking and hissing. The noise brought Maggie back to the present. She led her sister toward a bench close to the coal stove and urged her to sit down. "Please warm yourself while I summon the police," she urged.

Maggie stepped up to the ticket window and knocked on the glass. The stationmaster raised his questioning gaze to hers. "Yes?"

"I beg you to call the police. My sister was almost murdered tonight." She leaned closer. "It concerns the Altar Murders," she whispered, and watched his eyes grow round with awe.

He opened and closed his mouth like a beached fish, and then pointed toward the telephone on the desk. Maggie nodded. "I'm ever so grateful," she added. Hearing male voices outside, she threw a glance toward the door. Had the men followed them all the way here? She would scream for help if they stepped inside.

But the door opened and there was Thaddeus Webb, larger than life, filling the room with his presence. Sergeant Horridge was with him, and they saw Maggie simultaneously.

"Maggie!" Thaddeus called out. "I've been frantic with worry."

Relief washed through her. Maggie wanted to throw herself against him, but the curious stares of the travelers halted her. Instead she pointed at her sister huddled before the stove. "Leonora," she said. "They were going to kill her."

Now that he knew she was safe, Thaddeus was furious at her foolhardiness. "I could kill *you* for traipsing off to Richmond in the middle of the night, alone."

"It's hardly night," she said, her anger rising. She had just faced death, and here he was, berating her. Ignoring him, she led the men to her sister, who barely dared to look at them, embarrassment staining her cheeks. Leonora tried to pat her hair into place, and she pulled the blanket more tightly around her.

"I say!" Thaddeus exclaimed, and unbuttoned his heavy coat. He wrapped it tenderly around Leonora's shaking shoulders and gave her a handkerchief to mop her face. He turned to Maggie. "What happened?"

"I've asked the stationmaster to fetch the police." Maggie told Thaddeus and Sergeant Horridge about the robed men in the basement, and the altar on which she'd found Leonora. As she finished her story, the door opened and four blue-uniformed police officers entered, carrying truncheons.

"What's going on here?" one of them demanded, looking suspiciously at Leonora. "To walk about in public without proper clothes is indecent conduct."

"Never mind that," Maggie said, exasperated. "I can lead you to the men involved in the infamous Altar Murders."

"Altar Murders—?" they gasped in unison. "Not again!"

"Yes, right here in Richmond."

"She's right," Thaddeus said. "That's the house where I was brought, the place that I couldn't find again later."

"Hmmm. We well recall *that* incident," the oldest constable said suspiciously. He eyed Septimus Horridge. "Who are you?"

"I'm Sergeant Horridge of Scotland Yard, and I've been working on this case from the outset." He explained to the officers about Leonora's predicament. Then he turned to Maggie as the Richmond constables muttered among themselves. "Can you show us the house?"

"Yes . . . but who will look after my sister? We can't leave her here alone."

"I'll stay with Miss Winston," offered the youngest constable, evidently relieved that he could avoid facing the altar murderers.

"Come along then," Maggie said, after patting her sister's shoulder. "We'll be back soon," she told her reassuringly.

"I'll see to it that she gets a cup of hot tea and is tucked away from these curious gawkers," the constable said, and stepped over to the ticket window.

Thaddeus held Maggie's arm, and she sensed his boiling anger. "I can't believe you did this," he spat. "If there hadn't been a key in the basement door, they would have overpowered you, don't you see?"

"I couldn't very well let them kill a defenseless woman without trying to save her," Maggie said, drawing herself up.

"You're foolish beyond belief. They might have killed *you*," he yelled. Then, seeing her distress, he calmed down. "Maggie, I was so worried. The thought of losing you made me crazy."

She smiled through a haze of tears. "I'm grateful

that you care, but let's leave the subject for now. Sergeant Horridge might want to know that one of the murderers is my uncle, Rupert Merton."

"Extraordinary, if it's true," Horridge replied. "I'm sorry this had to happen to you."

They turned down Sparrow Lane. The wind whipped veils of snow through the air, stinging their faces.

"Here we are," Maggie said, pointing at 542 Sparrow Lane. The house lay in utter darkness. "It looks like we're too late. They obviously fled after they lost track of us."

The police officers stalked up to the door and let the knocker fall. The sound reverberated through the rooms, but no one responded.

Sergeant Horridge tried the handle, and the door swung open with a creaking noise. Truncheons at the ready, they entered quietly. Thaddeus was right behind then, after motioning to Maggie to stay outside—a futile order.

She tried to peer around him, but there was nothing to see in the hallway. Thaddeus lit a gas fixture on the wall, and the dim glow showed the door to the basement. Maggie shuddered with apprehension as she smelled the incense.

"I recall this scent," Thaddeus murmured. He opened two doors and looked inside. "But the rooms were so dark then, I can't recognize them."

"The men were in the basement," Maggie said to the constables.

They advanced to the open door and looked down the steep stairwell.

"I'm certain they aren't here," Maggie said as the men started climbing down. The flambeaux had been extinguished, leaving a stale, smoky odor behind.

She followed last, loath to once more see the altar where four women had most likely lost their lives.

Why? She wondered if she would ever find the answer to that question.

"No one here," the first constable said. "And I don't see any altar, Mrs. Hartwell. Are you sure it was here?"

Sergeant Horridge held the oil lamp aloft. Maggie instantly noticed the spot where she'd dropped the torch. Remnants of a charred piece of rug were still on the floor, and beyond the threshold, oil gleamed.

"See? This is where I hurled the oil containers." She stepped gingerly into the room, careful not to step in the shards of glass and oil. The carpet was soggy, but there was no altar, no candelabras, no strange wall-hangings, no robes, and no chanting men.

"They were here just half an hour ago," she said. "Can't you smell the incense?"

"That doesn't prove anything," Sergeant Horridge said. "However, I believe you. They knew it would be only a matter of time before we arrived, so they packed their paraphernalia and left. I'm sure that they disposed of the body Webb saw on the altar when he was here."

Maggie sighed in disappointment. "At least they know we know. They cannot practice these strange rituals again."

The sergeant shrugged. "They'll start up somewhere else if I'm not mistaken."

Thaddeus held out a gleaming object he'd lifted from the floor. "One of the scarab rings," he explained, and dropped it into the sergeant's hand. "A group of men in London all wear this type of ring—including Mrs. Hartwell's uncle."

Twin spots of red glowed on Maggie's cheeks at the thought that her uncle was at the heart of the Altar Murders. "I didn't suspect a thing," she murmured. "I truly didn't. I thought Uncle Rupert was odd, but not *insane*."

"There's no blame on you, ma'am," said one of the constables.

"All we can do now is discover what Miss Winston has to say. You'd better come down to the police station, all of you," the Richmond constable said. "Besides, you cannot travel back to London with Miss Winston until we find some decent clothing for her. She has endured a terrible ordeal." They shook their heads and went back upstairs.

Thaddeus threw Maggie a veiled glance as if he was about to say something, but he seemed to change his mind. Evidently, he had decided not to upbraid her again. They left the house and walked up the street. The snow was coming down heavily, turning nature into a fairy-tale landscape, but Maggie could not enjoy it. She had too many questions on her mind.

They returned to the station house to find Leonora much improved, a tea mug in her hands. She didn't look much like the calotype she'd sent. There was some color in her cheeks, and with her cloud of blonde hair and deep blue eyes, she was very attractive. Something stirred in Maggie's heart—pride?—at having such a comely sister.

"We'd better all go down to the station," the sergeant said, and scrutinized Leonora's boots. "At least you can walk in the snow with those. 'Tis only half a mile down the road."

Without protest, they all filed outside, Maggie relieved to get away from the curious glances of the people in the station. They walked in silence to the police headquarters, Maggie supporting her sister who stumbled occasionally with fatigue.

The drab, white-painted room was the Richmond police office. There were sputtering gas globes in the ceiling and a stove in a corner. Desks were laden with papers, but also tins of sweets, teacups, and packages covered with grease spots that spoke of homemade sandwiches.

"Here, Miss Winston." The sergeant pulled a chair close to the stove. "I'll nip next door to my old lady to see if she has some garments to lend you."

They waited in silence until he returned laden with female garments, even carrying a hat with a simple velvet hatband. Blushing, he placed them on a chair. "I hope these will fit you." He pointed at another door. "You can change in the coat closet."

Carrying the clothes, Maggie followed her sister. The closet was large, with a gas lamp and rows of uniform jackets and coats. The air smelled of cigar smoke and gas fumes.

Still shivering, Leonora dropped Thaddeus's coat and the blanket. She looked very thin under the shift, and so pale that she was faintly purple. The shock had done that to her, Maggie thought. In silence, she helped her sister to dress, feeling a flurry of tenderness. How she wished they had grown up together.

"Much obliged," Leonora whispered. "I brought you a present from home, an embroidered picture of the house Mama and I lived in." She shrugged forlornly. "It's gone now. I don't know what those hoodlums did with my luggage."

"We'll find it somewhere. I'll ask the police to look around the house where they kept you locked up."

"They took all my clothes so that I couldn't escape—except my boots, since I had to visit the outhouse at the back of the garden." Her voice trembled. "It was most humiliating."

Maggie hugged her sister, her heart brimming with sorrow. "Yes . . . I can't imagine how you survived. Did the men . . . abuse you?"

Leonora shook her head. "They weren't interested in me that way."

There was a knock on the door. "Are you ready?" the sergeant asked impatiently. "We're waiting."

Maggie bound Leonora's blonde hair at the nape

with one of Victoria's ribbons that she had found in her skirt pocket.

Leonora stepped out, dressed in an ill-fitting black skirt and a flower-print blouse that sagged over her shoulders, and a gray cardigan. Maggie helped her back to the stove.

"Now, Miss Winston, if you would be so kind as to tell us the whole story," Sergeant Horridge said.

Leonora's bottom lip trembled, and she pleated the fabric of the skirt nervously. "When Mama died, I discovered that I had a sister living in London. I read Mama's journal, you see. She never told me anything about the past during the years we lived in Claremont—it's a small town due west of Richmond, Virginia—so I had to find out the truth for myself."

Maggie recognized the soft twang of the American South, and thought how strange it was to find her sister so—foreign. She knew nothing about this young woman, and it would take years to recount every memory that they ought to have shared together. Anger at her parents, who were to blame for her separation from her only sister, surged through her.

"I decided to travel here to see Margaret—Maggie." She gave her sister a wan smile. "I don't regret that decision *now*, but if you'd asked me two weeks ago, I would have answered differently. I met many nice people on the steamer, especially a young Englishman by the name of Anselm Ripley. He was so charming, so attentive, so well-bred."

"How did he approach you?"

"He asked me to dance at one of the dinner dances on board." Leonora sighed. "I was foolish to trust him. Right before the boat docked, he came to my cabin. I thought he would help me with my luggage, but instead, he offered me a glass of champagne to toast my arrival in England. A porter entered to take my bags. I drank, and a few minutes later, I grew dizzy as I was putting on my hat. He'd put something in my drink . . . I was powerless to fight him when he wrapped a shawl over my head and pulled me outside. Everything was a blur, but I was still clutching my hat, vaguely remembering that it was important."

"The purple plume," Maggie interpolated.

Leona nodded and continued. "Ripley stopped to make a telephone call, and soon after a carriage arrived. It wasn't empty, though—three men were in it. They overpowered me and hauled me inside, but I managed to drop the plume on the ground. One of the men—not Ripley—had traveled on the ship as well, a tall, dark-haired man in his fifties who'd stayed in our boarding house two days after Mama died. I never spoke with him on the ship, but he stared at me many times and he frightened me."

"That sounds like Uncle Rupert," Maggie said.

Leonora went on. "I don't know what happened then, because they drugged me, and I slept most of the time. The journey seemed to take several days, but I'm not sure. They kept me tied up in the carriage the whole time, except at mealtimes. Then we arrived here, which is Richmond outside London, according to the kind officer." She directed a smile at her erstwhile guard.

"Ripley didn't go with you?"

"No, once he'd made that call, he said good-bye, claiming he had business in the area. He paid a porter to keep an eye open for the carriage, and to carry my bags."

"And when you arrived here?"

"They locked me in a room, one man keeping guard every day. There were different men—all young, aloof types that barely spoke with me. When I asked how long they intended to incarcerate me, they said, 'As long as necessary.' They went through my luggage and took a japanned box that Daddy sent me five years ago."

"A japanned box?" Maggie and Thaddeus echoed simultaneously.

"Was it black and rather gaudy?" Maggie continued, now tense.

Leonora nodded. "Yes . . . cheap, but the only thing I ever received from Daddy."

"No message?" Thaddeus asked.

"Nothing."

"The men came for me once before, saying they'd found what they were looking for, but Mr. Ripley stormed into the house in a real taking, shouting they had stolen the wrong box at Maggie's. I've no idea what he was talking about."

Maggie faced the officers. "I had a japanned box as well, which I bought at the market two years ago and kept on my desk to hold odds and ends. It vanished mysteriously, soon after my sister's disappearance"

"Puzzling indeed," Septimus Horridge said. "It's evident that the men want whatever the boxes conceal."

"The strange thing is, when I got it from Daddy, it was empty," Leonora explained.

"Hmmm," Thaddeus said, rubbing his chin. "Could something have been hidden in the walls, or bottom of the box?"

"It's conceivable," Horridge said, "but we won't know until we find the boxes in question."

"Do you know what the men did with the box?" Maggie asked.

Leonora shook her head. "I never saw it again."

The Richmond constable asked Leonora to describe the men.

"Oh, dear. The leader was tall and slender, with the most piercing eyes. Called himself the Reformer and always wore a hood over his face in my presence. He wore American-style clothes except for an Oriental waistcoat."

"That might have been Uncle Rupert." Maggie

briefly told Leonora how her uncle had suddenly turned up at the hotel about the same time that Leonora disappeared. "He said he didn't know of your existence."

"We know now that we can't trust any of them. There was, of course, Anselm Ripley, and the other men of the group were young, handsome, seemingly well-to-do," Leonora continued. "They hadn't any odd features that would make them stand out. They called themselves the Twilight Brotherhood."

"Do you know anything about the rituals?" Thaddeus asked.

Leonora accepted a cup of tea that one of the constables had brewed. "They had them intermittently, but I was never present, until tonight. I could hear them chanting, a sound that rose to screaming, and I believe they danced. That would be at the climax of the ritual—when the women lost their lives. One of the guards told me." Leonora's voice faltered, and she gulped down some tea. "I can't describe the terror I felt under that roof."

Sergeant Horridge was deep in thought, leaving his tea untouched. "There might be a connection between the men, other than ritualistic. We know that all the victims were young and wealthy. The members of the Brotherhood obviously married the ladies for their money, then murdered them. Unfortunately, all the husbands had impeccable alibis," Horridge said. "We checked them." He glanced at Thaddeus. "In my wildest dreams, I never thought the Altar Murders would be connected to Miss Winston."

"An alibi can always be bought," Thaddeus said. "Perhaps they gave each other alibis. Ripley belongs to a club on the Embankment, and there's a possibility the others do, too. I'll find out when we return to London."

"The Brotherhood wanted Leonora's japanned box, so they abducted her, but why? Why couldn't they just steal the box from her? And then they searched for Mrs. Hartwell's box—another question mark,'' Horridge murmured.

"It's strange indeed, but once we track down the cult members, we'll discover the truth, no doubt,'' Thaddeus said.

"Miss Winston, why did you travel under an assumed name?'' Sergeant Horridge asked.

Leonora gave him a tired glance. "We ran a boarding house in Claremont, and—like I said before—after Mama's death, the man I now know as Mr. Merton, stayed with me for two days. He asked me many strange questions about my past, and I was afraid of him. He left, but to my dismay, I discovered that he'd followed me from Claremont to New York when I left for England. To make sure he wouldn't know on which ship I traveled, I used the name Laura Winter. But I guess it was in vain. I understand now that he was trying to discover if I still had the box that Daddy sent me.''

Sergeant Horridge nodded. "A devious man indeed.''

Leonora slumped in her chair, her cheeks even more pale than at the outset.

"We'd better go home,'' Thaddeus said. "Miss Winston badly needs her rest.''

"The last train has left,'' Maggie said.

"I'll ring for a local man with a cab,'' the Richmond sergeant said.

Rugs across their knees, and collars folded up against the cold, Maggie, Thaddeus, Leonora, and Sergeant Horridge returned to London. Still, they were almost frozen stiff by the time the cabbie halted in front of Hartwell's Hotel. Thaddeus gave the jarvey an extra gratuity to make up for the discomfort of driving back to Richmond.

"You'd better come inside and warm yourselves with brandy before spending any more time in this cold weather." Maggie noticed that Rafferty had swept the gathering snow up against the side of the house, and the white powdering of the windowpanes made the hotel seem welcoming on this special night of Leonora's first view of Maggie's home.

"Your hotel is darling. I love it," Leonora said with a warm smile. "I'm obliged to everyone here that I'm alive to see it."

Rafferty greeted them inside the door. Even he, who usually was impervious to rain and cold, had stepped inside on this night.

"This is my sister, Miss Winston." Maggie introduced Leonora, knowing that the servants quarters would soon buzz with gossip about her long-lost sister.

Maggie led the way upstairs to her sitting room. A coal fire glowed warmly in the grate, and Leonora was instantly drawn to it.

"My daughter, Victoria, will be thrilled to meet you," Maggie said, setting out glasses on a tray, then filling them with brandy.

"I wish I could see her now, but I gather she's asleep."

"No, she's at Margate with her governess, but she'll be back the day after tomorrow."

Maggie handed the glasses around, and touched Thaddeus's arm briefly, but he only gave her a long, searching stare. Was he still angry with her for going off to Richmond alone?

She raised her glass. "Welcome, dear Leonora. I wish our first meeting had been a happier one."

"Hear, hear," the gentlemen murmured politely.

Leonora blushed delicately and sipped her brandy. "I know I will consider this city as my home now, but I'd like to visit the mansion outside Sheffield someday."

"You'll be very disappointed," Maggie warned.

"I want to trace my roots," Leonora said with a sigh.

Sergeant Horridge downed his brandy and set the glass on the tray. "I must leave you for now, but I'm sure I will have more questions—if you don't mind, Miss Winston."

Leonora's lips tightened. "I will be more than happy to help you apprehend those villains," she said. "They have already ruined too many lives."

Thaddeus set down his glass as well. After giving Maggie a tender smile, he said, "Due to the circumstances, I will join the sergeant in his work now." He bowed to the ladies. "May you have a good night's sleep."

Maggie ached, yearning to hold him, but this was not the time. "Will you come back here tomorrow?" she asked.

"We'll see how the investigation goes. We must concentrate on catching the murderers," he said, closing the door behind him as he left.

Chapter 23

"**T**haddeus asked me to marry him and I accepted," Maggie explained as she brushed Leonora's hair later that night in her bedchamber. "We argue a lot, but I love him."

Leonora laughed. "Sounds like you inherited Mama's temper. She would get extremely angry, and then it blew over, as if nothing had happened. Mr. Webb's a wonderful man. He'll make you happy."

Maggie's curiosity grew at the mention of her mother. Here was a window into her past. "What was Mother really like?" She held her breath as Leonora watched her in the mirror.

"Very proud, very independent. That's why she and Daddy never got along. She told me once that he wanted power over everyone in his circle, and she would not be cowed." Leonora paused. "She was also gentle and kind, but rarely showed those traits to the world. I'm certain she missed you, but Daddy forbade her to take you. Mother changed her name to Winston in case Father ever decided to look for us. However, at some point he must have discovered where we lived since he sent me the box."

"Why didn't Mother write to me?"

"I think she felt guilty for leaving you in Papa's dubious care. She knew everything about you, though:

your address, your marriage to Mr. Hartwell. She had kept in touch with the family solicitors, you see."

As Maggie finished braiding her sister's hair, she set down the brush. "Father never bothered to contact me, but he might have asked the solicitors to discover my whereabouts. Like you, I did receive a box upon his death, but it was a different style. It was of rosewood with inlays."

Leonora rose and started pacing. "We have to find my luggage. Mother wrote down everything in her journal, and I know you would love to read it. It is the essence of who Mama was."

"The police sergeant in Richmond is going back to the house in daylight to search for more clues. They'll eventually find those men who kept you captive."

"If they have done anything to the journal, I don't know what I'll do. It's the only thing I have left of Mama. The boarding house wasn't a lucrative business, alas. We had a few sticks of furniture—nothing fancy, mind you. I sold them to pay for the funeral and the steamship ticket."

"You lived a frugal life. Did you have many friends?"

Leonora sank down on the bed, staring into the distance. "The vicar and the schoolmistress. I know the bank manager was fond of Mama, but she always kept to herself. Papa ruined her life so that she didn't dare to give herself to another man." Leonora sighed. "She turned bitter in the end, and she kept telling me never to marry."

Maggie sat down beside her sister and hugged her. "Let's make a pact not to make the mistakes our parents did, shall we?"

Leonora's lips trembled. "You're right. I like you, Maggie, and I wish I had known you when we were growing up."

"I, too, would have been happier with you and Mama, but we can't change the past." Maggie smiled.

"Soon you'll find some nice young man here in London. Did you have any admirers in Claremont?"

Leonora blushed. "Only a persistent boarder, but I could not conceive of marrying a man thirty years my senior."

"Father accused Rupert Merton of being your sire," Maggie said softly, wondering how Leonora would react.

Leonora's eyes blazed. "Impossible! Mama was a principled woman. She would never have cheated on Father, no matter how much she hated him. She took her wedding vows seriously."

"She had an unhappy life, but at least she had you," Maggie said kindly. Leonora looked so tired that Maggie thought she would fall down if she didn't lie down. "I asked Gertie, the youngest maid, to make up a bed for you in Victoria's room. She'll be your maid for now. I want to know that you're right next door to me."

Leonora's eyes were huge and frightened. "I'd rather sleep here, if you don't mind," she whispered. "I'm still afraid they will come back and find me."

"Of course you can sleep here. My bed is wide enough for both of us. But you don't have to be afraid. Sergeant Horridge promised to send two constables to guard the entrances. No one will be able to get in here without their permission." She patted Leonora's shoulder. "What you need is a good night's sleep."

Leonora hugged her impulsively. "You're so kind. I'm delighted that we're sisters." She crossed the room, her borrowed nightgown dragging on the floor. Maggie tucked her in as if she were a child.

"Sleep well," she said, and went to the bathroom to draw a bath for herself.

Maggie awakened early. Daylight had barely arrived when she staggered out of bed and stretched her tired limbs. Last evening's adventures had exhausted her, but after sleeping soundly, she was ready to tackle the day's problems. Leonora was still asleep, her hand tucked under her chin. She had tossed and turned in the night, but Maggie had barely noticed it, even though she was used to sleeping alone.

A maid knocked on the sitting room door, and after donning a dressing gown, Maggie went to accept the breakfast tray she had ordered on the previous evening. This first morning after her sister's arrival, she would share breakfast alone with Leonora. Soon enough, the servants would get to meet her. They must be bursting with curiosity right now. Gertie was the only one who had met Leonora, a fact she could brag about in the kitchen, Maggie thought with a smile. She unlocked the door.

It was Cecily who brought the tray. "What are those police constables doing outside our door?" she asked, setting the tray on the table. "The guests are suspicious."

"Well, we don't want to frighten them, but until the people who kidnapped Leonora are captured, we must have protection."

"I knocked on your sister's door, but no one was there."

"She slept here with me. She was too frightened to be by herself," Maggie explained, and poured herself a cup of tea.

Cecily eyed the bedroom door speculatively. "Gertie said your sister is quite lovely, and speaks with a drawl."

Maggie smiled. "That's true. Do you want a raspberry pastry? I see that Monsieur Andrè has made only the best to welcome my sister."

Cecily laughed and placed a pastry on a plate. "Yes, everyone is happy that she's safe. After all, there has been much speculation in the kitchen region." She chewed greedily, then said, "It's strange that Gertie is so late this morning. She's usually the one to arrive the earliest."

"Perhaps she's in Victoria's room, where she was to make up a bed for Miss Winston last night. She might be waiting to help Leonora dress."

Cecily shrugged. "I wouldn't put anything past Gertie, the nosy girl." She wiped sticky raspberry jam off her fingers with a napkin. "I will take a look."

Maggie finished her tea and ate half a pastry. She didn't eat much in the mornings. Contemplating whether to wake Leonora or let her sleep until the tea was cold, she stared at the bedroom door.

A sudden scream rent the air. Maggie started violently, cold sweat broke out on her hands, and she began to shiver as if the nightmare of last night had started all over. The scream came from the corridor, and Maggie rushed outside.

Cecily was running toward her, her face deathly pale. "It's Gertie," she said. "She's in Victoria's bed—dead."

Maggie stumbled against the wall as if the rug had been pulled from under her. "Dead?" she echoed.

Cecily nodded, sobbing hysterically. She staggered into Maggie's sitting room, and sank down on the first available seat.

Maggie took a deep breath to collect herself, but something inside her was close to snapping. Bracing herself against the wall, she followed Cecily inside and poured two stiff measures of brandy. "Leonora was supposed to have slept there," she said tonelessly, and pressed the glass into Cecily's shaking hands.

"I know . . ." the assistant said, her voice a hoarse whisper. She sagged on the sofa. "Gertie had such grand plans . . . she worked so hard to realize them . . . now she's gone . . ."

"Don't tell Leonora," Maggie said firmly. "I must inform the police." She downed the brandy in two gulps, still feeling as if her last shred of control was unraveling. "Wait here," she said, and went with precise steps to her bedroom. If she moved slowly, she might not shatter, she thought. The brandy made her light-headed but did not ease the dread in her chest. To her relief, Leonora was still asleep.

Maggie collected some garments, and pins to hold up her hair. In the sitting room, she discarded her nightgown and pulled on a shirtwaist and skirt. Like an automaton, she twisted her hair into a chignon and fastened it.

"Let's go downstairs," she whispered. "I don't think I can stand to look at Gertie."

Supporting each other, Cecily pressing a handkerchief to her mouth, they went downstairs. "Perhaps Gertie waited for Leonora to come up last night, and when she didn't, Gertie fell asleep in her bed," Cecily continued between watery sobs. "The room must have been pitch-black and the murderer—"

"And the murderer thought it was Leonora." Maggie left Cecily in the office and stepped into the foyer. The world seemed so strange, as if she was separated from it by a wall of terror.

"Rafferty, summon the two constables," she ordered. "Send them to my office immediately." *I must inform Thaddeus.* Filled with sorrow mixed with fear, she waited for the police. They came promptly, their helmets clutched under their arms.

"One of my maids was murdered last night," Maggie explained. She described to the two men how to find Victoria's room. *I will have to change my daughter's room. She can't sleep in a bed that contained a corpse.* "And I will give Sergeant Horridge a ring," she added.

The constables hurried upstairs, and Maggie walked stiffly to the telephone. She had turned into a wooden doll and as long as she stayed wound up, she would be able to function. If she stopped, she knew the apprehension would freeze her to the spot.

To her relief, she got hold of Horridge instantly, and he promised to come posthaste. *Victoria might have been killed, had she been here.* And how did the murderer know in which room Leonora would sleep?

Was someone at the hotel involved, after all? Maggie shivered at the ominous thought, fearing that they were in danger at this very moment if that suspicion were true.

"Cecily, go upstairs and lock yourself into my room with Leonora, and don't let anyone in, unless it's the police." She observed her assistant, who was slowly drying her tears. "Can you do that? I have to fetch Mr. Webb since he's involved in this case."

"I thought his assignment was over with the appearance of your sister, Maggie."

Not wanting to frighten Cecily with an account of Rupert's involvement with the Altar Murders, Maggie said, "The case has complications that have to be solved." She found one of her coats on the peg in the office, wound a scarf around her head, and pulled on a pair of mittens. She then made sure that Cecily went upstairs and entered her sitting room. "Admit Sergeant Horridge when he arrives, and tell him exactly what you saw."

"She'd been strangled. There were marks around her neck," Cecily said tearfully.

Maggie shivered, unable to listen any longer. "I'll be back in half an hour," she said, and fled downstairs.

It was still cold outside, but the snow had stopped. The sky was leaden, promising more to come. As Maggie hurried along Berkley Street, she waved at a passing hansom which didn't stop. Only after she'd crossed Manchester Square did one halt beside her. She gave the jarvey Thaddeus's address.

There was the familiar green door, and she banged the knocker. Rapid steps echoed in the hallway and she felt a surge of relief—which dissolved as Gavin appeared in the door opening.

"Hello, Gavin, is Thaddeus here?"

"Come in! It's freezing out," he said, and pulled her inside. "A cup of tea perhaps?"

"No, I need to speak with Thaddeus instantly.

Murder has been perpetrated in my home." Her voice shook, and again she had the sensation that her whole world was about to shatter.

"Thaddeus isn't here," Gavin said quietly. "Hasn't been here since yesterday."

"What! But he left my house late last night."

"He's probably working on something, or perhaps he went to his parents' house in Ludgate Hill. They aren't on the telephone, so to find out, you'll have to go there." He gave her a searching glance. "You look so pale. Do you want to stay here and rest? I can go."

"No! Thank you, but I couldn't bear the thought of waiting and worrying here."

She left the house, but turned around on the sidewalk. "If Thaddeus returns, tell him it's imperative that he visit me."

"Of course. I'm sorry about these awful things that keep happening to you."

Maggie could barely suppress her tears as she sped down the street. At Regent's Circus she found a cab, and counted every minute it took the driver to reach Ludgate Hill in the congested traffic. Everyone seemed to be outside this morning, laden with Christmas presents, no doubt.

Ludgate Hill was filled with buses, wagons, and pedestrians, workingpeople dressed in rough fustian and ragged dresses. The children looked pinched with cold. If it hadn't been for Horace Hartwell, she might have been one of these people, wondering if she had enough money for another meal.

The building where the Webbs lived was better than the others on the block, of solid brick and sporting a newly painted black door. Mrs. Webb had to work hard to pay the rent of a flat in this establishment, Maggie thought as she knocked.

Amintha opened the door. "Mrs. Hartwell! What a nice surprise," she said, and beckoned her inside. "Mother will be ever so excited." They climbed the stairs to the second floor where the Webbs lived. The first room of the flat was the parlor, threadbare and faded, yet it looked so clean that it literally shone, and every piece of furniture was clearly treated as reverently as if it were made of solid gold.

Beyond the parlor was the kitchen, and Maggie glimpsed two other rooms beyond that. Mrs. Webb was in the kitchen, kneeling, with Delia above her, standing on a chair. Delia looked ethereal, like a fragile lily, in her white wedding gown.

"Mrs. Hartwell, what a delightful surprise." Mrs. Webb said with a smile. "We're about to hem Delia's gown as you can see." Her voice was filled with pride. "Isn't she lovely?"

A lump formed in Maggie's throat. "Yes, very." Would she ever be a bride again? she wondered. "Is Thaddeus here? It's urgent that I speak with him."

"Thaddeus? Oh, no, we haven't seen him since last Sunday dinner," Delia said.

"And he barely stayed for dessert," Amintha chimed in. "I will fetch Father so that he can meet you."

Desperation spread through Maggie. Where was Thaddeus? She had an urge to bolt from the flat and go on searching for him, but she couldn't very well avoid her first meeting with Thaddeus's father. Amintha pushed him into the room in an invalid chair. Maggie's heart constricted when she saw that he looked exactly like Thaddeus, a thinner, older, white-haired replica. He had that same twinkle in the eyes, although Mr. Webb's eyes were blue. And his grin. Maggie could have cried when that smile she knew so well appeared on the old man's face.

"Mrs. Hartwell, a pleasure," he said, stretching out his gnarled hand, which was dry and cool. "Thaddeus is quite taken with you. Couldn't talk about anything else the last time he was here. I must say, I don't blame him."

"Silas!" Mrs. Webb admonished, blushing. "He's only teasing you, Mrs. Hartwell."

Maggie smiled. "My skin is thick after my verbal battles with your son, Mrs. Webb. I see now where he got his charm."

Mr. Webb chuckled. "You have a pretty turn of phrase," he said. "I look forward to spending a day at your dining rooms, Mrs. Hartwell. I've always liked a bit of good food and wine."

"I'm honored that you chose my hotel for the reception. And there are no complications to the plans." *Except murder.* "But, tell me, do you have any idea where Thaddeus might be?"

Mr. Webb looked thoughtful. "Did you ask Gavin Talbot?"

As Maggie nodded, he continued, "Sometimes Thaddeus takes trips to other towns to purchase the antiques they sell at the shop, but we wouldn't know where."

Could he have left without word to her? Maggie wondered. No, impossible.

She held out her hand to the old man again. "I'll see you tomorrow," she said. "And then it's Christmas." She turned to Delia. "This must be the best Christmas ever for you."

The young woman blushed. "Yes . . . I suppose so."

"You look lovely." Unable to suppress a quiver in her voice, Maggie turned to the door. Gertie would have no Christmas this year. How unfair life was. "I'll see you then." With a wave, she left the house. Catching a cab at the corner of Fleet Street, all she could think of was getting home. She prayed that Thaddeus was there.

Chapter 24

When Maggie returned to the hotel, Sergeant Horridge was there. They had removed Gertie's body, but a pall hung over the entire establishment. Guests whispered in the lobby and threw suspicious glances at Maggie. Would this ruin her business? she wondered, pinching her lips. She had worked so hard to prove herself to be a first-rate businesswoman.

She was filled with sorrow at Gertie's passing; success or no success, it wasn't worth the loss of a fine employee, who had also been Victoria's friend.

"We must notify her parents," Maggie said to Cecily in the office after hanging up her coat and hat.

"She lived with a sister in Soho. We can go there together this afternoon if you wish." Cecily looked wan, and her eyes were wide and dark with sadness.

"Yes . . . Have you seen Mr. Webb?"

"No, he hasn't been here."

Sergeant Horridge came down the stairs, his bowler hat in hand. "Gruesome business, this. I don't know how anyone could have entered the house with my guards at both doors."

"Have you spoken with Mr. Webb this morning?" Maggie asked, worry squeezing her heart.

"No. I haven't seen him since we parted last night. He said he was going to investigate a lead on Ripley, and

319

I returned to the Yard where I worked all night." He paused. "Your sister is taking this latest event hard."

"Leonora felt it was her fault that Gertie died," Cecily explained. "I gave her a sedative after the police arrived, and I also sent for the doctor to examine her, after the ordeal she went through."

"I'm grateful for all you've done, dear Cecily. I couldn't do without you," Maggie said with feeling. She then addressed the sergeant. "I suppose there's no clue as to who executed this crime?"

"Nothing obvious, but one thing is clear, there was no forced entry. I have another case to attend to, but I'll be back shortly." The sergeant placed his hat on his head.

Maggie saw him to the door, then steered her steps toward the stairs. "I must look in on my sister. I'd like to be there when she wakes up," she said to Cecily.

At that moment the telephone shrilled. Cecily went to the counter to answer it, then called out to Maggie, "It's for you—a gentleman."

Thaddeus! Maggie hurried across the foyer and gripped the earpiece. "Maggie speaking."

"Ah! My dear niece . . ."

Maggie went cold all over, clutching the phone as if it was the only thing that would keep her upright. "Uncle Rupert?" She waved frantically at Cecily, but the older woman had left the room. "Where are you?" Maggie continued, feeling lonely and afraid.

He laughed at the other end. "In London, and want to meet with you."

"I know that you were involved in the abduction of my sister. You knew about her all the time and didn't tell me. You were one of the awful men in the robes."

He laughed again. How could he be so good humored after what he'd done? "Yes, of course knew about Leonora; she had the box I needed. You must do me a favor, Maggie. I will give you an address, and you will bring me a box—"

"Box?" Maggie's breath caught in her throat. "What do you mean?"

"Your father gave you a japanned box—but not the one you used to keep on your desk. Maggie, listen to me, you must bring me the box your father gave you."

"The japanned box?" Maggie repeated woodenly. "You stole my box, didn't you?"

"Of course! I sneaked into your office to have a look around before I ever met you, on that first day when you weren't at home."

"And you had me abducted so that you could search my rooms, and you also stole the extra key. You were the intruder who almost frightened me out of my wits."

"How perceptive you are, my dear niece," he said in a sugary voice, then charged into his next outburst. "Your japanned box was useless rubbish, and I searched in vain for the real box!" he spat. "That's why I asked you to come to Richmond, so I could convince you to tell me where you'd hidden the box. But my plans went awry, and I wasn't there to meet you. The Voices demanded a sacrifice that night, and someone must have forgotten to lock the door in the hurried preparations."

Maggie gasped, holding the telephone closer to her ear.

Rupert continued, "Listen carefully. If you fail to bring me the box I want, your friend Thaddeus Webb will die. He's even now under lock and key here, and you're the only person who can save him." There was a slight pause. "Although his death will not placate the gods of my religion."

"What religion, and what does the box have to do with anything?" It was agony to pronounce every word. The beasts had Thaddeus. Her legs trembled so much she had to sit down on the wooden stool that was kept behind the counter. "What you believe, Uncle Rupert, is dark and evil."

322   MARIA GREENE

"You don't understand." His tone became pee-
vishly lecturing. "The world is ruled by gods residing
in seven spheres, starting with the Prince of Darkness
supported by a full range of demigods and satyrs, to
the Lord of Light. I am the Chosen One, the Reformer, who will change everything. I listen to the
Voices as they guide me every day. I must bring their
message to the world. Now bring the box—"

"What message?" Maggie's throat was dry with
fear. Revulsion made her skin crawl at the mere sound
of his voice.

"That people shall learn to obey," he droned on.
"Lives must be sacrificed for a nobler truth."

"You say nothing about peace, or the love of God,"
she said.

"Ah, *those!*" he scoffed. "Nothing but social rituals
the church has created to control people. No, you
must learn to listen to the Voices."

Maggie was so stunned she could barely speak.
"You actually hear voices?" There was the babbling
she'd heard last night when she'd come upon the men
around the altar. Were those the voices he was talking about? Were the men even now assembled, Thaddeus their next victim?

"Inside my head. Every moment of my day,"
Rupert said on a whining note. "They never stop.
And now they're urging me to get the box. We must
not delay the spreading of the Voices to the entire
world. The box, Maggie, bring the box—"

"What does the box contain?" Maggie leaned her
forehead against the edge of the counter, wondering
if she had the strength to utter one more word.

He sounded impatient. "Your father left a map, half
in Leonora's box, half in yours, and it describes the
location of a gold treasure." Rupert's tone became
cajoling. "You see, little Maggie, your father converted his fortune into gold, which he then hid somewhere in the Sheffield mansion. One of the solicitor

told me. Bully bribed him not to say a thing, but when I lived in New York, he tried to get me to confiscate Leonora's map in America. We would then share the gold.'' He snorted. ''He's an idiot. When I discovered—from one of the people in Claremont—that Leonora was traveling here to see you, I knew the map would be mine. All I had to do was track her, and then get your address from the solicitors. The gold would be all mine.''

He paused, and Maggie tried to still her mounting fear. ''Maggie, we need the map to find your inheritance, do you hear? The Brotherhood needs the money. *You*, dear niece, now have the opportunity to obey and serve the Voices of the gods. They will reward you, but not in worldly goods. You will be sworn in as a servant of the Voices.''

Maggie closed her eyes, thinking that if the Voices sounded like Rupert's, she would recoil with loathing. ''And if I bring the box, you will let Thaddeus live?'' Maggie held her breath.

''Yes—if the gods permit.''

''You shall have your box.'' Maggie thought about the beautiful inlaid box she'd given Thaddeus. That was the only thing Father had given her. It was in Thaddeus's house somewhere. Straightening, she pulled a notepad closer, her movements sluggish. 'What's the address?''

''Twenty-five Golden Square in Soho. And you must come alone. Since your sister's soul went to the first sphere last night, where she must conquer the demons, you'll have no support from her, and no more grievance. She was so terribly *vulgar*, don't you agree?''

Maggie didn't tell him that he'd killed Gertie—not Leonora. ''So you killed my sister?'' Maggie clutched the hard edge of the counter, her palms perspiring. Slowly, slowly, she recorded the address on the pad.

''Oh, merely helped her along. She was not needed any longer, since I have her box. Her part of the map was in a hidden compartment in the wooden bottom." He chuckled in contentment. "To tell you the truth, your sister'll do much better when she returns here to Earth in the next century."

"You think murder is justified?"

"The spreading of the cause is divine, so any action connected to that is holy as well." He paused. "Maggie, don't bring that tedious Sergeant Horridge. I know he's been trying to ruin everything we've worked for here in London. If you bring him—or even tell him—of our plans, Thaddeus will have to pay the price. He's the pawn of the gods now."

"I will hurry," Maggie said, her voice a hoarse whisper. "Don't do anything until I arrive."

"We have ways of finding out if you brought the police, so do please come alone. The law's views are so very narrow-minded, so *tedious*. They'll do anything to stop our work in the world."

Maggie nodded as if he was there behind the counter. "I understand." The line crackled as the connection ended, and the phone hung from Maggie's limp grip. "He admitted to murdering Gertie— whom he thought was Leonora—for the advancement of his mission," she whispered to herself. "And he has taken Thaddeus, and will kill him if I don't bring the box," she added. She slumped on the uncomfortable stool, covering her face with her hands. "I don't know what's happening. Why does the past come back to haunt me? Father wanted nothing to do with me while he was alive."

She had to pull herself together before the guests noticed that something was amiss. The first thing she had to do was to fetch the box at Maddox Street, and make sure that no one suspected her disappearance for an hour. If Cecily found out about this, she would insist on calling in the police, and then Thaddeus would die.

As she pulled on a coat and a hat in her office, she recalled that her uncle didn't know that Leonora wa-alive. *What if he is planning to kill me, just like he aimed to kill her?* He would. With trembling fingers, she wrote on the pad by the telephone: *Help! Send Sergeant Horridge to this address.* She underlined the Golden Square house number and signed her name.

Maggie was so nervous she could barely pull on her gloves. After slipping a loaded derringer that had belonged to Horace into her reticule, she slipped out the door, careful to leave unseen. Perhaps Rupert would explain the reasons her father had kept quiet about the money.

As if in a trance, Maggie flagged down a hansom at the corner of Manchester Square. It took her to Thaddeus's house on Maddox Street, and, to her relief, Gavin was there to let her in.

"I need to find the box that I gave Thaddeus," Maggie explained breathlessly. "It was rosewood, carved and inlaid. Have you seen it?"

"Yes, of course. He's quite proud of that box, keeps it on the dresser in his bedroom."

Without thinking, Maggie made a move as if to run upstairs, but Gavin halted her, saying, "Perhaps I'd better fetch it, since a lady would be reluctant to enter . . . ahem, a gentleman's bedchamber."

Maggie blushed, vividly remembering her shared nights with Thaddeus. "Yes . . . yes, you're right, of course." Twisting her gloves and wondering if she should tell Gavin about Thaddeus's predicament, she waited until he returned downstairs. She decided not to tell him anything as it would only slow down the process of rescuing Thaddeus.

Gavin came down, the box clamped under his arm. It was a handsome piece, and it struck Maggie as odd that her father had given her such a lovely last gift. Had he repented his past sins before he died? But why hadn't he told her about the map? The answer was clear: he hadn't wanted her to know. To the end, he'd rejected her. Perhaps the thought of the gold forever remaining hidden appealed to his warped mind, she mused angrily.

She clutched the box. "Thank you." Leaving, she wondered where the map was hidden. The cab had left, and while she waited for another one to pass, she examined the box thoroughly but, as far as she could see, there were no extra compartments, no loose walls. Yet . . . if what her uncle had said was true, the map would be there. It did sound as if the wood was hollow at the bottom, but the wood seemed intact, no hidden compartments.

She looked down the street, worrying that she would be too late to save Thaddeus. There were no hackneys in sight so, unable to wait longer, she ran toward Regent Street.

For all she cared, her uncle could have the map if he let Thaddeus live. "Rupert talked about the powers of the gods . . ." Maggie muttered to herself. "If there's any true justice, let Thaddeus live," she prayed.

She knew that Thaddeus was shrewd. He could take care of himself, but what if he was unconscious . . .

She wondered how to overpower the men and rescue him if Rupert went back on his promise. There was no knowing how many men would be there.

A murder would take only a matter of seconds. The thought of Thaddeus suffering made her long to rush even faster to the Golden Square address to make sure he was still alive, but she was winded and her side ached.

"How will I find the courage to confront the villains?" she asked herself.

Clamping the rosewood box harder under her arm, Maggie reached Regent Street and looked for a hansom. There was none available, so she started running south, toward Piccadilly, until she completely lost her breath. *Dear God, let me be in time.* She fough" the vivid images of what the villains would do tc

Thaddeus if she arrived too late. She passed Conduit Street without finding a hansom, and the buses were too full to halt at the bus stop. Hot and weak with worry, she traversed the busy thoroughfare to Beak Street, veering to avoid a crossing sweeper. It had stopped snowing, and the temperature was rising, melting the snow into slush.

From Beak Street, she ran south until she reached Golden Square. The sky was a sullen gray as if threatening to smother the city with a blanket of rain. The failing light gave the facades of the town houses a dark, secretive look, and lamps were lighted inside to ward off the gloom. She counted the numbers until she reached 25. The curtains were drawn across the tall Gothic windows and there was no sign of life within.

Her box almost slipping from her trembling arms, she knocked, knowing she had to act before she lost her courage completely. She had a wild urge to put the box down and bolt from the square, but Thaddeus was there, and he needed her help.

The door opened a crack, and she stared in surprise. It was the man who had followed her along Oxford Street, and who had later abducted her. Shivering in terror, she couldn't find her voice.

"Mrs. Hartwell, I presume," he said with an ironic smile, eyeing the box. "I see that you heeded Mr. Merion's advice. Very wise of you." He motioned her to enter, and she could barely make her legs move forward. Swallowing hard, she followed the young man through a narrow hallway with a high ceiling. The air was stale and the atmosphere sepulchral. Maggie wondered if she'd ever leave this building alive.

The sound of male voices reached her. She entered a large room which stretched the entire width of the house. Her uncle was sitting on a hard-backed chair, and five young men were seated around him in a semicircle. One of them was Anselm Ripley, who was staring at her vacantly. The altar she remembered from Richmond was against one wall, near a tapestry depicting Oriental figures in various positions, surrounded by strange hieroglyphic signs. Candles burned in candelabras on the altar, and the room was wreathed in incense fumes. Scarves of smoke wove through the house.

"Ah! There you are Margaret," her uncle said jovially, rising to his feet. Only then did she notice the scarlet robe he was wearing. The hood hung down his back, and his face looked deathly pale against the vivid red.

"I brought the box," she said, her voice faltering. With a flash of terror, she hoped that Cecily would find her note by the telephone. If not, no one could save her if these men decided to kill her. But all she had been thinking of was Thaddeus's safety.

"Where's Mr. Webb?" she asked. "You promised to release him if I gave you the box."

The uncle smiled. "I did, but the promise might have to be broken." He observed the box from all angles. "Quite a handsome article, don't you agree?" he asked the young men, and they murmured their agreement. Maggie shivered as she looked at them. They seemed lost in another world, their faces calm and serene. What had her uncle done to keep them under his command? It was obvious that they stared at him in godlike devotion. A hookah was standing on a table, and Maggie knew from their dreamlike expressions, that the men had smoked it.

"Perhaps you don't have Mr. Webb in your custody, after all," Maggie said, hoping that her uncle had lied to her on the telephone just to get his hand on the box.

But, as that frightening thought crossed her mind, two of the men brought Thaddeus in from another room. He was reeling as if drunk, and Maggie noticed a large bruise discoloring his right temple.

His face lit up when he saw her, then darkened

"Why did you come here, Maggie, putting your life in danger?" he admonished.

"I had to, you must know that." She flew across the room, and wound her arms around his waist, supporting him as he stumbled to the nearest sofa. She couldn't believe these handsome, polite men could be involved in something so depraved as a cult that worshiped death and darkness.

Thaddeus was pale and evidently in pain. She sat close to him, trying to impart some comfort. As always, he seemed to give her more vigor. She would find a way to save them both. His hands were bound behind his back, the fingers bluish and swollen. Her gaze darted to every object in the room for something sharp to cut him loose, but the furniture was sparse and bare of ornaments.

"Why did you want the box, Rupert?" she asked, unable to say the word "uncle." Disappointment washed through her as she viewed her relative. "Do you think killing will forward your work?"

He caressed the inlaid wood, ignoring her question. "This is so much lovelier than the japanned box that Leonora received." He pointed at the black square article on the altar. "It contains the . . . the future . . . the means to establish my dreams," he said dreamily. He dropped the box to the floor and smashed it with a footstool.

"No!" Maggie screamed, half rising, but Thaddeus urged her back down.

"Don't annoy him," he whispered. "His mind is unhinged."

Rupert cried out in delight as he pulled a paper from the ruins of the box. With a triumphant smile, he brought it to Maggie.

She snatched it from his hand and glanced at it, recognizing the plan of her ancestral home and the garden behind it where roses and rhododendrons used to flower abundantly before neglect had set in. There was a marble birdbath in the rose arbor which was marked with an X and a long arrow pointing toward the ragged line where the paper had been ripped.

"What's this?" she asked.

"You do recognize the house, don't you, Maggie?"

"Yes, but this doesn't make any sense."

Rupert sauntered across the room and retrieved the other box. "Leonora's map contains the spinney and the stables, and combined, the two parts describe the exact spot where your father dug down his wealth." He turned to the men, spreading his arms wide. "Soon, very soon, you will witness the glorious rise of the Voices. The gods will speak to humankind, and the laws that uphold the universe will rule forever and ever."

Maggie shuddered at his singsong voice, and when the young men started swaying in the rhythm of his intonation, Maggie fumbled in her reticule, touching the cold handle of the derringer.

"You must find a way to leave, Maggie, and inform Sergeant Horridge. He'll bring his men to overpower these poor deluded creatures," Thaddeus whispered.

"They said you would die if I brought the police. I can't leave you here. Who knows what they'll decide to do." Maggie stared at his beloved face, yearning to caress away the strained look in his eyes. As she watched him, he seemed to calculate every possible escape route. "If you dash now, leaving the map, they might let you go. They got what they wanted."

"No," she whispered. "He won't let me go. He meant to murder Leonora last night, but accidentally killed Gertie instead. Besides, now he's admitted to the murder."

Thaddeus's eyes flashed with anger, and he strained against the ropes. "Blast! The maid—dead?"

Maggie nodded. "They mean to kill you as well unless Rupert keeps his promise to let you go."

Thaddeus smiled grimly. "I don't believe anything they say. That's why you have to fetch help."

"Perhaps they won't stop us from leaving." But as Maggie watched, one of the young men locked the hallway door and pocketed the key.

Then the men pulled their hoods over their heads, and holding hands, slowly formed a ring. A cold shiver ran down Maggie's back, and she fought back an urge to cry.

"What are you doing?" Thaddeus demanded as she stood on shaky legs. Without responding, she went to where her uncle was babbling in a toneless voice. She tugged the floppy sleeve of his robe, and he whirled around. His eyes were glowing strangely from the depths of his hood. He tried to enclose her in an embrace, but she recoiled. "You must let us go," she said. "You promised."

He laughed, a soft hissing sound that didn't sound human at all. The transformation frightened her. What was he turning into, a beast?

"The gods want a sacrifice. They are impatient for their freedom to roam the world, a gift I can give once the power has manifested itself."

"What power?" she asked hoarsely, a terrible fear welling up within her. *He had planned to kill them all along.*

"Wealth gives power. Only money gives the power to spread the message across the world."

Though feeling faint with terror, she made her voice cajoling. "But there's no reason to kill us, surely? We cannot stop your plans."

He flung out his arms dramatically, and Maggie flinched, expecting him to strike her. "Will you listen to the Voices, become obedient to their wishes, Margaret? Then I will fulfill my promise and let Webb go."

Maggie's thoughts raced. If she said yes, would he really let them live?

A sudden flare illuminated an oil lamp with a crimson glass globe on the altar, and the young men moaned in unison. As the light flickered red, their chanting rose to harsh cries. "The Voices want sacrifice."

Rupert heaved his shoulders apologetically, and a muscle twitched wildly in his jaw. "You see? The divine plan doesn't include you, my dear niece."

Anger shot through her. "How dare you claim to know what the divine plan is! All you worship is the power you hold over others. You're playing God, but you're nothing! *Nothing!*" she shouted. "You have no more power than anyone else. The voices you hear are in your mind—your sick mind."

The young men roared in anger, and Maggie felt a sharp pang of regret. She'd gone too far, but her wrath burned too strongly to quench now. As they closed in to take her, she pulled the derringer from her reticule and aimed it at the closet man. "I . . . will . . . shoot," she forced out, so frightened she could barely speak.

Just as she debated whether she would be able to pull the trigger, her uncle gave a downward chopping movement with his fist, striking her wrist. Pain shot up her arm. The pistol fell to the floor, where it went off with a deafening crack, hitting no one. One of the men picked it up and shoved it into his pocket.

As they closed in on her, she applied a sharp kick to the first man and, as he roared in fury, she gripped a chair and hurled it at her next attacker. Then Thaddeus was there, fighting right beside her although his hands were tied. As the men tried to subdue him, he swerved to the side, getting in a few crippling kicks.

Someone grasped Maggie from behind but, anger giving her strength, she tore herself free and ran toward the altar. Lifting one of the heavy candelabras, she flung it at her tormentor. Burning candles rolled on the floor, and, in an instant, the altar cloth had caught fire.

Rupert staggered toward her, screaming. "You'll

regret this, Maggie! You have violated the sacred altar. The Voices are very angry now."

"We'll all die together then. I'm not going alone," she shouted over the din of fighting men. Her uncle was slowly advancing on her as if in a trance. He threw back his hood, and Maggie cringed at the crazed look in his eyes. He'd slicked back his hair with macassar oil and the sharp bones of his face stood out against the feverish red spots on his cheeks. His lips were moving frantically in what appeared to be a prayer.

"The hunger shall be appeased, the sacrifice made," he said tonelessly as he flung himself at her, toppling them both to the floor.

Thaddeus roared angrily from the other side of the room. Maggie had no idea how he got away from his attackers, but he launched himself onto Rupert's back, pushing him off Maggie. However, the older man dodged Thaddeus's next attack, giving him a blinding blow to the jaw. Thaddeus rolled on the floor, frantically trying to regain his upright position—a futile effort.

Armed with rugs, the young men were trying to put out the fire which was now licking at the curtains.

The room filled with acrid smoke, and Maggie coughed. Her eyes burned as she pounded at her uncle who was straddling her, reaching out to throttle her. His ice-cold, bony fingers closed around her throat, squeezing until she could breathe no more.

Blood thundered through her head like a wild river, and she was vaguely aware of Thaddeus heaving all his bulk against Rupert. The older man's hands were dislodged momentarily, and through the clamor about the fire, she heard frantic banging on the door. A few moments later, the wood splintered and the room filled with blue uniforms.

"Police!" someone shouted, and Maggie recognized Sergeant Horridge's familiar tones.

Rupert was struggling to dislodge Thaddeus, who was much taller and heavier. The police separated the two men, and as Thaddeus slumped on the floor, Maggie saw that blood was streaming down his face. Sobbing, she crawled to him and held her arms around him.

"A proper set-to," Sergeant Horridge said grimly as he ordered the constables to tie up the robed men. He pulled out his pocketknife and sawed off the ropes at Thaddeus's wrists.

Thaddeus watched Maggie the whole time, and when his arms were freed, he folded them around her. "My darling," he whispered between coughs. "You were brave, but also reckless beyond belief. Of all the so-called investigation you did, this takes the fool's prize."

The constables had soon extinguished the fire, but the smoke hung heavy in the air. Together Thaddeus and Maggie stumbled toward the door, and he held her shoulders hard as if he never wanted to let her go.

The square was filled with spectators who gasped as Thaddeus and Maggie staggered outside. Leaning against the wall, they caught their breath. Maggie's eyes were streaming and sore, and her limbs seemed weighed down by lead. Thaddeus slumped against her, and she feared he was about to lose consciousness, but his eyes were still alert. The voices of the crowd rose as the robed men stepped outside.

Sergeant Horridge supervised the transferal of the prisoners from the house to the waiting police wagons. Rupert Merton gave Maggie a dark glance as he passed, and a flurry of unease skittered through her until she reminded herself that he was powerless to hurt her again. In the gray twilight he looked pathetic, every ounce of authority gone from the hunched shoulders.

When the prisoners were taken away, the constables guarding the door were bombarded with ques-

tions from the onlookers, but they waved them away.
"You can read about it in the newspapers tomorrow—it concerns the Altar Murders."

A roar went up as if the crowd wanted to launch
itself after the wagons and mete out instant justice to
the men who had tormented the city with the strange
murders.

Sergeant Horridge crossed to where Thaddeus and
Maggie were standing. "Will you come inside for a
moment and describe what happened here."

"You must have found my note," Maggie said as
she stepped into the house once more. The curtains
were blackened and tattered, the carpet soggy with
water. The stench of smoke filled the rooms.

"Your assistant contacted me. She told me about
your message by the telephone at the hotel. I came
just as soon as I'd gathered a few strong constables."

Maggie placed her hand on his arm. "I cannot
thank you enough. They planned to . . . to sacrifice
us on the altar."

The sergeant exchanged glances with Thaddeus,
who was rubbing his sore wrists. "Is this true?"

"Yes, you'd bloody damned well believe it! Forgive
my colorful language, but I'm furious. These men are
lunatics, and they would have killed us if you hadn't
arrived, Septimus."

"You should have contacted me immediately, Mrs.
Hartwell."

"They would have killed Thaddeus if I had brought
you along, so I left the note, hoping someone would
find it."

Sergeant Horridge shook his head and opened the
glass doors to a built-in bookcase. He pulled out one
book and read on the flap. "Belongs to Mr. Theodore
Fowler-Foss—he's the owner of this house." He
pulled out drawers and looked under tables and in
the corners behind an urn filled with dry pampas
grass and peacock feathers.

"What are you looking for, Septimus?" Thaddeus asked, massaging his sore head.

"We can charge them with their acts against you, but we need some evidence that the group perpetrated the Altar Murders. Suspicion isn't enough in court."

"There's my uncle's trunk," Maggie said, and pointed at a scuffed brown article with metal corners. It was covered with labels from many countries from all over the world.

"Eureka!" the sergeant said, and opened the domed lid, its hinges creaking.

Maggie and Thaddeus crossed the room to peer at the contents. First, there were layers of rich embroidered cloth of Oriental design, then a stack of books covered with strange signs. Thaddeus lifted one and flipped through the pages. "Seems your uncle was dabbling in black magic. But we knew that already." He read the titles of the other books. "*Letters on Christianity . . . Buddhistic Theories . . . The Ramayana . . . Hinduism: A Soul's Journey from Life to Life . . . Studies on Voodooism and Faith-Healing . . . Studies on the Dark Forces of the Mind.*"

Maggie shuddered in disgust. "I admit I always found him slightly peculiar, but a murderer? Never." She found one untitled volume and, the moment she read the inscription on the flyleaf, realized she was holding her mother's journal. Leonora would be pleased. Maggie cradled the book close to her heart as the sergeant shouted, "Aha!"

He was holding up a stack of papers, and a chart that looked like a family tree. "I think we'll have Merton's plans in black and white here." He flipped through the pages. "When we get down to the Yard, I'll confront him with this. These include the names of the murdered women and some other female names. Perhaps they would have been future victims."

Maggie tried to peer over his shoulder as he mum-

bled to himself, but she could not read the crabbed
writing.

"Looks like all the young men he ensnared in his
plan were from fine, if impoverished, families."

Maggie and Thaddeus exchanged glances. "Yes, it
fits, but Anselm Ripley appeared to be a man of
means," Thaddeus said.

"These men keep up a front. Their families might
have been wealthy in the past, and they live on small
legacies of what's left. Your uncle was careful when
he chose his followers." He shuffled the papers and
glanced at the chart. "If you recall, the ladies who
were murdered were wealthy, and without families
that might have stopped a liaison with one of these
young, enterprising men." He showed them the
chart. "If you look here, you can see that each member's name is connected with each of the victims.
Someone called 'Shadow' was supposed to marry a
Miss Porter." He barked a laugh. "At least her life
will be spared."

"Why would anyone keep such condemning evidence?" Thaddeus commented.

"My uncle thought the murders righteous, a part
of a greater divine plan. He thought himself untouch-
able by the law," Maggie explained.

"His was a devilish plan, my dear Mrs. Hartwell,"
the sergeant said grimly, and rolled up the chart. "To
fund his mission, he made the young followers marry
wealthy ladies. When the brides were sacrificed, the
men were the sole heirs to their fortunes."

"Rupert thought what he did was for the good of
the world." Shame for her uncle overcame Maggie,
but she pushed it away. She was not to blame. Drawing herself up, she held out her hand to the sergeant.
"Thank you for your invaluable help," she said.
"Without you we might have been dead by now."

He stared at her in surprise before reluctantly taking her fingertips. "Merely doing my job," he said.

"We'll keep the maps and boxes as evidence for now, but you'll get them back soon." He smiled suddenly. "I ought to thank *you* for solving the case. I expect you will be the key witness at the trial."

"Yes . . . I suppose I must." Maggie was loath to see the villains who had tried to kill her and the man she loved, but she knew she had an obligation to help.

"I must leave now. Lots of questioning at the station, I'm afraid."

Thaddeus led Maggie toward the door. "It's time for us to return home."

Maggie was still carrying her mother's journal, which she longed to give to Leonora. She would read it as soon as she found a quiet moment. "Victoria will be back this evening. I'm glad she didn't have to be involved in this." She wound her arm through Thaddeus's, remembering their fight last night.

"I suppose the assignment is finally over, Mrs. Hartwell," he said with a smile. "Your sister has been found, and a fortune in gold as well. After Christmas we'll travel up to Sheffield and dig up your legacy."

"I tremble at the outrageous fee you will charge me—especially now that the wooden box is destroyed and I'm due to inherit a gold treasure."

His smile warmed her, and she blushed.

"In fact, I'm slightly embarrassed that you had to rescue me and not the other way around," he said teasingly. "I don't see how I can charge you much."

"How modest," she chided. "Tell me, what happened to bring you here?"

"When we parted last night, I thought I'd investigate one of the members of your uncle's group. I remember seeing Fowler-Foss that night when I was attacked outside the music hall and brought to Richmond. Horridge informed me in a note after I returned from Liverpool that he'd discovered that Ripley and Fowler-Foss were friends. I had the devil's own time tracking Fowler-Foss down since he wasn't in this house, but I followed Rip ley last night to various haunts and I came upon them together. As I stalked them, I discovered that Fowler-Foss had invited Ripley to Golden Square. This town house has always belonged to the Fowler-Fosses, but young Theodore hardly ever used it. And when I arrived here last night, I literally landed in the hornet's nest. Ripley must have seen me at some point, recognizing me. I was planning to contact Horridge about my find, but before I knew what had happened, they had ambushed me, knocked me on the head, and tied me up."

They were standing beside a hansom cab. The crowd was still staring at the house, and two constables guarded the door against curious people trying to enter.

Oblivious to the many stares, Maggie blushed as she looked into Thaddeus's eyes. "I don't know what I would have done if anything had happened to you."

He pulled her into his arms, smiling. The crowd cheered as he planted a firm kiss on her lips. "I had no intention of letting them get rid of me before I'd kissed you once more. This has taught me how important it is not to waste a single day—a single hour."

She sighed happily. "Yes. Let's go tell the world how lucky we are to have found each other."

"I wish it was our wedding tomorrow, not Delia's. I don't know if I can wait any longer," Thaddeus said with much feeling.

Chapter 25

◦◦◦◦

"**M**ama, Mama!" Victoria cried as she dashed past Rafferty at the door. The sky had cleared, and the cold swept into the house with Victoria and her governess. A wintry sunlight slanted golden through the windows in the soft interlude before twilight fell over the London buildings. "You should have seen the sea, Mama. The waves were as tall as mountains."

With a rush of affection, Maggie scooped her daughter into her arms.

"It smells like Christmas in here," Miss Lather said, smiling. She blushed as Thaddeus shook her hand, welcoming them back.

"Maggie asked the cook to keep a pot of mulled wine with cloves and cinnamon simmering for the benefit of Christmas scent. Would you like a glass?" he asked Miss Lather.

"Yes, please. How lovely!" she exclaimed as she viewed the decked hallway. Maggie and Thaddeus had wound spruce garlands around the banister and along the edge of the front desk. Mistletoe hung in the doorway to the restaurant, and pots of holly flanked every door. The table by the main entrance to the dining room was covered with a red embroidered cloth, and a huge silver bowl held the mulled wine. Slices of orange and lemon floated in the red liquid.

Thaddeus lifted a silver cup to Miss Lather. "Happy Christmas," he said, smiling. "May you receive a large raise on Christmas morning."

"Have you moved into room number seven for good now, Mr. Webb?" Victoria tugged at his coat-tails. "Can I have some wine, too?"

"No, you cannot," Maggie said firmly. "But I believe Cecily was preparing a cup of hot cocoa for you in the kitchen. When you've finished, we will dress the yule tree."

"Will you come with me, mama?" Victoria clung to her, and Maggie could not refuse the request. "Don't drink too much wine, now," she admonished Thaddeus, who chuckled and instantly downed his cup. They exchanged loving glances, and warmth filled Maggie.

Leading Victoria to the kitchen, she said, "I have something important to tell you, my darling."

"When I have my cocoa?"

"Yes, that's a good time." Maggie wondered how her daughter would react to the changes that had occurred while she was gone.

They sat in the private dining room beyond the kitchen, a room that was empty at this time of the day what with the cook busy preparing the guest dinners, and maids scurrying back and forth.

"Is the cocoa good?" Maggie asked, and fetched a tin of her daughter's favorite gingerbread. She placed two on a plate next to the cup.

"Now then, are you going to tell me all about Margate?" she began. She listened intently as Victoria prattled on about the sea and Miss Lather's mother. Evidently the trip had been a huge success, and Maggie was grateful that Victoria had been spared the tragedy at the hotel.

"Mama, you look worried. Have I done something wrong?"

Maggie looked into her daughter's large blue eyes,

and smiled. "No, nothing at all. I was thinking about everything that happened while you were gone. On the sad side, we will not see Uncle Rupert anymore. He has gone . . . away, and I doubt he'll be back soon."

"Oh? He was kind to me, and told such strange stories."

"I know." Maggie took a deep breath. "But, though we lost an uncle, we've gained another relative, my sister Leonora from America."

"You found her!" Victoria slapped the table to emphasize her delight. The cocoa was temporarily forgotten. "Can I meet her now?"

Maggie nodded. "As soon as you have finished your unpacking." How could she tell the harsh truth of the Altar Murders and Leonora's involvement to a six-year old? She decided it would be better to soften the reality. "She's still resting after the . . . trip. You see, she was lost for a while in England, and couldn't find her way here."

"Why, she must be simpleminded," Victoria scoffed.

"For shame, Victoria! You must never speak of a person thus." Maggie wiped some crumbs from the tablecloth, remembering Gertie's death. She decided to impart the sad news of the maid's death later, since her demise would upset Victoria. Right now she would broach the subject dearest to her heart. "I have another piece of news that I hope will please you." Maggie took a deep breath. "Mr. Webb has asked me to marry him. How would you like to have him for a father?"

Victoria jumped up from the table, scattering cookie crumbs in all directions. She threw her arms around Maggie. "I told him to ask you, Mama, and I'm so glad he did. I *knew* he would."

Happiness quivered in Maggie's chest, and tears

gathered in her eyes. "You little . . . *minx!* Concocting my future with Mr. Webb."

"You look happier now, mama." Victoria caressed Maggie's face. "Your lips are not so thin, and your hair is softer. But most of all, I like your smile. I had almost forgotten what it looked like."

Maggie could not suppress her tears as they flowed down her cheeks. She held Victoria close, sobbing into the shoulder of her daughter's pinafore.

"Shall we go and tell Mr. Webb now, Mama?" Victoria said. "He'll lend you his hanky."

Maggie laughed as she dabbed at her tears with Victoria's napkin. "Yes, he'll be pleased to hear that you have accepted him as your new father." Maggie squeezed her daughter's hand as they left the dining room. "In a way, he proposed to both of us. It's important to me that you like him."

"I'll tell him that I do," Victoria said, and darted across the hotel foyer to where Thaddeus was standing, talking to Rafferty.

"I have a new aunt, Mr. Rafferty, and Mr. Webb will soon by my father," Victoria shouted for all the guests ensconced in the stuffed armchairs to hear. Maggie heard a few stray chuckles and the hurried crackling of newspapers.

She blushed as she joined the group around the wine bowl. Rafferty held is stovepipe hat in his hand. "My warmest congratulations, Mrs. Hartwell," he said with a salute.

"Why are we all standing here?" Victoria asked, sniffing the wine.

"A wedding reception will be held here this evening," Maggie explained. "Mr. Webb's sister is getting married in an hour, and the party will arrive soon after that."

Victoria gazed at her future father. "What are you doing here then? Aren't you going to the wedding?"

Thaddeus tweaked her nose. "Yes, of course, but

it's most difficult to tear myself away from you and your mother."

Victoria's brow creased in thought. "Mostly from Mama, though. You're not going to marry me, after all."

Thaddeus tilted his head back and roared with laughter, and within minutes the entire room rumbled with glee.

What a wonderful Christmas after all, Maggie thought as her heart was flooded with love.

Delia looked like a glittering snow princess as she stepped through the hotel doors later in the evening. Her cheeks flushed gently as her straight-backed and handsome groom, Mr. Alan Turner, whispered something in her ear. He was tall and dark, and evidently very much in love with his bride.

"How lovely you look," Maggie said, holding out both her hands in welcome. She kissed Delia's cheeks, and was enveloped in a cloud of light perfume.

Thaddeus was right behind the glowing couple, pushing his father's invalid chair. Reminding Maggie of a primrose in her yellow gown, Amintha came arm in arm with Mrs. Webb, who was dressed in royal blue taffeta and ostrich feathers for the occasion.

They greeted each other, and Maggie was delighted to see Thaddeus's entire family under her roof. The twin boys, Ben and Tim, had already found Victoria at a table laden with candy and nuts which was standing right next to the yule tree. The girl was decorating the tree with paper angels, garlands of flags and tiny tin trumpets. The boys joined her, viewing the tree with enthusiasm.

The guests arrived in droves after that, among them Gavin Talbot, and soon the dining rooms resounded with chatter and laughter.

Leonora came down, looking pale and tired, but

she wanted to share in Maggie's success at hosting the reception. Maggie introduced her to Victoria. To Maggie's relief, there was an instant rapport between them. With a promise to tell them a story about a red Indian, Leonora helped Victoria and the twins decorate the tree.

Looking over the food arrangements, Maggie clasped her hands together in delight. This was absolutely her happiest evening ever, she decided. If the day got any better, she would explode.

Thaddeus joined her after greeting just about everyone in the room and placed a discreet arm around her waist. "You have stars in your eyes, and you wear the widest smile of anyone here tonight. I can count all your teeth."

Maggie chuckled. "Always a rare turn of phrase, eh, Thaddeus?" She gave him a hot glance. "I would like to throw my arms around you, right now."

He stood before her with spread arms. "What's stopping you?"

"I can't steal the limelight from Delia and her groom, now can I?" They were interrupted by a movement at the door.

Ahs and *ohs* swept the room as the cake was rolled in on a cart by a beaming Cecily. The cake was a multitiered confection with marzipan rosebuds holding swags of whipped cream around the perimeter of every layer.

The bride and groom were enjoined to take the knife and cut the cake, while advice on how to go about it was shouted from every corner. A cheer rose when the first piece had been cut and the bridal couple was feeding each other with a fork. Then Cecily and two of the waiters passed plates of cake and glasses of sherry around. The clatter of china and the din of conversation rose to a fever pitch until a spoon against crystal tinkled to announce the first speaker.

It was Mr. Webb, the elder, who from the depth of

his chair raised his glass high. "To my dear daughter and my new son. May your life together be filled with peace and happiness." He then went on to reminisce about his own wedding, and how his brother had fallen over the cake in a drunken stupor. After the laughter had died down, Thaddeus raised his glass.

Maggie's pulse thundered in her ears. She'd seen that reckless glint in his eyes, and she held her breath as he spoke. "To my little sister. Whatever Father just said goes for me too, except for the cake bit, but I have something to announce that will make all of you drop your cake plates in surprise."

The silence was deafening, and Maggie blushed to the roots of her hair. Thaddeus drew her close to his side. "For a moment, Delia, I must take some of your much-deserved attention, to tell you all the happiest of news. What could be a better occasion than this reception to announce another wedding—you're all invited to the ceremony, of course." He took a deep breath and looked deeply into Maggie's eyes. "Mrs. Margaret Hartwell has made me the happiest man in the world by accepting my proposal of marriage."

Ohs and *ahs* burst out again, and everyone raised their glasses in cheer as Thaddeus held up Maggie's hand and showed the ruby ring to everyone. "I hope Maggie will let me help her with the hotel business, but detective work is the job I prefer, and Maggie seems to have taken a liking to it as well. Haven' you, darling?"

Maggie didn't hear a thing, but she nodded. She was only aware of the velvet tenderness of his eye and the wicked smile she'd learned to love so much and of the infinite promise of their life together.